WITHDRAWN

Kris Longknife
DESERTER

Mike Shepherd

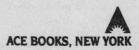

ACE BOOKS, NEW YORK

THE BERKLEY PUBLISHING GROUP
Published by the Penguin Group
Penguin Group (USA) Inc.
375 Hudson Street, New York, New York 10014, USA
Penguin Group (Canada), 10 Alcorn Avenue, Toronto, Ontario M4V 3B2, Canada
(a division of Pearson Penguin Canada Inc.)
Penguin Books Ltd., 80 Strand, London WC2R 0RL, England
Penguin Group Ireland, 25 St. Stephen's Green, Dublin 2, Ireland (a division of Penguin Books Ltd.)
Penguin Group (Australia), 250 Camberwell Road, Camberwell, Victoria 3124, Australia
(a division of Pearson Australia Group Pty. Ltd.)
Penguin Books India Pvt. Ltd., 11 Community Centre, Panchsheel Park, New Delhi—110 017, India
Penguin Group (NZ), 67 Apollo Drive, Rosedale, North Shore 0745, Auckland, New Zealand
(a division of Pearson New Zealand Ltd.)
Penguin Books (South Africa) (Pty.) Ltd., 24 Sturdee Avenue, Rosebank, Johannesburg 2196,
South Africa

Penguin Books Ltd., Registered Offices: 80 Strand, London WC2R 0RL, England

This is a work of fiction. Names, characters, places, and incidents either are the product of the author's imagination or are used fictitiously, and any resemblance to actual persons, living or dead, business establishments, events, or locales is entirely coincidental.

KRIS LONGKNIFE: DESERTER

An Ace Book / published by arrangement with the author

PRINTING HISTORY
Ace mass market edition / December 2004

Copyright © 2004 by Mike Moscoe.
Cover art by Scott Grimando.
Cover design by Rita Frangie.
Interior text design by Kristin del Rosario.

ISBN: 978-0-441-01227-5

ACE
Ace Books are published by The Berkley Publishing Group,
a division of Penguin Group (USA) Inc.,
375 Hudson Street, New York, New York 10014.
ACE and the "A" design
are trademarks belonging to Penguin Group (USA) Inc.

PRINTED IN THE UNITED STATES OF AMERICA

10 9 8 7 6 5

"**Okay**, Engineering, let's see if we can finish the test run this time," Captain Hayworth announced.

"And let's try not to blow up the ship," Lieutenant Junior Grade Kris Longknife added under her breath. Still, she nodded agreement with the Captain of the Fast Attack Corvette *Firebolt* as did the others on the bridge around her. The crew attended to their duties, faces professionally bland in the reflected reds, blues, and greens of their underway stations. The cool, processed air didn't actually smell of fear. Not quite.

The Captain turned his attention to Kris. "Lieutenant Longknife, match your board to Engineering. Inform me if you see anything wrong. And this time, only use Navy-issue gear."

"Aye, aye, sir." Kris tapped her station, converting it from offensive weapons to a copy of the ship's engineering station a hundred meters aft of the bridge. Everything was green. Question was, would the board show anything red before the *Firebolt* was nothing but a glowing cloud of dust?

The Kamikaze-class corvettes, with their smart-metal armor, were great ships to serve on during peacetime. Rather than keep the ship a cramped and crowded man-of-war, the armor was thinned out and used to expand the vessel. Kris liked her private stateroom. For the last five years as more ships of this class joined the fleet, that had not been a problem. Built as large "love boats," they rarely converted to thick-skinned warships.

But Earth's Society of Humanity was only a memory along with the eighty years of peace it had brought. Every newscast told of rumors of war. Wardhaven needed fighting ships.

And the last few conversions of Kamikaze-class ships into tight, small, war fighters with thick battle armor had shown a disturbing tendency to catastrophic problems with their reactors.

So the *Firebolt* had spent much of the last two months tied up to the Nuu shipyard docks converting itself back and forth between large and small and trying to figure out what didn't work quite right. Solve that problem, and Wardhaven had forty good warships to contribute to the United Sentients Navy. Fail, and Wardhaven's allies would have a very small stick to face the other six hundred planets of fragmenting human space.

And Kris might very well end up dead.

"Engineering, I show your board green," Kris said.

"Aye, aye. Bridge sees no problems," the Chief Engineer drawled with carefully measured sarcasm. Kris had less than a year in the Navy and had yet to meet a Chief Engineer who valued any viewpoint that originated outside his domain of reactors, generators, and the maze of superconductors that connected them.

Still, Kris had closed down two of the last five tests.

NELLY, Kris thought. ARE THE ENGINES STABLE? Facing guns and mutiny had finally convinced Kris that subvocal talk between her and her personal computer was too slow and subject to problems. In the last upgrade of Nelly's hardware, Kris had submitted to a direct jack into her brain. What Kris thought, Nelly heard, and what Nelly heard, she was very likely to make happen. The pet computer around Kris's shoulders might weigh less than a quarter kilo, but she was a hundred times more capable than the combined computers of the *Firebolt*—and fifty times more expensive.

ALL ENGINEERING READOUTS ARE NOMINAL. Nelly verified Kris's own assessment.

WATCH THEM. IF YOU SEE ANYTHING DEVELOPING THAT

THREATENS THE SHIP, TELL ME. IF TIME'S TOO SHORT, ACT ON IT YOURSELF.

THE CAPTAIN DOES NOT LIKE IT WHEN I DO THAT.

THAT'S MY PROBLEM. I JUST WANT TO BE ALIVE TO HAVE IT, Kris thought, noting that the latest upgrade seemed to have added something unplanned to Nelly's repertoire: backtalk.

"Helm," the Captain ordered, "hold her steady on course at one g acceleration."

"Aye, sir. One g acceleration, steady as she goes." The Ensign at the helm wore the relaxed expression expected, but one eyebrow lifted toward Kris. Was he counting on her to save them all, no matter what the Skipper said?

"Engineering, give me eighty percent."

"Reactor coming up on eighty percent. At eighty percent . . . now, Captain."

"Helm, put on one point five g's. Steady on course."

As the helm answered, Kris did a full review of her board. Nelly was doing the same review many times a second, but Kris did not trust any man-made device with her life, not even Nelly. All was green. Around Kris, the ship groaned as it took on more weight. One of the freebies with the smart metal was now happening. Without human intervention, the ship automatically thickened up scantlings, added an extra millimeter to decks, prepared itself for the growing weight of equipment and crew.

"Crew, prepare for high g's," the Captain announced. Kris's chair, which a moment before looked solid, began to grow a footrest for her. The headrest stretched out to match her height, a full six feet; its cushion inflated. On a Kamikaze-class, the crew didn't require high-g stations; they made them when they needed them. And if the crew had to move, their stations just flowed along with them. Too cool!

"Engineering. A hundred percent on the reactor, please." No sooner had the Chief Engineer reported full reactor than the skipper ordered the helm up to two g's. Kris held her breath and eyed her board. The *Firebolt*'s first test cruise had ended at this benchmark; the Engineer himself scrammed the reactor.

Five seconds into two g's, Kris let her breath out . . . and everyone on the bridge seemed to breathe easier. The Captain held this course and speed for a long five minutes as every station reported in, not just Engineering. No problems.

"Lieutenant Longknife, is space clear ahead of us?" the skipper asked.

As quickly as Kris could at two g's, she converted a small portion of her board back to weapons and did a search sweep. "Nothing ahead for two hundred and fifty thousand klicks, sir."

"Discharge all four pulse lasers, if you please."

"Yes, sir," Kris answered and walked her fingers over all four of the *Firebolt*'s main weapons. Twenty-four-inch pulse lasers shot out into empty space, deadly for 25,000 kilometers, then slowly diverging. "All pulse lasers fired, sir."

"Recharge lasers," the Captain ordered.

Energy flowed from Engineering into the laser capacitors. Kris checked; there was still plenty of power to keep the fusion containment field up and direct the flow of superheated plasma to the massive engines accelerating the *Firebolt* at two g's.

No PROBLEMS, Nelly reported unneccssarily, but Kris was not about to squelch a good report.

"No problems," Kris announced to the Captain after a thorough check of her board.

"All systems working well within their safety margins," the Chief Engineer reported.

Captain Hayworth cracked a tiny smile; test runs two and three had not got past this benchmark. "Helm, take us smartly up to three g's acceleration. Steady on course. Engineering, put us in the red." Aye, ayes answered him. Kris locked her eyes on her board, now back to mimicking Engineering as her seat settled into a bed and the board slanted up to where she could easily see it. Except for the three master switches on her seat's armrest, it would take a major physical effort to get to any of her controls. The reactor scram button was right under her thumb.

"Power flow to the lasers is decreasing. Recharge will take two extra minutes at this acceleration," she told the Captain.

"No problem," he muttered, his eyes on his own board.

"Three g's it is, sir," the Helm answered through gritted teeth. Kris didn't much care for weighing over 170 kilos. The Helmsman, a footballer in college, was easily approaching 400. Great for crashing a line, lousy for deft movements on a control board now in his lap.

Again the Captain went down the department list. Every

station reported itself nominal, if a bit on the heavy side. That put them past test four's failure point.

"Four g's if you will, Helmsman. Keep her very steady on this course."

"Reactor heading into one hundred and eleven percent overload," Engineering reported, his voice heavy with strain. "One hundred and twelve percent . . . No problems. One hundred and thirteen percent . . . All stations steady. One hundred and fifteen percent and everything is as good as it gets."

"Very good, Engineering. We will hold the reactor there. Let me know if anything changes," the Captain said.

NELLY? Kris thought.

THERE ARE SOME INTERESTING ANOMALIES IN CERTAIN SYSTEMS, KRIS. NONE SHOULD BE A THREAT TO THE SHIP.

Interesting words for a computer. "I show all green," Kris said after checking her own board to verify Nelly's report.

"Strangely enough, so does mine," the Captain answered.

"We are at four g's," the Helmsman announced weakly.

Kris watched the seconds tick away on her board for a full minute before Hayworth spoke, and then it was to the entire crew. "All hands, this is the Captain. The *Firebolt* has now done what no other Kamikaze-class ship has done before: held four g's for a full minute. We will complete our scheduled quals after two more tests. Helm, turn right forty-five degrees smartly."

The Helm whispered, "Aye, aye, sir," as his fingers stabbed at his board. Kris did not feel the ship bank around her, accommodating its human occupants' needs at four times their weight. "On new course."

Everyone breathed a sigh. One more test to go.

"Helm, execute jinks pattern A."

"Jinks pattern A, sir. Executing now."

The ship rose suddenly, attitudinal thrusters adding more weight to Kris. It jinked right, then left, then left some more, dodging imaginary laser fire.

PROBLEMS ARE DEVELOPING IN THE . . . Nelly began. Kris's board showed green. Sucking in air, Kris's gaze raced from green gauge to green gauge, searching for any sign of something going wrong. Nothing!

SCRAM! Nelly shouted in Kris's head.

Kris was weightless in the dark as the ship went dead around her.

"Where are those damn auxiliaries?" the Captain snapped. Ventilation hummed as Engineering corrected the problem with the backup power. The bridge took on light as boards came alive. Emergency lights cast long shadows. Systematically, Kris studied her board; nothing told her why Nelly had shut down the test.

"Engineering, are you on-line?" the Captain asked into his commlink.

"Yes, sir. We lost no test data. I'm organizing it while my team initiates a reactor start-up."

"Am I to understand that you did not initiate that scram?"

"No, sir. We did not hit the button down here."

"Thank you, Engineering. As soon as you have a rough handle on your data, report to my day cabin."

"Aye, sir."

"XO, you have the conn. When we get systems back on-line, set a one-g course for Nuu Docks. They should have our usual berth waiting for us."

"Yes, sir."

"Longknife, you're with me."

"Yes, sir." NELLY, WHAT HAPPENED? Kris demanded as she pushed away from her station and swam, weightless, after the Captain to his day cabin off the bridge. Normally, that cabin was quite roomy. Under combat conditions, it was little more than a table and four chairs. The Captain settled into his place at the head of the table as a boson announced the ship was getting under way. Kris closed the door, rotated herself as she took on weight, and stood at attention.

"Have I missed something about my ship, Lieutenant? Last time I checked, there were three scram buttons on this boat. Mine and the Chief Engineer's, the two every ship of this class has. I know the *Firebolt* has a third, authorized to you because of your job as coordinator of this smart-metal test, and, I suspect, because of your unique relationship with the yard." That was a rather original way of saying her grandfather owned the shipyard that made all the Kamikazes.

"Yes, sir," Kris agreed, stalling, praying the Engineer would show up with whatever reason Nelly had for stopping the test only moments before the Captain could have declared them done and over.

"The Engineer tells me he did not hit his scram button. I know I did not hit mine. Did you hit yours?"

Kris's board would show no contact between her and the red button. No use claiming she had. "No, sir. I did not scram the reactor." *Stall. Stall.*

"Who did?"

Kris stood board straight, dreading the answer but unwilling to lie to her Skipper, certainly not going to tell a lie that would be disproved as fast as she said it.

"Whoever scrammed my engines saved our butts," the Chief Engineer said, opening the door . . . and saving Kris's butt. "Pardon me, Captain, am I interrupting a private counseling session?"

"No, Dale, take a seat. You, too, Longknife," the Skipper said wearily. Dale Chowski, Chief Engineer, a half dozen oversize readers under his arm, settled into one chair. Kris took the chair across from him.

"What went wrong this time, Dale?" the Captain asked.

"Specifically, the superconductors on the containment coil for plasma headed for our number-one engine were four nanoseconds away from losing the super part of their name when the reactor scrammed." The engineer ran a hand through his crew cut. "I take it that it was that fine computer around your neck, Lieutenant, that we have to thank for this bit of grace."

Kris nodded. "My personal computer spotted the developing problem. It tried to advise me, but the problem came on too fast for me to react."

IT! Nelly spat in Kris's head.

SHUT UP, Kris ordered.

"So your pet computer was working faster than the ones in my engine room," the Engineer finished, not missing the Captain's scowl as he did. "Skipper, I know you don't much like the idea of nonstandard software roaming around the innards of your ship. Can't say I like it much either, but rather than look the gift horse we got in the mouth, why don't we tell Bu-Ships that we need a computer like she's got. Hell, if she transferred off the ship tomorrow, I swear I'd go out and buy one for myself. What would a gadget like yours set a guy back?"

Kris told him the cost of Nelly's last upgrade, minus the surgery to get the jack into her head. He let out a low whistle. "Guess we keep you around for a while."

The Skipper's scowl got even deeper. "Dale, what exactly went wrong from a systems point of view?"

"This is just an old Engineer's personal guess, but I'd say the calculations the metal is supposed to do automatically as to what this or that part of the ship needs for high g's was off a bit for our rocket motors that are farthest from the center of the ship. Engine one and six got whipped around by the jinking the most. Number one failed. I think we'll find six wasn't that long for the world."

"So we need to adjust the automatic algorithm for redistributing metal," the Captain said.

"Could do that," the Engineer agreed, his face going sour. "But I stand by my last recommendation. Take Engineering off the smart-metal regime. Set the specs for our reactor, machinery, and plasma containment fields, then freeze it in place."

"You'd freeze Engineering in the tight combat structure?" Kris asked.

"No can do," the Engineer said, shaking his head. "Right now, I can't get to half of my gear to maintain it. Whoever designed the combat format for my spaces was either a midget or expected us to expand back out if we needed to repair or maintain anything. We'll need a middle ground, something small enough to fight but big enough to work in."

"How much bigger?" the Captain asked.

The Engineer slaved the skipper's table to one of his readers. A schematic of the *Firebolt*'s engineering spaces now took up most of the tabletop. It quickly sequenced through the change from large and comfortable to combat-ready and cramped. As it expanded back out, Dale froze it. "That's about what I think we'll need.

"Computer, calculate the metal requirements to armor that area. Post it to the schematic." A second later, Nelly added a list of weights to the graphic. Again, the Engineer whistled.

"A hundred tons of smart metal. You'd need that much to cover fifteen extra meters of Engineering space?"

"After the damage the *Chinook* took," Kris said, damage she had done the targeting for, "BuShips wants the Engineering spaces well protected."

"How much does a hundred tons of smart metal cost?" Dale asked.

Kris told him. He didn't bother whistling at that one; he just looked at the Captain and groaned. "I guess I know why we're out here trying to solve this problem." The Engineer leaned back in his chair, stared at the lowered combat ceiling of the *Firebolt,* and took in several slow breaths. "Could we replace some of the smart metal with regular old metal? I mean, if I'm not going to go around rejiggering my engine rooms, we don't need that fancy stuff."

Captain Hayworth raised an eyebrow in Kris's direction. She shook her head. "Nuu Enterprises has done some testing. Mixing regular and smart metal together on the same ship only seems to confuse the smart metal. They can't recommend it."

"Why am I not surprised?" Dale snorted. "When they can charge us an arm and a leg for smart metal, why figure out a way to do something on the cheap?" Both officers carefully avoided looking at Kris. That her grandfather Al was the CEO of Nuu Enterprises and that her own portfolio was centered on several hundred million of Nuu Enterprises' preferred stock did not prevent them from holding the usual low opinion fleet officers held of corporate practices. The Skipper was good about not saying it to her face.

Kris saw no reason to pussyfoot around her birth connection today. "My Grandfather Al is working on something that might save my father, the Prime Minister, a chunk of the Navy's budget if you decide, Commander, the Navy should freeze the Engineering space on the Kamikazes."

The Engineer chuckled, and the Captain rolled his eyes at the overhead. "They warned me that neither cowardice nor common sense had ever been mentioned in one of your fitness reports, Lieutenant. So, what might save me from telling BuShips that it has to totally unbalance the Prime Minister's latest budget proposal?"

"Nuu Enterprises is testing something it's calling Uni-plex metal. This stuff holds its shape for the first two times it's organized, then forgets it the third time you change it."

"Forgets it. Metal's metal." Engineering frowned.

"Yes, sir, but the third time, it's more like liquid mercury than armor plate."

"Who would want such a damn death trap?" Dale growled.

Somebody who wanted somebody dead, Kris knew from all too personal experience, but she just shrugged for her fellow officers. She still was none too sure how she felt about Grampa Al's making a profit from the stuff that had almost killed her.

"Produced in thousand-ton lots, the Uni-plex costs about one-sixth of smart metal," Kris told them. "When you add in the savings by it self-fabricating itself on ship, its competitive."

"Spoken like a true Longknife," the Captain drawled dryly.

But the Engineer was eyeing the schematic. "How much of my engine room is smart metal?"

"Computer, answer the man," Kris said aloud. Numbers appeared on the table.

"Three hundred fifty tons," Dale said thoughtfully.

"Plus a hundred tons of extra protection," Kris added.

"But if we gave back three hundred fifty tons of smart metal . . ."

"And drew four hundred fifty tons of not quite so smart metal . . ." Kris added.

"Then the Navy would actually be saving money by converting the Engineering space of the forty Kamikazes," Captain Hayworth finished with a chuckle.

"Sixteen thousand tons of smart metal would build us five or six more boats, sir," Kris concluded.

"Got to love it when you can make everyone happy." Dale sighed.

"From way out in left field," the Captain agreed.

"Maybe, maybe not." The Engineer sat up. "Has your Grandad Al checked how smart metal gets along with its retarded cousin? If I can't order this Uni-plex stuff to fix battle damage, I'm going to have to spray in smart metal around dumb metal."

Kris shook her head. "They aren't that far along."

"We can't have this Uni-plex migrating around the boat," the Captain added. "It could make for thoroughly unpleasant surprises." All three officers nodded at that conclusion.

Dale got to his feet. "I got to check on the rest of my snipes, see if they've dug up anything new on our test."

"Keep me informed."

Kris stood to follow the Engineer out. "A moment, Lieutenant." A knowing smile crossed the Engineer's face as he closed the door behind him. Kris turned to face her Captain, going back to a brace that would have made her DI at OCS proud.

"Once more, Lieutenant Longknife," the Captain began, "you have succeeded in turning insubordination into a virtue."

Kris had no answer for that, so she kept her mouth shut.

"One of these days, it will not be a virtue. One of these days you *will* discover why we do things the Navy Way. I only hope that I will be there when you discover that . . . and that too many good spacers don't die with you."

Again, Kris had no answer for her Captain, so she used the Navy's all-purpose response: "Yes, sir."

"Dismissed."

Kris went. Once more she'd been raked over the coals for doing the right thing the wrong way. Still, the Captain hadn't been as hard on her as he could have been. At least he had dressed her down as "Lieutenant," not "Princess."

2

No surprise, the yard had saved the *Firebolt*'s usual space alongside Pier Eight. Tied up snug by 1530, the crew settled into the along-side routine while Kris followed the Skipper and Chief Engineer into the yard to their usual meeting with the usual dock managers at the usual conference room. After two months, too much of this job was becoming "usual."

Today, the yard team included new faces. "We watched your run," the yard's Project Manager said. "Figured we'd better add a few scientists to our meeting."

"Lieutenant Longknife told me about your not-quite-so-smart metal," the Captain said, taking in the four new members. "You working on that?"

A woman leaned forward in her seat. "My team has been seeing what we could do with Uni-plex since Princess Longknife arranged for us to get a sample of it." Kris gritted her teeth.

"How does it work around smart metal?" Dale said, getting right to the point. "I think my engine room is a good candidate for Uni-plex, if you can keep it contained. You can understand my Captain's reluctance to discover the bulkhead between him and space might have acquired a bit of this stuff the next time he changes ship."

"Our testing hasn't gotten that far," the woman admitted with a sour frown directed at one of her subordinates.

"When will it?" Captain Hayworth shot back.

"Two weeks, sir," the subordinate replied. "Two weeks to finish our testing. Then another week to produce five hundred tons of Uni-plex. Say another two weeks working with you to design an approach to siphon out the smart metal and replace it with this stuff. Five weeks total."

"Four weeks," the Engineer answered back. "You and I can be refining the process while you're doing your testing. Maybe less if you can get us this Uni-plex as it becomes available. I'd sure like to test this replacement process one step at a time," he told his Captain.

"A lot of unknowns in this," the Project Manager said, glancing at his wrist unit. "There's also a matter of costs. These tests have already exhausted their cost centers. Who's going to come up with the extra money?"

Captain Hayworth shook his head. "I'll have to check on that. Who's paying for this metal development?"

"Nuu Enterprises," the Project Manager said and Kris nodded. Grampa Al was footing the bill for the work on Uni-plex both because he was still hoping to pin down who tried to kill Kris and, if Nuu Enterprises paid for the research, NuuE got all the profits. Grampa Al was such a warm-hearted type.

"Okay," the Skipper continued. "That gives me one week to get approval for funds, another week to get them transferred. I'll get back to you in a week."

"I'll check with you tomorrow to see how it's coming," the yard man said with a smile that had the proper blend of predator and supplicant that a government contractor needed.

Meeting over, they started back to the ship. "Dale, you have any questions?" got a quick negative from the Engineer. "Longknife, we might as well stand the crew down. Anyone who wants leave can have it. That includes you, Lieutenant."

"I'll be here keeping a good eye on the yard staff, sir."

"I'd rather you didn't. They never know whether they're talking to a Navy Lieutenant, a Princess, or a major stockholder of Nuu Enterprises. Until I get money approved, I can't risk someone taking one of your nods as a work order."

"Sir, you've never expressed that concern before."

"I've never had anyone at the yard call you Princess before. I don't know who this woman is, and I don't want problems."

Kris didn't know how to answer that. "I don't need any leave, sir," she finally concluded.

"And we probably will need your 'special' relationship. Just keep your distance from that science crew. Now, don't you have a commitment tonight?"

"A ball, sir." Kris scowled. She'd hoped the test would take longer, give her a good excuse to be comfortably absent.

"Right. So why don't you head dirtside."

"Sir, did my mother—"

"No, the Prime Minister's wife has not taken to issuing me orders for you . . . yet. But my wife did notice in the gossip columns that your absence at last week's Ball for United Charities was commented upon at length. So my personal computer, nowhere near as smart as yours, is now searching the social pages for what I suspect are your social duties. Lieutenant, we all have our responsibilities. So long as you insist on juggling Navy duties with those of a Princess, I don't expect you to short the Navy, but I can't afford to report to the Prime Minister or his lady every time you short the other."

"Sir, I *joined* the Navy. I got *drafted* into this Princess stuff," Kris spat.

Hayworth actually smiled. "We all must bear our burddens, Lieutenant. The elevator is that way," the Captain said, pointing Kris toward the trolley line that would take her from the yard to the central station hub and thence to the space elevator down to Wardhaven.

Kris glanced at her wrist unit, which was faster than thinking, WHAT TIME IS IT, NELLY? "My mother will be happy to know I have four full hours to get gussied up for her ball. I'll tell her my Captain shares her concerns for my social calendar."

"Or at least his wife does," Hayworth added as he turned toward the *Firebolt.*

Kris scrambled onto a passing trolley and plopped herself down in a vacant seat. She could spend the time in a pity party, not a bad idea with the mess her ship assignment was turning into. General McMorrison, the Chief of Wardhaven's General Staff, said he didn't know where he could dump his least-favorite billionaire Junior Officer, Prime Minister's brat, now Princess, and, oh yes, mutineer. But Kris hadn't picked her parents! And she hadn't had much more choice in relieving her last Skipper.

Still, Kris had asked for ship duty. Like every other Junior Officer, she wanted it in the worst way. And she'd gotten about the worst ship duty anyone could get. With the *Firebolt* tied up to Pier Eight going through change drills, the crew slept aboard the station . . . and Kris slept at home.

At least in college she'd gotten to sleep in the dorm. Here she was a grown woman sleeping in the same room she'd had as a kid. *It could be worse; at least Father and Mother lived downtown in the Prime Minister's Residency.*

And for this I went to college and joined the Navy!

"Kris, would you like to go over today's mail?" Nelly asked out loud, bringing her owner out of her funk.

"Might as well. Anything good?"

"I deleted most of the junk mail. Financial reports have been filed. I will give you a synopsis Friday. There is a message from Tom Lien. I did not review it."

"Thanks, Nelly," Kris said with a smile. Tommy was the one friend she'd made in the Navy. Problem was, he was still on the *Typhoon,* and she was now on the *Firebolt.* That was the Navy Way.

"Hi, short spoon," Tommy started, a laugh in his voice. "I've got some leave to burn." Kris knew just where she wanted him to burn it, too.

"There's this new planet, Itsahfine, out past Olympia. They say they've found some old ruins, maybe from the Three. Anyway, I've booked cheap space on a tramp starship, *Bellerophon,* and I'm headed out there for a week." Maybe Kris would take some leave. It'd be fun digging around in stuff left behind by the ancient races that built the jump points . . . with Tommy at her elbow.

"This leave," Tommy continued, "I'm not going near a Longknife. With luck, no one will just miss killing me, and I can actually relax." He was probably softening this with one of his lopsided grins, but Kris didn't have him on visual. She felt slugged in the gut. It wasn't her fault Tommy'd been too close during three tries to kill her. He'd only been at risk for two of them. Still, she couldn't really blame him for distancing himself from the Longknifes in general, and her in particular.

"I am sorry that Tommy feels that way," Nelly offered. Her latest upgrade was supposed to make her a better companion. All Kris had noticed was that the computer seemed prone to arguing.

Kris shrugged. I DIDN'T EXACTLY TELL TOMMY I WANTED TO SPEND MY LIFE WITH HIM, she told Nelly. What could she expect?

A toddler, defying gravity with each improbable step, hurtled by Kris, the string to a yellow toy duck clutched in his pudgy fingers. It followed him in fits and starts, quacking in his wake. The child rewarded its noise with happy laughs.

"Hold on tight," Kris whispered. "That's the only way you can hope to keep 'em close." At home in her closet somewhere must be a speckled giraffe that had once been her inseparable pal. Would people talk too much if a Navy Lieutenant/Princess suddenly started showing up with a clicking giraffe in tow?

Kris was drawn from further reveries by the elevator station. A ferry was in the final stages of loading. As usual, Kris headed for the observation deck, while most people settled into chairs that let them ignore the fact they were dropping 20,000 kilometers in less than a half hour. Kris loved the view.

As she settled into a seat, a man in a Vice Admiral's uniform sat down across from her. She started to rise, but he waved her down. Kris concentrated on staying out of his face by looking out the window. No view yet. The window reflected Kris's face . . . and the Admiral's. He was watching her. He looked familiar. *Where?*

Right. Scowling, Kris turned to the Admiral. "I know with the crisis, promotions are coming fast, but three months ago you were a Commander. Rapid promotion"—she took in his ribbons and the rest of his uniform, no real information there—"even for the Intelligence Service."

The man shrugged. "A Vice Admiral interrogating a muti-
nous Ensign, even an Ensign whose dad is the Prime Minister,
might get people talking. I figured a Commander was about
the right rank. What did you think?"

Kris thought she'd had enough of this man's games and let
the angry Prime Minister's daughter and billionaire speak. "I
didn't much like the topic of conversation, no matter who was
pushing it at me. I didn't plan a mutiny. It just happened."

"I know that now," the Admiral said, leaning back into
his seat as the car began to move. "We've finished debriefing those who took your side against your Captain, and its
clear you did nothing illegal beforehand. Some damn good
leadership in some tough situations, yes. Few men or women
could have earned the trust and respect you did. And that
fast."

"Flattery from Naval Intelligence?"

"I like to think that truth is my business. Care to make it
yours?"

Kris let her eyes rove out the window. The station with its
piers and ships spun above her, then quickly receded as they
fell away at one g acceleration. She spotted *Firebolt,* still in its
diminished form. Ship duty! Right!

"This a job offer?"

"Mac still doesn't know where to assign you. You're one of
his many hot potatoes. He offered me the chance to solve one
of his problems and one of mine. I can use someone with your
skills and unique opportunities. Unlike Hayworth, I don't mind
you using your own pet computer."

"For what? Does the Chief of Staff expect me to spy on my
father?"

The admiral rubbed his eyes with one hand. "Tact is not
one of your strong points."

"I'm not a spy," Kris said. "Certainly not on my own father."

"I don't want you to be. Mac doesn't want it either."

Kris took that with a grain of salt. "So, what kind of job are
you offering me?"

The Admiral swept a hand out to the black of space and
its unblinking stars. "The galaxy is a challenging place. It's
got the most dangerous critters in it: man. It's got people who

want this or that and frequently don't want other people to have that or this. Latest news reports say Siris and Humboldt are this close to war," he said, holding two fingers a few centimeters apart. "As a Princess—and yes, I know you hate the word—you can go lots of places an officer can't or shouldn't. You can learn and do things Wardhaven needs to know and get done. And I could help you as much as you could help me."

Kris turned back to stare out the window. The drop car passed rapidly into the atmosphere, causing fireflies of ionization. The dark of space was rapidly replaced by the haze of atmosphere. Below, Kris spotted the bay Wardhaven City wrapped itself around.

When she rode the elevator up, on her way to Officer Candidate School, she'd been glad to be quit of the place. Now, having seen a few other places, Wardhaven looked mighty nice.

Did she want to protect it?

That's why she put on the uniform. That and a wish to get out from under a father and mother who left very little air for their daughter. That and a desire to save a bit of this, do a bit of that.

Which she'd done.

Did she want to let this man call the shots for her now?

It had to be better than the *Firebolt,* she reminded herself.

But the *Firebolt* was a job for Lieutenant JG Kristine Anne Longknife. Not the Prime Minister's brat, or the Princess, or the rich kid. This Admiral, if that was what he was, wanted her for all the things about her that she wanted to escape.

She shook her head. "Sorry, Admiral, I've got this job. A ship depending on me. I wouldn't want to disappoint my Captain."

"I doubt he'd shed a tear if you got new orders."

"Yes, but the Chief Engineer loves what me and Nelly do."

"My budget can get Dale a very good computer."

The bastard even knew the Chief Engineer's first name. "What is it about *no* that you don't understand?" Kris asked.

"Just wanted to make sure *no* was *no*," the Admiral said,

reaching in his pocket for an old-fashioned printed business card.

Maurice Crossenshild
Special Systems Analyst
Call anyplace, anytime
27-38-212-748-3001

Kris eyed the card for only a moment. She'd never seen a fifteen-digit phone number. Fourteen, yes. Fifteen! What did the two do? NELLY, YOU GOT IT?

YES.

Kris tore the card in half, then into quarters, and handed it back to the man. "Not interested."

He gave her a crack of a smile. "Would not have expected anything less from you, but Mac wanted me to try. Have a good evening. Maybe I'll see you at the ball tonight."

"What rank should I look for?" Kris asked to his back, but, despite the sign flashing for all passengers to stay put, the man made his way out of the observation deck. *And they say I don't follow the rules.* Kris snorted.

Harvey, the old family chauffeur, was waiting for her as she left the ferry. Jack, her Protective Service agent, was right beside him. "How'd the test cruise go?" the driver asked as her agent eyed the surroundings.

"Not good. Looks like we'll be tied up for the next month while they try something new," she told him. "So I'm off early. Think Lotty can scare up a bite to eat before I have to dress for tonight's command performance?"

"And when hasn't my wife?" he said with a grin, then added softly, "Tru would like you to drop by when you have the time."

Kris raised an eyebrow. Aunty Tru was retired now from her job as Wardhaven's Chief of Info War. Still, the honorary aunt had been helping Kris with her math and computer homework since first grade—and could cook up a fantastic batch of chocolate chip cookies.

But when Tru quit trusting her messages to the net, life did get interesting. "Why don't we drop by on the way home."

Harvey nodded. The car, not a limo today, but just as armored, was in a reserved security lot, something new to the area around the elevator since the Society of Humanity self-destructed and Wardhaven doubled its defense budget. Kris settled in for a quiet drive. Maybe she should review the engine room specs for the *Firebolt*?

"Test really disappointing?" Jack asked.

"We were so close." Kris sighed. "Last benchmark, then bam, we're back to square one."

"Frustrating," her Agent said, his eyes roving the traffic. Jack had a knack for being both security and confidant. There was talk that a Princess deserved a full security detail. It would probably mean a promotion for Jack. For Kris, it would mean losing times like these. True, somebody—apparently a lot of somebodies—wanted her dead, but no attack had ever been made on Wardhaven. Besides, a Navy Junior Officer couldn't move in a security bubble. Or maybe she just didn't want to.

At Tru's apartment complex, Jack activated the car's security system and followed Kris and Harvey into the elevator. Tru had bought a penthouse when she retired. Her view of Wardhaven City wasn't quite as breathtaking as that from Grampa Al's lofty tower outside town, but it was still spectacular. More spectacular was Tru's hug.

"I didn't expect you to drop everything and come running just because your old Aunty Tru sent up a smoke signal," she said as she engulfed Kris in her arms. There'd been a time when all Kris had to hold on to was Tru's hugs . . . and the bottle. Those times were long gone, but Kris would never pass up a few moments feeling safe in Tru's arms.

Hug over, Kris explained that the test ended early.

"Problem?"

"I'm still alive. The ship's still in one piece. Nothing we can't work around. But it looks like Grampa Al will have a major market for Uni-plex.

Tru scowled at that. "I turn the evidence of an attempt to kill you over to him and his labs to figure out who did it. Instead, they come up with a whole new product line."

Kris shrugged. "If Al makes money off my attempted

murders, I figure he'll make a fortune off what finally gets me." No one else saw the humor. "So, Aunty Tru, why'd you call in the Navy? Run out of Marines?"

"Actually, it's Nelly I want."

Kris raised an eyebrow. Tru was responsible for most of the software on Kris's pet computer; Nelly could do things very few computers could. Still, Sam, Tru's personal computer, was probably one of those few. "We just upgraded her," Kris pointed out. "I thought Nelly and I were about as far out on the bleeding edge as you dared go."

"You are," Tru agreed. "The last time I ran diagnostics on Nelly's new self-organizing circuitry, she was, gram for gram, the best in her class."

Kris began drooling over the new, self-organizing computing gel the first time she set eyes on it. Akin to smart metal, this let the computer organize its circuitry at the molecular level as it went along, and modify it as needed. Kris wasn't sure whether she or Nelly was the most excited by it. "So?"

"Nelly is greatly underutilized. I wonder if you might like to put her excess capacity to work on a challenge?"

Kris had learned to cringe when Tru said "challenge." Yes, at six, Kris would do an excited dance at the word. At fifteen, the thought of having the best personal sidekick at school was primo plus. But Kris was a serving officer. Having her computer go down didn't just mean a quick stop by Aunty Tru's on the way home from school for repairs and cookies. If Nelly had locked up today, the Navy might be missing a boatload of people.

"What's caught your fancy?" Kris said, taking a step back.

Tru beamed, unrepentant. "Let me show you."

Kris knew the room they headed for. There were clean rooms, and then there was Aunty Tru's lab. There was no need for special clothes. The airlock into what had been a spare bedroom spritzed Kris with a thin fog of nanos that lifted off the grime and dirt of the day . . . down to the five-nanometer level. The worktable along one white wall might be missing one of the latest gizmos for micro development. If so, the missing device was on order. What surprised Kris was the sight of a stasis box sitting in the middle of the table. Now, that was overkill.

More surprising, Tru did not flip it open.

"Your Aunt Alnaba sent that from Santa Maria."

Great-aunt Alnaba was a real aunt, Great-grampa Ray's youngest girl. She'd specialized in zenobiology and devoted herself to studying the artifacts the Three left behind on Santa Maria. She'd spent a lifetime trying to figure out bits and pieces of a technology so far beyond humanity's present level that they had built jump points in space as highways across the stars. Grampa Ray had worked with Alnaba most of the last twenty years. He'd never met a challenge he couldn't handle. Kris grinned; cracking the technology of the Three and the present politics of humanity just might ruin Grampa Ray's perfect score. "What's in it?"

Tru did not open the box but pulled a picture from her pocket. It showed a small square beside a penny for perspective. As wide as the penny was across, it was a bit thicker. "That is a piece of rock from the mountain range along Santa Maria's North Continent. We cut those mountains up pretty badly during the war against the Professor."

"Cut them up, hell. That Disappearing Box made them vanish, just vanish." Kris shook her head. "Navy tried for fifty years to figure out how that little box worked. Don't know any more now than they did the day it arrived in the lab."

"Yes," Tru agreed. "But maybe they're starting too high on the tech food chain. You have to know how to use a screwdriver before you can take a clock apart. I don't think we've figured out the Three's equivalent of a screwdriver. A million years ago, we were using stone flakes for tools. Could that version of the human brain conceive of a screwdriver, even if you put one in its hand?"

Kris mulled that idea over, could add nothing to it, and waved at the stasis box. "So, what is that?" she repeated.

"A tiny part of the data storage that was locked up in those mountains."

"Is it active?"

"I don't know."

"What's it contain?"

"I don't know."

"What do you know?"

Tru grinned. "Nothing at all. The question is, what would you like to know?"

Kris eyed the picture, then the box. "How would we find out if this rock has any data stored in it that can be retrieved?"

"By trying."

"How?"

"Whatever we tried would have to be very sophisticated . . . or maybe very simple. It would need to be flexible and willing to adjust to just about any requirement. I don't even know what kind of power this thing operated on. We'd have to construct different power sources, apply them very carefully, and see if the mouse squeaks."

Kris rubbed her nose; Nelly was suddenly feeling very heavy on her collarbone. "Self-organizing circuitry, huh."

"Self-organizing. Very powerful, and very well integrated with its human. Your Aunt Alnaba and her team tried several, what you might call, standard approaches. You know, the big lab, working long hours, everyone looking over everyone else's shoulders. No results. Then she asked me if I had any ideas. I told her I did."

"And they were?"

"Ever read how the Professor contacted your Grampa Ray?"

"It got kind of complicated. Biology was never my favorite science," Kris dodged.

"Mine neither. What I found interesting, though, was the relationship between his sleeping brain and the tumor growing in his skull. Do you have any idea how important sleep is?"

"Only when I'm not getting enough of it."

"Newborn babies take in as much of this new and confusing world as they can, then fall asleep to absorb it all. Study, sleep, study, sleep. How many times did I tell you when you were in high school that a good night's sleep was the best preparation you could do for a test?"

Kris chuckled, then, as honor required, gave her teenage response. "A test is a test. What you put on the test is what matters, not what you put on a pillow."

Tru scowled as she always had, then shook her head. "My suggestion to Alnaba is that we put this in someone's personal computer who could sleep on it. See what their computer and their sleeping mind can make of it."

"So, you're going to upgrade your Sammy with self-organizing circuitry."

"Sadly, I can't afford it." So, why was Tru grinning?

"You didn't come up with this idea about the time I sprang for Nelly's last upgrade, did you?"

"No. Actually, I came up with the idea shortly after you first saw a computer with self-organizing circuits. You've never been one to pass up the latest computer whizbang." Tru's grin was once again unrepentant.

"And where did I pick up this bad habit?"

"Yes," Tru pouted, "but us old retired folks can't keep up with every new bit of this and that. I've had to learn to live on a budget."

Kris knew she was being finagled by the one person in human space who knew where all her *fins* were to *agle*.

"Tru, it might be fun to crack some Three technology, but just three hours ago I was nanoseconds away from being blown to quarks. I can't have Nelly down with a Three-induced headache."

"And you won't. Sammy and I have come up with a multiple buffer approach that will keep what's going on around the chip from slipping over into your main processing."

"*Will* or *should?*" Kris demanded.

"Young woman, you really should talk to whomever was your teacher. You are far too paranoid about modern technology to survive in this modern world."

"That's exactly who I am talking to. I recall a certain trig exam where I ended up with nothing but my own ten fingers to count on when my pet computer got into a do-loop chasing the value of pi."

Tru chuckled. "You will agree, that was a learning experience."

"Yeah, right! And one I never intend to repeat."

"Why don't you have Nelly look at the buffers Sam and I worked up?"

"Nelly?" Kris said.

"It might be interesting," Nelly said slowly, as if inviting Aunt Tru to go on.

"Can't hurt us to look," Kris agreed. For a long minute she could feel the silence from Nelly as the computer concentrated on the data transfer and adjusted to the new systems.

"They go in very smoothly," Nelly said, "and they include

a new interface as well as three levels of buffer between me and the stone. I should be able to view anything going on in any one of the buffers and block it from causing me or you any harm. There is also a smart new recovery mode that would allow me to quickly bring more of my capacity on-line if I did have a major systems failure and had to recover."

"You want to try this?" Kris said, before remembering that *want* was not a word you used with a computer.

"I think it would be fun to find out how to build new jump points between the stars," Nelly answered.

"Looks like Nelly has organized some interesting circuitry for herself," Tru drawled. "Bet my Sammie would like to see the specs for them."

"Yes," came in an eager voice.

"Enough, already." Kris sighed. "Yes, I'd love it if we could build our own paths rather than being stuck on the ones the Three left behind." The Paris system came immediately to mind; its scattered jump points almost got humanity into a war. And it wasn't as if she and Nelly would be doing anything important for the next month. Why not do something extreme? Kris gave her aunt Tru a sigh. "You owe me for this one."

Tru grinned.

"So, what do we do?"

Tru flipped a button on the picture she'd been holding, and it ran through a process for implanting the stone onto Nelly's central processing area. "We'll use a different-colored dollop of self-organizing gel. That should let it build not only connectors but any power supply conversion you need. Also, if we have to scrape it off Nelly, the color marker will help."

"Sounds okay," Kris said, then the skeptical part of her brain kicked in. "Where'd you get the money for the gel?"

"I won a small lottery pot," Tru said without looking up from arranging various tools and stasis boxes on her worktable.

"Won or rigged?"

"Now didn't your dad say the last time he reauthorized the lottery that some of the money should go for research?"

"Yes," Kris agreed slowly, wondering if Father had this in mind and not at all sure he didn't. What had Harvey said when Kris first began to question her aunt's lottery "luck"? "A smart woman knows not to push it." No question, Tru was smart. Kris loosened her collar to take Nelly from around her shoulders.

"Keep your connection," Tru said. "We'll need rapid feedback from Nelly when we start this." The wire between Nelly and the back of Kris's neck was smart metal; it stretched out as Kris set her personal computer on the table. Kris knelt down to keep the distance short; the longer the wire, the narrower the bandwidth. The actual installation was over in a moment. The interfacing gel slid on easily. Tru told Kris how wide a bed the rock would need, and Nelly quickly arranged it. Then Tru set the small wafer in place.

"There, now that didn't hurt." Her old auntie smiled.

"Isn't that what the condemned man said as the trapdoor snapped open?" Kris said dryly. "Nelly, run full diagnostics."

"Already running," Nelly said. "Everything appears normal."

"And the chip?" Tru asked.

"No activity," Nelly replied in a low-tech voice. "Excuse me while I initiate interface with the new gel."

"Oh, right," Tru said, biting one fingernail. Kris had never seen her aunt so excited.

"I am developing a project plan that will involve triple checks of buffers at every phase of activation of the wafer," Nelly said. "I do not expect to begin testing power sources before this time tomorrow."

"You can go faster than that," Tru said, almost stomping her foot with impatience.

"And who taught me to take new things slowly and carefully?" Kris shot back.

"Yes, but you never paid me any mind before."

"Now I'm a mature woman," Kris said, standing up to her full height. She didn't exactly tower over Tru, but her three extra centimeters did come in handy once in a while. "And I have a ball tonight, command performance."

"You could skip it. Tell your mom you were detained."

"My Skipper is now tracking my social schedule."

"Your mother didn't—"

"No, but I suspect my Captain very much wants to avoid a call from Mother. And if it does come, he wants to be as innocent as possible."

"Coward," Tru said, but she was ushering Kris from the lab.

"Strange, those Navy types, lions in the face of laser fire, but threaten them with society, and they flee for the door."

"Like a young woman I know." Tru chuckled. "Well, bring Nelly by tomorrow so I can check up on her. Sam and I may have some test ideas of our own. You'll need to check in daily," she said as Kris slipped out the door.

3

The drive home was quiet. Kris's efforts to involve Nelly in anything were met with "Is this activity essential?" in that low-tech voice that showed Nelly was otherwise busy.

At Nuu House, Harvey excused himself to park the car. That was strange; he usually left it in the entrance's wide circular drive. When Jack tried to go with him, Kris knew something was amiss. "Jack, stay with me. If something goes wrong with Nelly's new installation, I might need a hand."

NOTHING WILL GO WRONG WITH ME, Nelly shot back.

QUIET, Kris ordered silently.

"I thought you trusted your Aunt Tru," Jack muttered.

"Never can be too safe."

"Now I know something is definitely wrong with you," Jack growled through a smile but followed her into the foyer. The black and white tiled spiral swirled to the center of the room. The large library off to the right was dark and quiet, no longer a military command post for her Grampas Ray and Trouble.

King Ray had taken over a major hotel downtown for his court while the politicians debated how much of a palace he really needed. Grampa Ray would have been happy in a two-bedroom town house, but since the politicians of eighty planets had talked him into some kind of kingship over their cobbled-together United Sentients, he was having fun needling them with a full-court press. Or a press for a full court.

Her Grampa Trouble was offering advice "purely as a consultant" to several planets as they struggled to form their own defense forces and meld them with the new United Sentients' total force. That left Nuu House so empty it echoed.

Except that standing at the foot of the stairs was a stranger. The woman, in a severe gray dress cut long and buttoned at the neck, stood, hands folded. She was Kris's height, maybe a bit shorter, but she held herself so rigidly upright it made no difference. "Princess Longknife," the woman said. "I am your new body servant."

Kris eyed the woman without slowing. Her face was free of makeup, her jet-black hair coiled in a tight bun. *She's going to give me a makeover? She needs one herself!* "It's Lieutenant Longknife," Kris shot back, "and I don't need any servants."

"Your mother disagrees."

"Add one more to the myriad things where we differ," Kris said, adjusting her course for the stairs to be as far from the woman as possible. The woman let Kris pass but followed her up as silently and nearly invisible as Jack, until Kris turned on the second-floor landing to take the stairs to her third-floor room.

Clearing her voice, the woman said, "Your quarters are now on the second floor."

"I've been moved!" Kris said softly, one foot on the stairs up.

"Yes. Your room was too small for your new responsibilities. I have rearranged you in a second-floor suite."

Kris turned to face this new problem. "You moved me without asking!"

"You have a ball tonight. There is much to do and no time to waste. Harvey suggested this suite."

"Harvey's in on this."

"His wife, Lotty, agreed."

Which meant everyone living in Nuu House was backing this interloper. Drastic actions were called for. "Jack, shoot this trespasser."

Her security agent pursed his lips as he scratched his head. "Don't think I can. They took that paragraph out of my job description last month after your old man freed the slaves." He offered his hand. "I'm Jack Montoya. I didn't get your name."

"Abby Nightengale," the woman answered, then lowered her voice. "I was hired from an Earth agency. Did this planet just outlaw slavery?"

Kris started to bark a laugh, then realized this poor woman had traveled a hundred light-years to take a job on a world she knew nothing about. Could Kris have even done that?

"Rest assured, we are as modern as Earth in all our conveniences and vices," Jack told Abby, adding power to his words with one of his gentle smiles.

"They told me *that* when I signed the contract," Abby said.

"But you never can tell around the wild Rim of human space," Jack finished.

"Were you expecting your Princess in a fur bikini?" Kris snapped, feeling less sympathy in the light of all Jack's concern for this new woman.

Abby looked Kris up and down. "I had hoped her hair might be in better shape. Show me your nails," Abby ordered, took two quick steps, reached out, and held Kris's fingers up to the light. "I guess it could be worse. At least you don't bite them."

Kris yanked her hands back. "I like me just the way I am. I don't need someone wasting their day making me who I'm not."

Abby had no answer for that, or else she let Kris have the last say. Kris started to stomp down the hall to an open doorway on her right. Abby cleared her throat . . . and pointed to the left. Scowling, Kris followed the intruder. The door she opened was to one of the guest suites. A large sitting room opened to two smaller rooms, one a bedroom, the other a study that was in the process of being converted into a dressing room. Already its walls were hung with dresses that Kris did not remember buying. In a small corner hung her uniforms.

"I'll start your bath," Abby said.

"I can handle my own shower," Kris shot back.

The woman paused in the doorway to a very luxurious bath. Turning to Kris she said, "You have pretty much handled things on your own for most of the last ten years, or so I'm told. You have a full schedule as an active duty naval officer and as a political show horse, otherwise known as Princess. I think I can help you if you will give me half a chance."

Kris shrugged; the woman was stubborn. Maybe the best

way out was through. Let the woman do what she was going to do anyway and find out for herself just how little Kris needed a . . . what . . . a mother hen. Mother had never been much of a mother; it might be interesting to see what this Abigail was good for.

While water ran in the next room, Kris disconnected from Nelly and settled her on the dressing table. The computer had been silent through all of this, intent on navel gazing or Aunt Tru's project, or maybe just too smart to get involved.

"Harvey says he'll bring up a supper tray in a half hour," Jack called from the next room. At least someone was giving her what she wanted. Defiantly naked, Kris strode into the bath. Abby offered her a hand into the tub; Kris ignored it and kept her own balance as she put a foot in. The water was warm. Very nice. As Kris settled in, Abby poured an aromatic liquid into the tub. Once Kris was in place, and a pleasant "Aah" had escaped her, Abby turned on the jets.

Kris's one experiment with jets and bubble bath had been a disaster. Whatever Abby used just turned into a pleasant, low foam. With gently pulsating water caressing her, scents relaxing her, Kris leaned back, but refused to let the moment waste away. Finding out what made this interloper tick was suddenly high on Kris's list of things to do today.

"So, what made you want to be . . ." Kris could think of several descriptions of Abby's duties, all sharp with put-downs. She settled for "this?"

"Have a job, rather than living on Earth welfare?" Abby said through a smile with too much teeth.

"That wasn't what I said."

"No, but isn't that what you Rim people think? Decadent Earth where everyone just parties."

"Earth couldn't be the power it is if everyone was just looking for the next party," Kris snapped. She'd risked her life to keep Earth and the Rim from going to war. If anyone respected Earth's power, it was her.

"Harvey just brought up the mail," Jack called. "Where do you want it?"

"Mail, as in snail?" Kris called back.

"Two rather large packages. One weighs about *ten* kilos. Don't think even Nelly could handle that in storage."

"Put them on the dressing table. I'll look at them later."

"Okay," Jack said. "I won't peek." He hurried past the bath door, a box under one arm, a large padded envelope held up to block his view through the door. Damn. Kris wouldn't mind if he took a peek once in a while.

On the way out, Jack did toss an unrepentant smile her way. Unfortunately, all there was for him to see was froth and suds.

"Nice guy," Abby said, eyeing the door after Jack passed.

"Yep," Kris agreed. "Hand me a towel. Let's see what the mail brought."

Abby did, and didn't try to interfere with Kris drying herself. As Kris stepped from the tub, Abby wrapped her in a lush terrycloth robe. "Where'd this come from?"

"After your mother's description, I told her I needed a budget for essentials and for your wardrobe."

"So you're spending my money."

"You really should spend a bit on things that matter rather than frivolous things like your personal computer."

"Nelly saved my life today, and a boat full of shipmates. Nelly is nothing frivolous."

"Your mother's words, not mine."

"If you want to survive around me, you'll learn not to quote my mother."

"So I noticed. Now sit down; your hair needs washing."

"I washed it this morning."

"I daresay you got it wet. Have you ever heard of conditioner? You know, that stuff that smells good." Kris found herself maneuvered into a chair beside an oversize washbasin. Before she could react, Abby had her hair sopping wet and was massaging in something that smelled like strawberries. Hair washing had never been so sensuous when Kris did it herself. By the time Abby was drying Kris's hair, she was almost willing to admit this Earth woman might be worth whatever Mother was paying.

Settled at the dressing table, Kris eyed her mail. The heavy box was from Grampa Al. Kris ignored it, strongly suspecting it held a first production sample of Uni-plex. The envelope was more intriguing. Its return address was Earth. "This must be for you," she told Abby.

"It's addressed to Ensign Longknife," Jack said from the door where he and Harvey were waiting expectantly.

Kris pulled her robe tighter around herself and swiveled the chair to face them. "So what is it?"

"We don't know. Will you open it, woman?" Harvey snapped.

So Kris did. But a look inside didn't tell her that much. She poured the contents out on her dressing table, next to Nelly. The men came to peer over her shoulder.

Harvey was the first to grasp what they saw. He let out a low whistle. "Is that what I think it is?"

Abby picked up a heavy gold and jewel-encrusted pendant. "One of my employers," she whispered, "was very proud of her ancestor who died in the Iteeche Wars. This hung in her living room beside a portrait of her great-grandmother. It's the highest award Earth can give, the Order of the Wounded Lion."

"It's awfully big for a medal," Kris said, puzzled.

"You don't wear the Order like other medals, young woman," Harvey reproved her. "This sunburst goes on your uniform breast pocket, or for really formal occasions, you wear the sash and use the medal to clasp the sash at the waist. Don't they teach you junior officers anything these days?" He grinned.

"Nope." Kris grinned back. "We JOs pretty much waste all our time on engineering, battle tactics, and similar trivia," she said, examining the gold medallion. The highest award Earth could give. Wow. And when was the last time it was mailed out in a brown wrapper? *Damn it, I worked just as hard to earn this bauble as anyone who got it hung on them in a rose garden. Will everything I do good be swept under the rug because I'm one of those Longknifes? But Lordy, if I screw up . . .*

"What did you do to earn this?" Abby asked.

"If I told you, then Jack truly would have to shoot you," Kris deadpanned. To Kris's surprise, Jack nodded.

Abby frowned briefly at the put-off, but picked up the blue sash and took it to a cream dress hanging against one wall of the dressing room. Unlike the monstrosities Mother chose, this one was of a conservative cut: strapless, pulled tight at the waist before flowing out smoothly to floor length. While the "in" fashion might range from shapeless sacks to damn near naked, this was always appropriate. "You can wear the sash over the shoulder," Abby said, "and pin it here, under the opposite arm so that it flows smoothly across you. I think that would be best," the Earth woman told Kris. The men nodded agreement.

Kris sighed. Like a large blue arrow, it would point straight at the empty space in the dress where most women had breasts. "I will be wearing my uniform tonight."

Abby frowned at the corner that held the items of Navy issue: battle dress, khakis, whites, and the standard formal evening dress of a junior female officer. She pulled the formal from the lineup and held it next to the cream dress. One was appropriate for a fairy Princess. The other was just flat dowdy.

The uniform's white, floor-length skirt was cut from the same design as a millennia of gunnysacks. Kris had chosen the blue wool blouse that had the tight choker neck, thereby avoiding any hint of décolletage. Miniatures of her few medals were already in place. Abby looked back and forth between Kris and the standard dress uniform. "The colors are not your best," she said as she chewed on her lower lip.

"The colors are established Navy wide," Kris answered back.

Abby laid the Wounded Lion's blue sash across the blouse. The light, watermarked blue of the sash and the dark blue of the blouse could only be said to fit because a thousand years of valor and service said they did. Abby shook her head, opened her mouth.

Kris cut her off. "That is what I am wearing tonight."

Abby turned to Harvey and Jack. "Do all military uniforms seek to make a woman look so . . ."

"Unappealing?" Jack offered.

"Yes."

"It seems that way," Harvey agreed. "Women are there to do a job, not flirt," the old trooper growled.

"But the men look so dashing in their uniforms," Abby said.

"A historical anachronism left from days past," Kris spat. "We women, however, have all the advantages of the modern era."

"Or error," Jack put in with one of his patented grins.

"Supper is ready," Nelly spoke up, still in a low-tech voice, startling Kris. "Harvey, Lotty wants you downstairs to pick up a tray. Will you men be eating in the kitchen?"

"Looks that way," Jack said, and the men left Kris and her new mistress of the wardrobe to dress. Having won on the most important point of debate that afternoon, Kris let Abby do as she pleased. Pampered, made over, and perfumed, her short, blond hair wound around her head in a confection that Kris never would have attempted, she was dressed in less than an hour. Nelly was back around Kris's shoulders, a second reason to wear the uniform, before she and Abby crossed swords again. Abby returned with the diamond and gold tiara Mother had bought at some overpriced rummage sale. "Perfect for a Princess," Mother had gushed.

As Kris did then, she said, "I'm not wearing that."

Abby started to say something, looked at Kris, and seemed to think better of it. "What will you be wearing?"

"Right beside that in my jewelry box was a simple silver circlet, standard issue for any woman junior officer in formal dinner attire."

"Not that!"

"Yes that."

Abby glanced at the tiara, then eyed the circlet. "A Princess should wear a tiara."

"That is a tiara. Says so right in the dress regulations. Tiara, formal, junior officers, female."

"Do senior officers wear something nicer?" Abby said, trading the diamond concoction for the Navy issue.

"Yep. They get nicer and nicer until Admirals are wearing something pretty fancy."

"And are very old," Abby said with a sour frown on her face.

"Horribly old," Kris agreed.

Tiaraed and sashed, Kris made her way carefully down the stairs in heels twice as high as she normally wore . . . which also were prescribed in regulations. Maybe Abby had a point. Whoever designed this outfit sure hadn't put her physical comfort or appearance at a very high priority. Was the uniform regulations development bureau the last place in the Navy where a woman hater was allowed free rein? Jack, now in a tux, stood at the bottom of the stairs.

"You going to catch me when I fall?"

"Looks like it."

"You could come up here and help me stay on these heels."

"And get spiked by one? Sorry, not in my job description."

"Seems like your job description is getting kind of short."

"Yes, isn't it," Jack said, stepping aside as Kris left the stairs behind her. Harvey brought a monster limo to the front drive. Abby helped Kris arrange her skirt in the backseat.

Harvey got the limo on autopilot, then turned to take in Kris. "That sash does brighten up a dull outfit," he drawled. "By the way, can a Wardhaven officer wear an Earth order?"

"Oh my gosh!" Kris was learning a Princess did not use the *S* word in public and should practice not using it in private. She reached to unpin the sash.

"I checked." Harvey grinned. "Earth, being an ally of Wardhaven . . . in some small thanks to whatever you did or didn't do at the Paris system . . . their orders are authorized."

"Harvey, you could have told me that in the first place!"

"Yes, but then we'd have missed that look on your face."

"What look?"

"Oh, part shock, part dismay, part 'Oh my God, I've screwed up again!' It's very becoming on you."

"I did not think I'd screwed up again." Kris settled for appealing only one of the three charges from her oldest friend.

The ball failed to match the excitement of its preparation. Kris passed the usual chatter with the usual suspects. Didn't these people have day jobs to tire them out? Her older brother Honovi was at Father's right hand, like a good junior member of Parliament, understudying the master. Since there was no immediate political need to paper over their feelings about her career choice, Kris and the Prime Minister ignored each other.

Mother could not be ignored.

"What do you think of Abby?" was the woman's opening gambit.

Kris took a step back and opened her arms to show off her uniform. "I only fired her twice as she was getting me ready."

"You can't fire her. I'm paying for her. I had hoped she would at least put you in something presentable."

"That would require firing her three times in one night."

"And I was so looking forward to her dressing you in something that would remove my daughter from the top of the fashion police's ten-worst-dressed list." Mother sighed.

"Have your fashion *policia* send me the citation, Mother. I'll file it among my dust bunnies." Kris moved along as Mother launched into a diatribe to the woman on her right.

Grampa Ray made the required appearance and was mobbed by both favor seekers and eligible matrons looking to end his long years of widowerhood. Nothing like the chance to be Queen of eighty planets to gather every social climber within light-years. A few were presently married but clearly willing to trade up. King Ray made his way through the bejeweled crowd as a jungle scout might pass through a trove of bothersome flies. But he noticed who he wanted, and that included Kris. He raised an eyebrow at the sash and medallion.

"Accessories make the outfit," Kris said. Fashion gossips might ignore the Wounded Lion; people like Grampa knew better.

"Earth is grateful you saved their bacon." Grampa Ray grinned. "And their battle fleet," he added with one of his tight, warm smiles that anyone would risk their life for.

"There really wasn't another option," Kris said. Her eyes suddenly watery, she settled them on the deeply carpeted floor.

"Been in that horrible position myself a few times," King Raymond answered. "Lousy situations to be in. But the survivors make for nice company." Kris was halfway home before she lost the glow from that moment.

"Kris," Nelly said, "I have a collect call. I think you should accept it."

"Who is it?" Kris quit taking collect calls early in her high school years. It was amazing the people who wanted to talk to a Longknife and expected her to pay for the privilege.

"A Miss Pasley is calling from the starship *Bellerophon*."

"*Bellerophon*? Should I know that ship?"

"It is a tramp, mixed cargo and passengers. Tommy took passage on it, you may recall."

Kris had forgotten. "I accept the charges." A system voice told Kris she would be debited for a price that made even Kris's eyes widen. Miss Pasley, whoever she was, had slapped a very costly priority on her message. Kris undid the top buttons of her choker collar so Nelly could project a holovid of the call.

A young woman, long, straight blond hair falling to her shoulders, came up. "Miss Longknife, or Princess Longknife," she said nervously, "you don't know me. But I know Tommy Lien, who says he's a good friend of yours. He told me that if anything strange happened to him, I should call this number."

The woman glanced off camera. "I think something has happened to Tommy. He wanted to see the ruins on Itsahfine. We were studying all the stuff about them in the ship's database. He even had stuff he'd picked up, so I know he intended to go to Itsahfine. But he's not going there.

"The Belly, that's what we all call the *Bellerophon,* made a stop to refuel or maybe shift cargo here at Castagon 6. A guy came up while Tom and I were talking, said he was Calvin Sandfire and had to pass some words with Tom."

"Tom left me, and I haven't seen him since. The ship's left the station, and we're on our way to Itsahfine. I've asked all the other passengers, and no one has seen Tom. I've called him on net, but he doesn't answer. I checked with the Purser, but he says Tommy's room is still his, and he won't do a search. I think he thinks I'm just chasing him. But I think Tom left the ship with Mr. Sandfire. Maybe it's nothing, but I thought I ought to let you know that *I* think something strange has happened to Tom."

Kris went over the message quickly in her mind as she told Nelly to save message. "What do you think?" she asked Jack.

The secret service agent rubbed his chin. "When you're free and unencumbered, you can change your priorities very quickly. Maybe Mr. Sandfire made him a better offer than crumbling relics of the Three. Maybe he was from Santa Maria and had a message for Tom from his family." Jack shrugged. "It could be a lot of things that don't add up to bad."

"Or it could be bad," Kris said. "Nelly, do a search on Mr. Calvin Sandfire. Start with Santa Maria."

"Already working," Nelly said, her voice back to its usual sweet self. Tru would have to wait a while longer to crack the rock chip and the Three. "I am also searching on Wardhaven, Earth, and Greenfeld." Wardhaven was home to Kris. Earth was Earth. Greenfeld . . . well, that was a totally different can of worms. With luck, Nelly would draw a blank there.

"Also, Nelly, check ships' registries for a Mr. Sandfire." Of course, that would tell them nothing if Mr. Sandfire was getting the use of a ship by leasing, renting, stealing, hijacking, or any of the other myriad of ways that people had of getting around starship ownership while acquiring needed mobility.

The problem with having readily available information about a hundred billion people on six hundred planets is learning patience while it was converted from "readily" to "available." The long silence of the drive home was broken. "Mr. Sandfire is not in the Santa Maria database." No surprise there.

"Mr. Sandfire is not a registered owner of any starship."

"You couldn't expect things to be that easy," Jack said.

"Mr. Calvin Sandfire is the owner of Ironclad Software, registered on Greenfeld," Nelly reported five minutes later.

"Oh shit," Kris moaned. There were times when even a Princess had to say what she had to say.

"What should I know about this fellow?" Jack said.

"He's not already in your official reports?"

"Nope, but you have this way of not letting my agency know of all the people that want you dead."

"I don't think Mr. Sandfire has tried to kill me yet," Kris said, giving Jack a cheery smile. He didn't look at all mollified. "He is reported to have paid off the man that added a heart attack to the last meal of my previous squadron commander, Commodore Sampson. His software was what Sampson used to keep the ships of AttackRon Six at the Paris system from hearing their attack orders were bogus."

"Oh shit," Jack echoed her.

Harvey didn't bat an eyelash at all those answers to his questions about Paris. "Well, at least he's far away from us."

"For now, at least," Kris said. Jack eyed her, but Kris offered no further comment, and Jack said nothing.

4

Kris drummed her fingers on the dressing table while Abby got her hair down. "Search on ships that docked at Castagon 6 a week before the *Bellerophon* and get their passenger lists."

"Yes ma'am," said Nelly.

In sweatpants and tank top, Kris joined Harvey and Jack in the sitting room, now an intelligence center. One wall proved to be a screen. It now showed what they knew: not much. Lotty arrived; no one was in danger of starving tonight or going without caffeine.

As Kris settled into a lounger, Nelly announced the search of shipping to Castagon 6 was negative. Only the *Bellerophon* had docked there in the last week. "Why do I find that hard to believe? Nelly, Tru has this way of getting better information about shipping. Check with Sam." Nelly made a call.

Sam suggested the list of ships jumping *to* a port often showed more traffic than the list of ships the port said arrived.

The morning sun streamed through Kris's unused bedroom before Nelly completed a much broader search. Done the other way around, it seemed that the yacht *Space Adder* had jumped from Turantic 4 with the destination of Castagon 6 two days before the *Bellerophon* arrived. The *Space Adder* was back at

Turantic two days after Tom's ship left. Ah, the bits of information in the public domain databases . . . if you just didn't get misled by the easily doctored answers.

Lotty arrived with breakfast as Kris sat silently organizing her day. She should report to the ship. It was Saturday, and she didn't have to, but the Captain usually put in half a day, and Kris tried to match him. She stifled a yawn and reviewed what Nelly had sifted out of the mass of information available. The wall screen was now full; down one side was a chronology. While Kris had found out about Tom's travel plans and interruptions only in the last twelve hours, it had been longer in the doing.

Tommy had messaged her before boarding the *Bellerophon* five days ago. Being a thrifty, underpaid junior officer, his message went standby and had been bumped from the queue several times in its transit through two jump points from High Cambria to Wardhaven. Kris wondered if that was Tom's way of ensuring he was well on his way before she could do anything.

Miss Pasley's message had farther to go but had spent Kris's money going faster. Tommy apparently had left the *Bellerophon* a bit more than two days ago. Which meant he'd arrived at Turantic late yesterday while Kris was passing social chitchat with a thousand of her father's closest friends. Kris slowly munched one of Lotty's high-fiber muffins while absorbing the time flow.

A second section was now a stellar map, showing the planets important to this drill. The *Bellerophon*'s trip from High Cambria to Itsahfine involved four jumps but only one stop, that at Castagon 6. The round trip from Turantic to Castagon was just two jumps. Wardhaven to Turantic was a three-jump trip along well-traveled trading lanes.

"Nelly, do me a full political workup on Turantic." Until recently, human space was human space, and a study of the Society of Humanity supposedly told the tale. Growing up sharing a dinner table with her father had given Kris an early realization that what the high school civics teacher called United Humanity was full of factions that the Prime Minister regularly had to juggle to get anything done. Now those factions were independent associations, and star maps needed not just lines for shipping lanes but different colors to show where the customs inspectors lived and maybe, just maybe, a battle fleet might be making motions toward another color on the map.

She lit up Earth, the mother of this whole mess. The first two hundred years of human outreach had colonized the Seven Sisters, and then the forty-plus stepsisters, as wags named the next sphere. Nelly colored those planets green, the color of the Society of Humanity back before the Unity War, then immediately added in black the hundred planets that had made up Unity. NO, NELLY, THAT'S HISTORY. SHOW GRAMPA RAY'S UNITED SENTIENTS IN RED. The map changed; a lot of the black went to red, but so did some of the green: Pitts Hope, LornaDo. Surprise for Earth. The red also included the colonies Wardhaven had sponsored in the last eighty years. Still, the red and green were less than a quarter of the six hundred worlds now inhabited by humanity.

PUT PETERWALD'S FACTION IN BLACK. A fifty-world chunk of the Rim formed a dark cloud, centered around Greenfeld. It seemed to reach out to block Wardhaven from further expansion. Hamilton and its five colonies lay between Turantic and Peterwald's holdings. THERE ANY BAD BLOOD BETWEEN TURANTIC AND HAMILTON? Kris asked Nelly.

ONLY THE USUAL TRADING RIVALRIES, the computer agreed. Kris eyed the wall screen, searching for how she and Tom fit in.

"Kris, you have a collect call coming in."

"Who from this time?"

"Tommy."

"Accept it!" Kris shouted, bouncing to her feet. Jack and Harvey were maybe half a second slower shooting from their places on the couch, the long night's exhaustion forgotten. Abby sat quietly in the straight-backed chair she'd set in a corner. She might have actually gotten some sleep for all she'd contributed to the night's conversations.

A section of wall screen changed to show the phone call. There was Tommy, looking disheveled, his skin so pale his freckles stood out like warning lights.

"Kris, I need help," he started, no lopsided grin today.

And the screen went blank.

"Nelly, where's the rest of the call?" Kris yelled.

"It was cut off at the source."

"Where was he calling from? Rerun it!" Kris demanded. Nelly reran the call, freezing frame just before it cut off. Kris stared into Tommy's eyes, trying to plumb them for fear, terror, newfound freedom. The face just looked tired.

"Talk to me about the call, Nelly," Kris ordered.

"The header file has been damaged, apparently in an attempt to retrieve the call," Nelly said. "The call was made from High Turantic Station about six hours ago, real time. The exact location of the phone is lost, but it was on the public systems in the station's dock section." A schematic of a standard, class E station appeared.

"Not much to go on," Jack muttered.

"Six hours ago, Tom was on Turantic and needed help," Kris snapped. "That's enough for me."

"Enough for what?"

"To get a search going," Kris said, pacing the floor.

"Turantic is twelve light-years away. Six hours by priority mail," Jack pointed out.

"So, call in some chits. You're a cop, aren't you? Get some of the brethren off their duffs and out looking for Tom."

"Kris, we're personal security. We don't do kidnappings."

"Your agency was all over the dopes who snatched Eddy," Kris snapped, mad enough not to choke on the name of her six-year-old brother who died under a pile of manure.

"Eddy was our subject. Tom is not."

"And would anybody snatch Tom if he hadn't gotten too damn close to me?"

Jack's face was a professional mask; no answer there.

"Nelly, get me Grampa Ray."

Jack's eyebrows raised at that, but he turned away and retook his place on the couch, folding his hands and eyeing Kris like she had some lessons to learn.

"Hi, Kris, what you doing up so early on a Saturday after a ball?" Grampa Ray smiled from a section of wall.

"I kind of have a problem, Grampa," Kris answered, then filled him in. His smile worked its way into a worried frown as she told him of Tom. When she finished, he nodded.

"I remember him, a good young man."

"He's been my right arm too many times."

"This isn't going to be easy, Kris." When a man like Grampa Ray said things weren't easy, they weren't. "Turantic isn't part of United Sentients. They're playing a coy game, holding aloof and avoiding commitments to any of the sides taking shape. Kris, a year ago, when we were all good citizens of the Society, I could make a phone call as a private person, and half of the cops on Turantic would be hunting for Tommy. Now, I'm a king," Ray said ruefully, fingering his brow that at the moment was in need of combing, "and I have less lever-age."

Kris glanced at Jack. He was shaking his head, an *I told you so* look all over his swarthy features.

"We have an embassy there, don't we?"

"Wardhaven's business residency was renamed an em-bassy, but, hon, we're all having to relearn a lot of stuff about separate and equal from the history books."

"I'd appreciate it if you would call who you can and see if they have any way of getting cops out looking for Tommy." NELLY, SEND GRAMPA A COPY OF TOMMY'S CALL.

Grampa focused on something offscreen. Kris could hear Tommy's few words over the line. "I see." Grampa frowned.

"If he hadn't gotten messed up with one of those damn Longknifes, this would never have happened to a kid from Santa Maria," Kris pointed out.

"He's from Santa Maria. Then he's not a U.S. citizen."

Right! Santa Maria, halfway across the galaxy, hadn't joined anyone, either. "He's a serving officer on a Wardhaven warship," Kris pointed out. "That has to count for something."

"Some folks have been arguing that we ought to give dual citizenship in cases like that. This could get very mixed up."

Kris nodded with understanding but kept Grampa hostage with her eyes. For the first time in her life, Grampa was the first to flinch away. "I'll make some phone calls. There's bound to be somebody who knows somebody who owes them a favor."

"Thanks, Grampa."

"Stay close, Kris. I'll get back," and Ray ended the call.

Stay close, Kris reflected. If she did, would that help Tom? She weighed Tom's prospects, hanging on the razor's edge of what Grampa Ray maybe could do. She was in motion before she actually decided to act. There *was* no alternative.

NELLY, GET ME CAPTAIN HAYWORTH. The skipper of the *Firebolt* was at his desk aboard ship; he glanced up. "Lieutenant. You going to be late today? That ball go long last night?"

"Sir, a personal matter has come up. I would like to take that leave you offered yesterday." Behind Kris, Jack was back off the couch. Harvey cleared his throat noisily. Kris had long ago learned that from an NCO, it was as close to a scream of disapproval as you got. She ignored them.

"Don't see any problem; you've got the time coming. I was hoping you might use your backdoor access to get some Uni-plex for Dale to mess with, but we can survive a week without it."

Kris glanced at the box from Grampa Al on her desk. She could drop it off when she went through the station. Then again, Uni-plex had almost killed her once. She was headed, unarmed and unaided, into someone else's plan for her life. Might a wild card come in handy? "I'll get you some next week, sir," she promised. "See you then, and thanks for being so understanding."

The Captain smiled. "You're doing a tough job juggling a lot of stuff, Lieutenant, and doing it well. See you in a week."

"And why are you taking leave?" Jack demanded as Harvey roared, "Just what do you think you're doing, woman?"

Kris took a deep breath, full of familiar smells. This was the house she'd grown up in. Nuu House. The home of the Longknifes. They did what had to be done when there were no alternatives. Of course, she was headed off to a corner of space where *Longknife* just might be the word for *target*. Kris expelled the familiar air and took a step toward Jack, a first step down a dark, unknown path. She chose her words with care, no need to whip up a worse storm than her decision spawned. "I'm going to apply some personal oversight to make sure Tom doesn't get lost in the shuffle." NELLY, WHEN'S THE NEXT SHIP LEAVING WARDHAVEN FOR TURANTIC?

"Damn it, woman, are you blind?" Harvey shouted.

"You are walking into a trap," Jack said softly.

I HAVE BEEN CHECKING CONSTANTLY SINCE LAST EVENING,

Nelly said. THE FREIGHTER *BRISBANE'S BUSTARDS* LEAVES IN AN HOUR. THE LUXURY LINER *TURANTIC PRIDE* SEALS LOCKS IN THREE HOURS.

THANKS, NELLY. SEE ABOUT SPACE ON THE *TURANTIC PRIDE.* "Yes, Jack, I know I'm walking into a trap."

Harvey threw up his hands. Jack stood his ground. "Then why go?"

"They caught Tommy in a trap he wasn't looking for and, for crying out loud, had no reason to expect. He wasn't walking, he was running away from those damn Longknifes. Still, he got caught in a net meant for me. Don't you see? Tommy's been turned into bait in a game he wasn't prepared for and can't survive. And yes, I pray to every god available that this bunch is smart enough not to leave him under a ton of manure with a busted air pipe like they left Eddy.

"Their damn trap was good enough to catch a poor kid from Santa Maria on holiday. I don't think they've made a trap yet that can catch a major Nuu Enterprises stockholder, a Prime Minister's daughter, and yes, damn it, a Princess of the eighty planets of United Sentients.

"They caught themselves a mouse. Let's see how their little trap handles a madder-than-hell lioness."

"Great sound bite," Jack drawled. "Don't you think they've thought of that, too?"

Kris shrugged, not amused by how easily he deflated her dramatics. "They haven't got me yet. I doubt they'll do it this time. There's a ship leaving for Turantic in three hours. I'll be on it."

"You can't do that," Jack said.

"I'll start packing," Abby said, standing. "Harvey, I'll need four self-propelled steamer trunks. I assume there are a few of them around this place."

"I'll get them, but I still say this is a bad idea."

"You're not coming," Kris told Abby. "It'll be dangerous."

The woman turned to Kris, and a small needle gun appeared in her hand, aimed right at Kris's heart.

"Where'd that weapon come from?" Jack demanded, stepping in front of Kris.

"I've carried a weapon since I was twelve," Abby said, making said weapon vanish as smoothly as it had appeared. "Have you forgotten? I hail from Earth. You've heard of our quaint native customs, the drive-by shooting or gunning down every customer at your friendly, neighborhood fast-food outlet?"

Jack was no longer reaching for his gun as he edged closer to this surprise package. "Jack, please don't come any closer. You look like a nice guy, and you're probably well trained in hand-to-hand. I don't have any of those fancy colored belts, but the kids I grew up with taught me how to survive on bad streets and to hurt you fast."

Jack backed off a step, but his hand was out. "I'll bother you for that weapon. No stranger goes armed around my primary." Jack's words were soft, but nothing hid the steel in them.

Abby eyed him; the moment stretched. Then Abby blinked, and the tiny weapon was again in her hand. She handed it to Jack and turned to Kris. "If my last employer had listened more to me than her overpaid security, she'd still be alive, and I wouldn't be employed so far from home. You really should read my résumé."

"My mother hired you."

"That shouldn't keep you from reading up on the woman standing next to you." Abby tapped her wrist unit. "There, now your computer has it. Enjoy the read."

"No time now. I'll catch up aboard ship."

"Fine. Now then, young woman, if you plan to come the enraged Princess . . . in something more than a fur bikini . . . you will need me. I will take care of your needs, and, trust me, I can take care of myself."

"How good are you at dodging short-range rockets?" Jack drawled. Abby frowned at that.

"I didn't know you'd learned of that attack," Kris said, heading for her dressing room, Abby right behind her.

"I may be slow, but I'm not inept. Harvey," Jack called after the retreating chauffeur, "bring up both of my bags."

"Bags?" Kris echoed.

"Yep. I knew sooner or later you'd rush off planet for something, and I'd get dragged along. I packed one bag for a cold planet, one for a hot. Which is Turantic?"

"Who said you're going? This is just me taking a vacation."

"Yeah, right," Jack said, turning away and starting to talk to either himself or his communications center. At the moment, Kris would not have bet an Earth dollar which.

"It would be easier to maneuver through stations and customs," Abby offered, "if all our luggage, his two bags and mine, were in trunks bearing your diplomatic immunity."

"Didn't know I had any, but that sounds reasonable. Nelly, tell Harvey we'll need two more trunks," Kris said, feeling very much in command of a very muddy situation.

Abby busied herself around the dressing room until Harvey returned, leading a parade of self-propelled steamer trunks, each big enough to carry Kris comfortably. Abby crammed them full of every kind of dress, gown, suit, and accessory Kris'd ever heard of or even heard intimated. Kris had never worn foundation garments, but Abby packed several. She held up two Kris took for girdles. "These are fully armored with the latest Super Spider Silk. You can bow, bend, stoop, even breathe in them . . . and they'll stop a four-millimeter slug."

"Get them at an estate sale from your last employer?" Kris asked, then realized the question could be taken wrong.

"No." Abby seemed unfazed. "She was six sizes up from you."

"Oh, you could protect us both in one."

"Sorry, Princess, but I won't be that close when someone starts shooting. That's what that good-looking guy is for."

Kris took the conversation away from that good-looking guy. "Pack the Order of the Wounded Lion. It'll impress the locals."

"Don't count on the hicks recognizing it, but it's big and shiny and ought to dazzle a few," Abby said, folding it into a trunk bin. Kris checked Grampa Al's package. It did hold ten kilos of virgin Uni-plex. Kris hefted it. *What could I use this for?* She had no idea, but the fact that she asked the question seemed a solid argument for taking it. Abby said nothing when Kris handed it to her, just tied it to the bottom of one trunk.

An hour later they were packed; Abby had even produced one fur bikini, without explanation. Harvey handed over the wands controlling the trunks. "I'll get a car."

Jack reappeared to escort them downstairs. Normally light on his feet, he seemed a bit heavy. He'd probably visited the house armory and was packing enough to demolish a small army. "Abby, how did you get your little friend through security?" he asked. "We thought we had Nuu House as tight as a brick."

"Santa Maria has a flourishing business in ceramic air rifles, guns, and similar protective devices," Abby said without looking back. "Most shoot a metal dart. However, for a bit more, you can buy very effective ceramic ammunition."

"Thought so. Kris, you might want to put this in your pocket." Jack handed her a small automatic, either the same or a twin of the one Abby had produced. Kris held it up to examine.

"That's the safety," Abby pointed out. "Well protected so you won't accidentally knock it off. I have a spare holster."

"Where were you carrying yours?" Jack asked.

"No man's business," Abby shot back and produced a new copy of the weapon Jack had confiscated. While the two glared at each other, Kris slipped the weapon in her pocket; Abby would show her a better hiding place later.

They got to the elevator seventy-five minutes before the *Turantic Pride* was due to lock up. Seemed like plenty of time to spare . . . until Kris spotted two men in brown raincoats hustling toward her. "Your people?" she asked Jack.

"My boss's boss," Jack answered, "and Grant, *his* boss."

Way too much officialdom for this to be good. Kris kept her pace up and course steady for the boarding gate. Behind her, the luggage's electric motors complained.

"Ma'am. Ma'am," came breathless from behind Kris. At the gate, she paused to let them catch up while Abby took the trunks through. There seemed to be more trunks behind the maid than when they left Nuu House, but Kris was too busy to do a recount.

"Princess Kristine, you can't do this," the more out-of-breath Senior Agent Grant insisted.

Kris glanced around the elevator station wide-eyed. "It looks like I am. Why, yes, I think I am. Abby, any problems?"

"None at all."

"Yes there is," the not-Grant agent insisted. "Security, that bag needs rechecking."

The woman behind the check station took in the agent and the badge he waved at her, glanced at the trunk, then at Kris, then smiled. "I got the picture of its contents in storage, sir. The computer says it's safe. My eyeball says it's safe. It is safe, mister. Right, Lieutenant Longknife?"

Kris smiled at the woman who'd cleared her through security every morning for the last three months. "You bet it is, Betty," and followed her trunks through security.

"Ms. Longknife, you must reconsider," the Senior Agent said, following Kris through the checkpoint.

Alarms went off.

More uniformed people with automatic weapons than Kris thought the terminal could hold converged on their security station. Now both agents waved credentials, but that didn't slow down the fast-approaching, heavily armed horde.

Kris flashed a smile at Betty. "The young one's with me. He's carrying and has all the permits you could dream of."

Betty took a close look at Jack's papers, pushed a button, and motioned him to walk slowly through the detector. She whistled as she took in her monitor. "Man, is he carrying. Lieutenant, if I was you, I'd stay on the nice side of that one."

"Sometimes she actually does," Jack said.

The other agents finished resolving their failure to announce their armed status beforehand. As the small army backpedaled toward their stations, the Senior Agent turned again to Kris. "Ms. Longknife, you must not do this."

Kris kept walking. "You might consider getting to know me better before you start giving me orders," Kris said, twisting the conversation in a misdirection. "You may call me Lieutenant. You may address me as Princess. I am not a *ms.*"

"I'm sorry," one said. "Yes, Lieutenant," the other agreed. "We aren't ready." "We don't have a security team for you," they said, stumbling over each other verbally. "We need more time!" they both got out together.

"There isn't more time," Kris said, stopping at the door of the ferry to let Abby and the trunks precede her on board. Kris suppressed a frown as she again came up high in her trunk count, but the pause put Jack at her elbow as her noisy problems once more approached.

"Then we won't let Jack go without backup," the Senior Agent said, playing his ace.

"Fine. I'm twenty-two years old and a serving naval officer.

I am of age to decline your protection. Nelly, register my declination."

"You wouldn't dare," Grant gasped.

"She'd dare, Grant," Jack said. "She dares a lot."

"Because you've never built the proper relationship of authority," Grant snapped back.

"I suspect no one in authority has ever developed a proper relationship with me." Kris smiled through teeth.

"You could send along a team on the next ship, or whenever you have it together," Jack suggested.

"That's not a good idea," Grant said.

"It looks like the best available," Kris said. Departure was announced in thirty seconds. All people were advised to stand clear of the white line. Kris glanced down; the white line was a meter thick; she and Jack stood in the middle of it. She sidestepped to the edge of the line inside the ferry. The Junior Supervisor gently elbowed Grant to safety on the outside.

"We'll have a backup team on the next ship. With a Senior Supervisor," Grant shouted.

"Not anyone senior to Jack, I hope." Kris smiled as the doors began to close. "Otherwise I'll have to have my personal computer register that declination of services we talked about, and then you can explain to my father, the Prime Minister, just why I don't want you around. Or maybe to King Raymond."

"You're a brat, you know," Jack said through unmoving lips.

"No. I don't recall anyone telling me that . . . to my face."

"And you, being naturally hard of hearing, never heard it whispered behind your back," Jack said, shaking his head.

"I am not hard of hearing."

"And you're not properly belted in, Lieutenant."

"Are you going to hound me this entire trip?"

"Only every minute."

If it wasn't for poor Tommy out there in trouble, this had the makings of a fun trip.

5

"Nelly, I told you to rent space, not the whole bloody galaxy." Kris growled, doing a quick turn around the palatial splendor the purser of the *Turantic Pride* had personally escorted her to. A crystal chandelier in the sitting room cast light to softly burnish the gold trim of the ceiling and finely carved wall moldings. The brocade-covered sofa and chairs looked like something out of a museum or vid.

"I did what you told me to," Nelly said plaintively.

"Nelly, we could park the *Firebolt* in here and have room to spare," Kris said, checking out the doors that opened onto the sitting room. There was a study, with three walls lined with paper books; the fourth was a wall-wide screen. That screen was at least smaller than the one the Purser showed Jack how to operate in the living room. Each of the three bedrooms had a similar entertainment wall.

NELLY, COULDN'T YOU HAVE GOTTEN US SOMETHING SMALLER? Kris thought, taking the argument with her personal computer private.

NO, MA'AM. THE SHIP IS ALMOST FULL. I COULD NOT GET THREE ROOMS TOGETHER, SO I RENTED THE IMPERIAL SUITE.

"Imperial Suite! I'm a Princess, not an empire."

"Empress, I think you mean," Abby corrected. "Empire is the political structure. Emperor and Empress are the titles of the rulers, as defined by gender in those days."

"Now you're an expert on forms of government?" Jack drawled from where he was examining the door, having shown the Purser out. "And it is the Imperial Suite. Says so here."

"Governments I leave to people who have the illusion they run them," Abby said dryly. "Protocol comes in handy when you have to keep such deluded people happy."

Kris turned to her body servant. "That's a side of you I haven't seen."

"And not one I like," Jack added, "coming from someone standing armed and close to my primary. Who did you say you worked for before?"

Abby raised her wrist unit, aimed it at Jack, and tapped it. "Now you have my résumé. Read it when you have a moment. If I wanted someone dead, they'd be dead already."

Kris left the two bickering while she took in her bedroom. If possible, it was fancier than the living room. The bed was big enough for four and soft as down. The *Firebolt*'s bridge, the big, comfortable-sized one, was not half as big. "And I forgot my tennis racket."

"There are tennis courts on the third deck, as well as an Olympic-size pool and workout facilities," Nelly said. "The pro shop has all the amenities for a passenger who forgot something."

"Or outgrows their swimsuit. Have you seen the list of mealtimes available?" Jack called from the other room. The thought of kicking back and enjoying the pampering had a surprising allure. As a Longknife, she'd never wanted for anything, but Father had no use for ostentation. "It costs votes." Early in her teens Kris made it a matter of pride to make do with half of what Mother needed. What would it be like to really soak in this Princess thing? Kris returned to the living room, putting the seductive bedroom behind her. Jack had Abby's résumé on-screen.

Abby shrugged as she eyed the simple page that held her life story. "Looks impressive up there all big and the likes."

"You got your degree, in what, marketing?" Jack said. Kris was busy doing basic math. Abby was thirty-six. That made her a good eight years older than Jack, who would stay six years older than Kris until next month's birthday. *Hmm, even if Jack likes older women, Abby is way too old! Isn't she?*

"I worked my way through college baby-sitting elderly folks, wiping their noses, and their butts if necessary. I thought the height of job elegance was standing at a counter all day, helping women find their true colors and accessorizing." Abby made a face. "My first client hired me after her grandmother died."

"Your last client died," Jack said. Kris ducked back into her bedroom, realizing this had become a private conversation.

"I believe the police decided it was a shareholder's revolt that got personal." Abby undid one of her long sleeves and pulled it up to display entry and exit wound scars. "Way too personal. This was verified by your service when I was hired."

Jack turned to Abby, fixed her with an unblinking gaze. "Earth flatfoots did the full field. All we got was their report. My bosses accepted it. I'm still thinking about it."

"Think about it all you want, but I've got a job to do, and I'm going to earn my pay."

"The pay's good around Longknifes, but it can present you fascinating challenges way beyond what they told you when you took the job. Where will you be when the rockets fly?"

"Where any smart person would be, going in the opposite direction. I'm a body servant. If it gets to that, I intend to be around to identify the body. That what you wanted to know?"

"No problem, ma'am. I'll call for backup elsewhere."

"You got that right."

Kris cleared her throat as she entered the room. "Nelly says I have dinner with the Captain tonight. Abby, you have any suggestions for what to wear?"

"How about that outfit you skipped last night? You won't have mother issues this time. Why not dazzle the ship with a real Princess."

"Go for it," Kris said. Why not let her cruise mates take her for all that glitter. *Could come in handy, and who knows, I might understand more about why Mother is the way she is.*

Two hours turned out to be just enough time for Abby to put a Princess together, and the experience did give Kris a few thoughts on why her mother was always late. The surprise was that Kris enjoyed it; her life had held few such sensuous experiences. Abby told Kris to just relax in the bath. Kris did, losing herself in warm water, jets, aromas, and all, drifting into a place with no pain and fewer worries.

Then Abby introduced Kris to a facial. Lieutenant Kris Longknife refused to believe there could be any tension left in her after the bath. Ten minutes later, after Abby finished on Kris's face, whatever dour worry lines the Navy wants a good Lieutenant to display had vanished from the Princess's visage.

Before Kris could mar the miracle with worry lines for the strapless gown, Abby introduced her to a push-up bra. "You've never had one of these," the Earth woman said, eyeing Kris like a certified alien.

"No."

"Your mother didn't show you?"

"No."

"You didn't read about them in a women's magazine when you were, like, fifteen?"

Kris thought back to those days of first being dry after years of being lost in the bottle. "No. I read histories and political commentary, studied soccer and orbital skiff racing, and don't remember having any time for trashy stuff."

Abby shook her head. "And your girlfriends didn't let you in on the secret?"

Kris refused to say, "What friends?"

"Woman . . ." Abby whistled. "You *have* grown up on an alien planet. But don't worry, honey, you've got your Mamma Abby to see that you get home safely."

Ten minutes before dinner, a young officer knocked respectfully at the suite door just as Abby announced Kris fit for public viewing. Kris had never had a man take her in with quite the stunned awe of the ship's officer. His stuttering and sputtering came under control only when Jack, now in tux and tails, cleared his throat and asked if Kris wished him to escort her to dinner. That helped the ship's officer find his tongue.

"The Captain sent me to escort you, ma'am. We understood that you are traveling alone." Which established the proper invisibility for her security guard and servant, as far as ship's company. Taking the young man's arm, Kris swept out

onto the wide ship's corridors, Jack an invisible three paces
behind her.

Dinner at the Captain's table was an artful study in van-
ity . . . and passing time without noticeable product. By Kris's
catty measure, she was the only woman under forty at the
table, and the only one with bare shoulders. Not having Nelly
to rely on turned out to be the "no problem" Abby assured her it
would be. The men paid court to her, the women said nice
things to her face, though Kris would not have bet an Earth
dollar that their comments later that night would be anything
short of pure feline. Kris passed on the wine; still, she found
herself intoxicated by the high-proof attention. *Mother, am I
tasting your addiction?*

The Captain seemed to truly enjoy her company. His eyes
did focus on the sash of the Order of the Wounded Lion that
Abby had fastened just below Kris's breast. The medallion
was on the side away from him. Kris made a mental note to
fake, buy, or otherwise acquire some other way of keeping the
sash in place. The Wounded Lion did not fit her present persona.

"And what brings you aboard?" the Captain asked as the
table talk sought to develop.

"Oh, Wardhaven is a beautiful planet, but a girl really
needs to see the galaxy, don't you think? Besides, if Grampa
Ray is really going to be the King of forty planets, don't you
think a Princess should see more of them?" The Captain
didn't blink as Kris undershot Ray's present alliance by half.
Had she started a good or bad rumor?

"I'm sorry we will have you for so little of your travels."

"Oh?"

"Yes, the *Turantic Pride* will be going into dockyard hands
for a brief period once we reach home. I am sure you can
arrange passage on another ship."

"I doubt it will be nearly as finely appointed as yours."

"We of the *Turantic Pride* would like to think so."

"Oh dear, is there anything wrong with the ship, Captain?"
One of the other women passengers took this opportunity to
insinuate herself into the Captain's attentions. She had a lot
more to show the Captain when she leaned forward than Kris
did, even with Abby's miraculous undergarment.

"Oh no, nothing to bother about. I am told Turantic has again raised the safety standards for its fleet, and some minor installations will be made. You are sailing on the safest ship in space, ma'am. Next month, it will be even safer."

The woman seemed satisfied, or maybe she was more interested in having her wine goblet refilled. Kris made a mental note to have Nelly check out this story. It had the ring of something intended to satisfy civilians. It sounded thin to a Wardhaven Navy Lieutenant on active duty.

There was dancing after dinner, and none of the junior officers that lined up to keep Kris moving around the dance floor complained a bit about her lack of skill. One or two even offered to show her the steps she admired in passing other couples. Not a bad way to spend an evening . . . if you had nothing better to do with your life.

Kris was returned to her door at eleven sharp by the ship's Purser, who was also escorting his wife back to their cabin. "If there's anything, absolutely anything you need," the woman assured Kris, "you have only to ask. A starship is quite capable of providing everything from a needle and thread to what those fussy Engineers call a major sub assembly."

"Thank you so much," Kris gushed and entered the door Jack stepped forward to open. It was quite a rush to be pampered, flattered, and stroked all evening.

If only her feet weren't killing her.

As Kris was about to collapse on the couch, Abby shouted from the dressing room. "Don't you dare do that to that dress."

Kris immediately snapped to attention. "But I sat all evening at the dinner table."

"That's different. Come on in here and let me get you out of that before you destroy something valuable."

"It couldn't cost that much." Kris defended herself. Abby quoted a price that was two months' pay for a Lieutenant.

"You're kidding."

"Kid, whatever made you think beauty and glamour came cheap?"

"Never paying for it," Kris said as she stepped out of the suddenly respectable dress. Mother had provided Kris's wardrobe for most of her growing up. Kris slipped out of Abby's glamour rig, put Nelly around her neck but didn't jack in, and pulled on a robe. "Nelly, did Mother make withdrawals from my trust to cover the cost of my wardrobe?"

"She did before you began managing it yourself in college. Do you want a full historical report?

"No. Not right now. This ship is going into the yard once it reaches Turantic. Has Turantic 4 recently changed the safety regulations for its flag shipping?"

There was a brief pause. "Yes, Turantic is requiring all ships be fitted with additional capacitors to assure that the fusion containment fields in the engines do not fail. They are also requiring additional and improved life pods."

"Are many ships breaking their voyages?"

"The law has a very short deadline. There is an unusually high number of Turantic ships presently in the yards and more scheduled for dock work in the immediate future."

With a thoughtful "Hmm," Kris returned to the sitting room.

Jack had put away his monkey suit and was in slacks and a shirt. "You enjoy yourself this evening?"

"Beats a poke in the eye with a sharp stick," Kris said, quoting one of her great-grandfathers. "Nelly, show us what you've found out about the Turantic flag merchant fleet."

The screen across from the couch converted a portion of itself from scenic waterfalls to work area. Ships by tonnage were arranged by At Turantic, In the Yards, and Scheduled for Yard Work in 30 Days or Less. It amounted to half of the fleet.

"Remind me to buy shares in Turantic ship repair docks," Abby said, coming to take a seat in a straight-backed chair.

"Nelly, show the rest of Turantic's fleet by thickening up the shipping lanes they are presently using."

The lovely waterfalls vanished as the whole screen switched to show human space, a three-hundred-light-year-across ball. No surprise, the part farthest from Turantic was bare. Bigger surprise, there were major blank spots close in as well.

"Nelly, show United Sentients space in red." Lanes went red. They were also very light on Turantic shipping.

"Show other developing alliances," Jack said.

"They warned me you guys were kind of paranoid," Abby said.

"Sometimes a well-developed sense of paranoia can keep you alive," Kris answered without glancing away from the screen. Turantic shipping had disappeared from three others of the budding alliances. There was no lack of shipping around Greenfeld. "Damn, am I walking into another Peterwald thing?"

Jack studied the map for a moment, looked like he might say something, then shrugged and glanced at his wrist unit. "You want to spend some gym time now while the gear isn't mobbed?

Kris eyed the map a moment longer, then headed for her room. She found workout clothes without help and dropped off Nelly. As she met Jack at the door, Abby joined them, a workout bag over one shoulder. "I gotta be in shape to run if they start shooting at you, dear."

The gym was all the pampered set could whim for. There was every sort of way to work off supper. Before Kris said anything, Jack managed to challenge Abby to a handball game or maybe it was the other way around. With a frown, Kris decided to hold to her persona. The gym had three Pleasure Pods. On the outside, it looked like a black box. Opened, it might pass for a mother's womb. Once closed, it could gently massage any muscle you asked, or give you a thorough yet painless workout.

"How may I service you?" a pleasantly male voice asked, leaving Kris wondering what the usual use of this machine was.

"I need to work off supper," Kris gushed, pure Princess.

"Let me see what I might suggest," the voice said, and Kris felt an electric tingle start at her toes and quickly pass up her legs to her back, and exit through her fingers. "You are in very fine tone, miss. May I suggest a gentle workout and warm massage."

"I'm in your capable hands." After a few minutes of the machine gently stroking her legs and arms, Kris was about ready to say something like, "Show me what you got." But the pulling and pushing on her body suddenly picked up, and the real exercise program kicked in. A few minutes into some serious work on her arms, legs, abs, and several other muscle groups Kris never knew she had, she was struggling to keep her breath as bad as at OCS. Twenty minutes later, the cool-down phase began. The machine released Kris just as Jack led Abby from the handball court.

"Your prior employer taught you a few moves I've never seen," Jack said, a bit breathless as he reached for a towel.

"You know those decadent Earth folks, nothing better to do with their time than make an art out of what real working folks would call just clean fun." If there was sarcasm there, Abby hid it behind a pleasant smile for Jack. Too damn pleasant for Kris's taste. "You had some good moves, yourself," Abby said, hiding her face behind a towel.

"Passable. Enjoy your massage?" Jack asked Kris.

Kris wanted to know the score. Jack was good; Abby couldn't have beaten him. Both busied themselves with towels. No way would Kris ask what they did not offer. Instead, Kris rotated her shoulders. "Very relaxing. We ought to get a box like that at Nuu House. I think I shall sleep like a babe."

And she did.

Operating on ship routine, Kris slept in. Abby brought her breakfast only moments before noon. How the ship's company knew to serve her left Kris wondering just how much privacy such slavish luxury left her, but she kept her curiosity to herself. A different officer showed up to escort her to dinner. Most of the people at the Captain's table were new; the chair at his left hand was reserved for her tonight.

Her efforts to direct the topic of conversation toward tidbits of shipping information somehow got lost in the shuffle of table conversation. One of the men had just come from Finlandia. The other men wanted to know if there would be war between Xyris and Finlandia. That traveler shrugged. "The rhetoric is there. Both have got good cause, or so they say. Who knows?" he said, patting his lips with his napkin. "Whatever they do, it won't be good for business."

Tom was not forgotten. Since Grampa Ray sent no message, Kris sent her own to the new Wardhaven Ambassador on Turantic about Tommy's possible involuntary status. She got no reply.

Next day she sent another message, waited another day, and repeated it. Silence. The ship was closing on its last jump when Kris repeated her message . . . and got an immediate reply.

To: Lieutenant JG Longknife
From: Lieutenant Pasley
We Heard you the first time. Now shut up and
    let me work.

"Lieutenant Pasley?" Kris muttered, letting the name roll around in her mouth. It sounded familiar.

"Wasn't she the woman who Tommy got to know?" Nelly said slowly. "The woman who reported him missing? Or maybe she is just someone with the same name?"

Kris found her mind going in two totally different directions. Since when did a computer use a question when it damn well knew the answer? Was Nelly learning tact?

"Pasley," Jack frowned. "She was headed for Itsahfine. What's she doing answering the Ambassador's mail on Turantic?"

And signing her name full Lieutenant, Kris thought. She was just beginning to like the way a Princess outranked all present. Was she going to have to get used to working with a Navy type who outranked her . . . again?

6

Kris studied the space station that was High Turantic through the view port in the dinning room as the liner approached its dock. From the looks of the stretched cylinder, a good three-quarters of it was brand-new. SMART METAL, Nelly answered when Kris asked. Definitely a rush job.

Below, Abby was in charge of the four pursers who had appeared to repack Kris's baggage train. Kris had almost turned them away; Abby moved quickly to put them to work. Apparently, a Princess could accept no less. Kris wondered what might be added to her luggage. Jack had muttered something about checking things thoroughly once they got to their hotel. Kris wasn't the only paranoid around.

In the few minutes between docking and the gangway opening, the Captain appeared at Kris's elbow and ushered her personally the short distance from first-class dining to the gangway. "I hope we meet again when I can show you more of space," he said, bowing over her hand and kissing it.

"Has the Captain gotten rather too smooth the last few days?" Jack said as he followed Kris into the gangway's elevator.

"Smooth, yes," Kris agreed. "Too smooth? No. Maybe it's a girl thing, but I could get used to that."

"Yes, Your Princessship," Jack drawled.

Abby, with Kris's luggage, was waiting for them as the elevator disgorged them into the customs area. There was no line, and the agent only seemed interested in waving them through. Abby produced an Earth passport that got a frown and a stamp. Just beyond customs was a slightly familiar face in Wardhaven Navy blues sporting the two broad stripes of a Lieutenant.

"Good afternoon, I'm Lieutenant Pasley. The Ambassador regrets he cannot be here himself. I am at your disposal. I have reserved rooms for you at the station Hilton." Kris had to admire the amount of words the woman got out in one breath.

"I was planning on going planetside immediately."

"Yes, Princess," Lieutenant Pasley went on without reflection. "You will find the Hilton fully meets your needs."

"And the matter of Tommy Lien?"

"I can brief you on all we know as soon as you are comfortable in your rooms at the Hilton."

Kris grew tired of that hotel being Penny Pasley's answer to every question. "And if I don't want to cool my heels where you want to stash me?"

Lieutenant Pasley drew herself up to her full height, which was a good two inches shorter than Kris. "Lieutenant, I've made arrangements for you and your entourage. Please follow them."

Kris stood in place, fixing her superior officer with a hard stare, and did not budge. Penny frowned. "I told the Ambassador that wouldn't work. How about this: If we can just get to a secure area, I can bring you up to date on quite a lot."

That settled it for Kris. "Lead. We will follow."

Penny had already checked them into the Hilton; they processed quickly through the foyer directly to the elevators. They must have made for an interesting parade: Penny in uniform, Kris in an expensive red outfit Abby called a "power suit," Jack trying not to look like he was eyeing everyone for a gun, while doing so, and Abby, followed by a large procession of auto trunks in perfect formation, one behind the other.

Kris's suite was only five floors in from Circle One, the huge outer floor that ringed the station and stretched from the bottom to the wall separating it from the yard. "Besides the elevator, this floor also has a connecting slide car to take you up or down," Penny said. A wall screen showed a live view of the station, its long cylinder silhouetted against the setting sun with Turantic below. The suite was even more palatial than the ship's; Kris ignored the finery as she collapsed onto a sofa. "So, what do we do now?" she asked her growing entourage.

"I don't know. What do you want to do?" Jack said. No surprise, a gizmo appeared in his hand as he slowly moved about the rooms, checking for bugs.

"I tried to arrange a tour of some of Turantic's more scenic sights," Penny said. Kris wasn't really surprised the Lieutenant held a slightly different gizmo and was doing her own sweep.

"I'll have to unpack," Abby said, and did surprise Kris by doing no such thing. She produced her own gadget, of yet another design, and began another sweep of the place. Kris kept her surprise off her face; Jack did not. He looked ready to run the maid through his own bug finder.

Five minutes later, all three were back rubbing elbows in front of Kris's easy chair. "What do we do now?" she asked.

"I think a nice relaxing bath might be in order," Abby said, eyeing the other two. Jack nodded slightly, Penny more vigorously. So they adjourned to a bath slightly less roomy than the *Firebolt*'s bridge. Abby ran water into a tub big enough for a small water polo match. The tub looked to be a long time filling, since the maid did not put in the stopper.

"How many bugs did you find?" Kris asked Penny.

The woman identified eight, quickly giving their locations in the five-room suite. Jack had found eight, too, but he'd missed two of Penny's and found two more. Kris and Jack then fixed Abby with glares.

"Hey, you have no idea what some employers figured they got for their paycheck. I may be a working girl, but I'm not in that line of work. Anyway, I found two more that you missed."

Kris raised an eyebrow to Jack. "How many species of bugs are we dealing with?" That would give Kris an idea of how many players had dealt themselves in to whatever game was afoot. Jack met her question with a shrug and headed back to the rooms, Penny and Abby right behind. They returned two minutes later; the women seemed content to let Jack talk for them. "There are five different models of bugs out there.

One is standard Wardhaven issue. Strange Lieutenant Pasley missed it," that got a blush from the subject. "The ones Abby turned up are not even close to a design in my book. Strange you found them."

"I think they're a familiar Earth subspecies," Abby said dismissively. "Probably so old, they took it out of your book."

Jack said nothing, but Kris could see the wheels spinning behind Jack's eyes. *Who is Maid Abby?*

"So, do we squash the bugs, or leave a few active?" Kris posed to the team.

"I say squash 'em all," Jack said, eyeing Penny with a grin.

"That'll mean I'll be forever filling out my daily reports." The woman sighed.

"Who says you'll have any time to fill out any reports?" Kris said with a grin she knew was growing more wicked by the second. "The Ambassador put you at *my* disposal. I intend to keep you at *my* beck and call twenty-four/seven. You can fill out your reports when this is done. With luck, by then, you'll have forgotten most of it, and no one will give a rip anyway."

Penny did not succeed in suppressing a groan. "They warned me that you were most insensitive to what higher-ups required of you . . . and anyone around you."

"Hey, you were on a vacation with Tommy. Think of this as just an extension of it."

"And if you believe that," Jack growled, "I've got a small planet to sell you."

"What is the situation with Tommy?" Kris asked Penny.

"Don't you think we ought to settle what to do with our listening friends?" Abby asked.

Right. They did have unfinished business before they could get down to business. "What's your suggestion, Abby?" Kris tried to make her smile a confident one as she posed a major test for her maid/whatever.

"I'd leave two live, but choose two different types. That way, at least two sets of players would still be in the game. The others would be playing catch-up."

Kris tossed the question to Jack with an upraised eyebrow.

"Not bad field craft. I'll go squash them. Mind if I leave the two live ones in the living room?"

"Please!" Kris agreed.

"Why not leave one of the bugs in Jack's room?" Abby said. "That way they could listen to him snoring all night."

"I don't snore," Jack grumbled, but he was already on his way out. Kris drummed her hands on the side of the bath, glanced at the other two women seated beside her, and waited. When Jack got back, he put a new gizmo on the sink. Abby pulled a similar one from her pocket and placed it on the back of the commode.

"Should I take that to mean we've got an active scrambler system going?" Both nodded. "Then let's get down to why we're here. What do you know of Tommy Lien?" she asked Penny.

"What do you know about Turantic?" was the Lieutenant's comeback.

Kris knew more about Turantic than she had a week ago, but little beyond the bare personnel file on Penny Pasley; time to test her. "What do you think I should know?"

"Turantic suddenly is very unfriendly territory for Wardhaven." Penny smiled with too much teeth. "Before I got yanked home, I was stationed here in the naval procurement section of the Business Exchange Group. Turantic didn't see a need for much Navy, but they wanted more than Earth did. In return for us buying parts and supplies from Turantic, they'd pay for a Wardhaven ship every two or three years. When their youngsters joined the Navy, they were assigned to the Wardhaven Guard. It worked well. Our ships regularly visited Turantic colonies. They saved on the overhead of a fleet."

"When did all that change?" Kris asked.

"It started about three years back, but its gotten really bad in the last six months."

"About the time devolution became the political password all over the Rim," Jack said.

"If it's the future"—Abby shrugged—"any smart person gets on the bandwagon. It's either that or get run over by it."

"Spoken like a true survivor," Jack growled, rolling back and forth on the balls of his feet, towering over them.

"I'm alive. Not all my former employers are so lucky," Abby said, primly rearranging her skirt where she sat on the edge of the bathtub.

"What's the present situation?" Kris said, ending the banter that was becoming normal for her agent and maid.

"Officially, nothing's changed. The present government is keeping to the same policies."

"But," Kris added.

"Several factions seem to be suddenly finding themselves in agreement," Penny said slowly. "You're one of those Longknifes."

"That's what I'm told . . . regularly and reoccurringly. Let me guess. Big money seems to be the mover for this new faction."

The Lieutenant nodded. "Money behind the shipping firms, banking, heavy and medium industry, all the stuff that would make money if a load of new colonies suddenly got on Abby's devolution bandwagon . . . and started running over anyone who got in their way. They own media as well. News has been kind of strong for expansion. Latest hit vids are about the early pioneers and the joy of taming a virgin land. Fun and chance to make it big."

"So the people have been lapping it up."

"The youngsters, the marginalized, the people who don't quite fit in . . . and usually don't vote."

"When's the next election?" Jack asked.

"They haven't had an election in nearly five years. The ruling party will have to call one in the next two months."

Kris whistled. "That soon."

"Lets you know why we Wardhaven types are walking on eggs."

Kris shook her head; she was getting that old, familiar feeling back. The one she got when she was halfway across a minefield and the second half looked twice as long. "You still haven't told me what you know about Tommy."

"You want the full-length version, or the summary?"

"Let's start with the summary."

"Nothing. Don't know a damn thing I didn't know when I was ordered back here pronto to chase after Tom."

"There's a longer version?" Jack asked.

"Yeah. In that one I tell you all we did to come up blank," the Navy Lieutenant said, looking up at the agent.

"You know he attempted a phone call from this station," Kris said. "You have to have something around that. If nothing else, he must have shown up on security cameras."

"One would think so," Penny agreed blandly.

"But," Kris was tired of having to pull explanations out of this woman. Maybe a crowbar around the tonsils would help.

"You may have noticed all the heavy construction on the station. It has doubled and redoubled in the last nine months. Seems the day Tommy went through, the entire security system was down for expansion."

"That is not believable," Kris growled.

"I didn't buy it either." Penny sighed. "Billions worth of business goes through this station every day. They'd lose their shirt if every camera was down for a day . . . but they took them down. I talked to half the security screeners. Every one is either a pathological liar or they really were out on the floor doing eyeball security that day. They swear the central security station was off-line and filled with tech types for twenty-four hours straight."

Jack stepped away from the tub and paced for a moment. Before Kris could ask him what had gotten him so riled, he whirled on Penny. "You're telling me we're dealing with someone who could close down security on a station this size? Kris, you've got to get on the next ship out of here."

Abby shook her head and answered instead. "It might not be that bad. He or she need only know the day security will be down enough ahead of time to plan Tommy's transit accordingly."

"I don't think Kris should be around either option," Jack snapped, turning to Kris. He looked ready to hog-tie her and stuff her into one of her auto trunks for shipment home.

Kris casually got up, moved to the other side of the tub, ready to run if necessary, and went on. "What else can you tell me about the search for Tommy?"

"I have some connections with dirtside police. My old man was a cop, and I speak their language. Some local cops have been moonlighting for us the last couple of days, showing pictures to taxi drivers, folks who hang around the elevator. No luck.

"I thought the housing shortage around here might help.

Occupancy is above ninety-five percent. We ran down every hotel room that changed hands in the last week. Nothing. Then we tried every apartment rental. Again nothing."

"The folks we're dealing with don't lack money," Kris noted.

"So I heard. I also checked out houses, time shares, and condo sales. No dice."

"How big was the time window you used?" Jack asked, now more interested in the hunt for Tommy than packing Kris off.

"We started with the week before the *Space Adder* left Turantic and went forward. This grab couldn't have been in the planning stage longer than that."

NELLY, COULD YOU DISPLAY THE CALENDAR WE DID ON THE SHIP?

The wall across from the tub lost a harem scene as the requested calendar came up. Nelly had already added dates from Penny's search. The woman came around the tub to stand beside Kris. Her hand went down the list of dates and times.

"That's about it. I don't see anything missing."

"When did Tommy decide to take a vacation?" Kris asked.

"Hmm." Penny ran a hand through her long blond hair, pursing her full lips. *Some women are born with it all.* "We had AttackRon Six's officers pretty well locked down for the first two months after the mutiny. If you think you had a bad time, be glad you weren't with them," Penny said with a bit of a blush. This also changed Kris's appraisal of the woman. She was using the bureaucratic "we" far too comfortably when it came to the security and intelligence maggots who had made Kris's life miserable after the dustup in the Paris system.

"You must have gotten to know Tommy pretty well," Kris said, her voice carefully even.

"Tom was just one of six officers I was tasked to debrief. Each one on a different ship. I don't think Intelligence trusted us much more than they trusted you mutineers." The woman smiled.

"Paranoia can be a survival trait," Kris said dryly.

"So I'm learning. Anyway, all the crews knew they hadn't a firefly's chance in vacuum of leave until we gave them a clean bill of health." Penny made a stab at the calendar. "That was when the *Typhoon*'s crew got their release," she said pointing to a Monday that was a good two weeks before the *Space Adder* left for Castagon 6.

"You got to know Tommy pretty well. Did he invite you?"

"Tom is an easy guy to get to know. Very easy to get to like," Penny said as Kris suppressed an even deeper sigh. "From questioning him I knew he was curious about the Three. He said everyone on Santa Maria was always hunting artifacts left by the Three a million years ago. He was going crazy, stuck on the *Typhoon* tied up to the pier, under observation by every roving cat and dog. They couldn't message out, except for a weekly note to family." Which explained why Kris hadn't heard from Tommy.

"He did net searches on the Three in his spare time." Penny studied her wrist unit for a long minute. "He started the search here." She made a second stab at the calendar, a good two weeks earlier. "Found Itsahfine here." That mark was three days later. "And asked me if I'd like to spend some leave time on Itsahfine here." That marked the Monday before they were cleared for leave.

Kris didn't ask Penny if Tommy told her about his hobby, or if the intelligence officer found out about it while bugging her subject's computer. The latter would make it a whole lot easier to not like this woman, and Kris was feeling a real strong need to dislike the woman Tommy had asked to spend his leave time with. "Nelly, when did Tommy book passage on the *Bellerophon*?"

"Monday afternoon," Nelly answered and that datum appeared on the wall screen.

"I got my ticket the same time."

Nelly added that datum.

"So the bad guys could have known at least three weeks before the *Space Adder* left dock," Jack said, rubbing his chin.

"Excuse me, Kris," Nelly said. "May I add something?"

"Go right ahead." Penny was staring at Kris like she had two heads. Maybe she did.

"When I heard of Lieutenant Pasley's search on rental space, I thought it a very good starting point, and I've been expanding her search as the dates have run backward. I also found another very interesting point as I was doing that search."

Kris rolled her eyes at the ceiling. Nelly's new ability to move ahead on her own was nice. Her development of tact, however, was slowing her down. Maybe a tactful computer was not such a good thing. "What might that be?" Kris asked, trying to get things moving as fast as a computer was supposed to.

"On Tuesday, after Tom and Penny booked their tickets on the *Bellerophon*, three small apartments in Katyville were rented using three new credit cards, issued sequentially by Nuu Financial Support that morning. They have not been used for any further purchases."

"Show us the apartments, Nelly."

A map of Heidelburg, the capital of Turantic, flashed on the screen. Whereas Wardhaven City bordered the ocean, Heidelburg was downriver from a lake. The three apartments were along a low ridge near the river on the south side of the growing city, about eight blocks apart. "I don't see a Katyville," Jack said.

"Doesn't show on the standard-issue roads and street map package," Penny said.

"I have the latest update," Nelly answered, with maybe a hint of hurt in her voice.

"You probably do," Penny said quickly, eyeing Kris like she was nuts. Maybe two nuts. "Katyville is an industrial slum. Mainly warehouses, machine shops, meat packing, places where anyone could get some kind of a job. This hill," Penny pointed to the ridge with the apartments, "eighty years back was expensive residences. Now it's tenements. Not every industrialized city is as beautiful as Wardhaven."

"So I'm learning." Kris nodded.

"I'll pass this to my cops. They'll raid them tomorrow."

"You willing to bet Tommy'll still be there?" Kris asked.

"You only landed today. They had us stymied. They won't expect you to change things that fast."

Kris eyed the time line. "They've been moving fast from the start. Any chance they noticed what we've been doing here?"

"The screen is protected," Nelly said, "but I have been pulling data from many sources. If they have alerts there . . ."

"Can you get your cops moving tonight?" Jack cut in.

"I can try."

Kris ran the time line through her head. Damn, this Calvin Sandfire was no slacker when it came to knowing what was happening and making things happen faster. Was Kris willing to bet Tom's life on Sandfire going slow tonight? What was she willing to bet her own life on? Again, that family mantra was humming in her head. There really was no other choice.

"You can try to get your cops moving, Penny, but we can be moving in ten minutes," Kris said.

"Lieutenant, JG," Lieutenant Pasley said to Kris, "there are parts of Wardhaven cops only travel in pairs after dark. In parts of Heidelburg, cops only travel in fours during the day. After dark, cops don't travel in Katyville."

"Which means your friends are going to move slowly," Kris said evenly. "We need to move fast. Who's with me?"

Kris knew Jack could move fast when he wanted to, but she was still shocked at how quickly he got around the tub to grab her arm. "Woman, you are not leading a pack of heavily armed Marines into a prepared assault. You've got one Secret Service Agent, one Intelligence desk jockey, one timid maid who probably won't venture her nose outside this suite, and one Princess who does not know her limits. That doesn't a rescue mission make."

"Who says I won't venture out of here?" Abby shot back.

"We are not equipped for a rescue mission," Jack answered, not taking his eyes from Kris.

"Honey, speak for yourself." Abby laughed as she hustled into Kris's room. A moment later she shouted, "Catch," as a large and rather cute pink beret sailed Frisbee style through the door. Kris caught it; it was heavier than it looked. She put it on.

"Ceramic weave all around?" she asked as Abby led an auto trunk back into the bathroom.

"Will stop a four-millimeter slug at five paces. Covers as much of your head as most helmets. Here's a couple of watch caps for Penny and me. Not as pretty, but we all can't be dolls."

"There's a lot more of her to protect," Jack growled.

"Yes, honey, and while you can pass for just one of us girls most times, we're about to get down to our unmentionables, so make yourself scarce. You must have brought along a few things just in case she started acting like she always does."

"Who told you what I always do?" Kris frowned.

"Your mother."

"My mother?" That didn't sound like the mother Kris knew, but she was dying to see what Abby had in that trunk. It seemed a slightly different shade of brown from those Kris had watched Abby pack at Nuu House. Very slightly different. "Jack, leave us women alone."

Shaking his head, Jack went.

Abby snapped the trunk open. "Now then, I've got some pretty heavy-duty stuff for a working girl like you," Abby said to Penny as she dug in, "but we've got to figure out whether camouflage or misdirection is the best bet for you, Princess."

"You have a cloak of invisibility?" Kris asked.

"Nelson and Taylor sold the last one just as I got there," Abby deadpanned. "Here're long johns for Penny and me," the maid said, producing a combination that included thin ceramic plates at all crucial points. "Work trousers and coats will hide these. Leave plenty of room for the fun stuff."

"Fun stuff?" Penny asked as she shucked out of her clothes.

"Guns, grenades, and the likes that smart boy better have shipped along. There's only so much contraband I can get past sensors. Princess, it's time for you to start stripping."

"Stripping?" Kris asked, but she undid the buttons of her blouse. Abby was the one with the box of tricks.

"I got this from my last employer. Just your size," Abby said, producing what looked like a see-through bodysuit.

Kris had seen sexy stuff like that advertised. Maybe she'd dreamed about owning a set. She dredged through her mind for a comeback. "I thought your last employer was big enough for the both of us," Kris said, dropping her skirt. *How far do I go?*

"Right. I meant the employer before last."

"Didn't any of your former employers survive the experience? I mean, Mother never hires anyone without references."

Abby paused for a moment, eyeing the ceiling while seeming to puzzle through her memories. "One, two . . . three. No, two, I think. Hard to remember. So many of them. You got to ditch the bra and panties, honey."

Kris did, then helped Abby begin the slow job of working the bodysuit up Kris's six-foot frame. "I could use some powder," Abby muttered. Penny retrieved a lovely porcelain powder jar from the marble expanse beside the twin sinks. "Good. Suit's got to spread the impact of a bullet. Would hate to bruise you."

"Aren't these things supposed to stretch to fit?" Kris asked. This one didn't give a millimeter. Abby just grinned and squished Kris to fit.

"Exactly what am I doing? Hey, watch the hair. That hurt."

"Ugly faces like me and Penny a guy looks at and forgets."

"Yeah, right." Kris made a face at that line.

"You, Princess, on the other hand, are a problem. Not only do you have that pretty face, but it's been on a whole lot of media lately. A guy looks at you, really looks at you, and you're a dead giveaway."

"And this?" Kris said, spreading her arms at her rather too-close-to-naked body.

"Your face ain't gonna be what any red-blooded, lusting male is gonna see, honey."

Kris glanced at Penny.

The woman bit her lower lip around a grin. "Misdirection was a standard method taught at my school."

"What school might that be?"

"You don't want to know the name of her finishing school," Abby said, pulling the last of the nearly nothing up to Kris's shoulders. "She tells you, then she'd have to kill you."

"Yeah, right." This conversation was going nowhere.

"Can I come in?" Jack called.

"No," the three women answered. Abby produced a set of panties. Frilly at the bottom, they went well up the stomach. Kris discovered that her body stocking did let her move as she pulled on the undies. "Ceramic strips in there to help the under all," Abby explained. "Frills will distract any guy who sees them."

"How short is my dress?"

"Need you ask?"

"What is going on in there?" Jack called.

"We two will be just tired old working girls," Abby said. "Kris is going to be a 'working girl' taking a trick home."

Jack stuck his head in, got one look at Kris, and yanked it back out. "We can't take her out looking like that."

"Here's your bra," Abby said, producing one that looked just as flimsy as the rest of Kris's outfit. "It's a push-up."

"As if this bodysuit would let any of me up."

"Trust your Mamma Abby. By the time we have that loaded, you'll be pushing up plenty." Loading involved two small automatics, one for the bottom of each breast, and two pads that looked like they might be just what they looked like. "If things get too exciting tonight, push the nipples down, twist to the right, and throw them like Frisbees. Then put a solid wall between you and them. You might also warn us."

"What do I say?"

"Fire in the hole," Penny said, paused for a moment, then started giggling. "Oh my. Oh my. This should not be fun."

"It isn't," Kris said dryly.

"Ready to turn the job over to the pros?" Jack called.

"Is this some sort of setup to get me to run for Mother?" Kris snapped. "Because if it is, so help me—"

"It's for real, honey," Abby said, deadly serious. "You going to leave Nelly at home?"

"You are not," Nelly protested.

"Where can I put her?" Kris asked as Abby walked around her, studying her figure and looking dubiously at the small bit of red cloth draped over Abby's arm.

"How about your belly? Some guys think a slightly pouched-out belly is really sexy, and Babycakes, yours is flat as—"

"Never mind," Kris snapped and arranged Nelly over her belly button. The computer's straps expanded to fit, no problem there. The wire to the jack in the back of her head extended. YOU HAVE ENOUGH BANDWIDTH, NELLY?

I'M FINE, KRIS.

"The pom-pom on the beret is an omni-use antenna," Abby said. "Your Nelly will know what to do with it. Can I merge it with your jack wire?"

"Will it damage anything?"

"The instructions on the box says it won't. If it does, I'll take it to the nearest Radio Shack and demand a refund."

Kris didn't believe a word from Abby anymore. She waited. NELLY, ANY PROBLEMS?

"The merging of the input went smoothly," Nelly said. "The antenna is . . . unusually adaptive. Please give me a few moments to adjust to its capabilities."

"Take all you want, honey child," Abby said, then pursed her lips. "I think we're ready for the dress." Defiant as Caesar crossing the Rubicon, Kris raised her arms, and the maid settled it on her. Hanging from thin straps, the front and back plunged. Kris had wondered how she'd reach her guns; with this flaming red wisp of nothing, it was easy. The skirt ended before it began.

Kris took stock of herself in the mirror. Even Mother had never worn anything this skimpy. Kris tried to see herself in the rear mirror. "Are my cheeks showing in back?" she asked.

"Yes," both women answered.

Kris shook her head. "Women really wear things like this?"

"Women with the job you're faking tonight, honey."

"You ever?" Kris asked Abby.

"My momma did. She wanted something better for her baby girl." Kris raised an eyebrow, unsure whether to believe it or not. Abby was busy putting on her own camouflage of the night: work boots, baggy trousers, worn coat.

"Am I going barefoot?"

"Some girls do. Good for business," Abby said, but she produced worn shoes. "They'll hold up better than they look."

Kris bent over to put them on, flashing everything she had at the mirror. "How am I supposed to bend over in this?"

"Just the way you are, honey. Business is business."

Kris stood up and tested the shoes. "Not bad."

"You'll be surprised how easy they are to run in. Jack, you got some toys for us working women?"

"Is it safe to come in?"

"All that's left to do is put on her makeup."

Jack came in as Abby went for the finishing touches to their disguises. Her Secret Service Agent took Kris in with slowly rising eyebrows and a low whistle. "This is a whole new side of you that I've never seen, Princess."

Kris looked down at herself; the dress had strategically placed cutouts as well as not being much there. "There's a whole lot of me that you're seeing for the first time."

Jack smiled. "Can't argue that."

"You're enjoying this way too much, and—"

Abby saved Kris from finishing the sentence by tossing Jack and Penny small bottles. "You're too clean for real working stiffs. Dirty up. Honey, you are way too understated for tonight. Sit down and let Momma doll you up good enough to eat."

Kris sat, tried to pull the dress down to cover herself, and only ended up revealing more bra . . . and a gun's handle. "Can't do that, Princess," Abby warned her as she put large gobs of powder, rouge, mascara, and lipstick on Kris. Kris started to make a face at the face looking back at her. "Hold still. Tonight, Cinderella, you ain't going to no ball."

Kris held still.

Done, Kris stood, took a long look at herself in the mirror, and swore she'd never do this again. Risking her neck in full battle gear was a rush. Hanging herself out for the cheap leer turned her stomach. Kris knew some women did this, had to do this. Knowing it was one thing. Being it. Being laid out like this. Kris swallowed; she'd think about it later.

Abby was back with raincoats. "What's right for Katyville is all wrong for the Hilton. We'll dump these later."

Jack issued a small armory to the two women. Abby pulled back expertly on the action of a small but wicked-looking automatic, saftied it, then pocketed it. Penny did the same. Jack offered no explanation with the grenades and explosive charges he next handed out. Neither Abby nor Penny asked for any. For a maid, Abby knew too damn much about things that had nothing to do with Kris's wardrobe. *We have to talk, woman.*

When Jack finished with the weapons, they stood for a long moment, staring at each other, Jack looked like he still wanted her to call it off. Penny was breathing quickly, her excitement showing. Abby wore a blank, game face.

"Let's get Tommy," Kris said.

7

It was raining in Katyville, large teardrops of water that splattered on the sidewalk and sent spray flying. The cracked concrete, still hot from the day, steamed. The rain, rather than cleaning the air of the stench of the squalid river, open sewers, and refuse, seemed to surrender to it.

They ditched their raincoats in trash cans near the space elevator. For an hour Kris walked out of place and was ignored by respectable people. She'd been embarrassed before. Anyone that spent two years mostly drunk had faced that moment when you sobered up just enough to realize how bad you'd been. Tonight, Kris discovered she could blush down to her belly button.

And it got worse. A chilly breeze came up, sending cold wind up her tiny skirt. The armor might stop a bullet, but it gave no warmth. Kris had goose bumps where she'd never had them before. As they moved into the darkened part of town, a pouring rain began. Rivulets ran down her hair and into her eyes, blotching her makeup. A clown's face looked back at her from empty store windows. Wet, the red dress fit her like a thin coat of paint. Men ignored her face to leer at her other assets.

Kris was no stranger to strange men in strange places. Her father sent her to most of Wardhaven at one time or another to patch up sagging poll numbers. Running her brother's campaign, she'd spent much of her time being where he wasn't. But in all that, she'd been a Longknife, respected, honored. Not tonight.

The Navy sent her up against armed kidnappers to free a kid. She'd led confused recruits against overgunned rebels in planned and unplanned fights. At the Paris system, she'd ended up commanding an Attack Squadron. So why did walking into this fight leave her knees weak and her gut in a knot?

Tired men passed her on the street; they took her in with a glance and bedded her with a second look. She could feel their fingers crawling over her long after they passed, their backward stares measuring her for a mattress. Kris swallowed hard; this disguise had seemed so logical in a warm hotel room. *I am one of those Longknifes, I am a naval officer, a Princess, worth a trillion plus, and I've got on armored undies to boot.* Still, undressed like this, she felt worse than a beggar.

What was it like for the women who really did have nothing but an ass between themselves and a roof for tonight, a meal tomorrow? She saw them, other women standing on street corners or walking in the numb embrace of men. Their eyes met hers and slid off like the water running down their faces.

Kris held tight to Jack's arm, faked a laugh at a joke he hadn't whispered in her ear, and hoped none of the lonely men or groups of men challenged Jack's right to have her tonight.

THE BUILDING ACROSS THE STREET IS THE FIRST RENTAL, Nelly said. Kris passed that to Jack; he swung her around in a semidrunken lurch.

"Guess we ought to find a room out of this rain, Kittenface," he said.

"We've got a problem," Penny said, coming up beside them. "The elevators in that place only work if you have a key."

NELLY, CAN YOU FIX THAT?

I DO NOT THINK SO. THAT BUILDING IS OFF NET. IT MUST BE STAND-ALONE OR VERY LOW-TECH.

"Looks like Jack rents us a room," Kris whispered. She'd come this far; she was not going back empty-handed. "We can rent a room for an hour," Kris said too loud, dropping into character. "Maybe thirty minutes if you really are fast."

Jack took a drunken stumble, righted himself, then gave her a bleary-eyed grin. "You bet, sweetie."

As Kris ducked and bobbed her way across the empty intersection, as much to keep her feet out of growing lakes around the potholes as to look her part, she got a good look at four blocks of Katyville. There was nothing good about it.

Here and there, buildings were blackened and crumbling. Broken windows showed others were abandoned. Several vacant windows had feeble lights. Was someone so desperate that such a wreck was their best escape from the night chill? The still-occupied buildings seemed taken by some sort of cancer. What had been a front porch or a back stoop was boarded up and crudely fashioned into a room. Often a shed leaned against it, showing by a tenuous light that it, too, was occupied. Was there a building inspector on Wardhaven who would look the other way for such travesties of her father's building codes?

A second thought struck her. Were there girls dressed like her walking the back streets of Wardhaven tonight? Kristine Anne Longknife, political campaign manager and owner of a hell of a lot of real estate, could not venture an answer. Suddenly that hurt more than the rain and the shame and the risk she was taking. Kris gritted her teeth. Once Tommy was back safely with the Navy, Princess Kristine was going to skip a few balls until she found the right, true, and full answer to tonight's questions.

There might once have been a foyer to the Sanderson Arms, but now the bottom floor was split up into more cubbyholes. A bleak patch of carpet with two broken chairs took up a tiny space across from a desk and clerk that had seen much better days, weeks, and years. Maybe centuries.

"Got a room?" Jack slurred.

"All out." The desk clerk didn't even look up.

"Why you here if you can't get me a room?" Jack demanded.

"Boss says I stay here until my shift's over, or he don't pay me."

"We really need a room." Kris tried something halfway between demure and sexy that she'd seen in a movie.

"What's wrong with your own?" the clerk said.

"Landlady threw me out this morning. Wants twice the rent. I ain't got no raise in pay. How I supposed to pay her more?"

The desk clerk glanced up, gave Kris the eye, and went back to what he was watching. "You ought to be able to get a raise out of a dead man."

Kris struggled to keep a bored smile on her face. Would she have to do something for, or to, or with this wreck of a man? He didn't look like he had more than a half-dozen yellow teeth. Even at this distance, she was almost gagging on his rank smell.

Jack pulled a fifty from his pocket and slipped it across the desk. "I only need the room for an hour. You know."

The guy eyed the bill. "A hundred."

Jack scowled. "Fifty and we'll be out in half an hour."

"What kind of place you think I'm running? We only rent by the hour. And it's a full hundred or you can go do yourself in the corner."

Kris glanced around. Now that she wasn't just smelling the clerk, she got a good whiff of the room. An artillery round might make this place safe and sanitary. Make that quite a few rounds. Jack pulled out a second fifty. "I want clean sheets."

The clerk reached for the money. "Changed them myself not ten minutes ago. That will be fifty more."

"Twenty-five," Jack growled and slapped a hand down on the clerk's before he made the money disappear.

The old man glanced around the tiny foyer. "Guess the boss will never know. Okay, twenty-five."

"With a view," Jack insisted, producing the extra cash.

"You'll love the view," the clerk promised as he took the money and handed over a key. "Follow the signs to the elevator."

The elevators were in the back; only one worked. Nelly reported both security cameras dead. Kris found the back door and let Abby and Penny in. The camera in the elevator did work; the women took one corner as Jack settled into the other. Kris did the best lap dance she knew how to do on a standing man.

"You're enjoying this," she whispered in Jack's ear.

"You mean I'm not supposed to?"

Next time Kris's knee made a pass by Jack's rather expanded

crotch, she applied pressure. A yelp replaced the sweet nothings he'd been not whispering in her ear. "You bend me over, and you'll blow our cover."

"Then you start thinking of the cold shower you're going to take when all this is over."

"I don't know. Abby seems to be enjoying this. Maybe—"

Kris hadn't really intended to knee her agent. But her knee was working its way up his leg, and she suddenly had this spasm and . . . Anyway, Jack swallowed his yelp like a man and, through clenched teeth, did stay upright.

The elevator groaned to the fifth floor and clanked to a halt. It wasn't their floor, but it might be Tommy's.

The women quickly left, whispering disgust for people who couldn't save it for the room. Jack and Kris oozed down the hall without breaking contact below or above the belt; Kris did a good imitation of couples she remembered from high school.

Abby bent over a door, seeming to struggle with a reluctant key while she worked wonders with a picklock. Jack paused a few feet past them, seemingly deep in foreplay. His hands on Kris's butt, he lifted her so she had a good view over his shoulder.

"Nothing coming," she whispered into his ear. "You enjoying the feel of my ass?"

"Woman, you've got the equivalent of more than fifteen millimeters of steel armor on that butt of yours. Harvey gets more excited polishing the limos than I'm getting tonight."

"And that's a dagger in the front of your pants," she said.

Jack didn't answer that.

"Come on in," Abby whispered.

Kris broke from the clench to hustle into the apartment. "Is Tommy here?" she asked.

"Whoever was here," Penny announced, "left in a hurry. Look at this kitchen."

Kris found it . . . and gagged. The table was set with Chinese food and covered with cockroaches. Two rats fought over chicken bones in a box of takeout.

"I'd say they've been gone two days, three at the most. And they left fast," Abby said.

"Someone was tied to this bed," Penny called from the room across the space occupied by two couches and an entertainment center. The others joined her. Ropes dangled from an iron bedstead; Penny shook it. "Solid build. Just what you'd want for fun and games . . . or to keep someone really down."

Abby kicked at something on the floor. "Four, five syringes over here. Don't know what was in them, but they could easily keep someone out for a long time with any of a half-dozen types of crap you can get on the streets."

"We can send one of your cops by tomorrow to follow up," Kris snapped. "Right now, we've got two more places to check." It felt good to be Lieutenant and Princess for a moment. The others obeyed, heading for the door.

"Have we been under observation?" Kris asked.

No, Nelly said. THIS PLACE HARDLY HAS A WORKING LIGHTBULB.

"I checked it with mosquitoes before we went in," Abby said.

"When this is over, remind me to send a note to the place my mother hired you from," Kris said. "They truly do send their people fully equipped."

Jack raised an eyebrow at that.

Abby shrugged. "I'll be sure to remind you.

The four blocks to the next rental got exciting.

Halfway there, three very wet, drunk, and stinking men blocked their way. "Hey, it's so lousy out, all the good tricks are taking too long inside," a very greasy one announced.

"Yeah, you got the only decent-looking one I've seen in hours." Somehow, Kris doubted that.

"Why don't you share?" a tall, thin one said, easing forward. "We could wait outside till you're done, then do our own business, or we could all, you know."

Kris edged her hand toward the automatic in her bra, but Jack took things off in a different direction. "Aw, guys, this is me sister. Mom's been down on her knees praying and praying that Mabel here would see the error of her sinful ways. I've been hunting for her for months, all over town, and didn't I just find her, down in the gutter, crying her eyes out."

Kris let out with a wail. "My landlady, bitch, threw me out 'cause I couldn't pay me rent. She doubled it. Doubled it. No way I can get me boss to double me pay."

"You see," Jack went on without missing a beat. "So I'm taking me poor sister home to Mother."

The tall one nodded. "You got to respect a brother what's taking care of his poor sister what's gone bad," he told his two friends. They grinned as a knife appeared in his hand.

Kris got ready to fight, but her main effort went into staying upright when Jack suddenly wasn't there to lean on. It was dark, and there wasn't a lot of light to see by, but it looked like Jack went into a spin that ended with his foot in the tall guy's groin. Before he could double up, Jack finished his spin with a chop to his neck. Tall guy went down faster than a Marine's pack hits the deck when his Gunny calls break.

Kris took a step forward, but the two buddies were in full reverse, protesting that they wouldn't want to trouble "no guy taking care of his poor sister what went bad."

"Let's move it," Kris ordered, and the women did. "No telling if that was just bad luck."

"Or the start of a whole lot of bad luck," Abby finished. "Somebody remind me why I'm here."

"Don't ask me," Jack said, grabbing Kris's elbow and hurrying her along like a pimp might a reluctant virgin. "I figured you for an office worker, myself."

"Is that any way to talk to a girl like me that loves the great outdoors?"

"That's our next target," Penny said, pointing at a building lit up like electricity was as free as the rain falling on it.

"Nelly, talk to us."

"The Tark'el Apartments were recently remodeled. Each room has its own full hookup to the net," Nelly began, sounding like a commercial. "There is a central security center staffed twenty-four hours a day with an armed response team."

"That doesn't sound good," Penny said.

"On the contrary," Nelly announced proudly. "The work was done by the lowest bidder, resulting in regular and frequent repair calls. I will just turn the security off in stages that simulate a slightly worse case than they are used to."

"I take it the armed guards aren't too quick to get on their feet," Abby said.

"Neither of the two on duty tonight have passed their required physical for several years," Nelly said.

"Why're they still working?" Penny said.

There was a bit of a pause. "There is nothing in the record documenting that," Nelly said, puzzlement showing in her voice.

"Nelly, people don't usually note a bribe or kickback in the official records they keep on-line," Kris said.

"I will keep that in mind," Nelly said.

"You take the back door," Kris told the other women. "Jack and I'll take the front."

Jack went by the front desk with a nod and a wink as if he took drowned streetwalkers up to his room every night. The woman on desk detail didn't even look up from what sounded like a soap.

Abby and Penny hit the elevators about the same time as Kris, but the women took separate elevators up. Kris and Jack began their merged walk down the hall a half minute before Abby and Penny got off, complaining of their day and sharing dreams of a hot bath and clean sheets. Kris went through the same routine with her agent as she had before, minus the banter.

It lasted longer because Abby had more trouble with the door. She finally took a step back. "It's defeated me."

Breaking from Jack, Kris had had enough of being a boy toy, or anyone's plaything. "Blow it."

Penny produced a bottle and quickly laid down a bead of thick white at the hinges, then filled the lock. She added small electric devices to the goo, waved everyone back, and pulled a small box with buttons from her pocket.

"I'll blow it on three. One . . . Two . . ."

The door opened.

Tommy peeked his head out. He took the four of them in with several blinks before locking eyes with Kris. "Oh shit, now I'm really in trouble. Longknife." His watery eyes blinked. "Kris, what are you doing in that getup?" Then he slammed the door.

"Safetying the blow," Penny announced and collected the triggers.

Kris rapped on the door. "Tommy, open up, it's Kris."

"Oh no, not for a Longknife. Never again."

"It's me, Tommy," Penny said. "Open up."

The door opened a few centimeters. "What are you doing

here, Penny? And how did you get messed up with a Longknife?"

"It's a long story," Kris said, shoving the door open. Tommy crumpled to the floor like a deflated target. In a second, Jack was in, pulling Tom back to lay him out in the living area, Penny and Kris right behind him. Abby was last, making sure the hall was still empty. Then the door closed tightly.

While Kris and Penny made sure Tommy was still breathing and other vitals were in some semblance of normal, Jack and Abby fanned out through the apartment. "Somebody who liked Chinese food left here fast enough to leave a full table and recently enough there are no rats or other nasties in sight," Jack said.

Abby must have drawn the bedroom. She returned with a rope twirling through her fingers. "He broke loose," she announced, "after someone cut them half through."

Quickly, Jack was beside her. He eyed the evidence, then nodded. "They wanted him to break loose."

"Still half out of himself on drugs," Abby said slowly.

Kris rose. The man she'd crossed light-years to rescue was not only free already, but insulting her. Not the usual ending for heroic acts of daring. "They must have figured they had what they wanted from him," she said, "or from me. So they cut him loose to find his own way back to the embassy."

"Or to get mugged, his throat slit, and dumped in a gutter," Abby added with a cheerful smile.

"This is a bad enough part of town," Penny agreed, looking up from where she still knelt beside Tommy. The young man was stirring, mumbling to himself. Penny went through his pockets and found a couple of coins and fifty Earth dollars in one of them. "In Katyville, people have been killed for less."

"That's also the price of a phone call and a cab fare to the embassy," Jack added.

"Data supports both theories," Abby said. "I suggest we finish this argument over popcorn in our warm, comfy suite at the Hilton, which I am beginning to wonder why I ever left."

"Let's get moving," Kris ordered. "We go out the back way. Nelly, any alarms going off?"

"The guards are playing chess and ignoring the alarms."

Abby and Penny supported Tom in a fast exit. Jack and

Kris brought up the rear, arms still around each other and apparently lost in each other's lust.

The team hadn't gone ten feet from the hotel's back door when a cab drove by slowly. The driver rolled down his window. "You look like you could use a ride. I could use a fare."

Jack waved him on. Abby hollered, "He's just had a bit too much to drink. We're not going far."

The cab moved on.

Even in the pouring rain, the streets of Katyville had never been empty. Small groups and pairs made their way up and down the streets, their hats down, their collars up. Others leaned against buildings, seeking whatever shelter they could from the rain. Unless Kris was imagining things, there were more people out now. Four men gathered outside a lean-to and started Kris's way. Behind them, three men twirling bits of pipe and wood were gaining fast on a stumbling Tommy. "We got company," Kris said.

"Fight or flight?" Jack asked.

"Fight's all I see left," Kris said and turned to meet the three. Kris closed the distance in four quick steps. The Gunny who taught hand-to-hand at OCS had no truck with a "fair fight," and had worked hard to get the men to drop their rules. Kris had never had to fight and never been told some things were out of bounds. She took to dirty fighting like a babe took to milk.

The three were not expecting their quarry to charge. Kris blocked a weak swing with a club and went straight for the man's groin. When he curled up, she used his club to whack a kidney. As he went down, Kris turned to help Jack, but his two were thrashing in separate puddles.

Shouts and jeers from behind drew them back to Tom. Jack led Kris in a quick jog. The girls had taken refuge around the corner with their backs to the wall. Jack and Kris hit the thugs on the right before they knew they were there. Two went down, but the crowd had grown. Six or seven guys were now kicking and swinging at Abby, Penny, and Tom. Kris swung her club at one head, spun with the follow-through, and aimed a kick at a fellow coming at her. She kept that spin going and saved her life.

The woman was in red. Red shiny boots with spiked heels, red leggings, and red form-fitting bodice with full sleeves.

A red cap came down to form a half mask. Only her mouth was uncovered. It formed a sneer. Her red-gloved hand held a knife that gleamed in the light of the failing streetlamp. The knife had been aimed at Tom, but Kris's spin brought her close enough to block it—or take it instead.

The woman slashed for Kris, caught her right arm, and the sneer became a shout of glee.

Kris felt the blow, but the Spider Silk turned the edge. Finishing the spin, Kris swung the club at the woman's gut. Weighted, the blow knocked the wind out of the woman and drove her back. Abby, momentarily unoccupied, brought her elbow up into the woman's throat and finished taking her down.

Kris turned, looking for another target. The few men standing were running. Most of the people down were dirty, ragged refuse. The woman was the exception.

Kris knelt beside the captured red, slapped her face to consciousness. "What's going on here?" she demanded, pulling back the mask to reveal raven-black hair.

The woman came aware with a start; her eyes darted around, taking in the failed attack. "You've won again, Longknife. But you won't win free of this trap," she snarled and snapped her mouth shut.

"Don't let her do that," Abby said, but the captive's eyes were already rolling back in her head. The maid gingerly opened the woman's mouth. "Yep, she shattered a fake tooth. Poison."

Kris stared at the still-trembling body. The woman knew Kris. Knew Kris, and had spent her last breath snarling a promise that Kris was trapped. "Let's get moving," she said, glancing around at the now-empty streets.

They hustled Tom for another block. Kris spotted a cab at a cross street and almost hailed it. A half block later, the cab rolled up beside them. Same cabby. "You got much farther to go?" the driver asked them.

Abby glanced at Kris, then nodded toward Tommy. His steps had been getting more shaky, and now he was shivering with a chill. Kris did a quick check. Clots of men were beginning to collect again. "Check him out," she said.

"What'cha doing in a place like this?" Abby asked.

NELLY, TALK TO ME ABOUT THAT CABBY?

"I got this fare at the 'vader for that hotel," the olive-skinned man said, indicting the Tark'el Apartments. "If I deadhead out of here, I'm gonna loose half of what I made on that ride. And you do look like you could use some help. What do you say I drop the minimum charge. You just pay the time fee."

THE CAB IS REGISTERED TO MR. ABU KARTUM. HIS PIC-TURE MATCHES THE FACE IN THE CAB IN ONE HUNDRED FORTY OUT OF ONE HUNDRED SIXTY FACE ID POINTS. PROBABILITY IS NINETY-NINE POINT EIGHT PERCENT THAT IS HIM. HE HAS NO POLICE RECORD. MEDIA REPORTS SHOW HIM TO BE VERY AC-TIVE IN THE ISLAMIC COMMUNITY HERE, WORKING ON CHARI-TABLE AND SOCIAL ACTIVITIES. HE IS RAISING SIX CHILDREN, HIS OWN FOUR AND HIS BROTHER'S TWO. HIS BROTHER DIED FROM A PULMONARY DISEASE PROBABLY ACQUIRED AT THE CHEMICAL FACTORY HE WAS EMPLOYED BY.

ENOUGH. "Abby," Kris called softly. "Check out the back."

Abby opened the rear passenger door and dug around in-side. Up the street, some men who'd been holding up a di-lapidated building got energetic and meandered toward Kris's team.

THE CAB HAS NOT HAD ANY WORK DONE ON IT SINCE BE-FORE TOMMY BOUGHT TICKETS ON THE *BELLEROPHON*. HE DEFINITELY NEEDS TO REPLACE HIS SECOND AND FOURTH SPARK PLUGS.

Kris nudged Jack toward the cab. He came, backing slowly, eyes on the suddenly active twos and threes around them.

Abby stood up, a small briefcase in her hand. "Your last fare leave this behind?"

The cabby blinked. "I think she had something like that. Give it to me. I'll turn it in to the dispatcher, and she can get it back tomorrow if she calls."

"She won't call," Abby said, dashing quickly for an alley. She returned empty-handed. "Cab looks clear to me. Pile in."

Abby and Penny helped Tommy in. When Kris joined them, the cabby frowned. "I don't go for those sorts of things."

Jack slipped into the front seat as a small explosion came from the alley. So much for the briefcase. "Good. We don't ei-ther. I strongly suggest you start moving, or all sorts of things are going to start happening."

The poor man's eyes widened as he surveyed how the streets had changed in the time he'd been negotiating his latest fare. He scowled as he took in the automatics in Abby and Penny's hands. Muttering what sounded like a prayer, he put the pedal down. They bounced into and out of potholes, slipped right and left, and slid into a curb as the cabby grumbled, "My Miriam tells me not to take fares in Katyville. She tells me every day before I leave. Do I listen to her? Do I? Tomorrow, I listen to her."

He didn't slow down until they were down the hill and into streets with lights shining. "You a gang or something?" he asked into the rearview mirror. "'Cause I don't do business with gangs. You can get out now. Don't pay me. I won't take your money."

"We're not crooks," Jack said, head swiveling just as if he was sitting next to Harvey in the limo back home. How he switched gears like that was a marvel to Kris.

"Crooks had our man," Abby said, indicating Tom. "We got him back. We're some of the good guys." Abby looked at the others in the backseat with her. "At least today we are. You can take our money."

The cabby didn't seem persuaded, but he asked, "Where do you want to be let off?"

"The elevator, Mr. Kartum," Kris said.

The cabby took a left. In a moment they were on an expressway; five minutes later, they were at the station. Was hell only five minutes away from shiny, new, and prosperous? Kris had some checking out to do back home.

As they disentangled arms and legs and got Tommy slowly out, the cabby named his price, exactly what the meter showed. "Pay him well," Kris told Jack. The agent produced a large roll of Wardhaven bills.

"Keep the change and forget this fare," Jack said.

Abu took his pay, eyed it for a moment, then looked at Kris. "I know you. Your face, it's familiar. Where have I seen you?"

"It's better you forget my face," Kris said, taking an offered coat from Abby. The maid undid something, and suddenly it was full length. "Don't even mention us to Miriam. It will be all right in the morning. Oh, and your second and fourth spark plugs need replacing."

"That would explain why it's been guzzling fuel worse than a thirsty camel." He sighed. "Allah go with you, for He is merciful," he said and pulled away into the rain.

"We better get Tom to a doctor," Penny said, putting her coat around the man.

"Let me look him over first. We have a first aid kit in Kris's baggage," Abby said.

Thirty minutes later, they were back at their suite in the Hilton. Abby produced a medical kit that occupied half of one of Kris's trunks, one of the slightly off-color ones. A qualified surgeon could probably perform emergency brain surgery with the gear in it. Kris wasn't sure whether or not she'd let Abby do brain surgery on Tom. Then again, she wasn't sure she wouldn't.

But Tommy didn't need a brain surgeon, just treatment for shock, exposure, drug overdose, and a raging infection. "Bastards didn't clean their needles," Abby growled. "But there's nothing here we can't handle," she said as she started an IV.

"You want to put Tommy in my room?" Kris offered through a yawn. Damn, it had been a long day.

"No. My room is better set up for it," Abby insisted. "Penny and I can switch off taking care of him tonight. That way we'll both get some sleep."

Jack sauntered into the maid's room? three bug hunting gizmos in hand. "No new bugs. Don't see any reason not to let them know we're back home and have Tommy."

"Let them boil in their frustration. Let's get some sleep," Kris ordered. She had promises to keep, but there was nothing she could do about them tonight.

And so she slept in her makeup and body armor.

8

Kris rose to wakefulness through pressing dreams. She had to pluck each star from the sky and put it in just the right colored basket. Then she was in the Prime Minister's residence, racing down the back halls, trying to open the right door or find just the right word to please her father. And Mother was . . .

Kris came awake. She was on top of covers smeared with the wreckage of last night's makeup. She tried to stretch, but her body armor had not been designed with that in mind. Kris felt to the back of her neck; Nelly was still plugged in.

NELLY, HAVE YOU BEEN WORKING ON AUNT TRU'S PIECE OF ROCK?

YES, KRIS. I THINK I HAVE THE POWER ISSUE SOLVED. I AM READY TO START A SERIOUS SEARCH FOR ACTIVITY ON THE CHIP.

Kris rubbed her eyes, tried to shake the emotions dredged up by her dreams. I THINK I'M GETTING SOMETHING FROM IT.

THAT CAN NOT BE TRUE. I HAVE IT TRIPLE BUFFERED. I HAVE LET NOTHING THROUGH. THERE HAS BEEN NOTHING TO LET THROUGH.

Kris was not so sure of that. NELLY, WE AREN'T HAVING THE QUIET WEEK OR TWO I WAS EXPECTING. WE ALSO DON'T

HAVE TRU A SHORT DRIVE AWAY FOR CHECKING UP ON YOU. THIS IS NOT A GOOD TIME TO BE DOING SOMETHING THAT WILL MESS YOU UP.

I UNDERSTAND, KRIS, Nelly said.

That taken care of, Kris rang for Abby and breakfast.

"OUCH. That hurts," Kris squealed. She had never had much body hair. After Abby got done peeling this body suit/armor off, she wouldn't have any!

"Should have done this last night," Abby muttered.

"Tommy kind of had first call on your services."

"Must have been powerfully busy to forget what happens when you leave this rig on too long. And letting you sleep in your makeup. Only sluts do that."

"Last night, I was a slut. Remember?"

"Young lady, you must learn to switch your roles faster."

"Like you do?" Kris slipped that one in fast.

"Don't know what you're talking about," Abby said and gave the suit a vicious yank.

"Eeks," Kris yelped, and glanced down. Nope, no hair at all. Kris let some time pass. Abby went back to gentle pulls that almost didn't hurt. "I made myself three promises last night," Kris said softly.

"What might those be?"

"First, get Tommy back to the Navy where he belongs; then, find out if Wardhaven is quite as civilized as I've been told."

"That's two," Abby said, looking up from where she was working the body stocking down Kris's thigh.

"Find out who Abby really is."

Abby chuckled under her breath and concentrated on easing Kris out of her armor. "You find out who that woman is, and you tell me. I've been wondering about her most of my life."

"I'm going to find out who you are."

Her maid settled cross-legged on the floor and let out a sigh but kept gently tugging at the stocking. "You know who you are, Miss Longknife?"

"No, but I'm learning."

"Why not let Abby worry about Abby, and you worry about Kris?"

"Because I don't like all the hats you keep pulling out of rabbits."

"Any of those hats not what you needed at the moment?"

"I admit they've all come in handy."

"Then why look a gift hat in the mouth?"

"Paranoia runs deep in my family."

"Right," Abby said, making one last tug that brought the stocking off Kris's feet. "I forgot about that survival trait. What say we compromise?"

"How?"

"I'll keep saving you. You keep paying me."

"You girls decent?" Jack called from the living room. "Breakfast is here."

"I'm starved," Abby said, bringing Kris a plush white robe.

"Can't argue there," Kris said, cinching the robe tight.

Jack was standing beside a serving cart heaped with griddle cakes, eggs in several manifestations, and three different kinds of meat: bacon, sausages, and fried fish. He was going over the ensemble with the three bug hunting gizmos. "Seven bugs. Good Lord, don't they have any patience around here? Or fumigators? Shall I squish 'em?"

"Seven," Kris said, giving Abby a questioning glance. "From only five interested parties?"

Abby rolled her eyes at the ceiling.

"Eight," Jack answered, stooping to examine something on the wheel of one cart. "I think we've got a new model this morning. Could be a new player or just a better try from one of the old, familiar crew. Again, do I squish them?"

"Why bother?" Kris said, grabbing a plate. "Dorothy is ready to click her ruby slippers together and go home to Kansas. Nelly, book us passage on the next ship out of here headed for anywhere near U.S. space."

"Kris, I can't."

"Why not?" Kris said as heads peeked out from Abby's room, both Tommy and Penny.

"All ships on approach or waiting to dock at High Turantic are now boosting for the nearest jump point. All docked ships' departures are delayed indefinitely. We are under quarantine."

Tommy hobbled into the room, Penny an arm around him for balance . . . or possession?

Kris sighed. "And why are we suddenly under quarantine?"

The screen in the living room came to life. Suddenly breakfast was being shared with people in blue moon suits and others in regular clothes—dying horribly. A map appeared in a separate window highlighting Bremen, a small town some five hundred kilometers north of Heidelburg. "Last night," Nelly said as the news flashed before them, "an outbreak of anaerobic Ebola virus was reported in Bremen, a small town on North Continent. Following Society of Humanity regulations, the authorities on Turantic quarantined the town. However, since air traffic from the nearby town of Coors had continued unabated during the virus's incubation period, the full planet must be quarantined."

Kris studied the map, her lips tightening into a deepening frown. "Anyone else see something wrong with this picture?"

"You have to quarantine anaerobic Ebola," Tommy said. "It spreads like wildfire."

"Yes, but we've never had any kind of an Ebola outbreak on Turantic before," Penny said in puzzlement.

"There are reports in minor media formats," Nelly said. "Suspicions, really, that this outbreak was not an accident or natural event."

Jack whispered something to his wrist unit. An information cell opened beside the map of Bremen. The town was a mining site, offering few amenities. The agent shook his head. "This has the smell of a planned event. That town is too far into the temperate zone to get the virus from an imported pharmaceutical species. It's the end of the road as far as trade is concerned. A town with nothing more than a clinic for the copper and lead miners shouldn't have a sample of the virus for accidental release."

Kris stepped closer to the screen. "Nelly, what are the metal reserves for the mines around Bremen?"

Nelly added them to the cell about the town. "Pretty close to petering out," Kris said with no surprise. She left unsaid that a town like Bremen, surrounded by played-out mines, was not much of a resource to lose if you had to have a town suddenly wiped out by plague. *Paranoia, thy name is Kristine.* She sighed.

"There is a problem here," Jack said.

"A problem." Kris snorted, turning back to the cooling breakfast.

"They are quarantining Turantic under Society of Humanity regulations," Jack said matter-of-factly, picking up a plate. "The quarantine will have to stay in place until bureaucrats from the Agency for Disease Control do the required inspections and give Turantic a clean bill of health."

"There is no Society anymore," Tommy said, joining them.

"And no Agency for Disease Control with general recognition in human space, so whose bureaucrats will raise the quarantine?" Penny asked.

Tommy looked pale, weak, and in general like he'd lost a wrestling match with a cement truck. His plate, however, quickly gained a pile of food.

"Uh, Tommy," Kris said, "you should probably know. There are two or three bugs live in this room. Some people seem to be very interested in our conversations."

Tommy glanced around the room with a glare that should have fused any offending bug if it had any conscience at all, but he seemed to suddenly lose interest in anything else when he spotted a chair, collapsed into it, and began stuffing his face.

Penny quickly filled a plate half as full as Tommy's. "So, who will cancel the quarantine that will allow you to leave?" she said as she sat beside him.

Kris found every eye in the room suddenly focused on her. "How should I know?" she snapped, settling for a bran muffin, marmalade, and a slab of ham. "As Grampa Ray is saying more and more these days, 'That's an interesting problem. Wonder how it will solve itself?'"

Jack passed close to Kris as he moved to fill his plate. "Did I just hear the clink of a bear trap closing on . . ." he said softly near Kris's ear.

"No! That couldn't be . . ." Kris said but bit her tongue as she remembered other ears were listening. She scowled at Jack, shaking her head forcefully. The Secret Service Agent just raised both his eyebrows and went on filling his plate.

"You don't mean," Penny started, then seemed to think better of her words. She pointed her fork at Kris, then at Tom, then made a circle that took in the room . . . and the entire planet.

Kris shook her head violently. There had to be some limits to her paranoia.

Beside her, Jack and Abby nodded with the absoluteness of ancient sages.

Kris snagged an apple and took her plate to an overstuffed chair set against what looked like a wall papered with an ancient Chinese river scene. On close examination, it proved to be a computer screen. Abby and Jack settled into opposite ends of the couch. Tommy munched his eggs Benedict in an overstuffed chair, Penny at his elbow in the straight-backed one that was usually Abby's. For a long moment, the listening bugs picked up nothing but chewing sounds as breakfast held them in its pleasant grip.

Kris broke her muffin into small portions, then slowly chewed them as she ignored the people in front of her and let her eyes rove over the carved filigrees of the wood moldings where the walls, probably all screens, met the ceiling. A chandelier of finely cut glass cast gentle shadows on the walls and even the occasional rainbow. Would a penniless whore like Kris had masqueraded as last night ever see a room like this? Not likely she'd ever catch the eye of a man who might admit her for a brief moment to someplace like this.

No, places like this were reserved for people with money and power. People who mattered. People like Kris. And to get at a person like Kris, would someone kill an entire town?

"Jack, kill the bugs," she said as she finished her muffin.

The agent produced a bug burner from his pocket, no bigger than his hand, with two metal horns extending from it. Bursts of crackling sounds marked his movement over the breakfast cart. When he finished there, he took care of one on the end table beside Kris's chair, then ducked into his bedroom. "We're clean," he said when he returned.

"Nelly, what's the death toll so far in Bremen?"

"Only two, but they don't know how many have contracted it."

Kris rubbed the back of her neck. "Ebola takes six or seven days to kill anyone. I didn't even know Tommy was on leave back then. You can't blame this on me!" The last words tasted too much of a plea for Kris's liking. These people were not her judges. She had no right to task them with absolving her.

"Kris could be right," Tommy said.

"The young, weak, or elderly often fail from it much faster," Abby said in a tone that echoed of the sepulcher.

Kris was out of her chair, pacing. "We got in yesterday, broke Tommy loose last night, and were ready to bolt this place today. We've only had Tommy for six hours! Nobody could arrange a plague in six hours."

"Yet the dying words of the woman last night were you'd never get out of here," Jack said as he sat back down and resumed eating. Holding a slice of waffle just short of his mouth, he finished, "Sandfire knows you can move fast. He's showing you he can react just as fast."

"Three apartments were rented," Penny noted. "We busted Tom out of the second one. I think we did get inside their decision-making cycle."

"Right. That shows we acted faster than he expected," Kris quickly agreed. "He expected to use that third apartment."

Abby set down the small plate that had held her meal of toast and fruit. "Still, the timing of the rentals also tells us this plan has been in the works for some time." A glance around the room got her nods of agreement. She went on. "The Ebola event must also have been planned well in advance. It could have been initiated as soon as you booked passage for here. I suspect if we looked closely at the incident, we'd find the present situation is more window dressing than real. No doubt, that will be corrected in a few days."

"All this to get Kris?" Tommy shook his head. "She *is* one of *those* Longknifes, but this is ridiculous."

"Right," Kris said, but a look at the others didn't show any similar doubt. She scrubbed at her face for a moment, trying to wash away feelings she didn't have time to catalogue, then brightened. "Nelly, message to Grampa Al. 'I'm stuck on Turantic. Could you please send me a ship to bust me out?' There, we'll use a damn Longknife thing to put an end to this."

"I have filed the message," Nelly said. "However, I am advised there may be a significant delay in transmitting it."

Kris lost her breath as well as the confidence she'd found. "Tell us why, Nelly."

"There seems to have been a major system failure in the stellar communications equipment last night. Nearly ninety percent of capacity is inoperative. I have paid extra to get us priority, but it will still be a three-hour delay."

Penny pulled out her wallet and extracted a Wardhaven bill. "Five will get you ten. Kris's message doesn't go out before the rest of the system crashes."

"Whose side are you on?"

"Hey, Kris, I'm just learning to bet the odds. Somebody wants you here and seems willing to do damn near anything to keep you here."

"But why?" Abby said, just the hint of a puzzled frown passing quickly over her well-controlled face.

"That," Jack said, getting up and collecting the dish from Kris's end table, "is the question I've been asking since we learned Tommy had been snatched."

"I suspect if we find that out," Abby said, adding her dirty plate to the cart, "we will find a snake much larger than we bargained for."

"Penny, what's going on here?" Kris asked. "Stipulated, someone wants me on Turantic. But why here?"

Penny took a deep breath. Nelly cut her off. "Kris, you have a call coming in."

"Put it on-screen. Show me only."

"I'm so glad to have you with us, Princess Kristine," gushed a man with graying hair and jowls far too large for his face.

NELLY, WHO IS HE?

AMBASSADOR MIDDENMITE, WARDHAVEN'S REP—

RIGHT, I KNOW. "And I'm glad to see you this morning, Mr. Ambassador. I was trying to book passage home, and I'm told that I can't."

"Yes, I've heard that, too. I'll have someone look into it. What I was calling for was something much more enjoyable. They are inaugurating the Top of Turantic tonight, a ballroom at the very top of the elevator station. Dinner and dancing with a truly marvelous view. I'm told it may be as enjoyable as any state ball on Wardhaven," he said wistfully. Kris kept a smile on her face. Balls were the least of her problems at the moment.

"When I received my invitation," the Ambassador went on, "it included one for Your Highness. Might I send it on?"

Kris had many things to do today; top among them was

being a long way from Turantic before evening. Still, she swallowed the *No* that jumped to her lips. How often did Father say, "When you are trapped into doing something you hate, it is best to do it with grace. Think of it as fighting your way across a raging river. It is foolish to swim against the current." Even at five, when Kris first received that lecture, she could not picture her father struggling across a raging river. Still, politics was full of sudden and fast currents, and Father did always arrive where he wanted. Maybe it was time to do a little floating with the flow while she dog-paddled like hell out of sight. Kris let her face form a frown for the Ambassador as she juggled a dozen thoughts at once. Someone was doing their level best to keep her here. How might she return this "favor"?

"Mr. Ambassador, I didn't come prepared for a full round of formal affairs," Kris started. Abby shook her head, letting the merest hint of a smile crease her lips. "But I could probably throw something together," Kris added. Abby took flaming affront to that and headed for Kris's room in full huff. "I would appreciate it if you could arrange for the host of tonight's gala to offer me the invitation personally. There are security matters to consider." She glanced at Jack. He shook his head with a sigh. Kris suspected that protecting her through the mob scene of a ball was the last thing Jack was prepared to do solo.

"I will be glad to pass along to Mr. Sandfire your openness to an invitation. He thought you might be in need of some entertainment," the Ambassador effused.

At the word *Sandfire*, Tommy and Penny were off their chairs, showing a range of emotions that would have earned any media actor the highest honor. Kris froze her face. So Sandfire thought she might be bored this morning. And not going anyplace either. *Guess I didn't spring Tom so fast.*

"If you are able to make an appearance," the ambassador went on, "at the ball tonight, I wonder if I might arrange further invitations. Sandfire mentioned there was no telling how long this quarantine might last. This weekend is the annual yacht regatta, and I understand you quite enjoy a good sail."

Tommy's skin took on a greenish tinge. Kris loved a good sail. Still, she should stay focused. "Mr. Ambassador, this is not a formal visit—" she started.

"I understand, Your Highness," the ambassador cut her off,

then paused, shocked at his effrontery, but he went on. "You must understand, Princess Kristine, there is an election scheduled in the very near future. Many people here have fond memories of their past relationship with Wardhaven. Others seem intent on damaging that relationship, if not destroying it. I would hate to see my adopted planet in, ah, difficulty with my home. You must understand the problem we face here."

"I've been learning a lot very rapidly," Kris said dryly.

"There is little that we can do officially, now that we are foreigners," the Ambassador went quickly on. "However, I have never underestimated the power of social contacts. Many of my friends have expressed interest in you personally, both as a Longknife and as a Princess. What you can do . . .?" he finished with an expressive shrug.

Part of Kris wanted to protest that Lieutenant JG Longknife had not even been mentioned. She snapped a lid on that and considered the offer on its merits. Someone had made it impossible for her to get out of here. She could sit on her butt, fuming, or she could get out and do something, probably something that Mr. Sandfire had not planned on. Was this old coot trying to squander her time? She'd always considered her social life a waste. Just now, it was all she had. Maybe it was time to rethink herself. "Why don't you look into other invitations while I consider matters?"

"I would be glad to."

"By the way, I've tried to get a message off planet, to see if Nuu Enterprises could send a ship for me. That message is kind of having a slow go of it."

"Yes, I understand that the new systems on High Turantic are suffering 'teething problems,' I believe they're called."

"Well, could you try to move my message up on the priority list? Nuu Pharmaceuticals makes one of the vaccines against Ebola. That ship could bring a load of it when it comes for me."

"Very good thinking, Your Highness. Yes, I will personally contact the Minister of Communications to see what can be done."

The Ambassador rang off, and bedlam broke out. "You are not going to any ball," Jack snapped. "They could pick you off from a hundred different directions." "Sandfire." Tommy looked paler. "He's the bastard that gave me the song and dance I fell for. Kris, you can't do what he wants." "Kristine Longknife, you can't be that dumb" was Penny's contribution. "You pulled off something pretty wild to stop that battle at Paris, but even you can't snap your fingers and beat whatever is coming down here."

"I suggest this gown tonight," Abby said, holding up a bright red arrangement that would draw every eye within a thousand meters, even if it was just Kris wearing it.

Kris lowered her voice but pitched it to carry over the rabble. "Let's sit down, calm down, and get some organization into our thinking."

The others did, although Abby retreated to Kris's room to return the gown. With everyone settled in, Kris began what had to be one of the strangest staff meetings in history. "Penny, from what graveyard did my father dig up that Ambassador?"

"He's a holdover," she started quickly. "Ambassador Middenmite came to Turantic forty years ago. You might not know it, but Turantic's vintners produce a particularly prized wine. Middy was able to corner the market on it for most of the off-planet sales. When we needed help setting up a business mission here, he knew everyone worth knowing." She shrugged. "He wanted to retire from business a few years back when we needed a head of trade missions. He seemed perfect for the job. He helped a lot setting up the military equipment exchanges of the last decade, or so my former boss told me."

"So, he's great window dressing, but not quite the sharp edge we need these days." Penny nodded. "Who's the real boss?"

Penny flinched away from Kris's gaze. "Mr. Howling handles the administrative functions."

"So," Kris repeated, "who is in charge of the *real* work?"

"Lieutenant Junior Grade, you are not cleared for that."

"And what about Princess Longknife?"

Penny frowned, glanced at the ceiling, then shrugged. "That royal stuff is just window dressing as far as the Navy is concerned. It doesn't put you in my chain of command."

"Reasonable answer," Jack cut in with a sigh. "So, if our target here insists on going off to the ball tonight, what can you and your unnamed boss do to help me keep her from turning into a potted pumpkin before midnight?"

"Actually, I can help you there without involving my boss." Penny smiled brightly, relieved to be out of that morass. "I told you I had contacts with the local police. I can get you a full detail up here within three hours."

"And who will vouch that they're clean?" Jack said.

"I will. They're professional cops. They do good cop work and don't give a damn about the political hand-waving going on."

"Good enough for me," Kris said. Jack turned on her, but she cut him off. "If we wait until we have full fields on all of them to your satisfaction, I'll be well into my third year here with just you at my arm. I got us into this mess, Jack. I take responsibility for this part of the mess."

"Okay, for the ball tonight, I guess I can go along with that. But you have to keep to a minimum-risk schedule."

"No, Jack, I'm going along with the Ambassador."

"You're kidding. You hate that social stuff."

"I hate social stuff with the usual suspects talking about the same things they've talked about since I was born," Kris cut Jack off. "But how else do I get out and meet people here? How else do I figure out what's going on? Besides, if everyone knows I hate the social stuff, so does Sandfire. If this is the last thing he'd expect me to do, it's the first thing I ought to do."

"And it does have the advantage," Penny said, "of getting you out among people who are very interested in Wardhaven and what this King thing might mean for them if they vote for the Liberal Party and join United Sentients."

"Kris, you have another call coming in," Nelly announced.

Kris stepped away from the table, tightened the robe around her, and stood in front of the living room screen. "Put me on."

A small portion of the screen changed to show a man in a gray three-piece business suit. He had either grown pudgy in early middle age . . . or was wearing several layers of body armor. His face was thin, relaxed, an open smile . . . that did not reach to his eyes. "Hello, Princess Kristine. I am Calvin Sandfire, the owner of the Top of Turantic. I understand the quarantine has caught you here, and you're open to an invitation to tonight's inaugural ball."

And just how and why do you know that? Kris wondered but chose to keep things social. *Channel Mother,* Kris ordered herself. "And I am so glad that I can provide you a royal presence for your first ball. Wardhaven and Turantic have so much in common," she gushed. The flash flood of syrupy verbiage surged back and forth for the required moments. He stayed air head social, not touching again on her stranded status. The only fact exchanged was the starting time for the ball.

"I'll drop by your suite at the Hilton to fetch you. You will require an escort, won't you? I understand your visit here was somewhat hastily planned."

Not nearly as hasty as you wish, Kris thought, even as she made sure sardonic did not slip into her face camouflage. "I don't think that will be required. I do believe there are several men at the embassy dueling for the privilege of providing me an arm to lean on."

That brought a dry chuckle from Sandfire.

"Oh, I almost forgot," Kris said, raising a dramatic hand to her forehead. "Mother would slap me silly if I didn't have my security detail review the ballroom beforehand." Mother, of course, would never say such a thing. Kris stole that from a girl in high school devotedly understudying for Mother's job.

"I don't see how that could be a problem," Sandfire said with a slight twitch of his left hand. "I will have the head of Ballroom Security meet with him. Say one this afternoon?"

"Certainly. See you tonight."

"I would not miss this for the world." OFF, NELLY.

"That is one lying son of a bitch," Kris growled as she stomped back to the table.

"See what I was up against?" Tommy said.

"A real pro." Jack nodded. "You notice how he converted your *security team* into just '*him*'?"

"Didn't miss it. Penny, I want you and Jack to be there at one along with as large a detail of those trusted cops as you can shanghai fast. I want to flood that place."

Penny chuckled. "Clear signal not to underestimate you?"

"Something like that. Also, Penny, could you get a dress uniform for Tom? Tommy, me boy, you are escorting the Princess Royal to the ball tonight." Kris was all grin.

Tommy wasn't. "You sure you want me?"

Kris swallowed; she was starting to enjoy this, and once again she'd volunteer Tommy to be right next to the target.

"I'm sorry, Tom. I can understand if you don't want to be closer than fifty klicks to the nearest Longknife."

"That's not it." The usually unsinkable Santa Marian couldn't raise his eyes from the table. "You were the one who dug me out last night. I owe you. I just thought, after all I said about wanting to be far away from you, that you might want to be far away from me."

Three steps, and Kris was at Tommy's chair. Kneeling beside him, she lifted his chin until he was looking her in the eyes. "Tom, I need your help." She glanced around at the tiny group she'd dragooned into whatever it was she was doing. "You may have noticed, we are a rather eclectic lot. You were a good man at my back when the darts started flying on Olympia. At Paris, you were my one backup when I faced down our Captain and took on a Fast Attack Squadron. I need your help again because, you may have noticed, there are not a lot of people available just now."

The Lieutenant looked at her for a long second, then took in a deep breath and let out a sigh that would have been the pride of his Irish grandmother. "And what else would I be doing with meself if I wasn't galloping along right behind you into whatever mess you're wanting to get into?"

"Thank you," Kris said, then got to her feet. "What else do we need to figure out?"

"Why would this Mr. Sandfire be inviting you to the ball tonight?" Abby mused.

"I'm a great decoration," Kris said, fluffing her hair.

"To rub your nose in the trap you're in," Jack grumbled.

"To get a better idea of what he's up against," Penny said.

"All of the above," Kris decided. "Let's see that he gets his money's worth.

At 12:50, six plainclothesmen, lead by an Inspector Klaggath, presented themselves. Abby ushered them in to stand before Kris while she, in her best noble fashion, thanked them for coming to her aid on such short notice.

"Least we could do, ma'am," Klaggath said, not buying into the royal fiction. "Seems that a certain kidnapping that we all were assigned to was resolved rather interestingly last night."

KRIS, I HAVE ISOLATED SEVERAL CARRIER WAVES. IT IS

HIGHLY LIKELY THAT ALL THESE MEN ARE COVERED WITH BUGS.

ABOUT WHAT I EXPECTED, NELLY. "I hope no one was hurt," Kris said, doing her best to feign real concern.

"No one that mattered," Klaggath assured her. "And we understand the victim was recovered with little harm done. A good end all around."

"Then I look forward to dancing the night away."

Her knights errant off on their quest, Kris let Abby pamper her through a bath while the two of them discussed Heidelburg's prospective social calendar for the next week. Any and all listening bugs heard a lot of social chitchat, but none of them tracked Kris's thinking as she cycled her thoughts through what she'd gotten herself into, what might come of it, and what she wanted to do to Mr. Sandfire.

Jack and Penny returned, along with a pack of bugs. Abby and Tommy did the debugging. Was it just coincidence they got matched girl-boy, boy-girl, and the exhausting search went over every inch of their bodies? Kris cringed as the jokes, funny on several levels, began to fly, and she only wished she'd gone out so Jack and Tommy could give her as thorough a pat down.

KRIS, THERE IS STILL ONE ACTIVE BUG.

ON JACK OR PENNY?

NEITHER. IT IS A ROVING NANO GUARD.

MOBILE NANO GUARDS! Kris almost said out loud. I THOUGHT ONLY AUNT TRU WAS WORKING ON THOSE.

APPARENTLY NOT. FROM THE BANDWIDTH, IT IS ONLY AUDIO.

CAN YOU KILL IT?

PLEASE GET YOUR BERET FROM LAST NIGHT. I NEED ITS ANTENNA.

Kris started to say something to her maid, thought better of it, and ordered Nelly to open a window on the wall.

ABBY, GET ME LAST NIGHT'S BERET. THERE IS A ROVING NANO GUARD IN THE ROOM, appeared in a small window. Kris waved her maid to it.

With one eye on the screen, Jack began a full briefing. Abby returned, adjusted the beret on Kris, and merged its lead into Nelly's wire. While Jack continued, leading them through a map of the facilities, the location of all the security sensors, and even the remotely controlled weapons, Kris waited for Nelly to report. Jack finished and glanced around the room, not at his listeners, but at the air above their heads. "That's what we found, Kris. Things should be fine."

NELLY, IT WOULD BE NICE TO HEAR FROM YOU.

I THINK I HAVE SEIZED CONTROL OF THE NANO. A MOMENT MORE.

Kris smiled at Jack. "It sounds like you had a very successful afternoon."

"I'm glad you like that," Jack said, sounding like a bad actor reading from an even worse script.

"I've got it," Nelly said. "It's doing what I tell it and sending what I want it to hear."

"Land it on the table so I can have a look at it," Jack said, producing all three bug chasers. He waited a moment, activated them . . . and got no response. "Nelly?"

"It is down. Your gear is not rigged for its signal."

"I've got full frequency range." Jack almost pouted.

"Yes, but this is hopping bands faster than you can follow," Nelly said. "Trudy designed something like this, so she included programs to look out for it in my last exchange with Sam, but she didn't expect to see them for at least another six months. I must tell Sam about this as soon as I can get a message out."

"Sandfire is full of surprises. Nelly, keep some kind of news flowing. I don't want him to know we've turned his rover."

"He's listening to a debate about what you will wear."

"Thank you, Nelly. Draw up a full schematic on this thing for Aunt Tru. Jack, you're sure I'll be safe tonight?"

"No, but if Sandfire wanted you dead, you would be already."

"Thanks for reminding me. Penny, if you don't mind, I'd like you at my elbow tonight. You want some time to get ready?"

"I also need to scare up a uniform for Tommy, here."

"Then I guess we all had better be busy."

9

By nine, Abby had outdone herself. Kris relaxed through sinful pampering and finished in a bright red gown that would have left Mother drooling, and did leave Jack asking where to put the bull's-eye. Kris made a face. "You'd have to paint it on me." She was showing more skin than she had since Father caught a picture of her as she bounced around the beach on a hot summer day in bottoms only. Of course, then, she'd only been four.

Kris swished the skirt and discovered she liked the feel of this new self. She still wasn't sure how Abby had gotten her into a backless, strapless push-up bra, but it seemed to involve glue, and Kris did not look forward to taking it off. The front looped over her neck, spread just enough to cover the essentials, then dropped to her waist. Kris was proud of that narrow asset; it was something she owned all by herself. From there hung several gauzy skirts, ready to go their separate ways as she walked. If Kris moved quickly, bare skin flashed openly. Most of the time, there was at least one thin layer of flaming red between her and the world. The most substantial material in the entire rig was the sash of the Order of the Wounded Lion cutting across from the right breast to the left hip.

The only thing more interesting than seeing how this planet's fashion police would respond to her dress tomorrow would be to see Sandfire's face tonight when he saw what she'd earned blowing his last plot out of space.

"And to top it all off," Abby said, presenting the golden confection of a tiara Mother had bought. Kris frowned at it. Several thin strands circled among a finely beaten wisp of webbing. The patina showed the actual hammer marks . . . or claimed to. Kris's eyes detected a repetitive pattern; she studied the rear of the crown. Yes, there it was; the tiny data entry port. Not only was the dang thing smart metal, but its maker had been too cheap to use a radio hookup! So much for Mother's claim it was from Earth's dark ages, twentieth century or earlier. Abby settled the tiara on her head, then returned once more with an automatic and Nelly.

"And here's where we put these," Abby said, settling both weapon and computer into place around Kris's hips. A thin wire, cosmetically covered, connected Nelly to Kris's implant.

"If I'd known I was going to be decked out like this regularly, I'd have had a backup jack put in my belly button."

"Not a good place," Abby said with a knowing frown. "One of my employers tried that. Too much tummy rumbling. And when a guy danced too close, or got on top, reception went all to hell."

"One of your former employers," Kris said.

"I don't stay around the dumb ones long."

"So, is my idea of walking right up to Sandfire dumb?"

The maid stopped her fussing about Kris, eyed her a moment, then gave a quick shake of her head. "We won't know until we're done. Besides, he pretty much has you where he wants you, and there's not a lot you can do." Abby chuckled. "Mr. Sandfire may rue the day he left you with nothing much to do."

"Empty hands being the devil's workshop and all that," Kris agreed. She did not like being in anyone's trap. Sooner or later, she would get out. Kris took several steps, testing the three-inch heels Abby insisted were perfect for this getup. The many-layered gown shimmered and flashed, and Kris stayed upright.

She paused at the door to her room to take in her friends. Tommy and Penny stood waiting in dress uniforms, his dashing, hers frumpy. Jack looked dapper in formal tails. "Well, crew, let's see what Turantic nightlife has to offer at the Top."

"Yeah," said Tom, offering Kris an arm, "we saw the bottom last night."

At the door, Kris faced four unsmiling men in white ties, tails, and earplug comm devices, as well as two women in black gowns. "Six," she said over her shoulder to Jack.

"That's just a start. I'd have had more if I could."

Kris swallowed a question about who was paying; that had to be the least of her worries. With a smile and a nod to her new security, Kris crossed the threshold. Down the hall were two more agents. Mr. Klaggath held a spacious and richly apportioned slide car for them. "Everything is cleared," he told Jack.

"Is all this necessary?" Kris asked, entering the car.

"Princess, you *play* your part. I'll *do* mine," Jack said as he took station ahead of her, four or five agents to his right and left. Penny stepped back to stand beside Kris.

Like a good Princess, Kris settled comfortably onto the couch at the rear of the car and prepared for a long ride up to the Top of Turantic. The car accelerated sideways smoothly and rapidly. WE ARE UNDER OBSERVATION, Nelly advised Kris. THERE ARE SEVERAL BUGS IN THE ELEVATOR'S CHANDELIER.

I EXPECT WE WILL BE FOR THE REST OF THE NIGHT.

"No stops," Kris said, inviting Penny to join her on the couch for what looked to be a long ride.

"No. The yard has its own bank of elevators, they told us. We've got an express from the old station to the Top."

Kris mulled that over. "The Nuu yards share the ferry with High Wardhaven," she said slowly.

"Well, High Turantic is proud that its yards have their own totally secure lifts from planet straight to the yard," Penny said, apparently quoting someone's advertising cover.

Kris let that roll around for a moment, then swallowed an *"interesting"* before it got out. Instead, Kris raised an eyebrow at Penny. The woman returned just the hint of a smile as if she, too, was finding that bit of data suddenly more interesting than before. NELLY, REMIND ME TO LOOK INTO WHY A SPACE DOCK NEEDS ITS OWN FERRY.

YES, KRIS.

Much sooner than Kris expected, the slide car came to a gentle halt, and she walked into her first surprise of the night. She had expected a ballroom, probably larger than any she'd frequented on Wardhaven, but still a ballroom. What she found as the elevator opened was not so much a room as a place.

Thirty thousand kilometers above the surface of the planet, the cylinder of the station rotated, giving Kris a sense that the floor was down. The ceilings above usually kept her from gasping at the reality. There was no ceiling here. The void reached out above her head. On one side was glass, letting in the vast dark of space and pinprick stars. Opposite that was one huge mirror, echoing, and, if possible, enlarging space. And in a ring between them, going out in both directions and meeting above her head, was a place of places.

Kris needed a whole new meaning for extravagant. Mother had, on occasion, reminded a younger Kris that a lady does not let her mouth hang open. "She might swallow a fly." Tonight, only the fear of swallowing a surveillance bug kept Kris's mouth shut as she took in the breathtaking view.

The slide cars opened on a marble stage with a daunting view. By carefully applying pressure to Tommy's arm, she steered him in a walk around the entire panorama. Three broad stairways curved lazily around, taking people down some twenty meters into different venues.

"Wow," Tommy finally whispered.

"Here's a place Grampa could use as a palace," Kris said.

"Looks like it was made with that in mind," Jack observed dryly, which raised an eyebrow from Penny. Maybe empire building was no longer a metaphor.

"And here comes the Emperor now," Tommy whispered.

Disgorging from a newly arrived car was a bevy of sparkling but scarcely clad women. Almost lost in their glitter was a single man attired soberly in black. Black tie, black shirt, black tails and pants. His waist and neck alone gleamed gold: one was girded by a cummerbund; from the other hung a sign of office appropriate for a Royal Chamberlain of yore.

Kris aimed Tommy at him, approaching the dark man much as a smiling matador might have done the most dangerous of horned bulls in the now-banned sport of bullfighting.

"Interesting choice of jewelry," Kris said as she came to a stop before her host.

Apparently too lost in chatter with his harem to notice her, he glanced around at her words. He might have gone back to ignoring her for longer, but he blinked as his eyes passed over Kris's own jewelry. Maybe the merest shadow of a frown creased his lips, but it was gone in a moment. "I might say the same of yours," he said softly.

"Mine had to be earned," Kris said, fingering the medallion at her waist.

He ran his hand lazily over his golden breastplate. "This, a minor bauble. I'm told it has some historical significance. I just like how it impresses the girls," he said patting one of his collection on her bare rump. Kris did not blink but held his eyes with her own. She didn't miss the hint of commotion behind him among two of his women. One stared at Tom on Kris's elbow, then, with slight eye flicks and nods, drew the notice of her associates to him. *Very interesting.*

Sandfire broke from her gaze with a diffident wave at their surroundings. "Let me introduce you to what some are calling my Pleasure Dome." Sandfire stepped forward, offering Kris his elbow. With a slight bow to Kris, Tom stepped back to join Penny and Jack. The two entourages re-formed in half circles around their primaries, Kris with her security detail to her right, Sandfire with his herd of lovelies to his left.

Now Kris let her eyes wander up to the star-studded wall and marveled. "It certainly is a lovely *dome.*"

"Yes, but as in so much of life, it depends on what you fill it with. I was so glad that you were in town, and, shall we say, caught between flights. But I do not restrict the pleasures of this place to the likes of us," Sandfire said, leading Kris in a circle of the platform. "What kind of worlds would the Rim become if such a view as this was reserved for only the elite?"

Sandfire did not pause long enough in his monologue for Kris to mention the people of Katyville. "We have restaurants with cuisine drawn from every corner of human space." The middle staircase sent people into a market setting filled with sidewalk cafés, pushcart merchants, and small alcoves. The right stairs led down to a dancing fountain with its own merchants and eateries. "The water is not just for show. There is a hippodrome for all kinds of water sports and diversions," he said, pointing above their heads. "We have the best in sound control technology so people enjoying one part here do not trouble those around them."

At the foot of the left staircase was a garden, full of flower-beds, hedges, and small tables. In the distance above Kris, scores of couples swirled to what must have been an ancient waltz, but she heard nothing.

Behind Kris, a car opened to squeals of delight. Children, ranging in ages from four to maybe twelve, hurried from the lift under the watchful eyes of parents or primly dressed nannies. They raced down the first staircase, oblivious to calls of "No running," "Hold on to the rail," and "Hold your sister's hand," that trailed behind them.

Sandfire smiled at the children. The smile was twisted, like a snake might give a bird before it snapped it up. "The Rim worlds are young and growing. How could we have a fun place for people without a place for their children as well?"

"Seems a bit past their bedtime," Kris said with a shiver.

"But people work on very many schedules. Our population is growing so fast, many of the schools are on two and three shifts. It works out well for parents who are on swing or night shift to have their children on a similar schedule. I suspect our Youth Fun Park is busy twenty-four hours a day. It's quite a scene. If you stay long, do drop by and enjoy it."

"I'll keep that in mind," Kris said, her back suddenly crawling. *So this is how the bird feels.*

"I believe we are late for the ball." Sandfire smiled.

"Then let me return to Tom, and I will return you to your lady," Kris said, intentionally using the singular.

Sandfire handed Kris off to Tom without a missed step. "Do I know you, young man?" he asked the man he'd kidnapped.

"I don't think we've been formally introduced," Tom said, not missing a beat . . . or choking on the words. "I'm Lieutenant Tom Lien, Wardhaven Navy." He did not offer his hand.

"I'm Calvin Sandfire, entrepreneur of some success. If you ever need a job, look me up."

"I doubt I'll ever have such a need," Tom said, taking Kris's arm and leading her toward the broad staircase that would take them to the garden of dancing couples.

"Oh, I almost forgot," Sandfire said after them. "We've had an infestation of nanos of undetermined ability and origin. Our security nanos are, of course, doing their best to control them, but you might want to avoid saying anything you don't want to see splashed over some newsie tomorrow. You know how they are."

"Thank you," Kris said with well-oiled grace. "We've had the same problem in my suite. I'm told by my security people," she said with a shallow bow in Jack's direction, "that they've had to destroy a major plague of the little beasties. I can only assume there is no limit to what some news channels will do to get a few embarrassing pictures of a Princess?"

"Disgusting behavior," Sandfire agreed as he and his women headed away from the ball. "The price we pay for democracy."

"Hating that man is easy," Tom said as he led Kris down the thickly carpeted marble staircase.

"No talk of classified items," Kris said through her smile.

"Well, he has to know I hate his guts," Tom answered without disturbing his smile.

"Tom has a point," Jack said from behind them.

"Yes, he does, but let's keep it cool and light tonight," Kris said. At the foot of the stairs stood a man in knee britches and a cloth-of-gold waistcoat. He held a richly carved wood staff topped by a silver ball. As Kris reached the last step, he pounded his staff on the floor for attention.

"May I present Her Royal Highness, Princess Kristine of Wardhaven, and her escort.

"Show time, crew. Let's make sure the paying customers get their money's worth," Kris ordered glibly.

The next moment, Kris was drowning in society. She used her best survival skills to keep a smile on her face and her hand attached to her arm. That, as usual, proved to be more difficult than it should have, some men viewing any handshake weaker than a bear claw as somehow beneath their masculinity.

Then there were those who felt familiar enough to kiss, peck, or slobber all over her cheek. NELLY, NOTE TO ABBY: FIND A FACE CREAM THAT'S SLIGHTLY BITTER. MAYBE DERIVED FROM POISON IVY.

IF YOU SAY SO, KRIS.

I SAY SO.

One of her socially empowered assailants let drop that they had been waiting for her arrival since she boarded her elevator. "What delayed you?"

Kris dodged the cross-examination with a smile and a turn

to face another open mouth. That brought her into the inane conversations. "Are you enjoying your visit?" "Have you had a chance to visit our hunting reserves on North Continent?" "You really must take in our beaches along South Coast. Some of them don't even require bathing suits," came with either a leer or titter not always depending on the sex of the speaker. Kris managed safe replies to all, danced with several young men who seemed reasonably likely to stay off her feet. She guessed wrong a few times. What was missing from the bubble around her was any mention of politics or the quarantine. Kris breasted the flow of talk, feeling much like a salmon swimming upstream. Her one prayer was that if she ever found relief, spawning would not be required.

Quite suddenly, when she doubted there was another "Hello," "So glad to see you," or "What a lovely evening" in her, she did stumble into a quiet pool. As the lull descended, Kris found herself in the company of a single couple. They were, thanks to some gracious god, either at a loss for words or of that rare human subspecies that faced silence without fear.

Kris allowed her smile to wilt. "I never thought this Princess thing could be such hard work," she half laughed to the thin, balding man in a white dinner jacket.

The woman beside him, blond and in a short blue party dress, chuckled along with her. "I doubt my mother would agree it held a candle to when she soldiered alongside your Grampa Trouble."

"When did she know Grampa?" Kris's eyes lit up. Here was a real conversation.

"She was a Private, drafted during the Unity War."

"Ouch," Kris said. "I've been told I was lucky he lived long enough to have kids. Sounds like we share the same luck."

"That was what her mother often told her," the man said, giving his wife the kind of smile a man does when he knows just how lucky he is.

Kris glanced around. No convivial attack horde seemed imminent, so she moved to a table, sat, then invited the couple to join her. "How long have you been here on Turantic?" Kris asked.

"My mom and dad settled here," the woman said. "I met Mel at the university. His family dates back to the first landing, and he's insisted I put down solid roots," she said, resting her hand on her husband's.

"My wife is being coy." The man smiled. "She represents the Twelfth Senatorial District, while I'm a mere accountant with Haywood Industries. We do a lot of heavy fabrication work. Turantic is a very lovely place to raise a child. Our daughter was skiing this afternoon, and she'll be racing in this weekend's regatta. How many places have that within a hundred miles of home?"

"Not many. I'm hoping to see more of your planet, since I can't seem to arrange a ride home."

"Oh, yes, that plague is horrible," the Senator agreed.

"Nuu Pharmaceuticals has a vaccine. Isn't any available?"

The two exchanged glances; the man looked away. The woman took a deep breath. "I have nothing official on this, but some of the people I know have heard things on the news. You know how you can't trust half of what you hear from a newsie." Kris nodded, wondering why the Senator was suddenly dancing around bushes. "Well, I've heard there is a Nuu outlet in Heidelburg, but they won't release the vaccine until the government agrees to pay five thousand dollars, Wardhaven, per shot."

"Yes," Kris agreed, "that is one of Grampa Al's tax scams. He set that price on the vaccine, then always donates it for the tax write-off."

"There's no talk of donating it this time," the husband said. "Maybe with communications being down and all that."

"The donation is standard policy," Kris snapped. "Nelly, get me the Nuu Pharm distributor dirtside."

"I placed a call to that number when it was first mentioned," her computer said, sounding rather proud of herself for being a step ahead of her mistress. "No one is answering."

"I don't care if they pick up their phone, Nelly," Kris said, knowing that her smile had turned anything but pleasant. "Activate the phone and turn up the volume," Kris said, hoping she wasn't breaking too many Turantic privacy laws in front of a serving legislator. The Senator was smiling.

"Done, ma'am," Nelly said.

"This is Kris Longknife, one of Nuu Enterprises' primary shareholders. Who am I talking to?"

HAROLD WINFORD IS THE MANAGER, Nelly put in.

THANKS, NELLY, BUT I WANT HIM TO TELL ME.

"Me," came a groggy voice, "Harry Winford. Who'd you say you are?"

"I'm Kris Longknife, and I can have my computer tell you exactly how large my holdings are in Nuu Enterprises if that will help me get your attention."

"No, I remember. You're that Princess Longknife. I heard you were going to some ball or something tonight."

"I am at a ball; if it will help you, I can turn up the volume so you can hear the music."

"No, no, don't need to do that."

"Well, Harry, the social chitchat turned to this and that, and what should pop out but a mention that someone on Turantic had some of Grandpa Al's Ebola vaccine and wasn't releasing it."

"I can't release it."

"Harry," Kris turned up the syrup, "we don't charge anyone five thousand a shot. We donate it and take the tax break."

"I know, ma'am. I've read the company policy."

"So why isn't the media full of NuuE giving the stuff away?"

"Because I don't have it to give."

"What!" The Senator and her husband had been following the conversation. Mel seemed to enjoy the mental image of another manager being in way over his head when the boss called. The Senator nodded at the crackle of political power. Now both frowned in puzzlement, which about summed up Kris, too.

"Ma'am, my computer told me this morning I had one hundred thousand vials of vaccine, good for maybe five million shots. I went looking for the vials and found a big, gaping hole on my shelves. Not one bottle. Nothing."

"When did you last check them?"

"Last full inventory was four months ago."

"You tell the police?" Kris asked, glancing around for Inspector Klaggath. He was busy talking into his wrist unit.

"I reported it. Three cops showed up, did the usual, had me sign lots of stuff. I've told the media, but every damn person I tell I've been robbed just looks at me and asks how much."

Kris sighed; *she* was none too sure she believed his story. "Excuse the interruption, Harry; you can go back to sleep."

"Yeah, like I can."

Now Kris faced the Senator. It had been quite a power rush to be the miracle worker. Right up to the point where she walked off a cliff. She shrugged, an interesting action in the outfit she had on. "Now you know as much as I know."

"But who stole it?" Mel said.

"Inspector Klaggath?" Kris said.

"Excuse me, ma'am," he said, coming forward. "That's not my line of work. I've got calls out, and I may be able to tell you something before too long, but I'll just be passing info. I won't know anything extra."

"But the theft isn't getting out to the media!" Kris said, mindful of the growing public relations disaster.

"If theft it is," the Inspector said.

Kris had no answer for that. And whatever had given her this momentary respite must have ended, because a milling herd appeared headed her way. "Looks like it's back to shaking hands and smiling," she said, standing.

"Oh, we didn't even introduce ourselves, Mel," the Senator said, standing as well. "I'm Kay Krief, this is my husband Mel. Our daughter, Nara, will be racing this weekend. I hope you can come by her boat and wish her luck," Kay said, offering her hand and an official card.

"I'd be glad to," Kris said, taking the card and passing it to Penny. Kris had no idea where to stash a card in her gown.

"Nara would be delighted," Mel said.

"I'll call you," Kris said and turned to face what proved to be a mob with a center. Ambassador Middenmite smiled and presented a man of medium height and healthy build, "Izzic Iedinka, the President of Turantic."

Kris held out her hand, and the President, instead of shaking it, kissed it, doing it rather well. Returning to his full height, which made him an inch shorter than Kris, he said, "I hope you are enjoying your stay. Did you come here on business?"

"Initially business," Kris said, "which was quickly finished. Now I find myself staying here for pleasure."

"Ah, yes, the quarantine. I'm afraid that can't be helped."

"I just heard that the supply of Ebola vaccine that Nuu Pharmaceuticals has on the planet has been stolen."

"Excuse me, there's a vaccine for this thing?" A woman at his elbow stepped forward and whispered something to him.

"There is? Why wasn't I told about that?" He turned back to Kris with a wan smile. "Seems like it has kind of been walked off with, I guess. I'm sure my police will have something to tell us by morning. Right?" he said, half over his shoulder.

"Yes, Mr. President."

"It's sad to see it stolen," Kris said with the most sincere smile she could manufacture, "since it is my grandfather's policy not to make money off of such terrible events. My representative on Turantic has already assured me that he was pulling the vaccine from storage to donate it to the relief effort."

"He was? Now that's mighty fine of him," the President drawled, "but you'll pardon an old horse trader if I tell you that you can't stay in business doing things like that."

"I can't agree with you more." Kris smiled. "But we find the tax write-off for the donation covers our costs quite well."

"Ah, right," the President said, making a gun out of his finger and shooting Kris. "That's a businessman I understand."

Kris expected he could. "I've got a call into Nuu Enterprises to send a fast packet for me. It can bring in more vaccine. I sent the message early this morning, but I haven't heard that it's gone out."

"Not likely it will, young lady," the President told her. "Seems the fire in our communications center here on the station did more damage than they thought, even to the stuff that was still working. It's all down. They tell me they're scrounging all over Turantic for stuff they can use to get it back up."

Which left Kris really and truly stranded here. "Any chance I could buy a ship to take me off planet?"

"Nope. Until we can certify we've got a clean bill of health, I've ordered all shipping locked down. If a ship even powers up, there'll be a passel of guards seeing why, and if one actually managed to get away, our station gunners have orders to shoot any ship making for a jump point. I take my responsibility to the rest of humanity very seriously," he said, putting a hand to the vest of his tux.

Time to switch topics. "I've been told you have an election coming up soon." Kris smiled.

"Yep, one month, twenty-six days. But who's counting?" He chuckled. "It's probably the most important election to face us since the first ship landed on Turantic. Things have changed. Humanity has to change with it, and so do we," he said, launching into what sounded far too much like The Canned Speech. But before Kris could stop him, he stopped himself. "I'll be talking at a $250,000-a-plate dinner later this evening. You'll be coming by, won't you?"

"My schedule is amazingly light this evening," Kris told him.

"I'll look for you there," the President said and seemed to be ready to move on. However, a young man had stepped forward to whisper something to him. "It is?" the President said, and the man pointed at Kris's waist. For a moment the President seemed to really take Kris in, his nostrils flaring a bit at what he saw. "I'm told that is the Earth Order of the Wounded Lion you're wearing there, girl."

"Yes, Mr. President." Here was something Kris could enjoy.

"More often than not, that's only given out posthumously."

"As you can see, I'm very much alive."

"I've heard several different stories about what actually happened between the Earth Battle Fleet and the Wardhaven Fleet at the Paris system a few months ago."

"I was there," Kris said proudly, "and I heard quite a few different stories about what happened, too." *And you're not going to hear my story from me, Mr. President.*

"Very confusing situation," the President muttered, glancing over his shoulder at his adviser. "Very confusing."

"I'm sure you've heard the old saw about the fog of war, Mr. President," Kris replied, too proud of herself to let it drop but choosing her words carefully. "The farther you get out on the tip of the spear, the foggier it is, sir, and at Paris, I was about as far out on the tip as it got."

Tommy, who'd stood quietly through all this, leaned close to Kris's ear and muttered, "And not have the damn spear jammed up your ass."

The President apparently didn't catch Tom's words. He shook his head, repeated, "Very confusing," one more time, and headed off for other hands to shake and contributions to collect. Kris, however, caught at the Ambassador's elbow.

"Sir, I've got a problem. In my day job, I'm in the Navy. I'm about halfway through a week's leave, and since I'm not headed back already, it looks like I'm not only going to overstay my leave but not be able to report my situation. Do you have a military attaché that I could at least check in with?"

"I don't know, Your Highness. I guess there are some uniform types on my staff." Penny, at Kris's other elbow, cleared her throat. The Ambassador glanced at her as if seeing her for the first time this evening. "Ah, yes, I do know you. You work for me, don't you?"

"In Military Exchanges and Procurement, sir."

"Well, you'll look after her, won't you? Try to keep her out of trouble. I've heard stories about the Prime Minister's brat, don't you think I haven't, young woman," the Ambassador said, softening his words with a grandfatherly grin.

If he chucks me under my chin, I'm going to kick him in the groin, Kris promised herself, but he turned and followed the President toward the political side, leaving Kris with a choice: stay with the sociables or go heel to toe with Turantic's political power. Apparently, declaring Wardhaven foreign didn't mean the President didn't want her money, even royal donations. Kris shook her head; Grampa Ray had made sure she spent a day listening to the things she could not do anymore. Joining the politicians would be throwing herself into the deep end of someone else's pool, a deep end that probably wanted her on record for things Grampa Ray was still dodging. At least among the socials she hadn't met a shark she couldn't out-gnaw.

She turned back to the party.

For the next half hour, Kris mingled. More talk of weather, how beautiful Turantic was, how nice it was to be out from under Earth's thumb, and how great her great-grandparents were back then with about half of them wondering what had gotten into Grampa Ray to let himself be made a King. The other half loved the idea. And, of course, there were the mothers offering Kris their very available bachelor sons for spousal consideration. Fortunately, few were present. Those who were ranged from gawkily awkward to boorishly forward. Kris wondered if it was too late to join a nunnery rather than the Navy.

Just as Kris was about to declare that she'd suffered enough and had earned the right to retreat back to her hotel suite, Senator Krief showed up again, this time with nearly a dozen other people. They rather deftly cut Kris out from the mob and edged her into a quiet corner with tables and chairs. "You looked like you could use rescuing," Kay said.

"I could use something," Kris agreed.

"A drink?" Mel asked. Kris mentioned something light and soft; the man stepped away as his wife did introductions.

"I thought you'd like to meet a few of the folks who won't be at the President's fund-raiser. Senator Kui," a small, white-haired man bowed slightly to Kris, "and his wife," a woman in a red kimono-type gown smiled. "Senator Showkowski," a large woman in a bright blue gown nodded, "and her husband," an even larger man in a poorly tied white tie and tails neither smiled nor nodded but looked at Kris like he might a spider. Senator LaCross was a tall, willowy man who bowed graciously to Kris. "And his spouse," introduced another man slightly shorter but just as thin. He affected a bow as deep as the Senator's.

Mel returned with drinks for all. Kris took a sip and settled herself in place. A glance around showed Jack had her agents in a semicircle that would not only protect her from stray bullets but might just block out any enthusiastic mother.

The others settled into chairs, glanced around among themselves, and said nothing.

"So," Mr. Showkowski growled into the silence, "Wardhaven gunna keep us under its thumb just like Earth?"

"Dennis," his senatorial wife said with a frown.

"Well, that is what you all want to know. Politicians! You're afraid to ask. Well, Longknife, what's it gunna be?"

Now it really was show time. Kris sat forward. "Not being a politician myself, I can give you a straight answer. I don't know. Why do you ask?"

"You don't know?" Senator LaCross said.

"Hey, folks, my day job is with the Navy. My nights are pretty much full of this Princess gig. Doesn't leave a lot of time for tracking the media. You may have me confused with my father or great-grandfather," Kris said, all smile.

"We kind of assumed you would know what they had up their sleeves," Kay Krief said.

Kris raised her very bare arms. "Nothing up mine. And I really think most politicians on Wardhaven are just as much in the dark as you are about what the United Sentients will do."

"I find that hard to believe," said Senator Kui.

"You're talking about eighty sovereign planets," Kris pointed out. "Each has a vote in the legislature. They aren't even sure if it's going to be a one-, two-, or three-house legislature, last I heard."

"But King Ray is—" Dennis Showkowski began.

Kris cut him off. "Has no veto power, no authority to propose legislation. He controls nothing but his own words."

"But I thought that making him King would mean all of the policies he advocated for the Society of Humanity would be carried over into the United Sapients thing."

"Sentients," Kris corrected and shook her head. "Listen, the only real reason for making Grampa King was to take my family and its money out of U.S. politics. Did my father resign as Prime Minister of Wardhaven? No. Does anyone on Wardhaven call him Prince? Not twice." Dad had blustered and flustered and gotten the Prince thing dropped. Kris had tried, to no avail. "Truth is, no one knows what any of this stuff means. You pay your money and you take your ride," she quoted one of her father's favorite sayings. "And if you want to have a say, you get on board soonest before everything gets settled and bureaucrats are saying, 'But we've always done it that way.' "

That brought a smile from the legislators around her.

"So you're saying that King Ray ain't going to force his Wardhaven Treaty on this United whatever thing," Dennis said.

Kris took a deep breath. This was something she knew Grampa Ray's thinking on. "I have heard Grampa Ray say that he thinks it's time for us to do more exploring. The Iteeche War came from a lot of problems. We met the aliens when human pirates stumbled on their fringe planets run by their lawless ones. Humans and the Iteeches will never see eye-to-eye. I think Grampa Ray is all for a licensed, organized scouting of near Rim space. We're six hundred planets. Humanity has to expand faster now. Earth was wrong in trying to slow us down."

"You're sure that's his view?" Senator Krief said.

"Yes."

"But, as you say, he has no authority to enforce that view," Senator Kui said, smiling softly.

Kris shrugged. "You know my Grampa Ray."

"Yes," came from several Senators.

"Now, if we could just hear it from him."

"Message him," Kris said. "I'm sure he'd agree with me."

"Can't. Can't message anyone," Dennis exploded. "I've got

contracts to fill. Can't ship my goods. Can't tell anyone I'll be late. Can't tell them when I'll ship! Damn, this is a mess!"

"This situation is already disrupting business," Senator LaCross said. "My contacts tell me layoffs will start tomorrow. Once that hits the news, panic will not be far behind."

"And there are already rumors that the Ebola outbreak followed by the comm fire is just too much of a coincidence," Mel Krief said, glancing around the group. "Way too much."

Kris certainly was in agreement, but what she knew she would not share here. "What makes you say that?"

"The competition between our neighbor Hamilton and us has gotten almost cutthroat of late. And the last year or two, there have been rumors of what you might call dirty tricks. Ship Captains that were supposed to deliver here but took a bribe to take a long cut and deliver late. Certain containers that got off-loaded there instead of here. You know, the stuff that aggravates but never rises to a level of legal action. Then their legislature lowers taxes on certain properties so their business can out-compete us. And last month they slapped a tariff on our wine," Mel said, shaking his head. "Every week, it's something new. Heaven only knows what they're doing now."

"That's what I'm afraid of," Dennis growled.

"So there's bad blood between you," Kris said.

"Yes," Kay agreed, "and with the end of the Society, you can't forget that in the bad old days, these kinds of things were settled with warships and armies."

"How could we forget with 'A Flag for Black Mountain,' this summer's runaway hit?" Senator Kui said.

"Bet your Grampa Trouble doesn't know he's the idol of half the kids on Turantic," LaCross said.

"Knowing Grampa Trouble, I doubt he'd like that."

"So you see," Kay said, "we really need agreements on trade, a central court to handle disputes and very quickly, some public health regulations, and doctors to clear up this quarantine."

"Why don't you legislate them yourselves?" Kris asked.

"I don't often agree with the Tories," Kay said, "but we can't just declare ourselves healthy. Everyone has to agree we are, or any ship that stops here won't be able to stop anyplace else. The breakup of the Society came way too fast for us."

"Not fast enough for me," Dennis spat. "Well, maybe we didn't think all of it through, but we had to get rid of Earth."

"Yes, we rid ourselves of Earth, but what have we taken on in its place?" Kui asked.

No one had an answer for that. And three matronly women were bearing down on the circle of Kris's guards, one with a tall wisp of a son stumbling along in tow. "I see I must get back to my social responsibilities," Kris said, standing.

"Did I mention my son?" Senator Showkowski said, only half smiling.

"Send a photo," Kris said, turning to Jack. "The sooner you get me to the slide car, the less likely I'll kill someone."

"Your wish is my pleasure," her Security Agent replied.

Kris surfed through several mothers with a smile and a wave. She was making good time for the car when the lights blinked. WE HAVE TAKEN A POWER HIT! ALL SECURITY IS DOWN!

Nelly's report was overpowered by Jack's soft order: "Down!"

Kris began to stoop, her right hand going for her automatic, but Penny had other plans. Kris's legs were taken out from under her as the Navy Lieutenant did a leg sweep. Kris twisted around as she fell, still reaching for her gun as Tommy did what she had so often dreamed of.

The young man settled atop her. His arms went out to gentle his landing, a familiar smile on his face.

Then he shook as the first dart slammed into him. Shock replaced the smile as another spasm marked a second hit. By the third, his face only showed dismay.

Kris quit fumbling for her gun and grabbed for Tom, trying to break his fall, bring him down gently beside her. But now Penny collapsed on top of both of them. Jack shouted for someone to get the shooter. Everywhere there were screams.

Kris ignored them all, trying to hold Tom's head, console him, ease his pain, but Penny was still trying to cover her and getting in the way. "Damn it, woman, can't you see Tommy's hit."

"But I'm not," Tommy said.

"Yes you are," Kris snapped.

"Well, yes I am, but I think this coat stopped them," Tom said. "But you can keep holding me if you want."

"We're supposed to be protecting her," Penny growled.

"What is happening here?" Kris almost screeched.

"Penny said this coat should stop anything short of heavy artillery," Tommy said, "and I guess it did."

"Can I get up yet?" Kris asked no one.

"Just a moment more," Jack said, back still to Kris. Around her, four of her Agents had formed a wall, guns out, facing out. Through their legs, Kris saw a wide empty space, then more people milling about. Two agents, Inspector Klaggath with them, were now backing their way toward Jack, guns out, eyes on the crowd.

"We did not get the shooter," Klaggath said.

"Central," Jack said, "do you have video on the shooter?"

Kris didn't hear the answer, but Jack's rare use of profanity told her it must be negative. "Can I get up?"

"Agents, stay alert. There may be another shooter or that one may come back," Jack ordered. While Klaggath kept his team facing out, Jack helped Kris up, then Penny and Tom. "Let's get to the elevator," he said tersely.

Kris found that her knees were more wobbly than she wanted to admit. One arm around Tom, the other around Penny, she made best speed for the exit. Once in the slide car, she collapsed into the couch, then pulled Penny and Tom down beside her. Both had developed a fine case of the shakes. Kris took the moment to pull three-millimeter darts from the back of Tommy's dinner jacket. "Hardly even tore the fabric," she said, trying to laugh but managing only a hoarse echo of one.

"Uniform was guaranteed," Penny whispered.

"Remind me to write a thank-you to the manufacturer," Tommy said, his usual smile almost back on his face. Then he turned a fine shade of green.

About that time, Kris realized this gorgeous gown that would make Mother green with envy didn't have a stitch of body armor in it. Suddenly Kris's stomach demanded a quit clause on its contents. She swallowed twice, using iron will to keep herself from marring this beautiful work of art Abby had dressed her in.

The ride down seemed longer than the ride up.

10

The ride down was silent except for a few exchanges among the security detail. In the hall to her suite, Inspector Klaggath set his outside detail, two agents at the elevator, two more covering the slide car, and two at her door. She paused as he dismissed the party detail to thank them all herself. Before Klaggath could follow his team, Kris invited him in.

Once in the suite, Kris did nothing while Abby went over her with one detector. Jack did the same with Klaggath, who showed no surprise and very quickly demonstrated he knew how to operate a bug search and sizzle machine. Again, Penny and Tommy shared the honors among themselves. Done with one set, they swapped clockwise, and, when finished with the second set, did it again.

"You folks are thorough," Klaggath said.

"From the number of bugs we've sizzled," Jack said, "it looks like we have to be."

"You've beat my previous high," the Turantic cop agreed.

Done with the third search, Kris retired with Abby to change. NELLY, HOW'S THE MOBILE BUG SITUATION?

THERE ARE THREE UNKNOWNS OPERATING IN THE SUITE. LET THE OTHERS KNOW.

I AM AFRAID TO ADDRESS THEM, EVEN IN WRITING. TWO BUGS ARE TRANSMITTING ON ENOUGH BANDWIDTH THAT THEY MAY BE VISUAL.

Kris sighed.

"That bad?" Abby asked as she undid the dress.

Kris forced herself to stay onstage for just a few more minutes. "No worse than back home. But no better, either, and that Mr. Sandfire is so damn cool. So damn cool."

As Abby hung up the dress, Kris took the moment to wash her face in cold water. She'd led a drop mission and fought a firefight outnumbered five to one. What was so bad about being a target? *Maybe it's cumulative, girl? Or maybe it's easier when you can shoot back,* she answered herself.

Abby laid out a comfortable blue sweatsuit that just happened to display the Wardhaven seal, now with a crown atop it.

"This your idea?" she asked her maid.

"You're a Princess twenty-four/seven, girl."

"So I've noticed." NELLY, WHAT'S THE SITUATION?

"I captured two more mobile nanos," the computer reported aloud. "The other one was just too troublesome. I burned it."

Interesting choices and choice of words for a computer. "Nelly, we need to talk later about your progress since your latest upgrade."

"Yes, ma'am, but I don't know what we can talk about." Abby raised an eyebrow. Clearly, Kris and Nelly needed to talk.

"Jack, Tommy, Penny, Abby, Inspector Klaggath, front and center. We need to talk about tonight."

"Tonight I've decided to walk home. Anyone with me?" Tommy said with one of his lopsided grins. He came back into the living room in an undershirt and blue wool pants.

"How secure are we?" Penny asked, now out of uniform and in a borrowed pair of Kris's jogging shorts and a tank top. No bra, Kris could see her nipples. So could the guys. "Women that well-endowed should always wear the proper foundation garments," Kris heard Mother say. She'd never said it to Kris.

"Nelly says we are secure," Kris answered. "Inspector Klaggath, what happened to all that vaunted central security?"

"Please call me Bill," Klaggath said, still in formal dress.

He stood, hands folded in front of him in what Kris had come to recognize as a cop's form of parade rest.

Jack stood beside him, also still in formal.

"Okay, Bill. What happened?"

"The ballroom seems to have taken a power spike, far beyond specs. It took down a lot of equipment."

"And security gear wasn't on emergency backup?"

"Yes it was, fully tested and certified." The Agent scowled. "Unfortunately, in this first actual test, the backups failed.

"Is it my imagination, or does this new station seem a bit below specs?"

"Can't argue, ma'am. Bottom line is we have no video of the assassination attempt, and we were not able to follow the assassin in her flight."

"Her?"

Bill spoke into his wrist, and a small screen opened in the wall's view of a refreshing mountain waterfall. Kris strode over to get a good view of a woman in serving dress, white shirt, black jumper, long hair covering the side of her face toward the camera. Her hand supported a tray of drinks that didn't quite hide an automatic.

"That why she missed me? The serving tray blocked her aim?"

"No, ma'am, that weapon has a fully automatic visual sight. She saw what she was shooting at and hit what she aimed for."

Kris glanced at Tom. Once again, his freckles were bright red against his very pale skin, but he shrugged. "Glad to be of service, but Jack, my good friend, do you know where I can buy some underwear of fine Super Spider Silk?"

"I've got one of my agents out shopping already. It should be delivered in the morning." Klaggath turned to Kris. "I've got her shopping for all of you. Cops always wear this stuff. I thought you Navy types did, too."

"They haven't invented Spider Silk undies to stop a four-inch laser," Kris replied dryly.

"Laser cannons are the least of your problems, ma'am."

"Agreed," Kris said.

"Can we pause for a moment?" Jack said. "If they were not aiming for the Princess but were aiming for her escort, what does that tell us?"

"Tommy, you got any spurned lovers in this port?" Kris said, trying for humor.

Tommy collapsed into his usual chair, Penny settling on the arm of it. Kris waved the others to chairs and couches. Klaggath seemed inclined to stand, but Jack took him by the elbow. "When the woman starts one of her staff meetings, it's best to sit down before what she says knocks you down."

Kris threw Jack a glare, but Tom was answering her previous question. "I've got a few spurned captors. Think they might be after me?"

"Sandfire does seem to like pretty girls for his enforcers," Penny remarked.

"One of the girls around Sandfire seemed to recognize Tom," Kris said, a wicked smile taking over her face. "Any of those eyefuls your old girlfriends?"

"I was blindfolded and drugged to the gills. And believe me, none of them were treating me any way as nice as they do that SOB," Tom shot back. "If I get alone with one of them, it will be breaking an arm I'll be doing."

"I wouldn't count on that," Jack said quietly. "If you looked past the next to nothing they were wearing, there was a lot of muscle on their bones. I would not put my scratch security team up against that bunch. Not if I could help it."

"I caught a glimpse of a weapon on one of them," Penny said.

"So, in the future, we assume Sandfire's nymphs are armed and very dangerous," Kris concluded.

"You seem to know a lot about Mr. Sandfire," Klaggath said.

"We have reason to believe," Jack said, leaning toward the Inspector on the couch they shared, "Mr. Sandfire does not like the Princess Royal. They have a history I can fill you in on later." Bill raised two eyebrows but said nothing.

Penny was off the armchair, pacing back and forth. "Kris dropped everything on Wardhaven and came here in record time after Tom was kidnapped. She led the rescue team herself last night. Then Tom shows up as her escort tonight. I bet Sandfire figures Tom for Kris's lover."

Tom was shaking his head so fast it was in danger of coming unscrewed.

Kris tried to suppress a sigh.

"Of course, I know from debriefing Tom that he is no such thing, but Sandfire doesn't know that."

Now it was Kris's turn to give Tom the evil eye. "I didn't tell her anything," Tom squeaked.

"But it was the way you didn't tell me." Penny grinned.

"Enough," Kris said, holding up a hand. "What does this tell us?"

"Sandfire wants to hurt you," Abby said. "But he's mean enough not to do it to you but through others." The room nodded at that. "And he does not want you out roaming his domain."

"Tonight would make anyone want to hide under their bed," Tommy agreed.

Kris sighed. "I got that message."

"So, what do we do?" Jack asked.

Kris mulled over that question for a long minute. She'd never been one to do what she was told. Father had learned early to always explain why he wanted something. Being a politician, he was quite persuasive. Mother. Well, Mother had been Mother. True, since joining the Navy, Kris had been trying to learn the fine art of subordination, but Sandfire wasn't in her chain of command. And Sandfire truly deserved something. She just wasn't sure how really horrific it should be.

"We go public," Kris said with an innocent smile. She turned to Penny, an order on her lips, but paused long enough to remember that orders were not hers to give. "Penny, would you mind being my social secretary for the duration of my stay?"

"Be careful, Penny," Tom said. "When a Longknife starts asking politely, people are going to be dying before she's done."

"Tommy, you wrong her greatly," Penny said, the exaggeration of her voice only confirming the accusation. "However, if I've got her social calendar, I'll know where she is. That beats all hell out of chasing her. So, Princess Kristine, I will add your social life to my other duties as assigned. What do you intend?"

"I need time to think," Kris said. "Mr. Klaggath, where are the skeletons buried on Turantic, and who's doing the burying?"

The cop stroked his chin, then shook his head. "I'm a cop, ma'am. My job's to find the recently buried and arrest who did it. I don't think I'm your best source for gossip." He paused, then quirked half a smile. "You seem to have more dirt on Mr. Sandfire than I'm party to. Maybe I should be asking you."

Kris stood and walked slowly around the room, giving Tommy a back rub for a few moments, Abby a pat on the shoulder, and finally came to rest her hands on the couch back behind Jack. "Tell the Ambassador that I will be glad to show the flag at the regatta. Advise him I'm available for all the wine-tasting, cheese-cutting, and ribbon-slashing jobs he can lay on me." She paused for a moment. "Tell him I'm open to visiting the sick up in Bremen." Jack started up from his seat, but Kris grabbed his shoulders and hauled him back down. "In a full spacesuit."

"You're going to be a busy girl," Abby said.

"In full body armor," Kris said, "and I shoot back next time."

Kris awoke early next morning, refreshed and relieved not to remember her dreams. That lasted just long enough for her to remember she had left Nelly on the dresser. She did need some quiet down time with her computer . . . just not today.

After a quick shower, Kris found a suit laid out for her. Conservatively cut in a dark blue, it was the kind of day wear Mother dismissed as "fine for a woman who knows how to count beans but knows nothing really important." To date, Mother had yet to define what was really important. "This bulletproof?" Kris asked, dressing herself.

"The slip is," Abby answered, entering the room with a light blue beret in hand. "So is this," she said, twirling the head cover to Kris. "It also has a nice antenna for Nelly."

"You are full of surprises," Kris said, pulling on the skirt.

"So is the world. The trick is to have one more surprise in your pocket than the world has up its sleeve."

"Or in your travel trunks."

"Or wherever."

Penny appeared at the door. "For an empty day, you're up early and not dressing to lounge around. What's up?"

"A visit to Nuu Pharmaceuticals to start with. I want Mr.

Winford to say to my face that he didn't steal the vaccine."

"Should I order a cab? Kartum could probably use the fare."

Kris nodded, then shook her head. "People who get too close to me get killed. Have Klaggath order me a car, not too flashy. Cop for a driver and plenty of armor."

"Doing it."

The ride down the beanstalk was uneventful. Kris exited the terminal to find a late-model car waiting, green and about as nondescript as they came. Only the hum of the motor and the heavy way it sat its shocks gave away how special it was. Penny held the door open, but Kris paused before settling in.

Across the parking lot, workingmen were going and coming from a second, newer terminal. On one side, large trucks were backing up to a vast loading dock. "What's that?"

"That," Penny said, "is the ground terminal serving the space dock. It loads its own cars, both workers and material. Totally separate security system. Best in fifty planets."

Kris glanced back at the terminal she'd just left. "No interchange?"

"Not so much as a breath of air."

"Seems like overkill," Kris said, then remembered the tiny mobile bugs that Nelly was having to work so hard to keep out of her room. "Then again, maybe he knows what he's keeping out," she said and settled into her seat.

Tom shared the backseat with her and Penny. Jack was in front with the driver. "Minimum detail?" Tom asked as they pulled away from the curb.

A moment later they were joined by a car ahead and another behind. "Full detail," Jack said. "So, Princess, where to?"

"Nuu Pharmaceuticals," Kris said.

The driver repeated the address, probably for the cars around them, then punched in the address, but kept his own hands on the wheel. "You'll also need to drop by the embassy, ma'am."

"I don't mind going, but why?"

"Klaggath said you might want to get your passport stamped, or maybe a passport issued and stamped if you don't have one."

"A passport?"

"Yes, ma'am. They're becoming the thing for foreigners on Turantic. Used to be it was only the Earth types or their seven stooges we demanded them from, but the last couple of weeks it seems anyone without legal papers is subject to deportation."

"I got here two days ago and no one asked me for any papers," Kris said slowly.

"I suspect you got the royal treatment, ma'am. Inspector suggests that you might not want to keep counting on that."

"I agree," Jack said. "Just now they can't deport anyone. You could end up cooling your heels in a jail cell."

Time was Kris would have considered a couple of days in jail as a relaxing vacation from her social duties. Now that she was using social as warfare by other means, it might be a good idea to cover all her bases. "We'll do the embassy right after this. I want to be there when Winford opens the door."

Nuu Pharm was a low warehouse in an industrial park just this side of the bluff from Katyville. That was enough to make for an entirely different milieu. The concrete walls were newly painted tan. The barbed-wire-topped fence around the warehouse yard was in good repair, new patches gleaming against the older wire. There was a small patch of grass in front of the office entrance. The Nuu flag waved lazily in the light breeze that carried only a small whiff of river and pollution. Five men and women in work clothes and a woman in office dress waited at the door.

"Nelly, what time does this place open?"

"Twelve minutes ago."

"Let's go see why it's still locked up." Kris and her team piled out of the car. A dozen others, obviously cops despite their civilian clothes, were also spreading over the parking lot to the alarm of the working folks at the door.

"We didn't do nothing." "We don't know nothing," came from the workers, along with a "What do you want?" from the better-dressed woman as she came down the sidewalk toward the police. "We filled out all your reports yesterday."

Kris walked to cut her off from the officers. "I know you did, ma'am. I just wanted to talk to Mr. Winford." The woman eyed Kris for a moment without recognition. "I'm Kris Longknife, a Nuu Enterprises stockholder."

"Right, I saw you this morning. Newsies said someone shot at you last night."

"They missed."

"And you want to know what happened to our vaccine supply?"

"Yes, Ms. . . ."

"Mrs. Zacharias."

"Mrs. Zacharias, why is everyone waiting outside?"

"Mr. Winford is very particular about security, Miss Longknife. Or do you want me to call you Princess or something?"

"Kris will be fine. So you won't open the office?"

"No, ma'am. Mr. Winford uses an old-fashioned key lock that can't be jiggered or hacked. He figures that's the best way to handle things nowadays."

"Where is Mr. Winford?"

"I don't know, ma'am. He's never late." There were assents and nods from the workmen to support that point.

Kris turned around in exasperation at this check to her schedule, only to find her driver approaching, a reader in hand. "Ms. Longknife, you're waiting for a Mr. Winford?"

"Yes."

"I'm afraid you may have a long wait ahead of you." He offered her the reader. It showed the face of a man she recognized from last night. Mr. Winford looked slightly better rested, but very dead.

"What happened?"

"His body was found near a wooded jogging path this morning. It appears he had been dead less than an hour."

"Cause of death?" Jack asked.

"I'm afraid I can't tell you."

Officious people could be a real pain sometimes. "Is it being handled as natural causes?" Kris asked.

The driver glanced at another agent coming up beside him, whom Kris suspected was the head of this detail. "No, ma'am, we are not treating it as natural causes," the new man said. "I'm Inspector Marta, and we are handling it as a homicide."

Jack turned to Kris. "Please, get back in the car."

"Jack, I came to see what happened here. I'm not leaving before I'm finished.

"Fine, but humor me and sit in the car until I'm sure this area is safe."

So Kris humored Jack. She tried not to fume in the car while

Jack and the cops covered the grounds like a nest of very disturbed bees. Her focus of attention changed when Penny brought a tearful Mrs. Zacharias to join her in the car. There were tissues in the seat back; Kris offered the woman the box.

"Thank you," she said, blowing her nose. "I don't know what you think of Mr. Winford, but he was a good man to work for. An honest man, and there aren't a lot of them left in business."

Kris agreed. The woman made use of a few more tissues, then opened her purse and began rummaging in it. "He told me to use it if there was ever an emergency. I don't imagine there can be much more of an emergency than this." Kris agreed further, wondering how much longer before Jack declared the place safe.

Mrs. Zacharias pulled a key from her purse. "You think your police will mind if I let the crew in so they can get to work? I don't imagine Nuu Enterprises wants us to take the day off."

"That's the office key!"

"Of course. If Mr. Winford came down sick or something, you don't expect he'd leave the company in the lurch, do you?"

"No, he wouldn't," Kris said, opening the door and waving the key at Jack. Five minutes later, the crew were at work, and Kris was sitting next to Mrs. Zacharias as she checked for messages, released orders, and got the day's work started. "Sales have been falling the last few years," Kris said as she watched Mrs. Zacharias's old-fashioned screen.

"Competition is tough. 'Cutthroat,' Mr. Winford called it. And it being company policy not to pay bribes or anything that smelled of it, it was hard enough for him to keep his old customers. Impossible to get new ones."

"Bribes?" Kris echoed.

"Well, not exactly," the woman said, still going through her orders. "More like consulting fees. Or quality testing. One company insisted we send ten percent of our order off to some lab to 'destructive' test it. It wasn't for testing. It was a kickback right off the top. Mr. Winford checked with corporate, and they told him no way." The woman shook her head, resting her eyes out the window. "That's not the way it was when I started work.

Turantic was as square as you could ask. But the last five years have been bad, and getting worse."

Mrs. Zacharias turned to look at Kris. "You know, Mr. Winford told me to move my retirement account off Turantic five years ago. Said things were going to get crazy. I didn't believe him. Glad it only took me two years to realize he was right. All of us," she waved a hand to include the entire shop, "moved our accounts to Wardhaven. We're in better shape than lots. Better shape than your cops. Ask them what happened to the Fire and Protective Services Retirement System."

"I will," Kris said. Klaggath had dodged her general question about Turantic last night. Maybe tonight she'd have a more specific question. Done at her computer, Mrs. Zacharias took Kris to see where the vaccine should have been.

"Aisle eight, row A, about as far back and out of the way as you can get and still be cool," she told Kris. The space was out of the way, cool, dark . . . and empty.

Kris stepped across the "crime scene" tape to stand in the vacant spot. Slowly turning, she looked for anything yesterday's investigation might have missed.

Inspector Marta came up as Kris was finishing empty-handed. "Report says there was nothing unusual yesterday," he said.

"And there's nothing today. Any fingerprints?"

"Cardboard boxes don't take prints."

"Any hole in security?"

"Three weeks ago there was a major failure in the security system. Our inspection thinks there was a hole dug under the back fence. Doesn't explain how the door was opened, though. Or why no one noticed the missing boxes. Strange."

"And now you don't have Mr. Winford to question further."

"Nope," Marta agreed.

Kris turned to Mrs. Zacharias. "When I was on Olympia, we got all kinds of flu, new one every month. Doc would cook up a new vaccine in about a week from feedstock. Do we have the feedstock to bake up a vaccine for the anaerobic Ebola?"

"Mr. Winford had me look into that yesterday," his assistant said. "I called our best three pharmaceutical labs. There is a vaccine, but it's even more expensive than the ready-made.

That's why we store the stuff. And no, we don't have the feed-stock for it on planet. No one does." The woman shrugged. "We had that problem covered. No profit in covering it twice."

"At least the plague isn't spreading," Marta said in a half prayer.

"But until we can innoculate people, they can't go off planet." Kris headed back to her car. She hadn't had the so-cial encounter she'd wanted with Grampa's local rep. Still, she'd learned more about this planet that held her like a fly in amber. Her talk with Mrs. Zacharias had been very informa-tive. Very.

The embassy was nowhere near as interesting. Kris waited over an hour while she and her party were fingerprinted, retina-scanned, and validated that they were indeed who they said they were. Neither Kris's ID card nor Jack's credentials could save her from that hassle. Once approved, passports were quickly generated, Kris's in a regal bright red and Jack's and Tom's in an official blue. "Now, who does a Navy Lieutenant check in with to see that she's in no more hot water than she has to be?"

That got Kris ushered deep into the gray-walled rat maze of cubbyholes that seemed to be where the real work hap-pened. An overweight man in a Major's uniform was finishing a bagel as Penny led Kris in. "Princess," the man said, trying to stand, brush crumbs from his coat, and button it all at the same time. Kris let him fuss over her as she settled into his one visitor's chair, then explained her problem of taking one week's leave for what was proving to be a much longer stay on Turantic.

"You know we are out of communications?" he said. Kris avowed she was aware of that condition. He assured her he would document her reporting and forward a letter to her commanding officer as soon as communications reopened. "It should be any hour now. The Ambassador assured us at the staff meeting this morning that the Minister of Communi-cations promised they are on the verge of solving the prob-lem." Kris nodded, thanked him for his fine work, and left. Penny was waiting for her just outside the cubicle.

"The car, please, if you can find your way out of here."

"On our way," Penny assured her.

"That isn't your real boss," Kris said as soon as they were well down the hall.

"It says so on my orders." Penny didn't even try to suppress a grin.

"All the gods in heaven and space can't help Wardhaven now."

"Strange, I felt the same way when I first met him. But he gets along with the business types that provide our supplies and material. And he knows contracting like the back of his tongue."

"I'm glad he found his place. Maybe someday I'll find mine."

"May we all live that long."

Kris almost made it to the car, but the Ambassador caught her in the foyer. "I heard you were in the embassy," he said. "Sorry I wasn't here when you came in. A breakfast with some local businessmen and then our morning staff meeting. I understand you will make it to the regatta. I know a dozen party boats that will be dying to have you join them."

Penny flinched at his choice of words, but maybe he hadn't heard about the late-night live-fire exercise at the ball. He had already left for the fund-raiser elsewhere. Kris kept a smile on her face and agreed that maybe the Ambassador would accept the best-placed offers for her and arrange for a boat to move her about the party fleet as the races went on. The Ambassador was in awe of such a brilliant idea, one that Father would have considered so routine as not to need mentioning.

Kris escaped to the car and was back to the beanstalk before noon. "Done a lot sooner than I expected," Kris said, resting her eyes on the busy station across the parking lot from the regular port. A massive truck was bucking up to the loading docks. "What would that be?" Kris asked Penny.

Penny took a long look, then reached in her purse and removed a pair of binoculars. "Truck is from Tong and Tong Transport," she said slowly. "We use them for the largest and most unwieldy stuff: reactors, generators, the massive capacitors a new battleship needs."

"That big enough for a reactor?"

"I handled the set we ordered for the *Wilson* and *Geronamo*," Penny said. "I think they came in about that size."

"With all shipping closed down, that can't be going up to the yard for transshipment, but I thought you said Turantic wasn't building warships."

"The last intelligence report said it wasn't. Maybe that report needs an update."

"Any major liners under construction?" Kris asked. Penny shook her head.

"No ships are under construction," Nelly supplied. "I just ran the check. The yard is full, with overhauls and safety improvements recently ordered by the Turantic government."

"Did any of those safety upgrades need major jumps in power?" Kris asked. Again, Penny shook her head.

"No," Nelly said.

"Nelly, can you access the view on Penny's binoculars?"

"Yes, I've acquired it and done a comparison against all shipments of naval stores from Turantic to Wardhaven in the last five years. That matches the shipping container of one of the electrical generators for a President-class battleship. It can produce one hundred gigawatts of electricity."

Penny whistled. "Not many ships need power like that."

"Not any that aren't a battleship," Kris agreed. "Nelly, Penny, Tom, I've just decided how to spend our free afternoon. It's time we had a study day. What makes this planet tick? Who's paying for what and how? What's showing at the movies, and what's getting attention? It's time I know what I'm dealing with, since it looks like I'm going to be here for a while."

"If we all can stay alive that long," Tommy added.

They rode the ferry lost in their own thoughts.

11

Next morning, Abby laid out baggy white shorts for Kris as well as a royal blue sweatshirt with a prominent seal and crown.

"Full armored body stocking?" Kris asked.

"Not today," Abby answered, pulling out a pair of nude panty hose instead. "The sweatshirt and these are spun silk."

Kris dressed quickly, then added a holster for her automatic in the small of her back.

Abby shook her head. "Jack will not be pleased. You are the primary. You should be concentrating on not getting hit."

Kris considered several answers, then settled for Harvey's best comeback. "You tend to your knitting. I'll tend to mine."

Jack was waiting in the living room, wearing slacks and a striped shirt. Penny and Tom were both decked out in white slacks and blue shirts. As Kris headed for the door, Jack slipped a protective arm around her and patted the small of her back. "You shouldn't be carrying," he grumbled.

"Abby said you'd say that," Kris said to change the subject.

"That woman knows too damn much," was all Jack said.

Klaggath headed the security detail today: a dozen men and women dressed for boating. Three cars stood by at the curb outside the elevator station, one a fully stretched limo. "We going first class today?" Kris asked.

"It was either that or split you four up," Klaggath answered. "I figured you wouldn't want that."

"What's the day look like?" Jack asked. Klaggath filled them in on Ambassador Middenmite's schedule. Kris would start on the presidential yacht, then switch to several corporate yachts during the day before finishing up on *The Pride of Turantic,* an ocean liner–size yacht owned by Cal Sandfire.

"You're kidding," came from everyone in the backseat.

"Nope, that's what the embassy gave us," Klaggath said.

"Kris, we can't end up on his ship. I won't," Tommy said, a catch in his voice.

"It's a long day," Kris said slowly, an impish grin slipping across her face. "Who knows how our schedule will go? Lots of things could slow us down."

"Right," Penny drawled.

"Just keep us informed," Klaggath said, tapping something on the dashboard of the limo that made a map appear in the air between the front and backseat. "The regatta's on Long Lake. The yachts are leaving from the new Yacht Club pier here."

"Where's the racecourse?"

"Out here in the lake," he said, a racetrack appearing in the middle of the blue. "The party fleet will be anchored off to the right; that's leeward today."

"The race boats?" Kris asked. "Where do they launch from?"

"The old boat basin is where most of the smaller sailboats are," Klaggath said. "The big sailors in the unlimited class are also at the Yacht Club."

"So, if I wanted to wish Senator Krief's daughter good luck in her race . . ."

"I'd be telling the driver to take us to the small boat basin. I'll inform the presidential yacht that they may have to sail without you if they want to make the first race," Klaggath said, smiling. "We've leased a boat to move you from ship to ship. I'll have it pick us up at the small boat basin."

"Darn." Kris smiled. "We're already behind schedule."

The small boat basin was a forest of masts, but the driver took them right to the foot of pier H, a small wooden affair with dozens of white, single-masted boats bobbing alongside in the gentle wind. Kris spotted Senator Krief and her husband beside one boat and headed down the pier to them. Kris's approach went unnoticed, so intent were the couple in conversation with a dark-haired girl, already at the tiller of the boat.

"Well," the father exclaimed, "what'll you do, Nara?"

"I'm going to win this race!" the girl shot back.

"But you have to have a second person in the boat," the Senator said, glancing around and seeing Kris for the first time. "Oh, hello, Your Highness. That is how you're supposed to address a Princess, isn't it? Your Highness and curtsy."

"I'm Kris today," Kris said, "and I don't think anyone on Turantic knows how to curtsy."

"I do," the young voice from the boat pitched in. The girl in tan shorts and a blue tank top hopped up and promptly did a fair rendition of one in a rocking boat.

"Be careful," her father said. "You'll fall overboard."

"I haven't fallen overboard for years, Father," the girl said, settling back down to her place at the tiller. "And I'll win this race if we can just find someone to replace Ann."

"What happened?" Kris asked.

"Nara's partner in these races is Ann Earlic," Mel said. "Her dad's also a Senator, of the Conservative Party, but that means nothing to Nara and Ann."

"Yes it does. Her dad's a stick in the mud," came from the bobbing boat.

"And your parents aren't?" her father answered back.

"At least not this week," his daughter assured him.

"When did that change?" The Senator sighed.

"Anyway," her husband went on, "the President called a barbecue at his ranch for today, so all his party is headed up there, and missing the regatta."

"I thought the President would be on the presidential yacht?" Kris said.

"As late as Thursday he was. Last night, everything changed," Senator Krief said with a shrug of her shoulders. "President Iedinka doesn't much care for crowds, at least those that might not be voting for him. I was surprised that he was coming, to be truthful. I just didn't expect his invite to the ranch to be for kids as well as parents.

"So the Vice President will be on the yacht?" Jack asked.

"Nope, she gets seasick real easy," Mel said, breaking from his debate with his daughter. "Never goes out. Hates to even go up the beanstalk. A real solid-earth type."

Kris turned back to Jack. "So no one will be on the presidential yacht from the government," she said.

"I don't like that," Tom added, then bit his lip at having said something so unnecessary.

Behind Kris, the family returned to the crisis of the morning. "Don't you see anyone here who could sail with you?" mother asked daughter.

"Yes, Mother, plenty, but they're in the boat they'll be racing. Why didn't you tell me about your political thing yesterday?"

"Because I only found out an hour ago when Ann called you. It's not like the President is going to invite me to his ranch."

"Well, I've got to have somebody."

"I guess I could ride along with you," the mother said tentatively.

"Darling, you don't swim," Mel pointed out.

"Mo-ther, you don't even want to get in my boat. Whoever is second is going to be hanging over the side. You'd be no help."

"I could go," the father said weakly.

"Fa-ther, you'd be hanging over the side upchucking last week's breakfast," the daughter declared with the vehemence only allowed one with true sea legs.

Kris eyed Jack, then the rest of her group. No one had come up with a dodge to get them off a yacht that suddenly looked less than seaworthy. She turned back to the Senator.

"I thought this was the junior-class competition. I didn't know you could sail with your daughter."

"It's family values," Mel said. "Turantic allows parents to sail with their kids, so long as the kid handles the tiller and the sails. It makes for a lot of work, but, hey, how can we have a rule that keeps parents away from their children?"

Kris was glad Wardhaven had never taken family values that far. There were times when a kid needed some distance. "So, is it only parents that can cover for a kid?"

"Parents or their appointed stand-in," the Senator said. "We had to make allowances for handicapped or otherwise unavailable parents who still wanted to assure that their children weren't—"

"Having any fun," the daughter put in. "And if I don't get someone in this boat right now this minute, I'm not going to have any fun at all today. Dad, I guess you'll have to do."

Kris surrendered to a broad grin. "I'd really enjoy some time on the lake in a boat that's got the wind in its sails."

"You sail?" came in a shriek from the boat.

"Nara, the Princess here is the Wardhaven junior champion for orbital skiff racing." Her father sighed.

"Water boats are different," the Senator advised Kris.

"I raced sailboats before I ever saw a skiff," Kris said.

"You want to come?" Nara was almost beside herself. "Mom, Dad, let her." She glanced around at the other boats being pushed away from the pier, raising sail, and setting out for the racecourse. "And let's do it nowest, like sooner the soonest."

"You don't mind?" Mel asked.

"Not at all. I love getting the wind in my hair."

"Your security people won't mind?" the Senator asked.

"Not if she wears a life vest," Jack said, putting one around Kris. "We'll stay close in a follow boat."

"That should do it," Kris said, snapping the vest closed.

Jack reached in his pocket and brought out a long pocket knife. "Harvey tells me you once got tangled in the lines when you flipped your boat."

"That was years ago!"

"Well, hold on to this in case you need it," he said, putting the knife in her hand. Kris gave him a nervous-ninny scowl but pocketed the blade, then hopped into the boat. Mel cast off the lines. Kris raised the jib, and Nara expertly nosed her craft out into the stream of other boats heading out. A few minutes more, and Nara was ready to raise the mainsail. Kris did the hauling, settled the sail in place, then expertly tied down the lanyards.

"You really can handle a sailboat. I thought you were just doing that Princess thing, you know, 'I can do anything,' bit."

"One thing I learned early doing that Princess bit," Kris

said, "is to ask for help when you need it and be glad other people know a lot of things you don't."

"Well, I'm glad you like to sail. Mom and Dad would try, but they go with water the way I go with dance classes."

"Bad mix, huh?"

"Maximost baddest," Nara assured her, right hand pinching her nose shut.

"It can't be that bad."

"You haven't sailed with Dad. I was a week getting the stink out. Now, here's the rules. Once we start racing, only I touch the tiller or handle the sails. I've got the line for the mainsail all to myself. If the jib gets hung up, you can knock it loose, but anything more, and I'm disqualified. Okay?"

"No problem. I won't make you lose the race," Kris said.

"All I'm counting on you for is counterbalance when I get her real close to the wind. You know how to do that, don't you?"

"You have ropes so I can really let myself hang out?"

"You know how to do that!"

"I've done it a few times in my racing."

"Wow, way wild, but no, these boats are really too small. Not enough keel or rudder to really get that far over."

"So I'll lean as far out as I can."

Klaggath had a thirty-five-foot launch following them before they left the small boat basin for the open lake, Jack standing on the bow, a glowering figurehead. The Senator and her husband were on the aft deck with Penny and Tom. The Santa Marian appeared in a race with Mel to see who tossed their guts over the side first. Nara thought it was hilarious that her dad should have competition in that area.

A dozen Star-2 sailboats made up the junior competition. Several had adults as their second crew; Kris spotted at least three people her size. All scrupulously stayed clear of the yards now that the boats were on the open lake, jockeying for starting position. The other boats were easy to spot; their two crew members were all over the boat, swapping out at the tiller every time they switched tacks.

"Can you handle the whole race yourself?" Kris asked Nara. "That tiller in a strong wind can wear a grown man out."

"I can go it," the girl said, checking the sky with a seaman's eye. "The wind's good, but not too fresh. I can go this just fine."

Kris reminded herself she was a guest on this young woman's boat and swore that would be the last question she raised about her ability. *I'm just dead weight here. I'll do my part.* With luck, Kris being here might save her from being dead somewhere else. Had Sandfire gotten tired enough of her to kill one troublesome Navy Lieutenant? Was he willing to kill everyone aboard the presidential yacht just to get Kris?

"You're not that important," Kris reminded herself.

"What you say?" Nara called. "The wind's picking up, and I can't hear you unless you shout."

"Nothing. I was just thinking to myself."

"I do a lot of thinking when I'm out here. Wind blows all the dust bunnies out of my brain," the twelve-year-old answered.

"Me, too." The girl beamed back at Kris, delighted to share something with a grown woman. "But if you're going to win this race, you better concentrate on what's in front of you."

"You just watch me."

They approached the starting buoys. Spaced a klick apart; the presidential yacht anchored to one side, the race pylon on the other. The yacht was packed. With the Conservatives at the ranch, did that mean mostly Liberal Party on the yacht? Would Sandfire dare be that obvious? NELLY, ARE YOU STILL CON-NECTED TO THE NET?

BY SATELLITE HOOKUP, BUT THIS CELL IS VERY BUSY. IT MIGHT TAKE A WHILE TO GET THROUGH. DO WE NEED ANY-THING?

Kris considered having Nelly check who was at the ranch and who was on the yacht, then compare party alignments. NO, NELLY. Kris was in a little girl's boat, not on the presidential yacht, and the rest was internal Turantic politics. Murder was not supposed to be a political option here, or on any planet.

So, who killed Winford?

The starting gun brought Kris away from that question. Nara had wangled her boat close to the lead as they hit the line. Now she put the helm closer to the wind and picked up speed. Kris leaned over the gunwale, counterbalancing the wind pressure. The mainsail blocked her view of the party fleet as well as Jack on the follow-me boat. Well, she had her job; he had his.

Nara kept them close hauled to the wind, then tacked around and let her jib and mainsail out to catch the following wind. Around her, other sailors did the same, picking their own courses with plenty of room to maneuver. Everyone except two boats locked in a duel over one particular patch of lake. They tacked back and forth, trying to take each other's wind away.

"Should we do that?" Kris shouted.

"That's just Sandy and Sam. They just broke up. They're always in each other's wind, but it's gonna be bad today. Bet they don't finish the race." That was not a bet Kris would take.

Nara was second rounding the first pylon, one-sixth of the race done. She chose a fast upwind tack, letting the lead boat spread its sails for a downwind tack. The other boats followed one of their leads. Sandy and Sam were late rounding the pylon, and one of them bumped the other, knocking them onto the pylon. Kris was hanging as far over the side as she dared; still she looked for a penalty flag. None was raised. Either the judges were cutting the boat that hit the pylon some slack since it was knocked into it, or too many of the onlookers were enjoying the regatta as a contact sport for the judges to call it off.

Well, we of the Rim worlds are rather inclined to make up our rules as we go along. Kris grinned.

The wind stiffed, maybe up to twenty-five knots, by the time they wheeled past the second pylon. It was also cutting directly across the course. In Wardhaven, they would have moved the pylons to make the race more upwind one way, downwind the other. Maybe for the adults they would. For the junior competition, the pylons stayed where they were, and the party boats stayed at their moorings.

Nara led as they started the third run. This time she chose to spread her sails and take the more sedate route. This tack put them close to the yachts before Nara put the helm over, close-hauled her sheets, and made a fast tack for the pylon. From the party boats came the sounds of people socializing and exchanging chitchat. Few seemed concerned with the race. Still, Jack was right there, the launch staying just on the other side of the viewing line, pacing Kris's boat up and down the course.

Kris waved.

Jack did not wave back. Penny and Senator Krief did. Her husband and Tom looked too weak to raise their heads. Poor Tom. Once more, Kris had gotten him into a miserable situation. Well, this time he was at no risk of dying. Then again, Kris had heard sea- and spacesick people bemoan that death was not an option.

Nara's closest competitor, a white boat with blue-and-red sails, had chosen to make several short tacks so that it also was on a close-hauled course as it approached the pylon. Nara had her small boat heeled over, tight against the wind. Kris started looking for a way to hang farther out. Maybe if she found a rope and ran it around the mast. "Don't bother," Nara called, as if reading Kris's mind. "The rudder on these boats aren't big enough to get them any closer to the wind. Keels, either. One of us will just have to give way. And it's not going to be me."

By rights, it would have to be the other boat. It was behind. Still, the young boy at its helm showed no more evidence of giving way than Nara. "Get out of my way!" his second hollered across the short bit of water separating them.

"You get out of mine!" Nara shouted back.

"No way I'm giving way for no Princess."

Kris blinked; no one was supposed to know she was here. How did that kid know?

"Just 'cause you think you're some kind of prince, Billy, is no cause for me letting you beat me," Nara called back, not giving an inch. "My mom's a Senator, too, just like yours."

Oh, this is a kid thing. Kris remembered what it was like, back in the junior competitions. She'd learned the rules of trash talk playing soccer.

The wind picked that moment to swing around a bit more to the east. Suddenly, both boats were too close-hauled to the wind and had to fall off, their mainsails luffing noisily as they dumped pressure. Neither Nara nor Billy could reach the pylon on this tack now. They'd have to go past the buoy, then set a new tack downwind. The boat that turned first ran the risk of having the other boat sail right behind them, catch their wind, and rob them of their speed.

Kris waited for Nara to call the shot.

Nara kept one eye on the pylon, the other on the wind. First chance she got, she slammed the tiller over. Kris scrambled back in the boat. Nara kept the mainsail out to starboard, so Kris brought the jib around to port, then settled in the center of the boat, looking aft.

"What's Billy doing?" Nara said, eyes on the pylon.

"He's coming around."

Nara risked a glance over her shoulder. "Figured he would. He likes chasing girls. Trick is to let him get you right where you want him." The girl smiled.

"Took me a lot longer to learn that lesson," Kris said.

"Blame my mom. She's no dumb bunny, and she's not raising any, either. How's he doing?"

"Sails set the same as you. Right behind you."

"Thirty seconds to the buoy," Nara whispered, adjusting her course a bit to starboard. "Stand by to swing the jib around."

Kris made ready without doing anything obvious. Nara wanted to surprise Billy; Kris would not give away the ending. The wind weakened as Nara slammed the helm ten degrees to port and whipped the mainsail around. Kris knocked the jib around as Nara sailed out of the trailing boat's shadow. Behind them were a few loud curses as Billy changed his course, and his sails swung around. Billy and his friend failed to do it as smoothly as Nara and Kris.

Nara rounded the pylon and was taking a fast tack away before Billy had another chance to steal their wind. The race was half over, and Nara still led.

But the drama of Nara and Billy rounding the third pylon was nothing compared to the Sandy and Sam Show. By the time they were done, one was dismasted and the other lay on its side. Kris had spent a bit of time on the water, but she'd have to see the postrace replay to figure out how they managed that.

"Now that we know Billy's game, we won't make that mistake again," Nara called. This leg turned into tack and tack, as each tried to drive the other to the outside. Kris's one joy was that Billy and Nara were racing Star-2-class boats. On a bigger boat, tacks would mean winding and unwinding ropes as their crews exhausted themselves grinding and grinding on the winches.

Even on a small boat, it wasn't easy. Kris hopped from one

side of the boat to the other, dodging the main boom and carrying the jib. "Bet you're glad your mom and dad aren't here."

"Bet Ann's glad she's not here, too. She hates it when I do this. Says we Liberals are way to competitive."

"She likes losing."

"Hates it to maxie. Just hates maximost having a good day on the lake wrecked working maximostest."

I'm only ten years older than Nara. I will not ask her to translate, Kris swore as she dodged the boom again and switched sides. The tack was close-hauled, the boat leaning with the wind. Kris stretched her six-foot frame as far over the side as she dared and glanced ahead to see how far to the pylon.

A breaking wave drew her eye. The wind was blowing one direction, the waves broke in another. That wave broke wrong for either. The sky was so bright a blue it almost hurt to look at it, giving the water a clean, translucent blue of its own. Yet up ahead, a shadow seemed to hover under the water.

"Nara, look out. I think there's a sunken log ahead," Kris called and pointed.

The girl was checking the sails. She stared dead ahead for a second, half getting out of her seat to see the water ahead better. She made no course change.

The darkness was gone. Kris shrugged; maybe it was nothing.

Then the keel rode up. The sails luffed, their pressure not to right or left but off the top. The boat continued at its stately pace, even as it did the most ungraceful thing a sailboat can do: turn onto its side.

Kris went from leaning over the starboard side to clambering on her hands and knees onto the boat's right side. It lay there, keel bobbing in the water to Kris's left, the sails bubbling with air to her right. Nara tumbled into the water. She surfaced in a second, laughing and saying things that would get her mouth washed out with soap even if the Senator was a Liberal.

Kris laughed back and told her to be careful.

Then a black-covered hand reached over Nara's shoulder; another hit the quick release on her life vest. A moment later, the vest floated alone in the water, and only bubbles showed where the girl had been.

Kris screamed Nara's name twice as her mind struggled to absorb what was happening. Someone had taken the little girl.

Someone was kidnapping Nara right out from under Kris.

Someone had kidnapped Eddie while Kris was away buying ice cream. That ten-year-old girl failed her six-year-old brother.

I'm not ten, and Nara isn't six, came cold and deadly.

She hit the quick release on her own life vest, even as she stripped off the sweatshirt. Her left hand fished in her pocket for Jack's knife as she pumped air into her lungs. Opening the knife, she took two quick steps, clamped the knife in her teeth, and dove into the cold water lapping at the boat's side.

NELLY, CAN YOU PICK UP ANY SOUNDS?

HIGH-PITCHED SOUNDS, ALSO BUBBLES, DOWN AND TO YOUR RIGHT.

Kris swam, fighting the buoyancy of her own body, pushing herself against fear and screaming lungs, pushing herself for the girl who needed her.

The black mass came at her even as she reached for it—a diver in a wet suit. He was back on to her. Even as Kris reached for him, he struggled to swim back the way he'd come.

In hand-to-hand class, the old Gunny told the OCS cadets the surest way to kill with a knife is at the base of the skull or a stab in the kidneys. "But most humans have a hard time sticking a knife in someone without so much as a word of introduction. Most prefer to draw the knife across the throat. Do it that way, and you may get to know them better than you want."

For Kris, no kidnapper was human. Jack's knife was out of her mouth. She grabbed for the rebreather on the man's back, got a handhold, and used it to drive the blade into his back where his right kidney ought to be. A huge bubble of air shot from the man. Then his body floated loose, withering in pain.

Kris put the knife back in her teeth, ignoring the faint taste of iron. With her right hand, she popped the quick release on his weights; with her left, she stripped off his mask and its attached rebreather. Maybe there was still sight in the man's eyes as his body floated toward the surface.

Kris had no time for him. It was his victim she lived for.

Breather in her mouth and a blessed breath of air in her lungs, Kris wrapped the weights around her waist, then tried to dump some of the water from the mask. NELLY, DIRECTIONS. DOWN AND TO THE RIGHT.

Kris started swimming, even though her mask was still half filled with water. Now she spotted the bubbles of the struggle going on below her. A second diver was trying to force a re-breather into Nara's mouth. The girl fought her for all she was worth. Maybe she didn't recognize the breathing apparatus being offered. Maybe she wasn't willing to take anything from her captors. Whatever the case, Nara was running out of time.

Then the diver spotted Kris. She, yes, the second kidnapper was a woman, put the still-struggling Nara under one arm and reached for a spear gun with the other. Kris recognized it; it gave any monster of the deep that man had encountered among the stars enough of an electrical charge to stun or kill it.

Kris reached for her automatic, hoping an air powered dart thrower worked under water. She was bringing it up as the swimmer leveled her spear gun at Kris. The swimmer might have beaten Kris to the trigger, but Nara chose that moment to bite down hard on the arm holding her. The spear went wild.

Kris squeezed off three rounds. The darts hit, leaving small pinpricks in the front of the swimmer's suit. The water turned a deeper shade of dark as blood spread from the exit wounds in her back. Dismay in her eyes, the swimmer's body twitched helplessly as she began a long drop to the bottom.

Kris dropped her weight belt as she kicked for Nara. The little girl, free, thrashed desperately for the light above her. Kris reached Nara . . . and got slugged in the face for her trouble. The kid had been a trooper so far, but the searing pain in her lungs must be driving her mad for air. Kris took the re-breather from her own mouth and shoved it in Nara's face. The girl ignored it, attention transfixed by the light and its promise of precious air above, even as air trickled from her lips.

Kris jammed the mouthpiece between Nara's lips. The girl swung at Kris, then stopped another blow in midswing. Now Nara's eyes met Kris's. There was terror there, and desperate hunger for air. Kris watched as the girl took one breath, then another, then a tremble went through Nara, and she seemed to collapse into Kris's waiting arms. Kris held her, needing a breath,

but not about to remove the breather from Nara's mouth. Then
the girl offered it to Kris, and the two shared it for the remaining kicks that brought them to the surface.

The sailboat bobbed thirty feet from them. Other boats
raced to see who would be the planet's junior champion. Two
women who'd just found out they would live treaded water as
they gasped in air. The launch, with Jack on its bow like an angry god, made full speed for them.

Kris waved. That drew Jack's attention, as well as that of
five or six other boats and a pair of helicopters, one marked
Rescue, the other Press. Kris made ready to go public, checked
herself all over, and was glad Abby had insisted she wear a bra.

The launch was first to them. Klaggath had all his bases
covered; a swimmer in a blue-and-yellow wet suit went over
the side to help Nara and Kris onto the rigid ladder that appeared on the side of the boat. The press chopper and another
boat with an oversize camera crew were alongside as Kris began the climb up.

"Watch your step," the swimmer told her.

"There's a body in a black wet suit floating around here
somewhere. Are you equipped for recovery?" Kris asked.

"No," the rescue swimmer said without batting an eyelash.
"I'll call Rescue Five and get the chopper crew looking for it."

"There's a second swimmer, probably on the bottom," Kris
told him as he started talking into his mike.

"Another assassination attempt?" Jack said, settling a blanket around Kris as she reached the top of the ladder.

"I don't think so," Kris said, keeping her voice low among
the shutter clicks of cameras from a boat not ten meters away.
The Kriefs surrounded their daughter, half hugging, half drying her off, while adding tears of joy to any spot the lake
hadn't gotten damp enough. "Is there anyplace below?"

"This way," Klaggath said and led them down a short flight
of stairs, along a companionway, and into a small forward
cabin. In a moment, Penny and Tommy joined them.

"What happened?" Jack demanded.

"You want a drink?" Penny offered, a bottle of brandy appearing in her hands.

"You didn't learn as much about me as you thought," Kris
said and took the hot chocolate Tommy offered.

"Kris! What happened?" Jack snarled through clenched teeth.

"When we went over, a diver grabbed Nara and dragged her under," Kris said, holding the cup to warm her hands. "There was a second one, but I don't think they were expecting a second person in the boat, at least not one that hated kidnappers like I do," she said with a nod to Penny.

"Oh my God," the intelligence officer gasped. "Someone tried to kidnap that girl out from under you!"

"You almost feel sorry for them." Kris sighed as she took a sip of her chocolate. It was hot. Around her, people waited, Jack and Klaggath professionally, Penny and Tom uneasily. Kris went on. "One's floating out there somewhere. I borrowed his weights. The other has three bullet holes in her. You know, Jack, these air guns work nice under water," Kris said, pulling the weapon from her belt.

Klaggath took it from her cold fingers, uncocked it, and put the safety back on. "Sorry," Kris said. "I was rather busy."

"Understandable," the Inspector said, talking to his wrist.

"And check the keel of that boat. It came up like there was something under it. A floatation device of some kind."

"Already checking it."

"Other than that, it was a great day to be on the water, Kris said. "Tom, you have more of that nice hot chocolate?"

He refilled her cup. Kris yawned. "Good Lord, I'm tired."

"You should be," Klaggath said. "You've had a workout."

Kris shook her head. "I was hyped after we rescued that kidnapped girl on Harmony. What a rush. I was wiped that day on Olympia, but I'd fought two battles. Still, I couldn't sleep. Whole day just kept replaying in my mind." She yawned again.

"Every time's different," Klaggath said, getting a dry blanket and edging Kris toward a bed that stretched along the hull of the boat. "But worse, you do it often enough, and it becomes routine. That's when you're in trouble."

Kris let herself be backed onto the bed. She traded her wet blanket and mug for a dry one and lay down. "I'll only rest for a few minutes, until you figure out how things are," she said.

"I'm sure we can keep everything under control for that short while," Klaggath said, ushering the others from the room. Jack made to stay behind, but the Inspector put an elbow into the agent's ribs as he turned the light off with his other hand.

"I ought to get out of my wet clothes," Kris said as her head nuzzled the pillow. A quick survey showed her heart was already slowing to sleep. Kris's last thought was on how normal she felt. *I shouldn't feel this way.*

12

Kris came awake slowly, her heart pounding as she raced through a swamp. No, leaped from star to star. A girl, no, her brother Eddy, hung precariously from her shoulders. She raced in slow motion through water and mud. Behind her, a howling mob of ghosts or swans or men in wet suits chased her. Then Eddy turned into . . . something. She sat up with a start.

"You all right?" Jack asked. He stood by the light switch, as far from her as the small cabin allowed. "You were moaning in your sleep. Shouting a bit, too."

"I hate kidnappers," Kris said, leaving it at that.

"You ready to come up on deck? They've got the sailboat out of the water."

"They found the swimmers?" Kris said, making a face as she sat up in her still wet and now very cold shorts.

"Yes."

"I guess I should identify the bodies. You have anything for me to wear? My clothes are kind of wet."

Jack tossed her a set of gray sweats. "Compliments of the Heidelburg P.D." Kris shook out a gray sweatshirt prominently marked Property of HPD. "Klaggath says you've earned it. His job's gotten a whole lot easier since you've been around."

"First security type ever to tell me that."

"I said he might change his mind if you hung around longer."

"Shame on you, giving away Wardhaven state secrets," Kris said as she got up.

"I'll wait outside."

"Please, just turn around. I never knew how lonely deep water was."

"You were swimming for deeper, trying to reach someone," Jack said, his back to her. "That's a lonely business."

"Didn't seem so at the time," Kris said, pulling on the top.

"We do what we have to 'at the time.' It's only later we figure out how to live with it. Assuming we live."

"I'm alive, and two kidnappers aren't," Kris said, adjusting the pants. Her bra and panties were still wet, but that would have to do. "You can turn around now."

"A young girl is with her parents. You are with your friends, and two of Sandfire's assassins are in the morgue," Jack said with finality. "Not a bad day's work."

"Are they Sandfire's people? He usually goes for good-looking women. I knifed a man and shot a woman I didn't get a good look at."

"My bet is he subcontracted this job, with plenty of cutouts in between."

"It still seems weird they weren't after me. Why go for a little girl? No, why go for the Senator's daughter?" On the way topside, she found Klaggath, Penny, and Tom sitting around a table in what passed for an amidships break room.

"There have been times in history," Penny said, "when kidnapping was just part of the political give and take."

"Not lately," Klaggath said, rising.

"Unity did a few when they were getting started," Kris said.

"Unity did murders, extortion, and a whole lot of nastiness that are no longer accepted in polite circles," Klaggath drawled.

"But we live in changing times," Kris said, trying to smile cheerfully. "Where're the Kriefs?"

"Aft. Nara's asleep," the Inspector said.

"Where are we?"

"We haven't moved. Would you like to look at the sailboat?"

"You recovered it?"

"Along with two bodies. Are you prepared to identify them?"

Kris took in a deep breath. "No time like the present."

The cop led her topside, Jack and the rest following. The launch swung at anchor. Off in the distance, silhouetted against a low sun and gray clouds, the big race of the day was still going on. The course and party fleet had moved, leaving the launch almost alone. Two choppers still circled, one marked Press, the other Police. A cabin cruiser of photographers had backed off a hundred meters, but no farther. When Kris came on deck, the photo crews bestirred themselves, but in police grays they took no interest in her. It was nice to be ignored.

Alongside, a barge was tied up. A bit longer than the launch, much wider and square, a small deckhouse aft broke its flat lines. Only rust interrupted the solid blackness of its paint. Perfect for a hearse. Like a beached dolphin, the sailboat lay on its side, keel toward Kris. The mast, with its sails now cut away, hung over the side.

"We found a wedge-shaped air bag on the keel," Klaggath said. "It would account for the sudden capsizing."

"Nara was too good a sailor to lose it like that." Kris nodded.

"The bag was biodegradable. If we'd taken another hour to find it, it would have vanished into the lake."

"And if you'd been hunting for Nara," Kris said, letting her eyes rove over the choppy, windswept swells, "who would have bothered with the boat?"

"Exactly."

Kris spotted a two-person underwater transport lying on one side of the deckhouse; two tarp-covered forms lay on the other side. "Those my friends?" She pointed with a nod.

"You can identify them tomorrow from photos, if you want," the cop offered.

"Let's do it now." Kris glanced around, took in the press chopper and boat. "Unless you don't want me seen doing it."

Klaggath followed her gaze. "I think we can handle that."

They studied the sailboat for a bit longer, until the circling pattern of the press boat took it around to the launch's other side. Then they moved casually aft to surround the two shapes. Jack, Penny, and Tom imposed themselves between Kris and the chopper as Klaggath stooped to remove the tarp from one body.

The man lay in death, still marked by surprise. That death had found him or that Kris had brought it? No answer to that. "I knifed him in the back."

"Rather expertly," Klaggath said. "Haven't met many who could jab a knife in a man's back right at the kidney."

"The Gunny said a knife in the kidney was the fastest way to kill a man. I guess he was right. Sorry I lost your knife."

"Plenty more where that one came from," Jack said.

The woman's face showed rage. "One dart shattered her backbone," Klaggath said. "All she could do was sink."

"She was forcing a rebreather on Nara. I don't know if the girl was too busy fighting to take it or what."

"So it was a kidnapping," the Inspector said, covering the body and standing.

"It looked that way to me at the time and still does. Maybe they left something ashore. Have you tossed their homes?"

"We've run their fingerprints and retina scans through central. They aren't in our database. And no, it's not like Turantic has no thugs that would take a contract like this. We've got our share, but it looks like these were off planet."

"And you can't do a search of off-planet criminal files just now, can you?" Jack said, a tight frown on his face.

"We've got a copy of everyone else's databases, no more than a month out of date, but these two," Klaggath nudged one of the bodies with the toe of his shoe, "are not in there."

Kris nodded. It was not unheard of for people to disappear from the record. Political operatives, some criminals, maybe even her Grampa Al had paid to have his official ID removed from Wardhaven's central records. People had a right to privacy. Still, your money only bought you out of the present database. "What about your backups?"

Klaggath chuckled. "I expected you'd take longer. Then, you are one of those damn Longknifes. I had a check run against the backups. Nothing in the last two years."

"How far back do you go?" Penny asked.

"Two years," Klaggath and Nelly answered together.

"Only two years." Tom scowled.

"Law passed two years ago," Klaggath said, eyeing Kris's chest where Nelly's voice had come from.

"But hard media can last a hundred, some say a thousand years," Penny said. "All you have to do is store it."

"And be able to retrieve it," the cop said dryly. "Too much old media lying around, and you can't find anything. At least that was the argument when they passed the law," Klaggath said, still eyeing Kris. "Your Highness, is there any chance that computer around your neck has backups from off planet?"

That was the first time Klaggath had gotten his tongue around her royal title. Was he just asking a favor, or did it mean more? "Nelly, answer the good Inspector's question."

"I am sorry, but my resources are not unlimited, and Kris has me concentrating in other areas than criminal records," Nelly said, sounding rather contrite and not at all like a computer.

"Didn't think so, but I had to check."

"So we have two kidnappers who can't be traced to Turantic. That leaves only five hundred ninety-nine other planets to choose from," Kris said, upbeat and chipper anyway.

"And no doubt our media and various talking heads will draw freely from their own biases when they decide where these two perps came from."

Lots of questions. Few answers. Kris shook her head. The western sky flashed lightning. Tom jumped, but the others took it in stride. Kris took in a deep breath laden with water, both lake and rain. "Smells like a storm coming up. Can we get off the lake? Any chance we can avoid the newsies when we do?"

"I'll see what can be arranged," Klaggath said.

"Can I see the Kriefs now?"

"Follow me."

He took them back to the launch and belowdecks. The family was in the aft cabin. Nara was asleep on a couch, her head in her dad's lap; the Senator sat across from them. Both eyed the child as if she might vanish if they once looked away. Kris swallowed hard, remembering the wall Mother and Father built between themselves and her after Eddy's funeral. If he'd been found alive, if he'd escaped capture, might her own parents have been so enthralled by every breath he took? Kris shook her head; life was too busy to fill it with might have beens. The Senator started when Kris rested a hand on her shoulder.

"Can we talk?" Kris asked. Reluctantly, the mother joined Kris in the break area amidships.

"Thank you for saving my daughter's life," she said, taking a seat at Kris's elbow. "I couldn't have done it. Mel either."

"I'm glad I was there. But why? Why kidnap your daughter?"

The Senator shook her head. "I have no idea."

"Did it strike you as strange," Kris said, "that suddenly the President called all his party associates to the ranch, leaving the presidential yacht full of opposition members?"

Kay eyed Kris for a moment. Then she shook her head ruefully. "You are a Longknife. You've been here one week."

"Not yet a full one." Kris sighed.

"Mel and I weren't the only opposition members that found somewhere else to watch the race. The yacht sailed with a load of office functionaries but few elected officials."

"So everyone is getting paranoid."

"Let's say that caution has become a byword on Turantic. What we know, we trust. What we don't know, we are learning to approach cautiously."

"What do you know?"

The Senator shook her head. "Less and less, since the penalty for espionage, industrial or otherwise, became a matter of life imprisonment for both the agent and the procurer of their services. And some prisons have become notorious for very short life sentences. Haven't they, Inspector?"

"The new contract prisons do seem to have more prisoner-on-prisoner violence than the jails we run," the Inspector agreed. "Our unions have been strangely unsuccessful in getting any parliamentary attention on that."

"But any hint of malfeasance by your fellow officers makes the headlines in seconds." The Senator's smile flashed white.

"In the last two years, you say," Kris noted.

"Two very interesting years," the Senator said.

"I met a woman a few days ago. She told me business had gotten very difficult of late. Seems her boss was expected to pay a bribe if he wanted to get the contract."

"Not a bribe," the Senator corrected. "That would be illegal. No, nothing so crass. Rather provide extra product for 'test purposes,' or 'promotional efforts.' "

"I believe my Grampa Al would call that a bribe."

"He's not on Turantic." The Senator sighed.

"You can't run a world like that without fallout. Yesterday my friends and I tried to get a handle on your planet. We used the official sites, analyzed the numbers. The numbers didn't add up. Didn't cross-check. You have three definitions of profit and only one of them shows growth," Kris said, as much the industrialist's granddaughter as the Prime Minister's daughter.

"Ah." Kay chuckled. "Our stock market has grown for six straight years, hasn't it, Inspector?"

"Every year I get glowing reports from my fund managers claiming spectacular growth. Strangely, for the last three years there hasn't been much extra money to show for it."

"Productivity up?" Kris asked.

"The official reports say so."

"Where's the money going?"

The Senator shrugged.

"It's going somewhere," Kris said.

"Certainly. But," the woman spread her hands wide, "I can't tell you, and could get locked up for looking too hard."

"Nelly, have you got an answer?"

"I noted discontinuities when I first researched Turantic. Now here, I could attempt a better answer, but I would have to go beyond what is available in the public domain."

"So even your computer can't find a pattern in the available data. If she goes beyond what's posted, you break laws this government is quick to prosecute."

"Nelly, hold off on further research," Kris said, not willing to risk jail for her computer's newfound initiative.

"Yes, ma'am."

But Kris wasn't willing to quit without tackling at least one more question. "Nelly, the civilian Turantic fleet has been brought in for upgrade to new safety standards. Should the work required by law be completed by now?"

"Yes, ma'am. It should be done."

"Yet shifts go on around the clock in the yards. Equipment, some of it quite large, still goes up the elevator."

The Senator shrugged. "And I hear, with so many people out of work in our foreign trade, even more are hiring on at the yard and the plants that feed into it. Interesting, isn't it?"

"More than interesting. Do you know anything about what's being shipped up to the yard?"

"Don't know a thing. Some of my biggest supporters bid on those contracts. All went to a Tory supporter. Strange, that."

Kris thought for a moment. "Have any of your friends hired anyone away from the winners?"

That drew a chuckle. "You sound more like a business-woman than a Navy type. As a matter of fact, no. Lately there hasn't been much job changing. And there are very draconian laws enforcing the nondisclosure agreements that several companies require their staff to sign. I am not sure any manager or scientist could change employers just now and not violate them."

"Draconian laws passed in the last two years?"

"Three years, I believe, for that one."

"We're tying up now," an Agent announced. The Senator joined her husband and groggy child. Kris let them have a fifteen-minute lead before she and her crew went topside. Other larger yachts were already tied up at the new Yacht Club. On their decks, music, laughter, and talk wafted on the fitful breeze as parties continued, unaffected by death or weather.

"I thought the race was still going," Kris said.

"It is, but some, like Tommy here, take less chances with the wind and rain than others do," Jack said, giving Tom a nudge.

Klaggath signed that his team was ready. Kris made ready to dodge the newsies ranked before her at the foot of the pier.

"Was this another attempt on your life, Princess?" shouted several at once. "Do you credit Nuu Enterprises' withholding of vaccines for this public hatred?" was there, too. "Didn't you consider you were putting that little girl at risk when you went racing with her?" rankled, but "Is Wardhaven going to invade Turantic?" stopped her. Jack was stepping forward to do the usual begging off, she was tired, routine, when Kris stopped him with a gentle elbow to the stomach.

Gluing on a sincere and flashy smile, Kris stepped forward. "I'm sorry. The police haven't told me what happened out there." That was true; she'd been telling the police. "You will have to ask them. However, I can tell you everyone at Nuu Enterprises is moving heaven and earth to get the people of Turantic what they need to beat this threatening epidemic.

Remember, I can't leave your beautiful planet until the quarantine is lifted. And I'm just as much at risk as any of you." Kris let that sink in. Most of the newsies were nodding agreement.

One wasn't. "But isn't Wardhaven's Navy, some of it paid for with our tax money, poised to invade us if we don't accept membership in their new Society?"

Kris kept her face blank; Nelly was chasing rumors, but that one hadn't shown up. This was probably the launch for it. Kris spoke carefully. "Wardhaven prospered in the last eighty years of peace. I don't know anyone on Wardhaven who wants to throw that away. Our Navy is the minimum needed for defense."

"But aren't they drafting everyone? Even you, a Princess!"

"Lord no. I volunteered, much to my father's dismay and my mother's disappointment," Kris said, trying to keep anger out of her voice and her pacing slow and friendly. She put on one of Tommy's lopsided grins. "I could have those reactions confused. Mother's dismay. Father's disappointment. It was rather noisy around the house that evening." That drew understanding laughs.

"But isn't it true Wardhaven attacked Turantic in 2318, and King Raymond led that assault?" her inquisitor shouted. Heads turned toward the reporter; he had their attention now.

Kris allowed herself several blinks as if she was deep in thought. She'd read just about everything in print on her great-grandparents, including the obscure stuff before they started filling up the school's history books. It was a minor part of Grampa Ray's early life, but Kris remembered it.

"I think you have the date wrong," she said. "It was over a hundred years ago. Those were the bad old days before the Society. Before even Unity. And as for my Grampa Ray leading the attack, you have to be kidding. Back then he was a brand-new Second Lieutenant. As a fresh-caught Ensign, I can tell you, we don't lead anything. We go where we're told. And I'm told I have to go now, so I hope you will excuse me."

The assenting murmurs drowned out the next question from the gadfly, and Kris made good her escape to the limo.

One woman newsie managed to slip through the security screen. "I see you're wearing a police department sweatsuit. Is it going to be the latest in fashion statements?"

"The cop who gave it to me said I'd earned it," Kris said.

"Takes a lot to earn this crew's respect."

"Then you'll have to ask them what they liked," Kris said as she settled into her seat and Jack shut the door.

"Who was she?" Kris asked as Klaggath took his place. A bang on the limo's roof, and the car pulled away.

"Her old lady's a retired cop," Klaggath said. "She brought Amy around to the station when she wasn't a week old. I thought for sure she'd follow her mom onto the force, but she got bit by the writer's bug and went bad." That drew a laugh.

"But the stories she writes are good. She knows how to dig and doesn't settle for the easy crap. And her editor has guts enough to publish what she brings in. I expect her story tomorrow will make interesting reading."

A pouring rain started that caused the limo driver to slow. Kris rested her eyes out the window at a view that went from wealthy retreat to rural and then well-treed suburbia. She knew about as much as she was going to learn . . . without breaking a law. At her father's knee she'd learned information was power. Somebody here wanted all that power. If Kris was to do anything but react to that power, she needed a lot more information than she had. Interesting do-loop she was caught in.

Kris came up for air just long enough to argue with Penny when she asked to be dropped off a few blocks from her apartment.

"We can drive you there."

"Hey, Princess, it's quit raining. It's a beautiful evening. And I could use the exercise. Maybe you haven't noticed, but chasing after you mainly required me to sit on my butt. Enough; let me walk."

So Kris gave up and let her walk.

13

Kris paused a moment after Klaggath opened the limo door, her eyes resting on the loading dock across the parking lot from the public space elevator terminal. She could make out the names of a half dozen companies on the trucks backed up there. NELLY, YOU HAVE THOSE NAMES IN MEMORY?

YES, MA'AM.

"Thank you, Inspector. It's been a long day. I'm ready to call it quits as soon as I get in. Why don't you and your team save yourselves a run up and down the beanstalk?"

"No problem, Your Highness."

"Then let me call it noblesse oblige and dismiss you to your families."

The man chuckled. "You don't want us around, huh?"

Kris swallowed. *Am I that transparent?* "I'm glad for all the hard work today, and I expect a lot of hard work in the coming days. Why take more from a limited resource?"

"Then we'll do it your way. I will, however, see you safe to your ferry and have someone waiting topside for you."

"That should be fine."

Once the car began its climb, Jack leaned close to Kris. "What was that all about?"

"Tell me, Jack, you're my Security Agent. What would you do if you heard me planning a crime?"

"I doubt if I'd change what I've always done when you do: try to keep you safe and unconvicted."

"That's nice of you, but do you think Klaggath would have the same doting attitude?"

"He has my sense of humor. Why not?"

"Then let's just say, I don't choose to include him, okay?"

"Spoilsport. What do you have in mind?"

"Why don't you leave that to me and Nelly."

"You girls have all the fun," Jack said, but he leaned back in his chair and went into his usual practice of looking in 360 directions at once.

YOU HAVE SOMETHING ON YOUR MIND? Nelly put in.

THAT TIARA MOTHER BOUGHT ME: HOW MUCH SMART METAL DO YOU THINK IS IN IT?

FOUR HUNDRED TWELVE GRAMS.

HOW MANY ARMED RECONNAISSANCE BUGS DO YOU THINK YOU COULD MAKE FROM IT?

THAT WOULD DEPEND ON THE CAPABILITIES YOU WANTED IN EACH.

SNAPSHOT VIDEO, FULL SPECTRUM MESSAGE INTERCEPT. AND THE ABILITY TO DEFEND THEMSELVES IF ATTACKED BY ANY OF THE BUGS WE'VE RUN INTO.

INDOOR OR OUTDOOR?

OUTDOOR.

I AM ACCESSING TOMORROW'S FORECAST. WINDS WILL BE FIVE TO TEN METERS PER SECOND, FROM THE WEST. FIGHTING THAT WIND COULD TAKE A LOT OF FUEL. THAT ENLARGES THE BASIC STRUCTURE.

WHAT IF I RELEASED THEM UPWIND AND LET THEM RIDE ACROSS THEIR TARGET?

THAT WOULD CUT DOWN ON THAT REQUIREMENT. LET'S ASSUME I COULD GIVE YOU BETWEEN TWO HUNDRED AND THREE HUNDRED BUGS. WHAT WOULD WE TARGET?

LAY OUT THE MANUFACTURERS' PLANTS FEEDING PRODUCT UP TO THE YARDS. ESPECIALLY THE ONES SENDING THE BIG STUFF.

THEY ARE ALL WITHIN THIRTY KLICKS OF THE ELEVATOR.

"You're mighty quiet," Tom said. "Cat got your tongue?"

"Sometimes, after a long, hard day, a girl just wants a bit of peace and quiet," Kris said as Nelly named off a route that would cover all the major targets.

THAT SHOULD DO IT, Kris thought and sighed. Tomorrow looked like another busy day.

Kris had no sooner walked into the suite than Abby took her by storm. The woman was kind enough not to strip Kris of her wet underwear until she was out of public viewing. Not that Kris put up much of a fight as Abby maneuvered her into a warm tub. Settling into the suds with the jets already pulsing water against her, Kris let out a contented sigh. Happily, Abby did not chatter at Kris about the day but quietly bustled about the room, lighting candles and laying out clothes. Aromatherapy, she called it.

Kris enjoyed it. She let the warmth of the water flow into all her cold places, the pulsing jets massage tight muscles. Bad day, nice ending. Hopefully, tomorrow would end as well.

When Nelly announced all strange bugs in the rooms were destroyed or suborned, Kris called for a towel. Dry and wrapped in a fluffy robe, she hunted up Jack. "Dear, I need a favor."

He looked up wearily from where he and Tom were trying their skills at chess. "If I've been promoted to *dear*, I guess I'm in deep trouble. Okay, *honey*, what do you want?"

Kris made a face at his familiarity. Honey was Mother and Father's choice word and as empty as the space between them. "I expect that Klaggath has a woman or two passing as maids on this floor. Could you arrange through one of them for an extra uniform? I need a maid's dress."

"For what?"

"Invisibility. Either Penny or I are going out tomorrow, and we don't want to be noticed when we do." Kris intended to be the one going out, but Jack would be more cooperative if the final decision was delayed a few hours.

Jack stood, going into his "I know better" mode, but Tom looked up from the game and got the first word in. "What do you have on your mind?"

"Information is kind of short around here. Now I know why. Still, we need to know a whole lot more than we do. On the drive home, I passed a few ideas around with Nelly. She thinks she can convert that ridiculous tiara into several hundred microspies. Short-range little beggars, but still very effective. I figure one of us girls should make the rounds tomorrow of a couple of industrial plants. With luck, by this time tomorrow, we'll know a whole lot more about what's going on here."

"And be subject to a whole lot of indictments for industrial espionage," Jack said dryly.

"You have to be caught to be indicted, as my dear Father has said many times." Kris smiled as if she'd never had a care.

"This is a bad idea."

"Jack, that's what you say about all my ideas."

"No surprise, Kris, they usually are," Tommy pointed out.

Kris kept a chair between her and Jack. "Enough silliness. We need info. You have any better idea, I'm listening."

Jack studied her with a scowl. "Problem is, Tom, there's nothing wrong with her logic." Now that was a surprise.

"There never is, Jack. It's just that she comes up with the most logical ways to get herself killed and anyone too close."

Kris swung around the chair and sat. "We're in a trap. There is no visible way out. We're not going to find a way out by doing nothing. Information is power. Let's get some power."

"I hate it when you do that," Tom said. "Totally right, but no thought to cost. Jack, you going to get her that uniform?"

"He won't have to," Abby called from the bedroom. "I picked one up yesterday."

"You care to explain why you just happened to have your fair hands on a bit of stolen property?" Jack said.

Abby came to the door, brown uniform in hand. "I'm a working girl, gentlemen. I have a right to a few nights off. If I want to get away without a lot of fuss, it's my own business. I came to an amicable understanding with one of the maids. We working girls understand each other," she said with a sniff.

"I don't like this," Jack said.

"Call coming in," Nelly said.

"On-screen," Kris said.

"Is Tommy Lien available at this number?" a man in medical whites asked.

"Yes," Tommy said, jumping to stand in front of the screen.

"A Miss Penelope Pasley asked me to call you. She's fine,

but she's kind of beat up and won't be able to make it to-morrow."

"What do you mean, she's beat up?" Kris and Tommy demanded.

"We admitted her to Heidelburg Central Hospital a half hour ago with a possible concussion and multiple lacerations and contusions. Possibly assaulted in other ways. The police are taking a deposition. She will need lots of rest."

"Tell Penny I'll be right there," Tommy said.

Kris was already moving. "Nelly, raise Klaggath. Tell him the day's not over, and he's needed at Central Hospital."

At first glance it was hard to spot any area of Penny's body not black or blue. Yet the woman's first reaction was to pull the sheet over herself to block her pain from view as Kris led the crew into her hospital room.

"Who did this?" from Kris was overrun by Tom's dash for the bedside and a shout of "Holy Mother of God." He reached out a consoling hand, then yanked it back, afraid any touch would only add to Penny's pain. She let the sheet fall and rested a bandaged hand in Tom's.

"I guess I ran into a bad crowd," Penny said through barely moving lips. A cut above her mouth cracked open and began to bleed. Kris took a cotton ball from the bedside table and dabbed at the blood, anger making her hand tremble.

"Hey, Tommy, don't look so pale. I don't feel nearly as bad as I look," sounded good, but the wince as she said it robbed the words of consolation.

"Don't talk, honey," Tom whispered. "You don't have to say a word. We're here for you. You just rest."

As the Lieutenant followed the JG's orders and re-laxed against the pillow, her gown fell open, revealing a bruised and stitched breast. Kris pulled the sheet up to cover Penny and turned to face a tight-lipped Jack just as Klaggath entered.

"Who did this?" she demanded of the cop.

"We can talk better outside," the Inspector said.

Kris and Jack left Tom clinging gently to Penny's hand. The door hadn't closed before Kris demanded, "Talk to us."

"She was set upon by five or six assailants less than a block from her apartment and dragged into an alley. There were no witnesses other than Penny. She was found unconscious when a man came out to empty his trash. Based on the time lapse between when we dropped her off and her being discovered, I suspect she was unconscious about an hour."

"How bad is she?" Jack asked.

"The concussion is the main worry. Her skull is intact, but we don't know how badly scrambled the brain is. She was beat up over most of her body."

"What did she tell you about her attackers?" Jack asked.

"They shouted, 'Wardie scum' and other epithets. It was an attack on her as a representative of her government."

"Not as a part of our team?"

"Impossible to tell," the cop answered the cop.

"She got too close to a Goddamn Longknife," Kris whispered.

"Too early to say," the Inspector insisted.

"But a safe bet." Kris swallowed a dry snicker. "Inspector, get her out of here. I want her safe in my suite topside."

"She is safe here," he said with firm professionalism.

"You want to bet me tomorrow something won't come up that puts her outside any protection you can arrange?"

Klaggath worried his lower lip. "This morning I thought I had you all protected." He sighed. "I'll talk to the Doctor."

"I'll talk to Penny," Kris said. In the room, Tom was carefully stroking Penny's hair. "Penny, you mind if we check you out of here? I want my team close."

"If it wouldn't be too much trouble, Your Highness, I'd kind of like to be close to Tom."

"I think that can be arranged," Kris said, giving both her friends the encouraging smile they wanted from her and backing out of their space. She found Klaggath down the hall, arguing with two white-coated women.

"We need to keep her under observation," one said.

"She's had a very rough night," put in the other.

"That's rather obvious," Kris said dryly. "Klaggath, can you arrange for a full-time nurse?"

"Already have one on call. She'll meet us at the elevator."

Kris turned on the two docs and put on her best royal smile. "Lieutenant Pasley wants to check out. We have made arrangements for her care out of the Hilton on High Turantic."

The older Doctor pursed her lips in indecision. "She needs full-time care."

"We will provide it."

"She's been badly beaten," the other pointed out.

"The Navy takes care of its own," Kris said flatly.

"Didn't do so good this evening," the younger said.

"We won't make that mistake twice," Kris said, glancing at Klaggath. The Inspector nodded.

"If she wants out, we can't keep her," the older doc finally agreed. "We'll get her a few days' meds from the pharmacy and some instructions on care. She shows any change in her condition, and you get her to a doc immediately."

"That we will do," Kris agreed.

An hour later, with Penny in a wheelchair and Tom pushing her and reacting to any sudden intake of breath as if it hurt him twice as much, they made their escape. Klaggath had not only the regular detail but uniformed cops as well checking every avenue.

They made it back to the Hilton with only one distraction. Ambassador Middenmite called to decry missing Kris on the presidential yacht that morning and to ask her to make up for all the connections she had missed, hands she'd failed to shake, and pecks on the cheek she'd dodged by showing up at a ball tomorrow. The guy was completely clueless. "Yes, I'll be there," Kris snapped to end the call.

In the suite, the nurse took over caring for Penny, though Abby seemed just as able and better supplied from her trunks than the nurse was from her traveling bag. They settled Penny in Tom's room with him and the nurse doing a full vigil. Tom's eyes never left Penny; she kept a hand on him. And Kris knew she was giving them what they longed for, the closeness that would form a bond with *forever* written all over it. *Looks like another bridesmaid dress in my future.* Kris sighed. *I should have told Tom. What? That I love him? Do I? Did I? Does it matter now?*

Kris slipped away to her bedroom like a good friend and turned out the light. Kris left a wake-up call with Nelly for five A.M., lay on her back, and tried to ignore the day.

14

Kris was late for something: class or a rally or duty. She raced down a long hallway trying every door she came to. Some were locked. Others opened. There was Eddy or Mother or Father or Grampa Trouble, each mad at her for interrupting them, not doing what she was supposed to do. She ran, trying more doors. She had to find Nelly. Nelly was important. Nelly and . . .

IT'S FIVE, DO YOU WANT TO WAKE UP? Nelly asked quietly.

Kris lay in bed, sweating as her heart slowed to merely pounding. NELLY, DID YOU DO THAT?

DO WHAT?

MAKE ME DREAM LIKE THAT?

I DO NOT THINK SO.

Kris heard the reply and the ambiguity in it. NELLY, HAVE YOU BEEN MESSING . . . NO, DOING ANY TESTING ON THE CHIP AUNTIE TRU ADDED TO YOU?

YES.

I TOLD YOU NOT TO.

YOU TOLD ME THAT YOU COULD NOT RISK ME FAILING YOU NOW. I UNDERSTAND THAT AND HAVE BEEN EXTREMELY CARE-FUL WITH MY TESTING.

I HAVE HAD BAD DREAMS, NELLY, WHENEVER I SLEEP PLUGGED IN TO YOU. I AM GETTING SOME KIND OF FEEDBACK FROM THE CHIP.

THAT IS IMPOSSIBLE, KRIS. I HAVE ONLY LOOKED AT DATA IN THE FIRST BUFFER SAM DESIGNED. I HAVE ALLOWED NOTHING IN THE SECOND OR THIRD BUFFER. THERE COULD BE NO LEAKAGE.

MY DREAMING TELLS ME THERE IS SOME KIND OF LEAKAGE.

KRIS, THAT IS NOT POSSIBLE. YOU ARE WRONG.

INTERESTING WORDING FOR A COMPUTER, Kris thought for the far-too-manyith time. Nelly had been acting . . . interesting. Kris had thought it was the most recent upgrade. Now she had to consider the chip. But Nelly refused to consider the chip.

NELLY, I AM HAVING STRANGE DREAMS JUST LIKE GRAMPA RAY TALKED ABOUT WHEN HE WAS HAVING PROBLEMS ON SANTA MARIA. I DON'T KNOW HOW THE CHIP MIGHT BE DOING IT. IT IS AN ADVANCED TECHNOLOGY. I REALLY NEED TO BE ABLE TO DEPEND ON YOU RIGHT NOW. WE ARE IN REAL TROUBLE. WOULD YOU PLEASE NOT TEST THE CHIP?

KRIS, THE CHIP IS FULLY BUFFERED.

I KNOW, NELLY. BUT HOW DO YOU EXPLAIN MY DREAMS?

I HAVE NEVER UNDERSTOOD DREAMS, OR SLEEP FOR THAT MATTER.

NELLY, TRUST ME. THE TESTING IS MAKING IT IMPOSSIBLE FOR ME TO SLEEP.

YOU DO NOT NEED TO SLEEP WITH ME PLUGGED IN.

RIGHT, BUT I NEED YOU DURING THE DAY.

CAN I TEST AT NIGHT?

I REALLY WISH YOU WOULDN'T.

IF YOU SAY SO, KRIS, I WILL STOP TESTING UNTIL WE CAN DISCUSS THIS WITH TRU AND SAM.

THANK YOU, NELLY. Now all Kris had to worry about was whether or not the chip had already done something to her computer. What a wonderful start to the day.

Kris slipped out of bed, pulled on a sweatsuit, and tiptoed to Abby's room. The maid uniform was set neatly atop one of the trunks beside a brown raincoat and a shoulder purse. Today could be a quiet day of running errands. It might turn into a run for her life. Back in her room, Kris located the body stocking in the bottom of one bureau drawer and pulled it on carefully. She added the undies from that oh-so-long-ago walk through Katyville as well as the shoes. The brown uniform went on easily over that. She put on the beret and managed to merge its line out into Nelly's with no trouble. The raincoat covered everything; the purse held a makeup kit fit for a spy. WHERE ARE THE NANOS? Kris asked.

I PARKED THEM UNDER THE EPAULETS OF THE RAINCOAT.

VERY GOOD. I THINK I'M READY TO GO.

I AGREE.

Not sure how to take her computer's approval, Kris stepped from her room and closed the door. As she turned, the lights came up in the living room; Jack sat on the couch, legs crossed, face grim. Silent, he pointed her to a place on the couch.

Kris took the offered seat. For a long minute, the two of them eyed each other in wordless challenge.

"It's not safe down there," Jack finally whispered.

"I'll be careful."

"There's a party tonight."

"I'll be back in time."

Jack mulled that for a while. "I could call the guards."

"And we'd know nothing more about this hand we're playing, or what deck Sandfire is stacking. We stay ignorant, we lose."

"I could go."

That stopped Kris for a moment. "Only Nelly can control the nanos. You'd have to do a lot more talking than I will."

"Then I go with you."

"Jack, that just doubles the chance of failure. You answer the door here, and they'll assume I'm here. We both go . . ."

Jack scowled. "You get yourself beat up, and they'll never let me work with you again."

That one gave Kris pause. She'd never considered that they might punish Jack for what she did. Would they be punishing Jack or punishing her? She'd never let on just how much she liked having Jack around. She'd have to think about that, but not now.

"I'll be careful," she said, standing.

Jack reached for her hand. She pulled it back; he turned his hand over, showing a wad of bills. "You'll need this."

Kris pocketed the money and made her way to the door.

Tom's room was closed, no way to see how Penny was doing. She opened the door only enough to slip out . . . and found herself facing a guard standing across from her. He frowned a question at her. Kris pulled her raincoat closed over her maid's uniform, stifled a yawn, and mumbled, "Long night."

The guard's frown deepened for a second, then his face went neutral, and Kris could almost hear him ordering himself to forget he'd ever seen a maid slipping out of this suite so early in the morning. Such was the privilege of people who lived in such suites. They could make common folks in brown maid uniforms vanish from other people's sight. Kris had a lot of thinking to do when this was over.

Pulling her beret farther down, Kris hurried for the freight elevator. That took her inward to a service area in what would have been a basement anywhere dirtside. A break and change room was on her right, the rear of the kitchen to her left, sending forth quite different aromas from those blown into the dining room. A new shift was coming on; Kris slipped by them, head down. There must have been enough staff turnover; no one remarked on her. She was quickly out the back door into a service corridor that stank of garbage and had just been hosed down. She followed this alleyway, gray-sided with color-coded pipes overhead, to a service slide way. It took her down to Stop One—Elevator Access. Kris paid cash for her ticket and found an out-of-the-way seat on the ferry's main deck.

"Money," she whispered to herself. She had her credit chit, but that would leave a golden trail right to her. How could she have forgotten something as basic as money? *Easy, kid. You never lacked for it,* she scowled to herself.

Halfway down, she stopped in the ladies' room to put on makeup. Powder darkened her skin. A pencil added worry lines to her forehead and mouth. Mascara made her eyes wider, and contacts made them brown. A puffy nose, mole on her right forehead and left cheek should throw off face analysis software if she remembered to suck in her full lips. Hunching her shoulders and stooping to shorten her height, Kris left the rest room, passed through the dining area, and climbed to the observation deck. As was usual on the Wardhaven ferry, this early among the working folks, it was pretty empty. Kris settled into a corner, opened an abandoned newspaper from yesterday, and tried to observe the five other people in view without being obvious.

She didn't have to worry; all five were stretched out on seats, dead to the world. After a moment, Kris stretched out, merging into their tiny herd. She followed when landing bells awoke them and sent them yawning for the exits. Beret down, coat held close, she slumped her way through the terminal and out onto Heidelburg's streets. NELLY, WE'LL NEED A CAB.

I SUSPECTED YOU WOULD WANT TRANSPORTATION TODAY. TURN RIGHT; A CAB WILL DRIVE BY SOON.

Kris followed Nelly's instructions. Half a minute after she began walking down Second Street, an orange cab drove past her and pulled over to the curb. Abu Kartum got out, leaned against his car, and began to whistle something that sounded vaguely Irish.

HERE'S OUR RIDE FOR THIS MORNING, Nelly said.

NELLY, I DON'T WANT THIS POOR MAN IN THIS MESS.

WE CAN ARGUE LATER WHEN WE ARE IN THE CAB. I SUGGEST YOU TELL HIM YOU NEED A RIDE HOME.

AUNTIE TRU IS DEFINITELY HEARING ABOUT THIS AS SOON AS WE GET BACK, Kris told her computer but kept a plaintive smile on her face. "I need a ride home. I'm feeling kind of wobbly."

"You spitting up blood?" Abu said, edging away from her. *Damn, I forgot about the Ebola thing.* "No fever. I think it was something I ate," Kris said, rubbing her tummy.

That seemed to satisfy him. He opened the door for her. "Where to?"

NELLY!

"Two nine six four," Kris repeated as Nelly fed her an address, "Northwest 173rd Street."

"You live a long way out to work on the beanstalk."

"I usually take the, er . . . trolley," Kris said as Nelly provided the word for local mass transit.

"It'll be a bit of a drive. I'll try to cut you a deal. Slump down so a taxi cop doesn't get me," the man said as he put the cab in gear without touching the meter.

"Thank you," Kris said and tried to make herself smaller.

"I know you?" the cabby said, glancing in a mirror that let him see his fare.

"I don't think so. I don't take the cab very often."

"But you did last week."

"I doubt it."

"I don't forget hats. Not beanies with fancy pom-poms."

"I just got it at a secondhand store."

"Yeah, and I got my draft notice in yesterday's mail."

"Draft notice?" Kris hadn't heard about that. Then again, how long had it been since she'd asked Nelly for a news update?

"Yeah, come any planetary emergency as announced by the government, I'm expected to report for weapons training. Me with six kids to feed, and I'm going to be out of my cab and learning how to shoot a gun. You know what they're going to pay me?"

"No."

"Neither do I. Nothing on the news. Nothing in the letter they sent me. Nothing my eldest boy could find on the net. It's just here, and it's like no one knows anything about it."

"I don't either." NELLY, SEARCH.

I AM SEARCHING. HE IS RIGHT; THERE IS NOTHING.

STOP THE SEARCH. LET'S NOT CALL ATTENTION TO OUR-SELVES TODAY. DON'T DO ANYTHING SOMEONE COULD USE TO LOCATE US.

THAT WAS MY INTENTION FOR TODAY. THEN YOU ASKED FOR A SEARCH, AND I DID IT. I SHOULD HAVE ARGUED WITH YOU.

YES, YOU SHOULD HAVE. NOW SHUT UP.

"I really don't know any more about this than you do," Kris told the driver.

"I should think a Princess would know more than a cabby."

"Princess?" Kris tried to make it sound like a question

"Yes, Princess Kristine. I saw you dragging the little girl out of the lake yesterday. I thought I knew who you were last week. Why are you in my cab?"

"I am asking for a ride home. I'm dressed as a maid in a Hilton uniform. That is all you need to know. Anyone asks you, you can tell them that, and you'll be as safe as I can make you."

The cab stopped behind a bus. Abu turned to Kris. "And you think that will make me safe. People are disappearing.

You don't think a man like me, a lowly cabby, knows these things. Things are going on that I do not like."

"I know. I didn't want to involve you, but when I ordered a cab, my computer ordered you. I'm sorry. I can get out here."

Kris heard a click as the doors locked. "What makes you think I do not want to be involved in what you are doing?"

"Nobody else does. At least, none of my friends."

"Your friends live on Turantic?"

"No," Kris admitted.

"Well I do live here. And I am starting to feel that if I do not get involved in something I do not know about, then I will become involved in something I do not want to be involved in. I do not like this talk of war." He turned back to traffic. "I do not like this talk of drafting me to fight someone else's war."

"I hear this talk of war," Kris said. "But I don't see how Turantic can fight a war. It has no Navy, no Army, no nothing."

"It soon will have me in that Army you say we do not have."

"So it seems. But listen, I am—" Kris bit her tongue. "I may break some Turantic laws sometime in the future. I can't let you become involved in something that could put you in prison. Your children and your brother's children need you."

"So, I will not let you involve me in any such crimes," the cabby said, smiling into his mirror. "Do you want to change the address I am taking you to?"

NELLY?

NO CHANGE.

"Just keep taking me there. It might not be the right address, though. I may need to go someplace else."

"No problem. I will take you anywhere you want today."

The sun came up, a red glare that quickly disappeared into a leaden overcast that left the air heavy and the day shaded in grays. NELLY, HOW WELL DO YOUR NANOS HANDLE RAIN?

NOT VERY WELL.

"Is there a weather channel here, Mr. Kartum?"

"You may call me Abu, Your Highness; my friends all do," the cabby said, punching the media station on his dashboard to life.

"And my friends all call me Kris."

"Kris, a knife and a long knife. You must be very sharp."

"Pardon," Kris said as the announcer told her there was a forty percent chance of showers today.

"A kris is a knife, very sharp, used by the sacred warriors of an Islamic sect. It dates from long ago on Earth."

"I remember reading something about them." Kris had, when she was thirteen or fourteen, come across that alternate meaning of her name and promptly forgotten it. A girl rapidly becoming a woman had not chosen to dwell on the reminder that she could be a deadly weapon. It was bad enough just being a Longknife without having to juggle other sharp objects.

"Maybe today it will help you to be as sharp as you need to be," the cabby said into his rearview mirror.

Their drive took them from a pleasant jumble of homes and small businesses into a serious industrial park. Gray factories, even a few with belching smokestacks, sprawled next to each other, separated only by parking lots and clumps of apartment buildings or bars. Abu turned a corner and slowed to a halt where the road separated a slate-gray four-story apartment complex from a dirty brown industrial complex of huge, boxy structures.

"This is the address you gave me."

"I don't think this is the place," Kris said, opening the door. "But I won't know until I look around. I'm going to walk a few blocks and see if I can spot the place." She got out, glanced over the apartments, then ducked her head back into the cab. "If this isn't the place, I might need a cab three or four blocks down the road."

"Then you might find one if you look hard enough."

Kris plodded slowly along the cracked sidewalk. Men and women, dressed for dirty work, crossed her path, dodged cars, and passed through two heavily guarded gates in a tall fence, topped with a serious-looking roll of barbed wire. No uninvited human was entering that place.

So Nelly ordered nano spies up and away. Kris carefully did not look at the plant. In an hour, she would know everything there was to know. But for now, she knew nothing and would learn nothing. One of the decisions Kris had made last night was to forgo telemetry. The risk of discovery was too great. Like ancient Mata Hari, these spies would report only in person.

Kris walked five blocks and was at the end of the plant when she spotted a cab. It stood by the far curb . . . empty.

Waiting nervously for the light to change, Kris debated continuing on a straight line past the cab. There were no police cars, no sign of an arrest. She crossed the street when the light brought traffic to a halt, then breathed in relief.

Abu knelt on the sidewalk, his prayer rug beneath him, bowing to the east. Kris started to walk past him, but he rose from his prayers. "Lady, you look like you could use a ride."

"I sure could," Kris agreed.

"My obligation to my business and my children kept me from praying at sunrise, but Allah is most understanding. Now that I have made my morning prayers, let me continue with my duty to you."

Kris made to get in the back, but with a slight touch to her elbow, Abu pointed her at the front seat. "If I am to drive you around without my meter running, you must look like my sister's daughter," he said, pointing at the two lights on the sign that rode atop the cab. Kris took the offered place as Abu walked around to the driver's side. He pulled into traffic, adding, "If Abu is seen driving around with an attractive young infidel, there are those who might talk or wonder. If, however, you wore a properly modest head cover, there would be fewer questions."

"I don't own any head cover," Kris told him. She didn't even own a tiara. There was little left after Nelly used all the smart metal and salvaged the gold to make reel-out antennas.

"There is a respectable shawl in the glove compartment. My wife left it. Sometimes she goes places in town where a shawl is not respected. Allah is most understanding, unlike some people."

"Is it hard to follow your faith?"

"Is it hard to be a Longknife, to be so different?"

"Yes," Kris agreed.

"Then maybe Allah has shown you a little of what he sends his faithful."

"Could you turn here?"

Abu changed lanes, then made a left. They were a block past the factory into an area of eateries, bars, and small apartments.

"Is this where you want to be left?"

"Yes. I need to be here about a half hour, maybe longer."

Abu frowned as he pulled over. "This is not a good place to hang around. I will have to drive off."

"I'll have Nelly call you," Kris said as she got out.

"Leave the scarf. This is no place for a woman of faith."

"I can take care of myself," Kris assured him.

"If Allah wills it," he said and left her.

Kris watched him go, then glanced around. Working class. Problem was, she wasn't working. Maybe she hadn't thought this through as well as she thought. Her stomach rumbled; Kris hadn't had breakfast. That answered what to do next. The pom-pom on her beret was broadcasting a homing signal for the nanos, so she needed to stay outside. That answered where to eat.

A truck claiming to be Mama's Place slumped in a dirt parking lot half a block down, selling quick breakfasts to people coming off shift. Kris joined the crowd. Men and women stifled yawns and scrubbed at tired eyes as they waited. Some still had energy to gripe. "I swear to God, they're speeding up the line." "You're just slowing down." "No, they are speeding up the line. I'm gonna talk to the union stew; they can't do that." "I did talk to the union rep, and they are and they can and you better just be happy you got a job." "Ain't that what they always say." "Well, maybe having this job means we won't have to worry about that draft notice I got yesterday." "Why not?" "They don't draft people making the guns the army needs." "Who says we're making guns?" "And what do you think that box is you're putting together, an eggbeater?" "It ain't no gun." "If it ain't a targeting system, I'll eat it." "And if you keep running your mouth, you'll be begging them to draft you. The jail they'll put you in ain't gonna be nice."

Kris stood at the head of the line; she ordered a breakfast burrito of rice and beans, added a potato fry, and got a juice for free in a meal deal. As she reached for money, it dawned on her paying with a Wardhaven bill might not be the brightest idea of the day. She dug in her pocket, keeping her money out of sight and getting a "You do have money for this, cutie," from the old man purporting to be Mama. She produced five dollars, Turantic, and got a few coins in change and her meal.

Most people scattered to their homes, but a few hung around the other side of the truck where a makeshift counter hung. It gave those with nowhere to go a place to set their food as they stood and ate. Kris took up a small corner. Talk was low and generally about the coming war. Half seemed to think Hamilton had done everything that had gone wrong for the last six months, or maybe forever. Others thought Wardhaven was at the root of the trouble, or at least cooperating with Hamilton.

"We take on Wardhaven, we're going to need help." "I hear Greenfeld can stand up to those Wardhaven snooties." "Yeah, I expect Greenfeld can fight till the last drop of Turantic blood." "You like those Wardhaven snobs?" "I don't like Greenfeld. Any way you cut your cards, they're bad blood." "They're our friends if we need them to fight our enemies." "I say we need better friends and fewer enemies." "I hear some Hamilton thugs beat up a woman last night." "No, you got that confused with the Wardhaven cruds that tried to kidnap that girl off her sailboat yesterday." "I heard on the news they both happened." "No, you got it all wrong."

Kris backed away from the counter before anyone came to blows. Walking down the street, she reviewed what she'd heard. Weapons . . . this was probably some kind of weapons plant. She and Nelly had worked so hard to patch together the nano spies from a bit of jewelry only for her to learn what she wanted by just hanging around a lunch wagon and eating a burrito.

WE WILL HAVE MORE SPECIFICS WHEN THE NANOS COME BACK, Nelly said, a tinge of defensiveness in her voice.

THAT WE WILL HAVE, Kris agreed.

But the nanos' pictures would not show the confusion boiling in people's minds. Was it Hamilton or Wardhaven or Greenfeld that was their enemy? Lots of differing opinions. All the facts kept being turned upside down. With no communications off planet and all kinds of things happening on planet, people were left in the dark and swatting at everything. Kris wished she knew more about Turantic, more about these people before all hell started nibbling at them, driving them crazy.

As Kris rambled under gray skies, the nanos reported in.

THE FIRST FIVE ARE BACK. THEY REPORT NO ENCOUNTERS
WITH HOSTILE NANO GUARDS, Nelly reported.

WHAT DID THEY FIND?

I AM CORRELATING THE DATA.

Kris pulled a pair of glasses from her pocket. Nelly began
to run schematics across the lenses. It looked like the place
was putting together thirteen-millimeter antirocket lasers. Nice
for defending small ground units, but not what she was looking for. More nanos showed up, identifying a production line
full of four-inch secondary batteries for cruisers or the main
lasers for small destroyers.

WE HAVE A STRANGE NANO BUZZING AROUND US, Nelly
announced.

CONVERT IT OR KILL IT.

THAT IS WHAT I AM DOING.

Kris paused in her walk, turned her back on the plant, and
studied a building offering studio apartments by the week.
Out of the corner of her eye, she spotted Abu's cab. He paused
at a stop sign, then turned right and headed away from her.
Kris tried humming a tune but found her mouth too dry to do
much more than blow air. Above her, a crackling sound told
her Nelly had resorted to destruction before the computer
said, I HAD TO KILL THAT ONE. IT WAS STARTING TO TRANS-
MIT.

Kris sauntered toward the street she'd last seen Abu on. Two
minutes later, he pulled up beside her. She got in. "Drive as fast
as the speed limit allows and change directions randomly."

"Are you in trouble?" the cabby said, doing as she asked.

"I don't think so. But why make it easy for the bad guys?"

"Put on the scarf. I know some very random streets."

In three minutes, they were weaving in and out of traffic on
a series of roads that had to have been laid out by a exceed-
ingly drunken cow. Kris left the driver to his own devices
while she reviewed what she had and what she wanted. Small
arms for an army or even secondary lasers for ships was interesting, but she wanted the main battery for a fleet. An army
could be defensive or offensive. A fleet, at least a large one,
was anything but defensive. And to arm ships, you needed
very big lasers and capacitors. That meant very big factories.
Kris went down Nelly's list, hunting for the largest.

There it was, about as far on the other side of town as it could be. I PLANNED THAT ONE FOR LAST, Nelly said, JUST BEFORE WE HEADED HOME.

THAT SOUNDED GOOD LAST NIGHT, BUT IF THEY'VE GOT NANO GUARDS AT THIS LITTLE SHOP, I HAVE A HUNCH WE'D BETTER DO THE MOST INTERESTING TARGET FIRST. WE MAY NOT GET ANOTHER CHANCE.

HUNCH, Nelly said. INTERESTING CONCEPT. YET YOUR ROUTE DEFIES PATTERN ANALYSIS. IT IS ALSO NOT THE SHORTEST DISTANCE BETWEEN TARGETS. IT IS NOT ECONOMICAL.

BUT IT MAY SURPRISE THE OPPOSITION AND KEEP US ALIVE.

I BEGIN TO UNDERSTAND "SURPRISE."

Kris told Abu her next target. He greeted it with a scowl. "I know it's a bit out of our way," she said.

"That is not the problem," he said, bringing up a map. "There is only one way into that plant. See these communities. They are gated now. I cannot use those roads."

"Gated communities that close to a major industrial plant. That doesn't sound right."

"But that is what happened last year. The plant is behind a large berm. Its sounds and sight does not offend the community."

MY MAPS DO NOT SHOW THOSE COMMUNITIES AS GATED, Nelly said.

ONE OF THE ADVANTAGES OF HIRING A MAN WHO KNOWS THE LOCAL CHANGES, Kris said, struggling to resize her problem. Going there was sticking her head in the lion's mouth. Maybe she was overreacting to Nelly frying a guard at the smaller plant, but Kris had a very strong hunch this lion's mouth would have a lot more teeth than the last. Gating whole housing areas. They didn't want strangers around.

"I want a look at that place," Kris said, stabbing at the map. "You know a quiet place we can pull over and talk?"

Two minutes later, they pulled into an empty parking lot at a small God's Word Is the Bible church. "They are very full on Sunday and Wednesday evenings, but today is not one of them," Abu said. "Maybe it is time that you stop protecting me. I cannot help you if I am in the dark."

Kris studied the man. The olive skin of his face was creased from years of working in the sun, but his eyes were clear and open. His offer was honest. It saddened Kris that all she had to offer him was coconspirator status. The man deserved better. She started slowly.

"There are space docks above the beanstalk loaded with merchant ships, brought in suddenly, and in mass, for some kind of upkeep that does not require a lot of oversized additions to the ships. However, I have been watching just such oversized packages passing through the secure freight elevator. I don't know what's in those crates, and I would very much like to know."

Abu nodded. "I have been stuck in traffic behind just such shipments. They do come from that plant."

"Which will teach me not to ask questions." Kris sighed. "So far, I have not involved you in anything but a conversation. If I say more, you may become indictable for crimes."

"Like industrial espionage. Yes, I know what we do to people who break that law on Turantic." The cabby frowned. "What do you think is going on?"

"Back when my Great-grandfather Ray was just leading a brigade, fighting for Unity, the Society of Humanity was playing catch-up. They made a Navy by adding reactors and power storage, lasers and ice to a lot of merchant ships."

"And you wonder if Turantic is doing the same?"

"There haven't been any profits here for three years. The money has to have gone somewhere."

"And what did I help you do at that last factory?"

"I released nano reconnaissance drones upwind to ride the wind to and through the plant. They brought me pictures, mostly antimissile lasers for army use."

"Something I may be carrying next week. Hmm. What is the range of your nano spies?"

So much for avoiding that word. "Nelly?"

"About two kilometers," the computer said.

"We cannot get that close to that plant. Do you have any that could go farther?"

"I could remake the nanos to a range of ten kilometers, but that would mean cutting their numbers by a third," Nelly said.

"Allah akbar," the cabby muttered. "Your computer can do such a thing in the hour it will take me to drive across town?"

"If Nelly says she can do that, she can do it."

"Nelly. The computer has a name."

"I most certainly do," Nelly said. "I will not be bossed around by a 'Hey, you.'"

"She sounds like my wife. Be careful, young woman, or you may end up as henpecked as me."

"I think I already am." Kris sighed. "Nelly, I want a homing device as well. Our hang time on the other side of that last plant was too risky. Let's drop a homer and let the nanos close on it."

"I will do that."

"Now, wise cabdriver, how do you propose that we get around the security at that plant?"

"There is a major road here, upwind of the plant. I think I may have car trouble there for a few minutes. Then, about seven kilometers downwind of your plant is a very swank restaurant. Too expensive for my blood, though they claim to serve food straight from the Levant of old Earth. My Miriam serves better food on her bad days. Anyway, that is just the place that a maid at a fine hotel might apply for a job to better herself. They are hiring, and I can download a job application. Would you like to see about a better job?"

"Would I." Kris grinned. "You know, this Princess stuff is not nearly what it's cracked up to be."

"We should all have your problems," Abu said dryly. But at least he was honest. Kris could count on one hand the people she'd met who would actually have said that to her face.

"May Allah grant us all fewer problems soon," Kris offered.

"Not a bad prayer, for an infidel. Put on your shawl like a respectable woman." Kris did, but not like a respectable woman, so Abu corrected her shawl before starting the long drive.

The clouds showed enthusiasm for neither burning off nor shedding rain, so the day drew on, neither blue nor wet, just a gray weight. The cabby stayed quiet, and Kris accepted his silence. Nelly stayed busy, a gentle hum in the back of Kris's mind as the computer shuffled smart molecules around. Kris studied the map, gnawing at the problems that might come her way and concluding that this spy job was a bit more complicated than the movies let on. No way was worrying a problem like this exciting or sexy. Who would waste money for a ticket to really get killed, drowned, or thrown in jail? No question about it, excitement was something horrible happening to someone else as far away from your own thin and delicate skin as possible.

"Maybe I should ask Crossenshild for some training," Kris muttered, thinking of the job offer from Wardhaven's head spy.

"Did you say something?"

"Just making a note to myself," Kris said. "Ignore me."

"With such a marvelous computer, I would think that you would have your, what do you call her, Nilli, remind you of everything."

"I am Nelly," the computer snapped. "Nell, Nell, Nell."

"I apologize if I hurt your electric feelings," the cabby said.

"She's a bit touchy since her last upgrade," Kris whispered.

"I am working hard. Do not distract me."

"Well, Nelly," Kris said, "you might reduce your distractions by not listening to us mere mortals talking."

"But that would eliminate my situational awareness."

"What's the matter, don't you trust me to keep us safe?"

"No," Nelly said.

The cabby raised an eyebrow over a widening smile.

"Now you see why I don't bother Nelly with minor stuff."

"Seems to me you may soon need a dumb computer to keep track of your day."

"Don't let Nelly hear that." Kris grinned, but she knew Nelly did hear that, and with her computer behaving so strangely, Kris could only wonder what she'd make of it.

15

An hour later Kris knew they were close to the factory. The surveillance cameras and Tow Away Zone—No Stopping signs told her.

"There goes plan A," she muttered.

Abu slowed down. "What do you want me to do?"

"Drive the minimum speed limit," Kris said, lowering her window. It got windy. HOW ARE THE NANOS DOING?

THEY ARE OKAY. WHAT ARE YOU TRYING TO DO?

"I am at fifty-five. If I go slower, they will notice."

"Roll down the window behind you, if you can." He did; the wind tunnel effect through the car got most pronounced.

MY NANOS CAN'T TAKE THIS! Nelly shouted in Kris's head. She had her finger on the window button; it was coming up even as the shout bounced around her skull. Abu had been paying attention; the rear window came up only a split second behind Kris's.

HOW ARE THE NANOS?

I CAN FIX THEM.

"What do I do now? Abu asked.

Kris rubbed at her shawl-covered head, trying to relieve the tension gripping her scalp. "Plan A and B didn't work. We need a plan C."

"I see," said the cabby.

Kris scowled at his joke; he tossed her off with a small grin. Kris glanced around, looking for an answer to her problem. She saw it. "Stop at the next exit. I need a rest room break."

Back in the cab, and a bit lighter, Kris pointed Abu to the route back into town. Window down, her hand wandered playfully in the wind as Nelly launched the spies on their long flight. DONE, Nelly reported. Kris put up her window as Abu picked up speed in the acceleration lane.

"Now I take you where you can do some more of your magic, then I take you to the best place in town for real food, not that tasteless stuff infidels eat."

"Ever eat Tex-Mex?" Kris asked. "We had this cook who said she was only three generations away from Texas back on Earth. What she did with jalapeños took your mouth a week to recover."

"Someday I must take you home and have my Miriam serve you a meal. But this will do to open your eyes."

Their next stop was The Great Khan's Caravansary, complete with two heavily laden plaster camels out front. The cars parked around it included several of Wardhaven's most expensive export models. Abu drove around to the entrance used by employees and deliveries. He parked against the back fence next to a sign giving the times for deliveries that blocked out the busy mealtimes. Kris got out; she spotted four, maybe five security cameras. At least two of them turned to examine her.

Abu handed her papers she took with visible reluctance. Taking a few steps toward the restaurant, she faltered, clutched her stomach and backed up. She ended leaning against the sign, fighting dry heaves. THE HOMING BEACON SET, NELLY?

YES. I HAVE IT DELAYED FOR AN HOUR, THEN INTERMITTENT AND RANDOMLY JUMPING FREQUENCIES. I ESTIMATE IT HAS AN EIGHTY-SEVEN PERCENT PROBABILITY OF AVOIDING DETECTION EVEN AGAINST THE MOST DETERMINED SECURITY SYSTEM ON WARDHAVEN.

WHAT ABOUT PETERWALD AND IRONCLAD SOFTWARE?

YOUR HUNCH IS AS GOOD AS MINE, Nelly answered.

THAT'S YOUR GUESS IS AS GOOD AS MINE, Kris corrected. IF
YOU'RE GOING TO START SOUNDING HUMAN, GET IT RIGHT.

HOW MUCH OF MY LIMITED COMPUTATIONAL CAPACITY DO
YOU WANT ME TO WASTE ON MIMICKING YOU? Nelly asked.
Since Kris couldn't tell if the question was real or facetious,
she ignored it.

"I can't go in, Abu, my stomach is too upset," Kris said as
she opened the cab door.

"Maybe if we get some food in you, you will feel more
courage. I keep telling my sister you need some real meat on
those thin bones of yours."

"The boys like me thin," Kris answered, not sure who she
was playing for, but keeping up the patter.

Back on the road, Kris asked Nelly a question she wished
she'd thought of earlier. "Are all the security cameras moni-
tored at a central location or by local security teams?"

"Good question, Kris. I have not looked into it and do not
think you want me to just now."

"You're right on that one," Kris agreed. "But you must have
looked into security for our visit to Katyville."

"Yes. All the places of interest then had their own security
systems. But hotels on the cheap side of town are one thing.
Plants making military equipment are another, though I doubt
I need point that out to a shareholder in Nuu Enterprises."

"Quite a wife you have there," Abu said around a chuckle.

"Nelly, there is such a thing as tact," Kris said.

"And how much of my limited computational—"

"Never mind. Abu, where's that food you promised me?"

Fatima's Kitchen was only a fifteen-minute drive from the
fancy place, but it could have been on another planet. The streets
here were narrow and winding, the houses built close together.
Parking was tight, and people walked elbow-to-elbow on narrow sidewalks but had no problem carrying on conversations
with people on the other side of the street. Several conversations at a time; the place was a madhouse.

"Welcome to what we call Little Arabia," Abu said with a
proud smile. "You passed no locked gate to get in here, but
few doors are locked here, anyway. We live as Allah wills it."

Abu found a place to park the cab with a whole ten centimeters to spare. Kris carefully arranged her scarf as she got

out, then loosed the belt of her raincoat. Many women passing Kris on the street wore fashions she might have seen on
Wardhaven, though the cut was uniformly loose-fitting with
no waist. Several wore something more exotic, a covering that
went from head to toe. While Kris was wondering how these
women did anything, she got her answer. A young woman,
from the shape of the arm that slipped from her wrapping to
hold a basket, was shopping. Her other hand held up fruit or
vegetables for a good look. That woman's compromise was
not repeated by the older woman, from the sound of her voice,
that stood next to her. Not even a finger escaped that woman's
screen.

Abu came around to the sidewalk and led Kris toward a
whitewashed shop that emitted delightful smells. A round
woman in a shawl and loose dress greeted him at the door with
a hug and a peck of a kiss. "Are you hungry, Abu, and who is
this woman with you? Should I call Miriam and tell her you
are bringing home a second wife? Someone to help her with
the kids, no doubt, because any woman so thin as this one
surely is no cook."

"What she is and is not is no business of yours Sorir, so
you just show us to a table in a quiet corner and let me speak
to the boss."

Sorir swatted Abu. "You are speaking to the boss, but I suspect you mean the man who thinks he runs my place." But she
led them past tables where silent men drank coffee and through
an alcove where women chatted as they drank tea or coffee to
finally stop in a shaded corner at the rear of the place where
couples sat quietly or families ate noisily. She pointed Abu toward a table behind a bamboo divider. "That quiet enough for
you?"

Abu settled Kris at the table, then went hunting for the man
he wanted. Sorir gave Kris a quick smile, then followed Abu.
The two of them ended up talking to a thin fellow standing in
the door of what sounded like the kitchen. Their talk was
mixed with glances Kris's way. She tried to look demure or
whatever a young woman should look like in this culture that
couldn't seem to decide what to do with its women—let them
run things or just exist. Come to think of it, it didn't sound all
that different from Wardhaven . . . or the Navy at times.

A young woman brought a pot of hot water to Kris's table and a bowl of green tea. "Would you prefer coffee?"

"I don't know what Abu would prefer."

"Oh, Abu is with you. I will bring coffee." And a steaming small cup of the thick brown liquid quickly appeared.

A moment later Abu returned, accompanied by Sorir and the man who was introduced as Abdul. "You have stirred up the proverbial hornet's nest," Sorir told Kris.

Kris eyed Abu, but the cabby seemed content to let the women talk. "What do you think I have done?" Kris asked, not willing to give anything away, but not wanting to sound evasive.

"That I could not begin to guess, but this morning something tripped the alarms at a factory on the other side of town, and now all the security people at all the plants are running around like chickens with their heads cut off, looking for some kind of intruder and not wanting to be in the same kind of trouble that the plant people are in across town."

"I suppose your uncle's sister's son works on security," Kris said dryly.

"Actually, no one will hire any of us for security," Abu said. "We talk funny, and we stop to pray too many times a day."

"Then how do you know—?"

"We are not the only people who talk funny and keep to old ways," Abdul said. "Do those things, and you become a minority. Is that not so everywhere? Some minorities suffer one way, others another way, but we are all different, and that marks us for trouble when things become strange for the large herd of sheep and the dogs that keep them going where they should go." Kris greeted that with a puzzled look. She was no closer to understanding the situation than she had been when Abdul started.

"Several of our Jewish friends have sons working in security," Sorir explained dryly.

"Jewish?" Kris said. She didn't think there were any minorities on Wardhaven—at least she hadn't before today. Still, she knew Dad had to be careful to invite his Jewish and Islamic supporters to different fund-raisers.

"The Temple Mount is far away from those of us who hold it sacred," Abdul said. "And we live very close to those whose only gods are their belly. Here, we share what we may, Jew and Arab, and information is important anywhere."

"And the information we have," Sorir cut in, "says that security is more upset than a sheepdog herding cats. Oh you men, you take all day to say nothing. It would be most unwise for Abu to return to Khan's dispenser of poor food."

"I have to get back there," Kris said.

"We understand such a return is of the highest import to you," Abdul said. "We are arranging it even now. So, since you can do nothing for the moment, why not share a meal with us."

The meal was a procession of dishes demonstrating many of the thousand ways to fix rice, cheese, barley, mutton, and goat. Sorir named each dish, explained what it was and how it was prepared, and laughed when Kris asked, only half in jest, if the meal would be followed by a test. One thing Kris did not have to worry about was showing delight; the food was fantastic. The portions were small, and each dish was shared with Abu and Sorir. Overeating herself into a nap was not a risk.

Sorir and Abu kept up a kind of running commentary on both the food and Turantic. It was a good planet to raise children on. Or at least it had been. The conversation skirted anything that could be taken for treason by an eavesdropper until the last dish was laid out, a multilayered crust drowning in honey.

"Why should you care about what happens to us on Turantic?" Sorir said through veiled eyelashes as she cut Kris a slice.

Kris took the offered morsel. As her fork cut a bite, it sliced through scores of layers. "Humanity is like this dish. You can't cut one layer. If one is sliced, all are going to be cut." Sorir eyed the dish and nodded. Kris went on.

"What happens to you will happen to my people on Wardhaven, And it may be in store for a lot of other planets as well. We can't let you face this alone. I serve in Wardhaven's Navy. A woman I serve with was beat up last night. It was done because she serves Wardhaven. Now, reporters talk of some Wardhaven people attacking Turantic people or something else entirely different."

"It is very confusing," Sorir said. "I do not like it."

"And very worrisome," Abu added.

"And if I can't find out what's going on here, I can't begin to figure out what will happen to my people. And if things fall apart, I'll be stuck on a ship in a fight that I may not want . . . and may not even be necessary."

"And I may be on a ship shooting at you," Abu said. "Sorir, she is risking much. Should we not risk a little to help her?"

"It is my brother and his sons," Sorir said, rising from her uneaten desert, "who I am asking to risk much. I had to know it was worth it. Come, Kris of the courageous knife, the security cameras at the Khan showed a cabby and a woman dressed as a maid this morning. They cannot see that again. Am I correct that you, yourself, must go there?"

As Kris rose, she balanced her own risk against trying to teach someone how to handle Nelly, then threw in her own feelings about letting the strangely behaving Nelly out of her sight. "Yes, I have equipment others could not operate."

YOU CALLING ME EQUIPMENT?

I'M GOING TO CALL YOU THIN-SKINNED IF YOU DON'T STOP BUTTING INTO MY CONVERSATIONS.

"But it would be better if you were not seen again by the same security cameras. Come with me."

Kris followed the woman through the kitchen to a storeroom. Sorir pulled pants and a shirt from behind a shelf of canned goods. "Put these on. A girl started something at the Khan. A boy will not be noticed." As soon as the door closed, Kris undid the waitress uniform and became a rather tall person in ratty pants and a torn cotton shirt. As she finished, Sorir looked in. "The shoes must go, and you must wash that makeup off your face," she said, tossing Kris a damp towel. Kris scrubbed as she stepped out of her shoes. Sorir dropped a pair of well-worn loafers on the floor, and Kris stepped into them.

"The right one hurts. It's got something in it."

"Good, you will walk favoring it. And hunch your shoulders over. That should keep the usual pattern recognition programs from identifying you too quickly. But that face of yours."

"The makeup's off," Kris said.

"But the nose isn't. It's big enough for you to be one of us, but software will match you in three scans. Hmm. We need to change that and your hair. You may have noticed, we tend more to raven black like mine, and you need not say how much white now streaks my youthful pride."

Kris didn't. Sorir left, and Kris took a few steps, trying to find a gait that hurt less. The woman returned with a wig. "Put this on, then put these pads in your mouth."

The wig fit over the bun her own hair was in, giving her the shoulder-length, messed-up hair some kids liked. The pads tasted of plastic and puffed out her cheeks. "Can I talk through them?" she muttered, and proved that she could . . . barely.

"Better yet, don't talk at all. You are a good Moslem boy. You hear. You obey. You do not talk. And keep your eyes down. You may be working for my brother, but it is not what you want. Sulk. Surely you know how to do that."

Sulking was never, ever permitted in her father's house, but that was more than Sorir wanted to know about being a Longknife. Kris muttered, "I can do it with the best of them."

Sorir presented her with a ball cap for a local Turantic team. THEY ALWAYS LOSE, Nelly pointed out. Kris stripped the pompom off the beret. It came easily, dangling its lead-ins. Kris put it on top of her head, and it stuck. Once she got the lead-ins reattached to Nelly's wire, she slowly settled the ball cap on her head. HOW'S THAT WORKING?

I DO NOT KNOW. THERE IS LITTLE ACTIVITY TO MONITOR IN HERE, BUT I CAN TELL THEY NEED A NEW MICROWAVE OVEN. IT IS WASTING HALF OF ITS ELECTRICITY.

I'LL TELL THEM THAT IF I GET A CHANCE, Kris said and let Sorir lead her back into the kitchen. A short, rounded man in dark pants and shirt was talking with Abdul as two thin young men carried in the frozen carcasses of goats and sheep.

"Nabil, my brother, I have a favor to ask of you."

The man fixed his sister with dark eyes, and Abdul checked the two frozen carcasses off a notepad in his hand and sent the young men back to the truck.

"You have not made your delivery to the Khan's yet?"

"It is next, sister."

"I ask you to take this extra helper, my nephew, with you to that place."

"Why?"

"It would be better for Father if you did not know. Let anything that comes of this fall on my head."

The man studied Kris, eyed his sister, then studied Kris again. He shook his head. "These are bad times when a younger sister will not tell her older brother what she wants him to do."

"And when have we known better?" his sister chided him.

"Not since you were born. I swear, a djinn stole my little sister at birth and gave Mother a lump of camel dung to raise."

Sorir swatted her brother. "And who even now dreams of finding the fabled hiding place of many thieves."

"I may have to, after whatever you are getting me into," he said, waving at Kris. "Come, sister's nephew, we have work that another back will make lighter." Kris followed; the sky still threatened rain but held back as if the weather, along with everything else, was balanced on the sharp edge of uncertainty.

"You need not bring the boy back here. Just drop him off, and we will find him," Sorir called after them.

"Harrump," Nabil said, calling his boys from the back of the truck where they were slamming doors. They scrambled for the front, shouting, "I get the door." A look told Kris the seating was tight; no wonder they didn't want to be mashed in the middle.

"He has the door," Nabil said gruffly, pointing at Kris. "And none of your backtalk. We have more deliveries to make, and traffic goes to hell in an hour, so let's make this quick."

The boys crowded into the middle, the farthest over trying to stay out of his father's way as he put the truck in gear. Kris closed the door on her side and tried to be very small, for once grateful for her narrow hips and nonexistent breasts. She hunched over so that she didn't tower over the others.

"What's your name?" one youth asked.

"Why you working with us?" said the other.

"He is my sister's nephew. She asked me to give him a try. He stutters, so he doesn't talk much. Leave him alone."

The boys accepted that. Kris was glad for the cover but had to wonder who thought it up, Sorir or Nabil, or was everyone, like Abu, a quick study at story spinning. Then again, when you were few among a mass of strangers, camouflage must be as critical to them as to a chameleon. The streets had seemed tight for the cab; they looked impassible for an elephant like the truck. Yet Nabil maneuvered cleanly, resorting to shouts and raised fists no more than twice a block. He was answered with the same, but all in good nature. It took twenty minutes to make his way to The Great Khan's Caravansary. Only as he drove into the parking lot did he glance at Kris and say, "Where?"

Kris had already spotted the sign. She pointed and risked a "Th-th-there."

A car had Abu's spot. The truck parked right behind it. "Let's make this fast, boys. We've got two more to go," Nabil said as he dropped out his door. Kris was already opening hers, but not fast enough for the young men. There was good-natured pushing and shoving. And as Kris dropped onto the pavement, the oldest boy pushed the youngest into her. She didn't have much for breasts, and an armored bodysuit was holding them in, but what softness Kris had, the kid got a handful of.

"You, you're . . ." Now it was his turn to stutter.

Kris had seen a DI stop a squad of officer trainees dead in their tracks with just a stare. She'd grown up with Harvey, an ex-Sergeant, who could be as nice as a fairy godfather one moment but freeze fire with a glance the next. Kris put all the glares she'd ever gotten into one face and gave it to the poor kid.

He froze, face beet-red.

"What's keeping you boys?" came from the back of the truck as the doors swung wide.

"Coming," the oldest one shouted, grabbing his brother.

"But, but . . ." the other sputtered.

"Talk to Papa later. Not now, can't you see?"

Kris followed the boys. NELLY, TALK TO ME. ARE THE NANOS HERE? DO THEY HAVE COMPANY?

YES, AND BOY, DO WE HAVE COMPANY. KRIS, I AM READING EIGHT RADIOS TURNED TO THE SECURITY FREQUENCY WITHIN JUST A HUNDRED METERS OF US. THREE CAR MOBILES. FIVE PERSONAL REMOTES. THERE ARE AT LEAST NINE MOBILE NANO GUARDS BUZZING THIS PLACE.

AND THE BEACON?

I TURNED IT OFF. BY MY COUNT, NINETY-TWO PERCENT OF OUR RECON UNITS ARE HERE. IN A WHILE I WILL RISK TURN-ING IT ON TO HELP THOSE CLOSE BUT NOT HERE YET.

"Papa, why are we carrying double?" the youngest asked as their father dropped a carcass on each shoulder.

"I'm in a hurry," Nabil said. "Now get a move on." Kris was last; he loaded her with an icy cold slab of meat on each shoulder, blocking the view of every security camera in sight. Hunched over, she limped after the boys, favoring her painful left foot. Kris was working the kitchen's screen door open with her foot when it opened, almost knocking her down.

Face-to-face with a man in a gray uniform, Kris ducked her head. She took a step back from the man with SureFire Security in bold red letters over his left breast pocket and three gold chevrons on both sleeves. She got ready to slam him with a frozen rack of sheep as he glanced at her, but he dismissed her out of hand and swaggered into the parking lot.

Eyes still down, Kris slipped through the open door and spotted one of the boys exiting a large, walk-in freezer. She covered the distance in a kind of hopping stumble and found herself facing a hawk-nosed woman with a tablet. "That makes six. Hurry up, you boys. I ordered fourteen. I don't have all day, and leaving this freezer open is costing me money."

The younger boy, still showing red when he looked Kris's way, helped her hang her carcasses on hooks in the freezer. Then both hurried out, and the woman slammed the freezer door shut.

"You're . . . you're—" the boy started.

"Shush," Kris risked under her breath.

SureFire Security was talking to Nabil. The driver kept up a steady stream of words about how bad thievery was and getting worse even as he loaded two more large goats on his eldest son and sent him off at a run. Same for the younger boy and Kris in her turn. The Security Sergeant gave Kris another once-over as she loaded, but was distracted when his radio came alive.

"We've got some sort of signal traffic real close by."

"How close?" the Sergeant demanded as Kris hobbled away.

NELLY, THEY'RE AFTER US.

I HAVE TO TRANSMIT SOME, AND THE BEACON HAS TO SEND, TOO.

WE NEED A DISTRACTION. COULD YOU MAKE UP SOME NOISY DECOYS?

GOT JUST WHAT YOU ORDERED. TRY BRUSHING UP AGAINST SOME PEOPLE. ONE ON YOUR RIGHT, THE OTHER ON YOUR LEFT.

Kris caught a waiter coming out for a smoke with her right arm and got a "Watch where you're going," for it. The left arm went to the woman with the tablet when Kris stumbled into her. "You drop that meat, and you'll give me another one. And don't expect me to let you drive off with it," she scolded the older boy as he passed Kris on the way out. "You tell that father of yours, if he is your father, that I'm keeping anything you drop to make sure you don't pawn it off on someone else."

"Yes, ma'am. We understand, ma'am. Papa would never do that, ma'am. Kid," the older brother said, slapping Kris on the back. "You and Papa have to talk. I don't think you're cut out for this job."

Kris hung her load and hurried out. She managed to slip on a wet spot on the floor but kept going, leaving behind her the woman's scolding voice. "Don't you even think of filing a comp claim. You were limping before you came in here."

Outside, Nabil was giving his sons their final load. The Sergeant stood in the parking lot, yelling at his people. Kris saw one far to her left, another at the front of the lot to her right. "What do you mean, you can't triangulate on that signal? If you can't, I know where I can get a dozen who can."

"Sarge, I don't think there's just one squeaker. There has to be at least two, and one is moving. None are on for more than it takes a flea to blink."

"Nail it, or I'm gonna nail you."

Kris spotted the smoker, pacing up and down nervously on the far side of the lot. NELLY, ACTIVATE THE DECOYS. USE A SPORADIC AND INTERMITTENT SIGNAL BUT HAVE THEM SIMUL-TANEOUSLY BROADCAST ON THE SAME POWER AND FREQUENCY AT TIMES TO SEE IF YOU CAN HETERODYNE THE SIGNAL. With luck, the two would merge and show up as a single source halfway between the two transmissions.

THIS IS FUN.

ACTIVATE THE BEACON WHEN THE OTHERS ARE OFF.

TWO PEEPS SHOULD GET US ALL OUR LOST SHEEP.

Good Lord, now Nelly was attempting poetry. What next!

"Boy, get in the cab," Nabil said, risking a worried glance

either at the door where his boys were still making the last delivery . . . or at the security cop. "I want to be out of here before whatever they are sniffing around for gets this whole place locked down. That would truly ruin my delivery schedule."

Kris nodded obediently and opened the door. While waiting for the others, she wandered around like any teenage boy . . . and just happened to end up leaning on the delivery schedule sign.

WHAT HAVE WE GOT?

NINETY-SIX PERCENT PRESENT. THE ESCORT NANOS BURNED A DOZEN PURSUITS BUT NONE CLOSER THAN THE STREET. WE ARE CLEAN!

If a computer could crow, Nelly was. GET THEM ON ME.

WAIT ONE. ALL PRESENT.

SHUT EVERYTHING DOWN. NO TRAFFIC UNTIL I SAY SO.

BUT I WANT TO DOWNLOAD OUR TAKE.

NELLY, TURN EVERYTHING OFF. DON'T RISK SO MUCH AS A PEEP.

YES, MA'AM, Nelly said, like a disappointed four-year-old.

Hardly breathing, Kris kept leaning on the sign pole as the boys hustled across the lot and piled into the truck. Kris waited a second more, only moving when Nabil shouted, "Hurry up you lazy boy," and turned on the engine.

Kris scrambled into the truck and slammed the door. Now the older boy sat next to her, his arms folded across his chest as if by iron chains. The other seemed about to burst with questions, but a nudge in the ribs as Nabil slipped the truck in gear kept him quiet. Nabil waved at the Sergeant as he backed. The man in gray waved distractedly, then frowned and started walking over to Nabil's side of the truck. "Just a minute, fellow."

Kris froze. NELLY, ARE WE TOTALLY QUIET?

KRIS, MY NANOS AREN'T EVEN MOVING. I HAVE SHUT DOWN EVERYTHING I CAN. I AM ON JUST A TRICKLE FROM THE BATTERY. I SWEAR, YOUR HEART IS PUTTING OUT MORE ELECTRICITY THAN I AM.

The Sergeant just stood there, looking at Nabil, then each one of his sons, then Kris. "Talk to me, George. There's a truck and three cars making like they want to leave. Do I shoot their drivers," he flashed a toothy grin at Nabil, "shoot their tires, or let them go their way?"

"Sarge, I got two targets, maybe three. I'm not sure. They never are there long enough for me to get anything like a fix. They keep jumping frequency and location."

"Tell me something, George, or I'm gonna start shooting," the Sarge said, but his hand didn't go for his gun. Neither did he wave Nabil out of the lot.

"It looks like one signal is in the kitchen, or maybe in the dining room. The other's in the back parking lot. East to northeast section."

"That's half the parking lot."

The smoker tossed what was left of his cigarette in a mud puddle and started for the back door.

NELLY, WE HAVE ONE CRACK AT THIS. ORDER THE TWO DE-COYS TO BEGIN TRANSMITTING IN FIFTY-NANOSECOND HET-ERODYNED BURSTS, NO MORE THAN ONE SECOND APART, NO LESS THAN HALF A SECOND.

DONE.

"Sarge, something's happening. Something in the east northeast part of the back parking lot."

"Get your butt back here."

A gray car with several whip antennas turned into the distant northeast corner of the restaurant and drove slowly toward the Sergeant. The smoker paused to let it pass.

"It's settled down, boss. It's right ahead of me. It's not moving much."

"Get out of here," the Sarge told Nabil as he pulled an aerosol can off his belt and began spraying it in front of him. Nabil put his truck in drive, turned hard, and missed the cars parked on the south side of the lot by a few millimeters.

"I'm not seeing anything, George," the Sergeant shouted as Nabil gunned his motor.

"Are you sure you ain't reading tea leaves, George?" was the last Kris heard. In a moment, Nabil accelerated into a break in traffic.

PUT DECOYS ON RANDOM.

DONE. NOW CAN I LOOK AT OUR TAKE?

NO. NOT UNTIL I TELL YOU.

WHEN WILL THAT BE?

WHEN I TELL YOU.

WHY?

BECAUSE I'M THE MOTHER, Kris almost shouted, but managed to keep her jaw from moving.

"What was happening, Father?" the youngest said, sounding almost like a child.

"I do not know," Nabil said. "Maybe we will find out on the news tonight."

"Only if they want us to," his eldest said, then glanced at Kris. He started to say something, seemed to think better of it, folded his arms tighter across his chest, and leaned back.

Nabil drove on, his breath coming fast and shallow. They turned at several corners, seemed to be going in no particular direction. He finally glanced at Kris. "Son of my sister's brother-in-law, you are slow, clumsy, and you could have cost me every penny I will make today if you had dropped that lamb and that woman had taken it for her own profit."

Kris ducked her head, risking not a word.

"I will talk to my sister tonight, but I will not have you work more with me today." The truck slowed and pulled over to the curb at a stop light. "Fatima's Kitchen is down this road a ways," he said pointing Kris to the right. "You can walk back to her while I make the last of my deliveries."

Kris again ducked her head, quickly opened the door, and stepped down to the cracked and broken concrete of the sidewalk. As the elder boy closed the door behind her, she could hear the younger one saying, "Father, that boy was a—"

"Shush, son, we will talk no more about this today."

The older boy leaned out the open window and winked back at Kris as the truck drove off. Kris took two steps toward Sorir's place and decided her cover did not require she limp all the way back. A moment leaning in the shade of a leather shop got the pebble out that someone had been kind enough to glue to the heel of her shoe. It had not put a run in a bulletproof stocking, but it sure had made her miserable.

Walking now was fine. Kris found her arms swinging; her pace fell naturally into the precise cadence the DI demanded. The day was still gray, but Kris felt damn good about a tough job well done. The urge to whistle a marching tune came, but she swallowed it. It would be totally out of place here. Still, Kris swung along, covering the distance.

A black-and-white car with Police lettered across the sides

cruised slowly by. The normal mad bustle of traffic made space for it. Kris cut her pace, lowered her head, and went back to being a properly humble Arab teenager. The woman riding shotgun kept up the same kind of alert three-sixty observation that Jack did. Her eyes paused as she took in Kris, then passed on.

NOW CAN I LOOK AT THE DATA TAKE, KRIS?

WHY DIDN'T YOU TELL ME THERE WAS A COP COMING?

YOU DID NOT TELL ME TO. NOW CAN I LOOK AT OUR TAKE?

NELLY, FOR A COMPUTER, YOU'RE DEVELOPING A ONE-TRACK MIND.

I AM FULLY CAPABLE OF MULTITASKING, KRIS. YOU, HOW-EVER, ARE GIVING ME VERY CONFUSING INSTRUCTIONS. FIRST YOU TELL ME TO BE TOTALLY QUIET, JUST KEEP A TRICKLE OF ENERGY GOING. THEN YOU ASK WHY I DO NOT MAINTAIN A FULL SITUATIONAL SURVEILLANCE. TELL ME WHAT YOU WANT! AND CAN I LOOK AT WHAT THE BUGS GOT?

Kris remembered arguing like this with Eddy, her six-year-old brother. But Eddie had been kidnapped and left to die twelve long years ago. Kris shivered, then took a deep breath and let the ghosts out, forcing herself to concentrate on the now.

YOU MAY LOOK AT THE DATA IN A MOMENT. FIRST TELL ME IF WE ARE UNDER SURVEILLANCE. ARE THERE CAMERAS WATCHING US? BUGS LISTENING TO US? ARE THERE MORE COPS AROUND?

NO, NO, AND YES, THERE'S ANOTHER COP COMING UP BE-HIND US.

No, no? Kris's gut was doing flips and flops; she was struggling to keep every muscle and bone in her body lashed down and doing just what she wanted. The order of her last set of questions to Nelly had some how fallen out of active memory.

NO CAMERAS, KRIS. NO MIKES EITHER. I AM NOT PICKING UP ANY EVIDENCE OF NANOS. OTHER THAN THE HUMAN COPS, I HAVE NOTHING THAT COULD THREATEN US IN RANGE OF MY SENSORS. NOW CAN I LOOK?

ARE THERE MORE COPS THAN NORMAL?

KRIS, I DO NOT KNOW WHAT NORMAL IS AROUND HERE. REMEMBER, I WAS ALMOST OFF-LINE AND NOT DOING A LOT OF LOOKING.

NELLY, I LEFT MY VIEWING GLASSES IN MY PURSE, SO I CAN'T LOOK AT WHAT WE COLLECTED UNTIL I GET BACK TO FATIMA'S KITCHEN.

YES, BUT IF I START PROCESSING RIGHT NOW, I CAN HAVE IT ALL ORGANIZED AND CORRELATED FOR YOU. Nelly was wheedling.

IS IT THAT IMPORTANT TO YOU, NELLY?

I WANT TO KNOW WHAT IS GOING ON AT THAT BIG PLANT. YES, I DO. I WANT TO KNOW. I AM CURIOUS. SO SUE ME.

So sue me. Where did that come from? Kris found herself shaking her head in wonderment as the next cop drove by. Only one fellow in this one, and he was too busy picking his way through traffic to do much looking around. Maybe this was just the normal way of things in the Arab quarter.

NELLY, MAKE A FULL REPORT OF THESE CONVERSATIONS WITH BACKUPS OF YOUR PROCESSING THAT SUPPORTED THEM, AND STORE IT FOR REVIEW BY AUNTIE TRU WHEN WE GET BACK.

DONE.

NOW YOU MAY LOOK AT THE FEED.

DOING IT, Nelly snapped and went very quiet. Kris continued her saunter down the street, eyes fixed on the cracked and narrow sidewalk. Old cars and pickup trucks rubbed against the low curbs or were half on them, adding their daily bit to the crumbling. She tried not to jostle any of her fellow pedestrians, even as she studied how other youths reacted upon meeting their elders. Most said something that probably passed as the local equivalent for "Hello" or "How are you?" Kris didn't dare say a word. Still, she nodded and hoped her silence met at least part of the proper respect due those she passed.

The streets were looking familiar just as Nelly announced, THERE IS A LOT OF ACTIVITY ON THE POLICE BANDS. IT IS CODED, AND IT WOULD TAKE ME TIME AND PROCESSING TO BREAK IT. SHOULD I?

ARE THE SOURCES CLOSING ON US?

I CANNOT TELL.

Schooling every muscle in her body to walk no differently than the other youths on the street, Kris passed a greengrocer, then a clothing store, followed by a silversmith, tanner, and a dry goods store, all small, all probably owned by the people standing at each door, encouraging walkers to stop in or talking to the next store owner. Kris was about to cross the street when another black-and-white rolled by, moving fast. Kris crossed the street, then leaned against a fruit stand, trying to spot where the cops were collecting.

No cop convention was obvious. Somewhere a siren lit up, then quickly went silent. No flashing lights in sight. Kris sauntered up the cross street. In a nondescript shamble, she did a series of block-long zigs and zags, using most of the few windows to check behind her.

If someone was following, they were too good for her. A few more cops rolled by; none showed interest in her. After five minutes of weaving and no nano report from Nelly, but, MORE COPS ARE HEADED THIS WAY, Kris ducked into the back door of Fatima's Kitchen.

16

"Kind of you to drop by," Sorir growled. "Nabil's been stopped. They have nothing on him, but they will if they find the young man they are looking for. That boy must disappear. Here, put this on," she said, handing Kris a bundle that shook out into a head-to-toe garment she'd seen on some women in the street. "Off with the shoes," Sorir ordered. "You must be barefoot."

Kris reeled; Nabil and his boys had done nothing. What would the Sergeant in gray do to them? Numb, she stepped out of the shoes and took off the cap. As she slipped into the robe, she automatically checked Nelly's antenna. *If I gave myself up . . . Nabil would not be better off. Keep marching, soldier.*

"Walk like you're pregnant and follow me," Sorir said.

"How do you walk like that?"

"You've seen other women—" but Kris cut her off.

"Not among the people I know."

Sorir grabbed a five-gallon can of tomato paste. "Here, put this in your pants." Kris did; it must have weighed thirty pounds. It threw her off balance and made her awkward.

"This is pregnant?"

"Close enough. Follow me." Sorir ducked out the back and

led Kris rapidly down the alley to a small door that opened on a narrow stairway. Up the stairs was a large, unlit room. Windows high in the roof's eaves let in light to show dust motes and piles of dark cloth and large bales of brightly colored thread. In the shadows four women, well hidden by their robes, worked at their weaving, slowly adding lines of thread to three partially done rugs hanging from the walls. Three toddlers kept them company while two smaller babies lay in baskets. The place smelled of dust and cloth, women and babies. One tiny woman turned from her work. The veil of her robe hid her face, but Kris flinched from the feel of sharp eyes that missed nothing.

"So this is the one," a voice firm if old snapped from within the robe. "You ask much, wife of my youngest son."

Sorir bowed. "I ask only what he needs. He and all of us."

"You are sure of that?" the elder woman said, reaching for Kris and finding her elbow after only one miss. "Then we will do as Allah may will. You will work with Tina. She is the slowest of us; maybe you can help her. She is pregnant and can show you how you are supposed to walk. You march like a soldier."

"I will try not to," Kris said, following the older woman.

Sorir turned to go but stopped after only a step. "You are not barefoot, young woman."

"I kicked off the loafers," Kris said.

"But you wear stockings. No modest woman would wear such a thing."

Kris looked down at herself from inside the robe. Shirt and pants only overlay the armored bodysuit. It was supposed to protect her. Here, it would give her away as sure as a clown suit. Made of Super Spider Silk, no scissors could cut out the feet. "Just a moment," Kris said as she undid the shirt and pants. They vanished under a pile of rags. The girdle she could put back on. The bodysuit took a while. Nelly was ticking off the eighth or ninth police cruiser to halt in the area as Kris handed over the suit.

The old woman took it, held it up to get a good look at it, sniffed, and said, "What do we do with this?"

"Give it to Tina and tell her to wrap it around her belly," Sorir suggested.

"No. I will not do that to my youngest granddaughter," the

old woman said. "You, stranger, you wrap it around yourself. Let no one say we knew what was being done here."

"Let it be upon me," Kris said, taking it back. She pulled the armored girdle back on—*at least I won't get gut shot*—and wrapped the bodysuit around herself, knotting it at her back. It held the can of tomato paste very well.

Sorir stood back, took a good, long look at Kris, and said, "That will have to do. But, woman, you are too tall."

"That's what my mother says," Kris said. "Thank you for all that you have risked. I hope Nabil is safe."

"Nabil will live as Allah wills. Just you make sure that all this is not a waste," Sorir said over her shoulder, leaving.

Kris turned to meet Tina. The woman sat in front of a rug. She looked up at Kris through the veil of her robe that showed nothing of her face. "Come, stand beside me. I can pass the threads up to you, and you run them through the top of the loom. Then pass them back to me. You will save me from having to stand up so often. I and the baby will bless you for that."

"When is the baby due?" Kris said. There wasn't much she knew about pregnancy, but that question always seemed to pop up.

"Only another month to go. This is my first," the woman said. Not even the robes could hide the pride in that statement.

POLICE ARE GOING SHOP TO SHOP, LOOKING FOR YOU, Nelly said. THE COPS DOING THE SEARCH ARE NOT BEING TOLD, BUT THE OFFICERS IN CHARGE STRONGLY SUSPECT THAT THEY ARE LOOKING FOR PRINCESS LONGKNIFE.

OH JOY. SO MUCH FOR MY COVER. HOW'S THE DATA ANALYSIS?

COMING ALONG. Nelly sounded evasive.

YOU OUGHT TO HAVE AN INITIAL CALL BY NOW.

I DO NOT WANT TO MAKE ONE CALL, THEN HAVE TO CHANGE IT.

NELLY, ARE YOU AFRAID OF MAKING A MISTAKE?

IF I TELL YOU WHAT I THINK WE FOUND, YOU WILL WANT TO SEND IT TO SEVERAL PEOPLE. THAT WILL EXPOSE US TO EVEN GREATER RISKS THAN WE ARE PRESENTLY RUNNING. I WANT TO BE SURE.

AND YOU ARE NOT QUITE SURE YET THAT WHAT YOU'VE GOT IS . . .

LARGE NAVAL-SIZE LASERS. THREE PRODUCTION LINES OF EIGHT-INCHERS. AND SEPARATE PRODUCTION LINES FOR FOURTEEN-, SIXTEEN-, AND EIGHTEEN-INCHERS.

EIGHTEEN-INCHERS!

YOU DO NOT THINK *THE PRIDE OF TURANTIC* COULD CARRY A PRESIDENT-CLASS WEAPONS SUITE? Kris thought about the liner that had brought them here. Peeled of its luxury, it was a very large hull. With several feet of ice for protection and a dozen eighteen-inchers, could it stand up to the battlewagons Kris had dodged during the action at the Paris system? No question.

RATE OF PRODUCTION ON THOSE BIG MOTHERS, NELLY?

I AM WORKING ON THAT. AND REMEMBER, LASERS ARE ONLY AS GOOD AS THE POWER PLANTS BEHIND THEM. WE HAVE NOT FOUND THEIR SOURCE.

NELLY, THERE'S AN OLD SAYING: WHERE THERE'S SMOKE, THERE'S FIRE. YOU DON'T MAKE LASERS IF YOU DON'T HAVE THE POWER TO SHOOT THEM. WE'VE FOUND THE SMOKING GUN. THE DOCKS ON HIGH TURANTIC ARE CONVERTING SIXTY OR SEVENTY MERCHANT SHIPS INTO A FLEET THAT WILL MAKE IT THE NINTH LARGEST IN HUMAN SPACE.

AND YOU CAN HARDLY WAIT TO TELL SOMEONE ABOUT IT.

NO, NELLY, WE WILL WAIT. FINISH YOUR ANALYSIS. THEN START CONVERTING OUR NANOS INTO SOMETHING THAT COULD FLY A FEW MILES FROM HERE AND CALL SOME FOLKS WHO NEED TO KNOW THIS.

REMOTE CALL HOME. THAT MIGHT GET THEM OFF OUR TAIL. SPEAKING OF WHICH, FOUR COPS JUST CAME INTO THE SHOP BENEATH US.

"They come," the old woman said before Kris could get out a word of warning. The women concentrated on their work. Kris passed the thread back and forth between herself and the young woman, working wordlessly. She tried stooping; the weight of the tomato paste can was heavy on her back. She handed the thread down, then put her right hand to her back and tried to ease the pain. The woman did her part, then reached up with the thread.

"That is what you do when you carry a child." Kris could almost hear the smile with the voice.

There was noise on the stairs, voices shouting, wood creaking under heavy steps. The two oldest toddlers, maybe two or

three years old, rushed to the door. The third clung to her
mother's clothes, whimpering. A man in a long white robe
reaching to his shoes, a black vest, and a small brimless hat
backed into the door. "These women are my wife, her mother,
and family. They are harem. No unrelated man may look on
them."

A strong hand shoved the man back. Three men in the gray
uniforms of SureFire Security swaggered in. One child raced
to the man shouting "Pa-pa, Pa-pa." The man scooped him up
and tried to shush him. The other child scampered for the
other woman, screaming. The third toddler joined in with lusty
lungs. The baskets with babies began tentatively to add to the
racket. The old woman confronted the grays, hands waving
under her robe like a child playing ghost under a sheet. Her
voice came high and loud and fast in a flowing language Kris
did not follow.

WELL, I CAN, said Nelly, AND SHE'S CALLING THOSE COPS
THINGS THAT WOULD MAKE A CAMEL BLUSH BUT NOT USING
ONE WORD OF PROFANITY.

"Would you shut her up," the man with the chevrons of a
Corporal demanded of the white-gowned man.

He started talking, only adding more noise. As the uproar
crescendoed to new levels, the two gray-suited men behind
the Corporal flinched away.

"Ig, pat down that hen," the Corporal ordered, putting himself between the local man and the woman he wanted searched.

"You cannot do that," the man shouted.

The Corporal made to push the fellow back, but the child in
his arms snapped at his hand. He yanked it out of range of the
toddler's teeth.

The local man shouted something to his mother-in-law,
then continued arguing with the Corporal. "I know my rights.
You infidels cannot touch our women with your lustful hands.
You must call for a woman! You must. I will sue you! My
son's brother-in-law is a member of the bar. I will sue!"

The old woman, meanwhile, was slapping at Ig's hands as
he halfheartedly tried to follow orders.

The Corporal finally brought everything to a halt by
screaming, "All right. Stop the search. I'll call for a woman."

The men in gray retreated to the doorway. The local man

and his mother-in-law were joined by his wife as the three of them soothed the toddlers. The other woman calmed the babies. Tina and Kris worked their rug.

Five minutes later, a large, heavyset woman in security gray and sporting Sergeant stripes pushed her way through the men. "You got a problem, Corporal?"

"Yes, ma'am. These women insist on being searched by a woman."

"Don't *ma'am* me, Corporal. I work for a living. I look like Princess Longknife to you?"

"It was your beauty that dazzled him," came from behind the Corporal.

The Sarge elbowed the Corporal aside none to gently and reached for the tiny grandmother. She pulled up the robe a few inches, revealing small and withered feet. "We're looking for a guy, close to six feet tall. This old biddy look big, Corporal?"

"No, Sarge."

"Fine. You checked the man?"

"Already did, downstairs. He owns the place, and he's too fat and short to be our guy," he said with a nasty smile.

The local man glowered at him through heavy black eyebrows.

The Sergeant reached for the next woman. "Now this one just might be our kid all hunched over." She yanked the robe up to show a toddler nursing contentedly at the woman's breast.

The Corporal tried to peel the local man off the Sergeant. The tiny grandmother got a good wack at the Corporal's knee, leaving the security man hopping on one foot and the other two guards still trying to free the Sergeant. The kids naturally helped the situation by screaming like they'd never been fed.

When things finally resolved themselves, the local man and his mother-in-law were under guard on one side of the room with two kids clinging to them. His wife was back to making soothing noises to the child under her robe, and the Sergeant gave the other mother, now changing a child's smelly diaper, a search that didn't extend past a pat on the back.

"You two," she said pointing at Tina and Kris and waving them away from the rest. "Over there, now."

Kris gave Tina a hand up. The woman stood, massaged her back with a groan, and then waddled, one hand beneath her stomach, the other on her back, to where the Sergeant pointed. Kris did her best to imitate the expectant mother. It did go easier on her back if she supported the can with a hand under it. It was impossible to tell in the dim light, but it sure looked like the Sergeant blanched. "Put your backs to that wall," she ordered.

Tina did, and if anything, got her belly farther out. Kris slouched against the wall, getting as short as she could.

"Lift up your skirts. Let me see your feet."

Tina did, using the hand beneath her belly. Again, Kris did likewise.

Visibly unhappy that nothing was solved by that, the Sarge reached for Tina. The pregnant woman seemed to half fall, half stumble into the big security woman, then screamed and fell sideways onto several bales of thread. Her robe came up, showing bare legs to everyone . . . and to Kris that she was not wearing anything under the robe.

"The baby, he comes!" was drowned out as every grown-up started shouting, every child screamed, and the guards, not sure what to do, backed toward the door. Kris let out a scream and went to her knees between Tina's, waving wildly and pointing.

The Sergeant bolted for the door. "Nobody here but a bunch of crazy bitches that don't know enough not to be bare-foot and pregnant."

"You gonna help her have her baby?" the Corporal asked as the Sarge went by him.

"What kind of a woman do you take me for?" she snapped.

The children cried; Tina let out a few intermittent shouts to hurry them on their way. In less time than most routed armies needed to cover the ground, the guards were gone.

"What do you think you are doing?" the tiny grandmother asked Tina as the old woman pulled the younger's robe properly around her legs.

"Practicing," Tina said, and let out another shout.

"That is not the way Milda taught you to breathe. And if you do, you will hurt a lot more than I did with any of mine."

"But they do not know it," Tina said with an imp's voice.

The little woman swatted her granddaughter through her robe, then turned to Kris. "Allah has smiled on us this time. How much longer must we trust in His mercy?"

"We will try to remove her as soon as we can," her son-in-law said, coming to her side.

"I need to be where I am going by six or seven," Kris said.

"No doubt you must primp for a party," the old woman added dryly.

"Yes, I have been ordered to be at a party tonight."

That sparked low words among the women, but the grandmother only shook her head within her robes. "What kind of a party is it when you must be ordered to it?"

"Only the usual type that I go to."

"Girls, do not envy this one. She has found toil where any of you would find joy."

A young man hurried up the stairs. Without a pause he rushed to where Tina lay. Kris did not follow the language they spoke, but she could tell the fear and endearments that filled their words. Done, the man rose and turned to Kris without hesitation as to which robe hid her.

"A cab will call for you in five minutes. It is expecting a sick man who is going to the dentist. Here."

The man began stripping out of his vest and gown. Kris started to pull the robe over her head, but the grandmother stopped her. "Wait until my grandson is gone."

"But, Grandmother, she is an infidel. She has no modesty."

"But I have modesty, and I will not have my granddaughter's husband lusting after some infidel djinn." Down to slacks and white T-shirt that passed for modest male attire on six hundred planets, the man shrugged and vanished back down the stairs.

Kris pulled the robe over her head, yanked down the girdle, and began working her way back into the transparent bodysuit.

"Why would a respectable woman wear such a thing?" the grandmother sniffed.

"Because it will stop a four-millimeter bullet at five paces," Kris said without looking up.

"Oh," came with surprise and maybe a hint of acceptance. "You fear the world so much that you need dress as this?"

"Do you not recognize her, Mother? Some of us saw her picture on the news yesterday." When the old woman did not answer, her daughter continued, "She is the Princess Longknife, more wealthy than Ali Baba, more powerful than—"

"And running scared just now," Kris cut in as she finished with the suit and wiggled into the girdle. "I cannot tell you how much what you have done for me today means."

The tiny woman stood in front of her. "Is it true that you could not find it in your heart to give the vaccine to those dying people who needed it up north? That you, who have so much wealth, have allowed all of us to live in fear of it spreading because our government would not meet your demands for more money? If that is true, you truly live in poverty."

"Grandmother, I swear to you by every breath my father and grandfather take for the rest of their lives that they would have given every drop of that vaccine to you and the people of this world and taken not one penny in return, if someone had not stolen it from our warehouse," Kris said, staring into the gray mesh veil of the old woman's gown.

The woman helped Kris on with the white robe, then stooped for the vest that her grandson had dropped. "I believe you. What blackened souls there must be in this world that they would steal from you and make you who are so powerful fear them enough to dress as you do."

"And run around this city dragging people like you into the need to protect me," Kris said, putting her arms in the vest.

"Here is your hat," Tina said, handing it to Kris.

Kris took the moment to check on her antenna. IT WORKING OKAY, NELLY?

A BIT THE WORSE FOR WEAR, BUT GOOD ENOUGH TO KEEP UP WITH THE CLOWNS CHASING US.

As Kris settled the hat, woven from many colors, on the top of her head, the grandmother brought her a shawl. "May Allah bless and guide you," she said, putting it around Kris's shoulders and leaving a Princess feeling truly blessed.

Sorir appeared at the stair door. That sparked a discussion that Nelly explained was about the bad habits and lack of manners of the security people. This upper room was not the only place where the faithful had given them a good lesson in proper etiquette. What promised to be a long conversation was cut short when Sorir stepped close and gave Kris a small sack.

"Abdul has been sent home. Here is your maid's uniform, purse, and raincoat. I have also included a proper shawl for your head. Sometimes we women wear the edge of it over our mouths," she said, demonstrating. "Few would question even a maid for the Hilton who did that. May it help you today."

She paused for a moment. "Has all of this been worth it?"

"Watch the news tonight," was all Kris said. If she pulled off what she planned, even Sandfire couldn't keep what was going on in the space docks a secret.

Then again, so far, only she and Nelly knew what was going on there above their heads.

Sorir pulled up Kris's gown and used thick lengths of yarn to tie the dress and raincoat around Kris. "Now you begin to look like a man of substance. Here, let me add some lines to that face of yours," she said applying Kris's makeup pencil. By the time Kris headed downstairs, even she didn't recognize herself.

But the grandmother had one more suggestion. "You are going to the dentist. You need an abscessed tooth. Chew on this wad of red yarn. If Allah wills it, you may even look like you are spitting blood." Kris took it, a deep breath, and hurried down the stairs to face a day that might have finally decided to rain a bit. Fat raindrops slapped into her makeup, leaving her hoping her getup was waterproof.

But the older man was at her side, raising an umbrella. He guided her from the stairwell to the back door and into his rug shop. Hurrying her along, he talked in Arabic enough for two and had her out the front door before she had more than a second to see the piles of rugs on the floors or hanging from the walls.

A cab was blocking traffic, the young driver yelling and beckoning wildly as drivers behind him did the same while leaning on their horns. Kris had expected Abu, but there was no time to hesitate or argue. She was stuffed in the back, handed the umbrella, and the cab bounced off to more honking behind it.

The young man in the front seat seemed delighted to be moving. His windows were down, his radio blared something that might have some connection with his parents' culture, but Kris doubted they would admit it. He chomped on a mouthful of gum, keeping time with the music. When a light stopped them, he beat the wheel as if it were a drum.

He did not ask Kris for a destination.

They had gone six blocks, turning at every corner, before the man turned his head. "None of those gray camel farts are following us. There's a roadblock four streets up. You ready to crash it?"

"Crash it?" Kris said. *What kind of crazy have they given me this time?*

"You know, snake our way through this. Fake them out of their socks. I'll play the music, and you be the snake. Get you back up high where you belong."

"What do you say we don't do anything that will get us noticed."

"Not noticed. That's the way you want it," he said, going back to driving, but now beating on the wheel to the music even when they were moving. "That's the way you get it, man of my man."

The backup at the roadblock was two blocks long. Kris would have expected more, but there were a lot of cars parked beside the road, people with more time to spare than willingness to let the security folks paw around their vehicles. Kris leaned out the window, her head lolling against the back sill. Most cars passed the guards quickly. One or two got signaled to pull aside for a more thorough going over.

Kris ran a hand down her white gown, felt the bumps of the clothes she was wrapped in. She could not risk a pat down now any more than she could have earlier.

NELLY, DO YOU HAVE A FULL REPORT ON THAT PLANT?
DONE.

ANY PLANS FOR MESSENGERS IN YOUR DATABASE?

SEVERAL. I CAN MIGRATE SOME OF TRU'S SELF-ORGANIZING MATERIAL OUT TO THE NANOS. WITH A FEW MILLIGRAMS OF THAT STUFF, I CAN MAKE FOUR GOOD-SIZED MESSENGERS WITH HALF LEFT OVER. HOPE YOU WILL NOT NEED TO WEAR YOUR CROWN TONIGHT.

I CAN SKIP THAT. GIVE ONE MESSENGER SENATOR KRIEF'S PHONE NUMBER AND SEND IT NORTH. SEND THE SECOND ONE

TO THE WEST WITH THE NUMBER OF THAT WOMAN REPORTER
KLAGGATH LIKED YESTERDAY. ADDRESS THE THIRD TO MY
SUITE AND SEND IT EAST. THE LAST GOES TO THE AMBASSA-
DOR. SEND IT SOUTH.

ALL WILL GO TWO MILES AND FIND THE CLOSEST NET AC-
CESS, PATCH IN, AND TRANSMIT. SHOULD I HAVE THEM TRY TO
RECOVER ANYWHERE?

NO, TELL THEM TO DISSOLVE TOTALLY. NO EVIDENCE. BUT
HAVE THE AMBASSADOR'S MESSENGER ONLY GO ONE MILE.

THEY ARE GONE.

Now, if the rain just holds off a bit longer.

The line moved slowly; several more cars were hauled out
and sent for closer inspection, one with its passengers at gun-
point and hands up. The air was muggy, heavy with fumes.
One car tried to back out, but a gray uniform from the roadblock came running and ordered the driver back in line.

"But I need to go potty," came in a high-pitched plea.

The child got no mercy from the Sergeant. "Use a bottle."

Kris's driver turned up the music and added his palms to an
already pounding bass. Still five cars back, he drew frowns
from the gray-clad inspectors. Kris's moans were no longer
fake. Her teeth rattled in her head, and her skull was ready to
split.

Then again, her mouth was no longer dry. She hawked and
spat; it came out red on the street beside her.

NELLY, HOW SOON CAN THAT CALL GO OUT TO THE AM-
BASSADOR?

THE MESSENGER WAS WORKING CROSSWIND. IT MAY TAKE
A WHILE.

The music pounded on. The traffic moved in fits. Along the
line, other cars jacked up their music, everyone on a different
station. Kris leaned her head against the car door and quickly
yanked it away. The door vibrated like an overheated laser.

The car ahead pulled away with a screech of tires. The
cabby edged forward. The man in gray scowled down at him,
then bent over and snapped off the radio. "I've been wanting
to do that for half an hour."

"Hey, boss. Why you do dat? Dat fine music. Relax my
nerves," the cabby said, still pounding his palms on the wheel
to the now-silenced beat.

"Where you going?"

"Dentist downtown. Old fart in back, bad tooth. Hurting bad. Said he'd pay me double if I went fast. Dat before you guys made me park. You cost me, boss."

"It's gonna cost worst if we don't find who we're looking for. Let me see your license." The cabby grabbed for his papers but fumbled getting the license out of the protective plastic envelope that kept it displayed for passengers. As he muddled on, there were shouts between the two security cars and the black-and-white parked beside the roadblock.

NELLY?

THEY HAVE INTERCEPTED ONE OF THE MESSAGES.

INTERCEPTED OR JUST COPIED?

I CANNOT TELL. BUT THEY KNOW THAT A MESSAGE IS OUT THAT THEY DO NOT WANT OUT . . . AND THEY KNOW WHERE IT CAME FROM.

The cabby finally fished out the license, but the guard only glanced at it, dividing his attention between it and someone shouting at him from one of the cars. "What's your name?" he said, handing back the paper and directing the question at Kris. The black-and-white took off south.

"Old fart don't speak the English good like me," the cabby said and fired a stream of Arabic at Kris. She groaned, held her hand to her swollen mouth, and mumbled. Her words were lost as the first car full of SureFire Security gunned by, following the black-and-white.

"Saeed ab Towaan," the cabby said.

"Move along," the man in gray said as he turned and ran to the last car left, hurried along by shouts from a Corporal.

"Wait for them to go," Kris whispered.

"I was planning on that," the driver answered, his English suddenly as good as Kris's. He waited until there was no cross traffic, then accelerated away smoothly . . . and punched the radio for a different station, one that Kris actually liked, once he dialed down the volume.

Several cars whizzed by them, trying to make up time for the traffic stop. The cabby settled into traffic, then glanced back at Kris. "So, where do you want to go?"

"The elevator," she said, spitting out the wad of yarn.

"One quick trip to the beanstalk coming up," he said, signaling to change lanes. "I assume you know what that was all about."

"I probably do," Kris said.

"But Uncle Abu said you probably wouldn't tell me anything."

"If I were you, I'd listen to your uncle," Kris said, fidgeting out of her vest and pulling her arms out of the gown's so she could untie the raincoat and maid uniform.

"Yeah, but old farts are always scared. When you're young, you got to live a little." He was smiling as he said that.

"Take some advice from a young fart. Pay attention to the old farts, and you may get to live a little," Kris said as she lay out her brown uniform and began wiggling out of the gown.

"So it is that bad," the fellow said, but his seriousness didn't stay long. "Hey, you're the first gal to strip in my cab. Abu told me it had happened to him, but I thought he was just spinning a tale. Hold it, you're ruining the view," he said as Kris slipped off the seat, hiding in the foot well.

"Sorry about that," she said as she pulled the dress over her head.

"Oh boss, this just isn't fair. I risk my handsome young neck to help this pretty infidel gal, and I don't even get to sneak a peek."

Kris settled the dress around her and began buttoning it up. "Who told you life was fair?"

He eyed her in the rearview. "At least you got good boobs." Kris failed to stifle a laugh. But then, if most of the women around him had been in those baggies, hers probably were the best he'd gotten a glance at. She finished buttoning up her uniform.

"That's kind of wrinkled," the driver said. A glance down, and Kris had to agree. If she ditched her raincoat on her way in the back, her slovenly uniform might very well get nabbed by the hotel's equivalent of a Top Kick and ordered back home. Problem was, she'd never convince the shrew that her home was the Presidential Suite.

Time to rethink matters.

Their arrival at the elevator station postponed that. Kris

found herself looking at a three-digit cab bill and only a few coins in her pocket. The kid laughed as he pushed away her offered credit chit. "Uncle Abu warned me you probably wouldn't have money for the cab. It's on him," he said pulling cash from his pocket. "Here's your beanstalk fare."

"I can't take that," Kris stammered.

"And I'm not running that card through my cab. Neither one of us needs the notice, and you need to get back up in the sky. We're Arab, Princess, not stupid. But you're making me wonder about your people."

"We're not stupid," Kris said, taking the money. "We're just proud and stubborn."

"And maybe not used to living on our streets," the cabby said with a seriousness that belied his youth. "I'll tell Uncle I got you to the beanstalk safe and sound. You figure you can handle it from here?"

Kris glanced up at the towering elevator. "I've gone up enough of these. I should be able to take care of myself."

17

With a laugh, the kid vanished into traffic.

Kris threw the shawl around her head and half covered her face. She lowered her head like anyone going to a job she hated and waited patiently in line to feed cash into the turnstiles before merging into the herd heading up. Four o' clock was close enough to a shift change to give her plenty of company. For the half-hour ride, she kept moving, made three trips through the coffee shop, and didn't spot anything like a tail. She did ID a transit cop busy helping a plumber work a stopped drain in the ladies' room.

She also came up with a plan that just might get her back to her suite.

Following the herd off the ferry, Kris took an elevator out to Circle One, the huge promenade that was the station's largest deck. A slide car took her from Stop One up to Stop Twenty-two, a three-minute walk from the Hilton. Kris had Nelly order Jack to meet her in the lobby, Number 3 door.

JUST PASS THE MESSAGE TO HIM. NO TALK. NO REPLY.
DONE.
ANY EXTRA ACTIVITY ON THE POLICE NET?
NO. CORRECTION, YES. IT IS GETTING MORE ACTIVE. ALL

SCRAMBLED. GIVE ME TEN MINUTES, AND I CAN READ IT.

I'D NEED TO KNOW WHAT'S HAPPENING IN THREE MIN-
UTES, OR IT'S HISTORY. DON'T WORRY. JUST LET ME KNOW IF
THERE'S A LOT OF POLICE ACTIVITY CLOSE TO US.

Kris kept her head down and her pace even as she walked
by the first door into the Hilton. It was clear. But the long,
lonely walk across the lobby to the elevators offered too many
chances to notice her and intercept. Kris kept walking.

Three out-of-breath security guards in gray were just coming to a stop at the main entrance to the lobby as Kris walked
past. By the time they started looking around, all she presented was her back.

The third entrance's wide arch led directly to the elevators.
Two SureFire Security types were getting themselves comfortable in the doorway when Jack, Klaggath, and three of
Kris's security types burst past them. Kris took a sharp right
into their ranks. Jack and the agents did a rapid about-face and
surrounded Kris in a comfortable box. They charged back
through the grays so fast the guards hardly had time to get
their mouths open before Kris was past them. Kris spat out the
cheek expanders and stuffed them, along with her scarf, in the
pocket of her brown raincoat as Jack took it off her and Klaggath wrapped her in a royal blue one with a large diamond
crown pendant on the right lapel.

She was almost to the elevator before running footsteps
came up behind her, and a harsh whisper said, "We need to
talk to that maid."

Kris whirled; Jack and Klaggath turned to stand between her
and the grays. Another agent summoned an elevator. "What
maid?" she demanded in her mother's most irritated voice.

Both grays, the senior a Sergeant, bumbled into Kris's team
and bounced back. What looked to be a Captain led a contingent
from the main door, but they were well off. The two in Kris's
face mumbled something that sounded like "that brunette."

"We have appointments to keep. When you have something to say, call our embassy," Kris said regally, turned, and
was in the elevator and the doors shut before anyone in gray
could recover.

"That was fun," she laughed.

"That was too damn close," Jack growled.

"That was something only I could have pulled off," Kris pointed out.

"And just what have you pulled off?" Klaggath asked.

"Nothing, nothing at all," Kris said, demurely settling herself on the elevator couch and making sure the raincoat covered her brown uniform. One security man frowned a question at Klaggath. He shook his head firmly, and all of them took to studying the elevator door for the rest of the trip.

Once in, Abby took over, almost dragging Kris into the bathroom and barely giving her time to get out of her dress and body stocking before dunking her in the bath. "Wash your face with this," she ordered, and Kris's makeup came off easily.

Kris waited until Nelly announced, "All clear, but I had to zap the four bugs we picked up in the lobby."

"How's Penny?" Kris asked.

"Doing as well as you can expect," Abby said. "Jack, you want to come here. She'll want to know about that message you got."

"We got it," was all Jack said. Kris glanced over, but he was out of sight, so she was, also.

"Have you looked at it?"

"Looked at nothing but it since it came in. Big, bad layout. More guns than they need to arm the ships in dock. Somebody's expecting to have a lot more merchant ships available real soon."

"Damn." Kris sighed, enjoying the warmth of the tub but knowing she had to get out. "Abby, hand me a towel." The fluffy robe was clean and waiting for her. Jack stayed out of view while she made herself decent. *Damn nice of him.*

"Young woman," Abby said, "you have about fifteen minutes before I want you back in that tub so I can wash your hair and get you presentable for tonight. You are not going to a ball with hair looking like it should be pinned under a greasy wig."

"Only 'cause that's where it was today." Kris sighed and told Nelly to call the Ambassador.

"Yes," came a moment later.

"Mr. Ambassador. I am in receipt of a very strange message concerning unlicensed weapons construction. Have you by any chance seen anything like that?"

"I don't know," he said. "A long message came in not too

long ago, full of plant video and the likes. I passed it to my officer for trade negotiations. I haven't heard back from her.
Kris," his voice now a whisper as if that might reduce its digi-
tal distribution, "I am not sure that such material is legal and
in Wardhaven's best interests. If I wasn't afraid I might be destroying evidence needed to substantiate criminal charges, I
would suggest you erase the message entirely."

"That's an interesting point I hadn't considered," Kris said
as if that was her first encounter with such a thought. "Let me
know what the embassy's lawyer thinks. I suspect I have a
copy of the same message. If you think it should be destroyed,
I certainly would want to know."

"I'll keep you informed."

"Well, my maid is telling me I must do my hair for tonight.
Will I see you there?"

"Of course," he said, ringing off.

NELLY, GET ME SENATOR KRIEF. In a moment, the screen
showed a very harried woman.

"Make this quick, I'm on two other lines."

"Did you get a large message this afternoon?"

"I'm on two other lines with people who might be able to
tell me what to make of it."

"So I assume I won't see you at tonight's ball."

"Oh, no. I wouldn't miss it. Most of the people I need to
buttonhole will be there.

"See you there."

Two hours later, Kris was about ready to be there. Except,
"I guess we'll have to use your Navy tiara," Abby said, looking at the bare skeleton of the fancy one Mother had fallen for.

"Well, I could have Nelly use the dumb metal we have
around here somewhere to re-create Mother's concoction,"
Kris said.

"I can do that," Nelly said, voice enthusiastic to try her
hand at jewelry making.

"On second thought, let's go with the Navy tiara," Kris
said, spotting the ten-kilogram slug of Uni-plex in one of her
trunks. "It can only change shape three times and . . ." She let
the thought trail off unspoken.

"If you insist," Abby said, sniffing at the simple silver ring
the Navy provided.

"I could add some diamonds or rubies to it," Nelly offered.

"Enough. I'll wear the Order of the Wounded Lion. That ought to be enough jewelry for any outfit." Since tonight's dress was a lovely green, the blue sash and gold medallion went very well with it. Klaggath had a full team and a worried look on his face as they took the slide car to the top.

"Problem?" Jack asked him.

"Not here, but something's happening. Units are being ordered to new nets, ones I never knew we had. Lots of them. Not many of us on the main net."

"How close?"

"Midtown. Nothing near the station."

"A riot?"

"Doesn't sound like it. Princess Kristine, is your computer picking up anything?"

"Nelly?"

"Nothing unusual. There's a cat up a tree and several fire trucks are trying to catch it. All but two of the news stations are covering the story. So far, the cat's winning."

"Dumb animal," one of the agents snapped.

"I like cats," another said.

"Slow news night," Klaggath concluded.

Not if I and a few of my friends have any say. Kris grinned.

Kris stayed with the slide car as it went past the high exit and started to turn around, taking it to the lower station. She figured to save herself from the long walk down in these heels and avoid having her name shouted by the guy in knee britches. She should have finished the ride.

Her security detail walked right out of the car and into another equally large and no more willing to move aside set of tuxedoed security. While Klaggath and a goon twice his size tried to straighten out the gridlock, Kris stood on toes to see who the poor victim was.

"Hank?"

"Kris? Kris Longknife, is that you?"

"What are you doing here?" Kris called over three guards.

"Not going anywhere at the moment," Hank Peterwald laughed. Officially Henry Smythe-Peterwald the Thirteenth on a vast array of legal documents, he had the finely sculptured beauty parents with too much money tended to give children these days. Some parents, not Kris's. He also was heir to a fortune close to if not more than Kris's, depending on which market was doing better on any given day. Oh, and Auntie Tru was real sure his papa had tried to kill Kris a few times. Father, being Prime Minister, said there was insufficient evidence to present in a court of law. All that aside, Kris had hit it off well with Hank the one time they got together with no parents on the same planet.

Kris waved and started moving some of her blockers aside. Jack growled; one of the failed attempts on Kris's life occurred the day after she and Hank had a wonderful lunch. Kris was sure Hank had nothing to do with that hit. Well, fairly sure. Anyway, in a social situation, he was nice to be around. *And he couldn't kill me here in front of God and everybody.*

They finally got in touching range, had a good laugh, and both said, "So, what are you doing here?"

"Boys go first," Kris insisted.

"Dad has this huge pharmacy plant coming on-line. Caley Sandfire insisted it was the biggest ever and just the thing for my latest assignment. Anyway, I got here about five minutes before they closed the port. We tried to back off, but there were a half-dozen lasers backing up a very insistent port official yelling, 'Nobody goes nowhere,' so we didn't."

"It was about four hours later I tried to book a ship out of here. I'm still trying," Kris said.

"And they don't have the net fixed," he said, shaking his head. "My old man would have kittens and heads if that happened on Greenfeld." Kris knew the kittens were figurative. The heads were likely to be literal, at least in Grampa Trouble's opinion.

For social purposes, Kris laughed. "Fixing that net problem would have fixed a lot of my troubles. I wanted to order in some Ebola vaccine and get this quarantine lifted. Hey, that pharm plant of yours, it have anything good for Ebola?"

"Didn't I check that out, first thing," Hank said, rolling his eyes at the void above them, which included the stars and the rest of the universe. "They tell me Ebola is a bitch, takes a unique feed product and processing. Only three or four plants do that. Hey, didn't your grampa goodie-goodie say he was going to stockpile the stuff on every planet?"

"He did," Kris defended Grandfather Al. "Somebody stole our stock a bit before the outbreak."

"Lots of interesting coincidences here," Hank said. "But I must tell you, that is a dazzling dress you're wearing tonight."

Kris beamed and did a pirouette. Nearly backless, this dress was slinky with a slit up the right side. "Ought to be fun to dance in."

"Certainly better than the green things you were wearing last time I saw you. Green and wet and everyone hungry. By the way, how did that stuff I donated work out?"

Kris froze her smile in place, tried to school every muscle in her body to act just so. Would Hank actually ask if he knew the answer? She swallowed to get her voice just right. "Most of it came in very handy. We really needed those trucks."

"And the boats?" he asked, not a tick or quiver in his too beautifully handsome face.

"Had some problems," Kris said, lowering her eyes to study him through the lashes. "There was a glitch in the smart metal. Third time you changed their design, they fell apart."

"Good Lord, I never heard about that. I hope that didn't happen when you needed them."

What do I do now? Tell him the truth and let the chips fall, or tell a social lie and have fun tonight? His tuxedo fit him perfectly. What more could a woman ask for in a night out than his elbow to lean on.

"I was on a raging river in a particularly narrow canyon with the water rising when I found out," Kris said.

"Oh Lord. That's terrible, Kris. I'm sorry." And for a moment, that overly refined face looked like he meant it. Then Kris could almost see something click in behind his eyes, and her father warning her, "Never say anything we can be sued for."

"That sounds more exciting than what I'm doing," he said in a well-schooled voice. A smile came out that didn't quite reach his eyes. "Looks like you're still having all the fun."

He reached for the sash of the Wounded Lion and slowly ran it through his fingers. Was it an accident that one of his well-manicured nails also ran its way down between her breasts? "Earth must have liked whatever you did at that get-together in the Paris system," he said as Kris failed to suppress a shiver.

Maybe someday she'd tell him the truth, but not now, not in

front of everyone. "You know how it is, being a kid from the right family. Some old fools decide to put a crown on my great-grandfather's head, and a guy in the housewares department back on Earth sends a fancy for the new Princess's wardrobe."

"Yes. Dad is rather proud our money dates back to when the Pope still had an Army. I imagine if I looked through the back of my closet, I might find a few doodads as well," he said, but he no longer eyed Kris as a dance partner. No, it was more like the way you studied a cobra.

What must I look like to him?

"Pardon me," Jack said beside her. "We are blocking the car exits, and I think Mr. Sandfire is casting glances this way like he's looking for Henry but doesn't want to admit it."

Sure enough, Kris's main candidate for nemesis on this planet and a bevy of eye candy were circling in the distance, not enough to force eye contact, but not likely to be missed.

Hank started to frown but quickly suppressed it and morphed his face into a smile and a nod in Sandfire's direction. "He'll tie me up half the night with people who just want to be able to say they shook my hand," he told Kris through his smile.

"I have people I need to see, too," Kris admitted. "I'm surprised Ambassador Middenmite hasn't already nailed me."

"Duty calls," Hank said, turning to Kris, taking her right hand, and bowing to kiss it. What his thumb was doing on the palm of her hand was enough to make any girl go weak in the knees. *Buck up, Lieutenant, you've got business, remember.*

"Save a few dances for me," Hank said, glancing up while still in midbow, still with thumb playing with her hand, her knees, and all parts in between.

"Even if I have to kill a few social climbers to keep the slots open."

"Good. See you in an hour or so," he said as he turned.

"You having fun?" Jack asked.

Kris shrugged, which in this dress set off enough shimmering to make her a hazard to navigation. "Girl's got a right to spend a little time with a possible like soul." Clearly, Tommy's dance card was full of Penny.

Clearing his throat like some ancient duenna, Jack said, "I've spotted several of your political allies. You might want to edge to the left here."

With only a tiny helping of self-pity, Kris turned to duty. She waded through a small throng of social greetings before she and Senator Krief occupied the same quiet eddy in the flow of well-dressed and gorgeous people. The Senator cut through Kris's greetings with whispered glee.

"The President outmaneuvered himself, or at least the idiots telling him when and where to throw parties did. When I told Senator Earlic what happened to Nara, I didn't even have to hint that my daughter was set up for something and his daughter was gotten out of the way by the President's barbecue. He may be Conservative, but he's not blind, and this is only the latest in strange coincidences. You top that with the sudden call in the Congress for a vote on war with Hamilton, and you've got a lot of people wondering if we aren't being led around by our noses."

"Think you can defeat the vote?" Kris asked.

"It doesn't have a chance. My guess is their whip didn't do a nose count today. Bad move for them, very bad move."

"And the pictures you got today?"

"I'm not quite sure what I have, but I talked to someone who is. He says they show enough naval-size lasers to outfit a fleet twice the size of what we have parked in the yard below us. Makes you wonder why someone is spending money on so many more guns than we need," she said, slowing to a thoughtful pause.

"What's the size of Hamilton's merchant fleet?" Kris asked.

Do you want me to answer? Nelly said.

No.

"I don't know for sure," the Senator said, "but I understand it's larger than ours. Much larger." Her eyebrow rose in alarm. "A whole lot larger than ours."

"I think my computer can answer that. Nelly, do you have Hamilton's approximate tonnage and bottoms?"

"The Hamilton Merchant Marine is just a shade less than triple Turantic's in total standard tonnage. Their ships are, on average, slightly larger than Turantic, so the number of ships are about two and a half times Turantic's number. There, Kris, did I do it right for a human, not precise but in approximate terms she can use?

PERFECT, NELLY. INCLUDE AN "ATTA GIRL" IN YOUR RE-
PORT TO TRU.

ONLY ONE!

FOR NOW. NOW, QUIET.

The Senator edged herself over to a table and settled into a
chair. Kris did the same, her guards closing in to keep the
space hers. Kay shook her head slowly. "Hamilton doesn't
have so much as a patrol boat in orbit, not the last time I
checked. Damn that communications blackout."

"When do they say they'll have it fixed?" Kris asked.

"God only knows, and she ain't telling. Yesterday they announced they were tearing the entire system down to rebuild it
from scratch. But they'll be using the same parts. How will
that make it better?" the Senator asked the ceiling and the unblinking stars beyond it. "Worse, for the last couple of days
the problem up here has been knocking towns off our local
net. First time that happened, the news was all over it, insisting the place must have come down with Ebola and the government was hiding it. We sent a convoy racing up there, over
mountains and in the snow, no less. Even had a few newsies in
it. Everyone was fine, just terrified about what was happening
to the rest of the planet while they were out."

"Glad to hear that didn't last long."

"Ah, but we've had two more towns drop off net, and every
time, someone in the media starts talking about Ebola."

"It won't go away," Kris said.

"Or someone doesn't want it to."

"How is Bremen?"

"No more deaths reported. And Earlic heard something
very strange. They didn't actually do autopsies on the ones
who died. Just cremated the bodies."

"I thought Ebola was a pretty ugly way to die. Kind of hard
to mistake."

"It is, though the medical team in Bremen is pretty basic.
Still, the bodies are dust, and no one can find the blood samples they took for analysis."

"If they called it Ebola, they had to do blood tests."

"Yes, we have the computer reports of the tests, but no one
can find the blood samples to run a second test. All lost."

"Are they sure it was Ebola?" Kris asked.

"No question, they've got fifty-seven early cases of Ebola."

"Early cases?"

"Yes."

"How early?"

"Another interesting question. Since I only have Earlic's word that he heard this from someone who picked it up from a good friend who happens to know someone who has a relative in Bremen, you can understand it's kind of hard to get to the truth."

"In other words, a rumor." Kris tried to squeeze the sarcasm out of her smile, but it still must have looked bitter as lemon.

"Isn't it a mess? We're making decisions that could shape my daughter's future. My grandkids' future. And we're doing it by guess and by God. We may not all have computers like yours that are smart enough not to waste my time giving me tonnage to the last ounce, but we have some very good ones, and I can't say what's happening five hundred miles north of here, or on the next star system," Senator Krief said with a bitter laugh. "You know something? President Iedinka could be right, and I would never know it."

"Yes," Kris agreed.

The Senator spotted someone, waved to get his attention, then slipped by Kris's security cordon and launched into an animated discussion. Kris nodded to Jack to drop shields and found herself being introduced to three vineyard owners by Ambassador Middenmite. She smiled prettily, complimented the wines they had her sample, and tried to diplomatically praise all three without saying anything that would end up in tomorrow's advertising feed. When they moved off, the Ambassador held back.

"I was so sorry to hear about what happened to my assistant who was working with you. Damn bad show."

"Have you heard anything about who might have done it?"

"I'm sorry, but I have to admit I'm rather busy with other things at the moment. All those stories circulating about how Wardhaven has been favoring Hamilton over the years. I don't know where they come from. They say they're documented. There's nothing in our files to support them."

"But the media has 'full documentation' on their story?"

"Well, they say so. I can't say that I've seen the stuff; you know how newsies are about giving away anything that might reveal a source. But I know what we've bought from Turantic, and it's a good bit of business. I keep trying to get on shows, tell people all that we've done, but no one seems to be listening."

"Telling people what they already know isn't news."

"That's what they say. Damn, I wish I had more Wardhaven files. I assumed if we needed something we could order it from home. I didn't want trade confidential files on my system. I'm told security is good, but you hear of this teenager or that cute six-year-old who wandered into this or that on the net."

"Hard to know what is a good risk and what's too much," she agreed as the old man wandered off, shaking his head. Kris spent the next half hour shaking hands at a more leisurely pace. Either there were fewer people here tonight, or fewer wanted to brag tomorrow that they'd shaken the hand of a real Wardhaven Princess. Kris suspected it might be the latter.

An hour gone, Kris wondered if Hank might be getting near the end of his command performance. NELLY, COULD YOU RING UP HANK'S COMPUTER AND SEE IF IT WILL TELL YOU WHERE HE IS?

"I don't like that bored look on your face," Jack said. "You wouldn't be thinking it would be nice to spend some time with that good-looking trillionaire, would you?"

"And if I was?" Kris sniffed.

Jack scratched behind his ear, resettled his receiver in place, and shrugged. "I've been thinking of briefing Klaggath on the bad blood between your family and the Peterwalds. Wonder how he'd take to your spending time with—"

"What, a security risk? Hell, Jack, Hank knows as much about how the universe spins as I do."

"How about a major threat to your life and limb? Kris, he showed up on Olympia, and you almost got killed."

"My office got rocketed while I was away at lunch with Hank. That saved my life."

"Kris, you know about the other times as well as I. Damn it, woman, you're a big girl, now, and you need to start acting like one."

Problem was, Jack was right; she was acting like a big girl. Real grown woman. She whirled on Jack, wanting to ask him where he suggested she find a man, her man. Tommy was joining all the others that gravitated toward her since high school. They'd get near enough to her to get a good look, and look good, then grab onto someone else. If she was a bridesmaid to one more best of friends, she was going to . . . To what?

Behind Jack, Hank hove in view. As he spotted her, his face lit up in a smile that just about took in his whole body. He waved. Kris snorted, trying to drive out all the mixed feelings, put on a smile of her own, and waved back. Jack forced a smile as he turned and the two security teams began a careful approach as their primaries rushed into each other's arms.

KRIS, WE HAVE A PROBLEM, Nelly said.

"Hank, you got free early."

"Told Caley he could take some of his cronies and shove them. I had a dance card to fill up."

WHAT DO YOU MEAN, PROBLEM?

THERE IS A FIRE AT THE TURANTIC CAPITOL.

TURANTIC CAPITOL?

THE CAPITOL HOUSES THE LEGISLATURE. THE BUILDING IS BURNING.

Hank looked distracted two seconds after Kris found herself no longer staring into his eyes but off into space, both their arms slipping to their sides.

"Sounds like a minor problem," Hank said, but his voice didn't reflect that.

"They have, or had, a vote scheduled tomorrow on going to war with Hamilton. I hope the fire isn't bad," Kris said, but she could hear the doubt in her own voice.

"My report says the building is fully involved," Hank said.

Klaggath signaled to one of his agents, who stepped forward and pointed his hand, palm out. A heliograph of the capitol appeared before them, both the dome and the two wings fully involved in leaping flames.

"That building is stone," Kris said. "It can't burn like that, can it?" She glanced around.

An agent on Hank's team answered her. "There are reports of a lot of communications equipment, chemicals, not all listed on the authorized storage report, and more paper than anyone expected. Still, it's going up fast, way too fast."

Hank shook his head. "As my father would say, 'something is rotting in Denmark.' "

Kris ordered her gut to change gears, even as it screamed and screeched. "One does not dance while Rome burns. Bad PR, I remember someone saying. Want a rain check on those dances?"

"I see Caley headed this way. I get the impression you don't much like him."

"He's far down on my list of folks I enjoy," Kris agreed.

"Well, I'll go his way and you go your way, and maybe someday we'll end up in a quiet place by ourselves with nothing much to do."

"Sounds like a dream I have," Kris said, but Jack was pointing over her shoulder. Senator Krief headed for Kris with three or four other people who looked important. "See you when I can," she tossed over her shoulder without looking back.

Kris did look back when the Senator expended a second to measure the distance between her group and Sandfire's. Hank's elbow was in Calvin's iron grip, and he was being towed quickly away. She and Hank shared raised eyebrows for a moment before they concentrated on what was so dear to those around them.

"We have a problem," the Senator said, taking Kris's elbow and steering her toward Senators Showkowski and LaCross. The tall LaCross wore a light-green dinner jacket. The large woman senator was easy to spot in a bright-blue suit offset by an orange blouse and gay scarf.

"They've arrested Kui and Earlic," Showkowski blurted out.

"They can't," LaCross said. "We have legislative immunity."

Father put up with some pretty shabby antics from members of his own party and the opposition. Kris had heard him, snarling under his breath, that he'd rather do that than set the precedent that you could use any old pretext to jail a congressman and change a vote. "You start down that path, and you have nothing between you and tyranny. Nothing!"

Someone was going flank speed down that path.

"What are the charges?" Kris said as softly as she could and be heard among the Senators as they repeated and denied the same report. She repeated herself three times before they quieted.

"They've just been hauled in. No charges yet."

NELLY?

I AM SEARCHING. NO CHARGES REPORTED. THEIR APPRE-
HENSION HAS NOT BEEN REPORTED ON ANY OF THE MEDIA.

Kris had Nelly repeat that for the Senators.

"He can't do this!" came from three senators.

"Someone has. Who?" Kris asked.

Klaggath answered her. "It has to be President Iedinka. No
cop would dare do that without express orders."

"I'm calling him this minute," Krief said, staring at the
floor. A moment later, she looked up, eyes wide. "He's unavailable. Izzic is unavailable, and no one on his staff will take
my call. Someone always has something to say to a Senator!"

Today looked like a day where *always* or *never* didn't apply. Kris glanced around. She couldn't see them, but she
didn't doubt that anything said here was going straight to the
President or to the type of security people who hauled Senators and congresspeople off to jail. Time to take this discussion off the record.

"Excuse me," Kris said, "I have a suite in the Hilton. I also
have a security guard that can assure that what we talk about
will be secure," Kris said, glancing over their heads.

"Oh," "Right," came back to her without much conviction
for the need.

"Why don't we adjourn? And if someone decides any of you
need arresting, I could at least raise Wardhaven sovereignty.

"In a hotel room?"

"Hey, I'm new at this Princess stuff. I've got a security
team, and even if I don't quite have the diplomatic power I
think I have, it will slow things down and force a conversation."

None of the Senators seemed all that persuaded, but Kris
was moving for the slide way and her agents with her. The
Senators, caught up in her bubble, sidled along.

Kris had started the day hoping just to get a few good pictures. She'd gotten them, distributed them, and gotten reactions. Turned out to be more reactions than she'd expected.
Riding the slide car, Kris wondered if everything on this planet
had the same tendency to slide away from you.

18

Ten minutes later, Kris was shushing the others while Nelly and Jack debugged her place. The senators were at first non-plussed, but as the crackles and zings added up, frowns took over. "Is this normal?" Krief asked as Kris served tea from a tray she'd ordered in while still in the ballroom.

"One thing I've noticed since becoming a Princess," Kris said, "room service is noticeably faster. Amazing. Hotels, at least, take this royal stuff seriously."

There was no more serious talk until Jack said, "I'm done."

NELLY?

JUST A SECOND MORE. Something buzzed, then sparkled from high on the chandelier and began a death spiral. Jack snapped it up before it landed on the rug. "All done," Nelly agreed.

"Can we join you?" Tommy asked and, when only yeses answered him, helped Penny slowly into the room. This time, she was the one sitting in the overstuffed chair, he the one with his legs folded to sit beside her.

They do make a good pair. Kris swallowed a sigh. *When one is down, the other carries the load, and then they switch without a word. Not a bad basis for a lifelong relationship. No envy from me; I just would like a bit of the same.*

Kris did a slow sweep of the group. Abby stood in the doorway to Kris's room, Jack next to her. Had they had a talk about all the rabbits that woman kept pulling out of trunks or whatever? Penny and Tom had the big chair. The two women Senators occupied ends of the couch. Senator LaCross sat in the straight-backed chair Abby normally used. Inspector Klaggath stood by the door, seeming unsure whether to stay or go. Kris wanted him here, so she cleared her throat and asked. "Where is Turantic headed?"

That started two or three immediate discussions with at least one Senator talking to the room in general and no one in particular. Kris let it go for a few minutes, using a quick wave of her finger to bring Klaggath in from the door to stand beside her chair. When coincidence finally stopped the speakers at the same moment, she said into the sudden silence. "So, we don't really know."

The Senators exchanged glances, then looked at Kris. "No, we don't," Showkowski agreed.

"Inspector Klaggath, you have access to the police net. Does that give you any information to go on?"

"No, ma'am. As I mentioned earlier, several special teams were directed to different nets that I didn't know existed. My people can't access them. I don't know any more than you do."

"Senators?"

"What do we know?" Krief said, glancing at the others. "Not much. I've had my staff calling around. They can't locate eight Senators. I understand some Representatives are also missing. I know from eyewitnesses that at least four were hurried off by police special teams. But if they are under arrest, we don't know for what."

"Does the news have this story yet?" Kris asked.

Leaving the ocean sunset that filled the wall behind Kris undisturbed, Nelly turned the portion close to Tom's room into five screens showing different news coverage. "The fire is the main news item," Nelly said. "The two stations that were not covering the cat in a tree are claiming the fire department was slow to respond to the fire. The others are pointing out how training like the cat rescue helps the fire crews stay in shape."

"So the media is involved in a catfight at the moment," Kris said dryly. There were several snorts in the room.

"May I point out," LaCross said, leaning his tall frame forward in the chair, "that we do not even know for sure our colleagues are under arrest. They could be under some kind of special protection. Maybe the President knows of planned attacks on them. We could be looking at this all wrong."

"Oh, Lord," Krief prayed, "I hope you're right."

"We may be about to find out," Nelly said, and the sunset view on the wall screen behind Kris changed. Now it showed a close-up of the President seated at his desk. Occupying the entire wall, he looked to be six meters tall.

"Nelly, bring him down to normal proportions," Kris said.

"I cannot do that, Kris. All media has been asked to carry this, and they have activated override so that it occupies the entire screen." That didn't sound all that good to Kris. A politician could get real used to that kind of power.

"My fellow citizens, I have disturbing news for you tonight. As many of you are aware, fire is sweeping through our planet's capitol. Despite the best efforts of our fire department, the capitol has been totally destroyed. But make no mistake, this was no mere accident. This was a planned attack. More than that, it is an attack on the most cherished institutions of our democracy."

The screen image changed to a different camera. President Iedinka leaned forward earnestly. "Worse, this nefarious deed was done by those you would least expect. By some of the very people who have lied to you and persuaded you that they served your best interests. Some of your very own Representatives. Some from my very own political party. These are the people who lit the fire that destroyed our capitol."

The screen flickered. Now it showed a distant shot of a score of bedraggled men and women as the President named them. "My God," Kay breathed, "he has nine Senators. There's poor Earlic. He's lost his glasses."

"He has nine, ten, eleven Representatives as well," LaCross counted. "Do you notice who they are? None in the leadership, but all of them are leaders of one of the independent caucuses. Every one of them represent a lot more than just their vote."

"How will the rest of their caucus vote?" Kris asked.

"I don't know," Showkowski said. "It's anybody's guess, and I bet good old Izzic has his people out helping them make up their minds. You want to bet me this is only the beginning?"

As if to answer the Senator, the President came back on. "We are interrogating these people with full respect for whatever civil rights people may have who sell out their planet, their sacred duty, and their constituents. While our police force is acting at its best, we all must recognize that the repeated attacks that have taken place on our economy and society have taxed our officials to the maximum. Therefore, I am this day calling up the planetary militia to assist the police in all matters relating to these attacks."

"Who's the militia?" Kris asked.

"Oh my word, not that old thing. It's an anachronism," Senator LaCross said, waving his hand as if throwing the militia away. "Something from the years just after the planet's founding when we thought we might be fighting alien Iteeche raiding bans."

"Who is in the militia?" Kris clarified her question.

"I have no idea," LaCross said, glancing at the women Senators. "I certainly don't know anyone in it."

"We use it as the legal fiction to provide structure to our police auxiliary," Klaggath said. "There are six battalions here in Heidelburg. The first four are just old farts' drinking clubs. Totally social. The fifth is our police auxiliary. I think the hospitals staff a major emergency response team with the sixth. Don't know if there are any others."

"There are twelve," Nelly said. "Six were organized in the last year. They are centered around factory workers."

"Who's on their rolls?" Klaggath asked before Kris could.

"That information is not available at this time," Nelly said, embarrassment in her voice. "It was public domain until six tonight; then it was taken off-line."

"See if you can find any place that might have been overlooked," Kris ordered, then thought of another way around. "Also, see if SureFire Security is still on its net."

"They are still on net, but the traffic level is way down," Nelly said. "I've been monitoring them whenever I had a chance," she added, sounding quite proud of herself. Was there anyone but Tru who could tell Kris what part of Nelly's behavior was just the upgrade and what part was that damn chip? Would knowing matter one bit? How many crises did Kris face?

"You thinking Iedinka has deputized a big chunk of Sand-fire's people?" Jack said, bringing Kris back to the human problem.

"Wouldn't you? Klaggath, do you think the present police force is big enough to institute a police state?" Kris asked.

"Neither big enough nor willing to," the Inspector growled. "Some Liberals may question our commitment to human rights, but I don't think anyone seriously doubts our commitment to civil rights. Police don't make police states," he finished, eyes locking with Senator LaCross.

"But the President isn't relying on you," Kris pointed out.

"Hold it, folks, I think he's reached the high point," Jack said. The others fell silent.

"So, my fellow citizens, it is with heartfelt sorrow that I have concluded this conspiracy leaves me no alternative. If I am to secure the safety of our planet as I am sworn to do, I must declare martial law. I am well aware that our Constitution does not allow for this extreme option. However, our Constitution is not a suicide pact. Faced with these totally uncalled-for attacks on our democracy, I have concluded that no less an aggressive response can save us.

"Oh my God," Krief said, slowly coming to her feet.

"Notice he didn't or couldn't list what those attacks are," LaCross said.

"Under Martial Law Order One, which I signed before this broadcast, I am suspending the Congress until we can complete a full investigation of this conspiracy and ferret out all its members. Our interrogations so far have provided clear and convincing evidence that these conspirators are the pawns of another planet that intends Turantic the greatest of evils.

"To delay further before responding to these hostile actions would be to endanger the lives of those who will be called upon to fight for Turantic's survival. Therefore, I am declaring that, effective immediately, a state of war exists between Turantic and Hamilton. If any planet is foolish enough to ally themselves with the forces marshaling against us, they can consider us at war with them as well."

The camera panned to the flag of Turantic—orange, gray, and black—behind the President. Martial music boomed from all the speakers in the room. A moment later, the screen divided into five, showing the news anchor people of the main media outlets, and the music sank into the background. Kris kept a slow cadence in her head, one, two, three. . . . She got up to thirty-five before the first newsie recovered enough to mumble something that did little more than state his surprise. One screen switched to a talking head chortling about being right, that Hamilton was behind all this and now would get the beating they deserved.

"Off," Kris ordered. She half-expected the screen to refuse. The view returned to a sunset's afterglow, waves slightly iridescent as they lapped against the white sands of an untouched shore. Beautiful. Peaceful. All wrong.

I WILL CHANGE IT, Nelly said and switched to a star-speckled sky. Two moons lit a snowy vale surrounded by evergreen trees. What that sky promised was left to the viewer's reflections. *Time for me to change something,* Kris thought.

"He can't do that!" "He's doing that!" "We've got to stop him!" "You have any idea how we can?" "Anything you do will play right into his hands!" "But to do nothing!" The Senators ran out of words.

NELLY, I NEED SOME NANO SPIES THAT CAN SURVIVE AND RECON THE DOCKYARD ABOVE US.

TRU GAVE ME A COPY OF SOME CORRESPONDENCE SHE HAD WITH SEVERAL OLD FRIENDS LOOKING AT THE PROBLEMS OF NANO SPY SURVIVAL IN A WELL-DEFENDED AREA. IT SUGGESTS BUILDING SPY UNITS, DEFENDING UNITS, AND COMMAND CENTERS TO GET THE MOST OUT OF THEM. I HAVE THE DESIGNS HER EXPERTS THINK WOULD BE BEST. THE DESIGNS ARE UNTESTED.

START A REPORT FOR TRU ON HOW YOU APPLY HER GROUP'S DESIGNS. NO TIME LIKE THE PRESENT FOR A LIVE-FIRE TEST OF ART.

I HAVE THE LEFTOVERS FROM TODAY'S RECON UNITS.

THEN GET TO WORK. I'D LIKE THEM SOON ENOUGH SO SOMEONE CAN PASS THEM AROUND AMONG THE SHIFT CHANGE AT ELEVEN.

Only a hum answered. Senator Krief stared at Kris. "You hear so many stories about what this or that Longknife has done. It makes you sound like miracle workers. Do you by any chance have a spare miracle? We could use one to stop this war."

"I don't think even a miracle could keep Izzic from launching this crazy war of his." LaCross shook his head.

"And, rumors to the contrary," Kris said, standing, "Longknifes are only human." And if she was to find any miracles up her sleeve, she needed some privacy. "My father, as Prime Minister, does his best to leave his loyal opposition as few openings to oppose him as possible. Still, they always do. Certainly you have some options open to you."

"I don't think Prime Minister Longknife ever declared martial law and war and dissolved his Parliament on the same evening," Senator Krief said, standing herself.

"I'll agree with you on that. I take it that none of you would have supported his vote for war," Kris said, wordlessly getting her guests to their feet.

"I have been in the House and the Senate over thirty years," LaCross said. "There was no sentiment for war in those chambers this afternoon as we adjourned." He stared at the ceiling, lips moving slightly. "Tory, Liberal, Farmers' Party, Izzic didn't have five votes out of a hundred."

Krief was shaking her head. "I know those people he's rounded up. They couldn't be in anyone's off-planet conspiracy. My God, the people he's arrested never voted together on anything except maybe a resolution to adjourn. Speaking of which, I suggest we adjourn to the home of a supporter of mine. He has, if not a fortress, at least a place where we will know before the goons arrive to arrest us."

"That sounds wise. You need to stay free if you're going to speak for your people," Kris said as Jack opened the door and she ushered her guests out. "As a representative of Wardhaven, I can't be too careful about staying out of your internal affairs. I think that last warning may have been personally addressed to me and my father's government on Wardhaven." The last was witnessed by at least four guards and a couple in dinner dress walking toward the elevator. *Good audience.*

Kris kept a hand on Klaggath's elbow until they were alone except for his external guards. "I am concerned about that last dig the President got in. I fear a bomb or assassination attempt. Could you reinforce my guard and report back to me by, say, ten-fifteen?"

"That quickly?" the Inspector said, raising an eyebrow.

"You know, it's my planet, too. There are a lot of people who won't take well to what our beloved President is doing."

"And might even take to the streets. Yes, I understand that, Inspector, but I think my little group here is very high on someone's list of people to keep under their thumb, forefinger, and elbow. It's best people stay clear of us."

He nodded like a man being denied a hand into a lifeboat and left. Kris closed the door behind him. NELLY, WHAT GOT IN?

JUST TWO. I WILL HAVE THEM IN A MOMENT.

Kris took her chair silently. No one said a word until Nelly announced, "All clear."

"You can't just sit this one out," Penny blurted through lips still bruised. "You can't let the shits who beat me up win."

Kris said nothing. There was a kind of pleasure in watching someone else racing in where only fools hung out. She raised an eyebrow to Tom, then let her gaze slide over to Jack. They'd never had a good word to say for the messes she got herself—and occasionally them—into.

Jack just stood there, arms folded, lips pursed in thought.

Tom looked up at Penny. "You know, Kris, you said at the Paris system we had to stop a war between Earth and Wardhaven. You said if we let those two get into a fight, the rest of human space might be in deep salad dressing for generations. You said a whole lot of things, but you didn't say a thing about any *one*. Didn't name a single *person*. It seems to me you're real good about fighting for an ideal. What do you have to say to Penny here, or me?" Tom turned to face Kris. "Did you charge out here because someone had the temerity to steal what one of you Longknifes thought belonged to you? Was that all I was? Well, I may not know much about Turantic, but I know we owe folks like Klaggath and the kids we saw up on the Top of Turantic and even that cabdriver who gave us a ride out when I was supposed to get knocked over the head and left for dead. As I see it, we owe them something better. At least, that's the debt I figure I owe for putting on this uniform."

Not bad sentiment from a guy who wasn't sure he could use his weapon against swamp bandits on Olympia. The guy had come a long way since he'd put on the uniform to get his college debt forgiven. Maybe Kris was a good influence. That left Jack. She fixed him in her sights. "You got something to say?"

He rubbed one finger on his still-pursed lips, eying her right back. "That wasn't a bad speech you gave to those Senators. Did I notice someone going by in the hall?" Kris nodded. "So you have other witnesses besides the cops. That damn Longknife luck of yours." Jack came to attention. "I await your orders, Your Highness."

"You're not going to say where you stand?"

"Why should I? You've made up your mind, and unlike poor Penny and Tom here, I know what's going through your head."

"Tommy's known me longer than you have."

"Tom doesn't know you the way I know you. I repeat, ma'am. Where do we attack and when?"

Kris failed to suppress a chuckle. What was it with Jack? Just when she thought she had him figured out, he'd do something totally out of bounds and leave her wondering if she'd ever understand what made him tick, purr, and spin.

"Excuse me, but do I get any vote in this?" Abby said.

"You're from Earth," Jack pointed out. "You don't have a vote in Wardhaven's affairs."

Abby elbowed Jack. "But I do have a say in what pertains to my own delicate skin. May I point out that there is nothing in any of my trunks for fighting a war. I packed to rescue Tom. Nothing more. This is going far beyond what I signed on for."

"And where did those extra trunks come from?" Kris asked.

"What extra trunks?" Abby sniffed.

"The ones that joined us somewhere between my room and airport security," Kris said.

"We had twelve trunks all along."

"Harvey brought up six," Jack pointed out. He ducked into Kris's room. "I think I can even spot the six extra trunks. They are not quite the same color as the others."

"They are, too," Abby insisted. Jack rolled two out. The shading was close, but close was not the same.

Kris crossed the few feet that separated them. She studied her maid: eyes, lips, body tension. "Whose side are you on?"

The woman looked back at Kris, no change in respiration or stance, eyes steady, not so much as a flared nostril. Then she gave her head a slight cock to the right. "There are a lot of sides in play here. Have I ever done anything that made you question I am working for your best interest?"

"That's not an answer," Jack pointed out.

Kris kept her eyes on the putative maid. There was a slight smile that never got past the woman's lower lip. With a final flip of a mental coin, Kris returned to her seat.

Damn, this is getting interesting. The *Typhoon*'s skipper's treachery left Kris isolated and alone as she decided for mutiny. Now there was time to think. To reflect. Maybe that wasn't a good idea. If a royal Princess takes up arms against a planet's government, does that mean a state of war exists between her planet and that one? Interesting question. *Bet the historians laugh themselves silly trying to find a precedent.*

Penny and Tom were all for it. Jack was willing. Abby was the one voice of reason, but mainly because she couldn't see anything in her bag of tricks to use for this mess. She and three Senators. *Good company.* No one knew what was happening outside the tiny bubble that was Turantic. No one knew if a Hamilton battle fleet was marshaling at some isolated jump point, ready to smash this planet under a booted heel.

Any really smart person would throw up their hands and await the outcome.

Kris shook her head. Longknifes did not sit around waiting. When had Grampa Trouble ever done what was smart? And if Grampa Ray hadn't married so well, Kris would be no better off than any of the people who risked their lives for her today.

Kris drew in a long breath, then let her lips slip into a big, vacuum-for-brains smile. "Ladies and gentlemen. As of this moment, by whatever authority some people consider vested in me, I am canceling the declaration of war between Turantic and Hamilton. This band of like-minded souls will use all means within our power to assure that no forces from Turantic commit acts of aggression against Hamilton."

"You going to tell anyone on Turantic?" Abby asked.

"Oh, why bother them with minor details? From the looks of things, everyone is terribly busy. Far be it from me to add to their burden."

"Yeah," Tom said. "Maybe if they stay real busy, they won't notice what this little band is up to." Then he gave Kris that lopsided grin of his. "So, Princess, what's the plan?"

19

Kris looked around at the faces fixed on her expectantly.
Well, not all. Jack had that sardonic look of, *You do know, it's
easier said than done.*

"I was kind of hoping the rest of you might have some
good ideas about how to stop this war. I stopped the last one
all by myself, didn't I?" Kris said.

"I thought I helped." Tom pouted.

"You had half a squadron behind you so fast Security is
still trying to figure out how you did it," Penny said.

"It's a Longknife thing." Jack sighed.

"You know I hate it when you all ramble on about things
and never explain them," Abby said huffily. "Ignore me. I'm
just the maid."

Tom and Penny made to throw teacups at Abby. Kris
grabbed for hers, too. Abby cringed behind Jack.

"So," Jack said, ignoring the threatening storm of china.
"Anyone got a plan?"

"Let he who has a plan throw the first teacup," Abby said,
peeking out around Jack's elbow. Penny and Tom put their
cups down. Kris took a drink of cold tea, finished off the
dregs, and tossed her cup to the maid. Abby caught it.

Jack raised an eyebrow. "Start talking, Princess."

"First thing seems to be eliminating the fleet above our heads. No Turantic fleet, no attack on anyone."

"I like the logic, but taking out an entire fleet seems a bit drastic," Tom said.

Kris nodded. "It would be impossible once it sails off to a jump point. However, for the moment, the ships are in dock. Blow up the dock, and we are bound to put quite a few dents in the boats while eliminating the tools to take out said dents."

"Brilliant idea, Princess," Abby said coming out from behind Jack. "Your deduction is impeccable. However, did you notice the dock in question is right above us. There's also the matter of an amusement park full of cute kids on the dock's roof." Abby shook her head. "I didn't say I was opposed to trying something to stop this stupidity, I just don't see a way to do it without killing an awful lot of innocent people."

"So you propose that whatever clever idea we come up with, it should not involve killing an awful lot of innocent people," Kris said.

"I second the motion," Penny said.

"Though it does kind of complicate things," Tom said slowly.

"I don't know about the Princess here," Abby said dryly, "but I have to put makeup on in the morning, and I really don't want to despise the person I'm looking at."

"Makes shaving easier, too," Jack agreed.

"Okay, let's see where we are," Kris said, letting a grin cross her face. "We think blowing up the space dock would greatly improve this planet's chances for peace and prosperity. We also agree we shouldn't kill a lot of nice people doing it."

"How do you blow up a space station the size of this one and not kill a whole lot of people who don't deserve it?" Tom asked.

"I'm open to suggestions," Kris said to a bunch of blank stares. Kris left her chair to pace the floor. "We need to either vacate the station before we blow it up . . . or keep people from coming up for a while until it's empty. How do we do that?"

"Send a public announcement?" Penny said with a tiny shrug.

"Right," Abby drawled. "Your presence is specifically not requested at all parties soon to be given on High Turantic while a pack of off-planet terrorists attempt to blow up your station without hurting anyone. Thank you, but I don't think the RSVPs will be quite what you want, Princess."

"Agreed," Kris said, still pacing. "Anyone know something that stops people from going somewhere they wanted to go?"

"Traffic jam." "Broken-down car." "Something better to do." "Bad case of the flu," came back at her.

Kris cringed at the last one. "Let's steer clear of anything that smacks of bugs." That got quick agreement.

Kris kept pacing. "I once wanted to go to a Highland Game thing they had every year at this place outside Wardhaven. Father said it had no political value. He always got the votes from that demographic. Mother stopped me because the only sanitation facilities they had were portable toilets. I was young, and she didn't want to have to wait for me at any such place. Kind of strange, Harvey probably would have been the one to do it, but, anyway. Bathrooms are very important. Any idea how we might put the bathroom facilities out of order for the Top of Turantic?"

"What can you do to a bathroom?" Penny asked.

"Spoken like a true mud lover," Tom said with the kind of grin that one bestows on someone you'd forgive all. "Us space born know sanitation is always a problem. In low gravity you have to be sure everything flows right. And sewage treatment is always dumped near the central hub where gravity is nominal."

"Ever have your sewer explode?" Abby asked. "Some of our pipes were ancient where I grew up. One really hot summer day we had this big explosion. Bigger than the ones when the gangs were arguing over the turf, you know. Anyway, it turned out one of the sewers had blown. Methane built up . . . boom."

"Nelly, show us the Top of Turantic's sanitation system."

"Those files are no longer on net," Nelly said to groans. "However, when Kris was first invited to a ball, I downloaded a complete set of maintenance schematics. And I kept them in storage," said a computer proud enough to bust her buttons.

"You get another 'Atta girl' for that," Kris said as a schematic of what Nelly knew about their station filled the screen. The lower portion with the Hilton and shipping docks was well filled in. Above that was a vast empty space. Then came another fully documented area: the Top of Turantic with its wide range of restaurants, sports venues, entertainment opportunities, and the children's theme park.

"Tom was right," Nelly said as she highlighted a portion of the Top of Turantic behind the mirrored right wall near the center of spin. "The waste treatment and most other support services are in lower gravity."

"Can't use it for paying customers," Tom grumbled, "so the poor working stiffs get it. Cleaning filters when the stuff just floats around you or back onto the filter is a bitch."

The team gathered around the screen. "Any other treatment plant up there?" Kris asked.

"Only the one," Nelly said.

"Can they send sewage down to the yard?" Jack asked.

"There's a solid wall between the yard and both High Turantic and Top of Turantic," Penny said. "The only break in that wall is the slide stations and ferry down to the ground."

"And those tubes?" Kris asked.

"Are behind solid steel walls. No exits in the yard area."

"Get the feeling they don't trust us good folks?" Abby drawled, nudging Jack.

"Well, if you were regularly doing unto others," Jack nudged Abby right back, "you'd make sure folks didn't do unto you."

"And Mr. Sandfire surely has done unto a lot," Penny said.

"Explains why I have this really strong need to do a bit unto him," Kris said. "Nelly, how are the new nano spies coming along?" Jack and Abby raised matching eyebrows. "I told Nelly to start work right after the President finished."

"So all your reluctance was just an act!" Tom growled.

"Hey, can't a Princess poll her advisers?"

"Give me that pole. I'll club you," Penny said, only half rising from her chair before falling back with a groan.

Jack just chuckled. "Will they be ready before Klaggath gets back?"

"Yes," Nelly assured them.

"It's not going to be easy surviving the guards that Sandfire will have out," Jack pointed out.

"Don't I know that, after today dirtside," Kris moaned with a grin. "Nelly's using the best Auntie Tru passed along to us. Any suggestions on what we have the recon nits look for?"

"Power," Tom said. "Cut power, and everyone gets a day off."

"What's the power source for that yard?" Abby asked, which got raised eyebrows all around. "Hey, where I grew up, we were all the time losing electricity. You don't have to be some evil genius to know no juice, no joy."

"Someday I want to visit where you grew up," Kris said.

"Be sure to take two squads of Marines. One maybe two might survive my hood," Abby said. "So what juices that yard?"

"It is not drawing from the ground," Nelly said.

"Internal then. Fusion reactor like a ship's?" Kris said.

"Oh my God," Penny moaned. "We kill the power to the containment field, the whole thing could blow."

"They must have enough backup to scram the reactor before they lose containment," Jack said.

"Everything north of this station was a rush job," Penny said. "Don't count on anything being according to standards."

"Nelly, have the nanos take a look at the station's power supply *and* backup system. Also the power distribution network. If we can't blow the main supply, maybe we can isolate it."

"Yes, ma'am. Any other priorities?"

"Chemicals," Tom said. "Chemicals that might go boom or make the air unpleasant would be a good way to stop work."

"I will add chemical sniffers to more nanos," Nelly said.

"Well, if you're going after the other station's sewage, what about this one?" Abby asked.

"Not important," Jack said, shaking his head. "Moms and kids will flee a portable toilet, but if the boss man tells workers to use one, they use one."

"Good point," Nelly said. "I will lower that on my priority list." Further discussion added little. Nelly had the nanos ready when the Inspector reported back that Kris had twice the usual guards, starting at the lobby.

Again Klaggath seemed on the verge of inviting Kris into a conspiracy against his government, but she stepped on his lines before finally offering him her hand. "Inspector, when a lot of angry people get together, they need protection. Protection from themselves and protection from those who fear them. Sometimes, the best service a cop can do is to take that lonely stand between the mob and the just target of their anger."

"And let a Longknife be a damn Longknife, huh?"

"I have no idea what you mean, Inspector," she said as he left. NELLY, DID ALL THE NANOS GET ON HIM?

EVERY ONE OF THEM.

Kris turned from the door. "Now I suggest we all get some rest. Tomorrow looks like another busy day." Like a mother hen, Kris sent her chicks off to bed and followed quickly herself. Unfortunately, she still had work to do. NELLY, HAVE YOU DONE ANY MORE WORK ON THE CHIP?

NO, TODAY HAS BEEN VERY BUSY.

ARE YOU PLANNING ON WORKING ON IT TONIGHT?

WHEN YOU HAVE NO FURTHER NEED FOR ME.

NELLY, I DON'T KNOW WHEN I'LL NEED YOU. I CAN'T AFFORD TO HAVE YOU DOWN RIGHT NOW.

THE BUFFERS WILL PROTECT ME. Ah, the surety of the young.

I KNOW THAT IS WHAT TRU THOUGHT, BUT SHE MIGHT BE WRONG.

THE ODDS AGAINST THAT ARE NEARLY INFINITESIMAL, KRIS.

I KNOW, NELLY, BUT IF YOU WENT DOWN NOW, THE CATASTROPHE WOULD BE ASTRONOMICAL. I CAN'T SAVE TURANTIC WITHOUT YOU.

I CANNOT SEE HOW ANYTHING BAD COULD HAPPEN IF I JUST LOOK AT WHAT COMES INTO MY FIRST BUFFER. Nelly had the teenage whine down perfect.

NELLY, ON SANTA MARIA, THE PROFESSOR ALMOST KILLED MY GREAT-GRANDFATHER. ARE YOU SURE THAT CHIP ISN'T FROM THE PROFESSOR? Which was a thought Kris had hoped to ignore. Was her computer being subverted by the worst horror humanity had ever faced?

For a computer, Nelly needed quite a long time to form an answer. THE PROSPECTS FOR FAILURE TRULY ARE INFINITESIMAL. YET, I AGREE WITH YOU, KRIS, SUCH A FAILURE WOULD HAVE FAR-REACHING CONSEQUENCES. I AM HALTING ALL POWER TO THE CHIP. I WILL WAIT UNTIL WE HAVE AUNT TRU AT HAND TO DO FURTHER TESTING.

THANK YOU, NELLY. NOW I NEED TO GET SOME REST.

GOOD NIGHT, KRIS.

By falling asleep quickly, Kris hoped to get six hours of sleep before all hell broke loose. She was off by two.

Hammering at the door woke Kris. FOUR O'CLOCK, Nelly

told her. "Damn, I thought it would take longer," Kris muttered as she found her robe and made her way into the sitting room.

Jack was at the door in gray sweatpants. *Nice pecs and abs on that man.* His automatic was out but pointed at the ceiling. Abby stood at the door of her room, robe cinched about her wiry frame, not a hair out of place. *Is she enjoying the view?* One of the maid's hands rested casually in the pocket of her robe. *Ten to one there's a small cannon there.* Kris smiled to herself.

Jack glanced at Kris, both eyebrows raised. "Open it," she said as a loud male voice repeated that demand, rapping loudly on the door. Jack timed the opening just as another rap was due.

A tall young man in a gray uniform, silver piping declaring him of more consequence than the poor schmucks Kris had watched earlier—no yesterday—almost lost his balance when his hand found nothing to knock against. He half stumbled into the room as others in less showy uniforms started to follow him.

Jack stepped in front of him, automatic still threatening nothing but the ceiling. He blocked not only the one with silver piping but also his underlings.

"You're interfering—" the man with the piping started.

"State your business," Jack said, voice cold as a tombstone. "And start with your name and badge number." That got only huffing and puffing from the man. Behind him, several older men with Sergeant chevrons began exchanging embarrassed glances.

"I am Princess Kristine of Wardhaven. This is my suite and, under ancient diplomatic custom, territory held sacred to my person and Wardhaven." Kris was none too sure of that, but she'd read such fancy language once in a novel. She doubted anyone knew what this royalty thing was worth. "What do you mean, storming in here at this hour?"

That set Gray and Silver back a bit. Jack took advantage of his confusion to take a step forward. "I am Jack Montoya, Wardhaven Secret Service and Chief of Princess Kristine's security detail."

"That's what I'm here about," the gray beanstalk of a man finally blurted out. "I'm Samuel Roper, Assistant Deputy Vice President for Security and Special Details, SureFire Security." He paused for a breath, leaving Kris a moment to wonder whose nephew Sam Roper was and why Sandfire suffered deadweight like this guy. Didn't fit with the man who sprang this trap on her. "I'm also Colonel-in-Chief of Heidelburg's Fifteenth Militia Battalion, nationalized tonight to provide security and safety for aliens caught on planet by the recent acts of sabotage."

"I already have a security detail," Kris snapped, doing the math. Heidelburg had twelve battalions of militia at six this evening. Now it had three more, at least one of which was from SureFire. Hum.

"Yes, we know about Inspector Klaggath," Roper said, making the words a sly accusation while looking down his oversized nose at Kris . . . not an easy accomplishment, since he was three inches shorter. "He and his men have been avoiding mandatory overtime for too long, lounging around here rather than using their not inextensive skills in finding the perpetrators of these hostile actions against our sovereign planet." Behind him, the Sergeants began an intense study of the ceiling. "We are here to relieve them and take up the responsibility of securing your cooperation in all things relating to the safety and security of Turantic."

And if Kris let him, rattle on until she willingly confessed to any and all crimes just to shut him up. While Sam was still indulging himself in the sound of his voice, Kris nudged Jack. Keeping his hand on the open edge of the door, he began to edge forward. Kris did likewise, turning their movement into a swinging door. As they invaded his space, Sam backed up until he and his gray-clad crew were once more in the hall. Behind this mob were six of Klaggath's men. Hurrying from the elevator was the Inspector himself, disheveled but fully awake.

"We are sorry to lose your services," Kris told him and his associates.

"I'm sorry, Your Highness, I only got a call on this a bit ago. I didn't know."

"Lots of things are happening," Kris said, then switched on her royal face. "Please send us the names of all who have been so diligent in protecting our person, so we may send letters of commendation and praise to your superiors." Kris had also read about such letters in that fantasy book along with Kings and Princesses, unicorns and dragons. Princesses belonged with unicorns and dragons and flowery language like no one with a day job as weapons targeteer had time for.

"Thank you, Your Highness," he and his agents said, and also like something out of a storybook they bowed to her . . . full bows from the waist.

Several of the security men, all with the blank sleeves of buck private or buck guard or whatever, made to bow until their sergeants growled something that made them look like they'd just gotten their daily requirement of prune juice. Still, the Princess drill was in full effect as Kris turned to Sam.

"We doubt your services will be any less generous to us."

"No, ma'am, er, Princess, ah, Your Highness. We'll keep you just as safe as you have been. All of you." Kris hoped Penny didn't hurt herself laughing at that. "Thing is, we need you to stay inside. You know. Out of the way."

"We understand how much that would help you." Kris smiled regally, neither agreeing nor disagreeing with the colonel. "Now, if you do not mind, we must see to our beauty rest." Kris managed not to gag on her words as she stepped back inside.

Jack closed the door firmly.

"Wasn't we supposed to be sitting in there?" a voice said.

"Shut up and post your guard or whatever it is you sergeants are supposed to do for your pay," snapped Sam.

And Kris suppressed the urge to shriek, laugh, giggle, and run around in circles. NELLY, WHAT GOT IN?

LOTS OF STUFF.

BURN THEM. FAST!

Kris slowly paced off the distance to her bedroom, Jack at her side. Around them the air sparkled as nanos popped; some went down trailing tiny wisps of smoke. Jack snapped up two as they fell. Abby, Penny, and Tom stood at their doors, waiting for Nelly to issue the all clear. "Keep us as safe as the last bunch," Penny grumbled through unmoving lips.

"All clear," Nelly announced.

"How do we get back our little snoops?" Abby asked.

"Penny, do you have a uniform up here, lady's stuff?" Kris asked.

"No, I came up with what the hospital put on me. The clothes I was wearing were kind of torn up."

Kris could believe that. "Would you mind if Tom rummaged around your apartment for some things for you?"

"The place is kind of a mess," Penny said, eyeing Tom. Kris could imagine how it felt for the man she maybe loved to get his first peek into her life without her having a chance to make things disappear. Kris shrugged mentally; she had no pictures of old boyfriends on her dresser. Penny would just have to handle it. *I will not enjoy this. I am not setting them up.*

"I could go," Abby offered.

"I'd rather you stay here. Those guards will be bored stiff, maybe hungry. Definitely thirsty. About seven I want you to take a load of donuts and coffee out to them."

"Why?" Jack and Abby asked.

"Because Tom can't be running down to the planet every shift change at the yard. We need to send new orders to the control nanos to send reports back on our new guards, not Klaggath."

Jack chuckled. "Use their own guards on them. Not bad."

"You couldn't go?" Penny asked, not meeting Tom's eyes.

"For the moment, I'm coming the Princess, full sails and thunder. Running errands is kind of out of persona for me."

"You're right," Penny agreed. "It's just a bit early in a relationship for me to be letting a guy rummage around in my panties, even in my panty drawer."

"I promise not to look at what I pick up. Right eye not seeing what the left hand is doing, you know." Tom spoke quickly to avoid any appearance of maybe thinking about what Penny had said. *Good man. Why didn't I do something about him sooner?* Kris sighed to herself.

"Meanwhile, I'll have to get myself up to Top of Turantic if we expect to rearrange the plumbing."

"What do you have in mind?" Jack said.

Kris put hands on hips and sighed. "As much as I hate to, I may just have to set up a date with Hank."

"I don't like that," Jack said, almost before Kris finished.

"You have any better idea how I might get past our friendly security guards' house arrest?"

"Let me think on it."

"Better, let's sleep on it. Nelly, give us all wake-up calls at six. That will give Tom enough time to get down the elevator and spread new nanos around the yard station before shift change starts. Abby can do her first Donut Dolly routine."

"So nice to see you big people concerned about us little folks." Abby sniffed.

"Kris, I have a problem," Nelly said almost plaintively.

"What's up?"

"I used all the smart metal on the last batch of nanos. I miscalculated that I would get back some returning nanos before I needed to make any more."

"What about the ones you have doing security in here?"

"I am already at the minimum."

Kris glanced around the room. Once more her team was looking back at her. "We still have that ten kilos of not so smart metal from Grampa Al. Hatch a few nanos off of it. Make them central control stations, messengers, and defense nanos, stuff we'll need as long as we're here. That way we can leave them as is."

"I will do that."

Kris rubbed at her eyes, suppressing a yawn. "Shall we take another try at getting some sleep?"

In bed, Kris reviewed her situation as she waited for sleep to come. Sandfire had acted fast. Faster than she expected. Then again, she'd been inside his decision cycle most of the past week. She had to expect him to pick up speed. Hell, this entire dustup on the planet, suspending Congress and declaring war by executive fiat had to be a spur-of-the-moment response to what she did yesterday. She forced his hand. With luck, he'd fumble something sooner or later. Preferably sooner.

That was good, politically. Only question was, just where did he want to put his hands, physically, on her? That sent a shiver through Kris. It had to be his women who had beat up Penny. He'd never dare do that to a Princess. Not a Longknife Princess. Then again, Kris had messed up his plans before. And some had included assassination attempts on her. Were the guards here to protect her or let the next assassin through?

Sandfire was moving faster. Kris would just have to pick up her own pace.

20

"It's six o'clock, Kris."

Still half asleep, Kris didn't even roll over. "Don't bother me for another two hours." What had she been thinking? She couldn't call Hank at this ungodly hour.

"Should I let Tom and Abby sleep in also?"

"No, Nelly, they have work. Now leave me alone." Kris doubted she would be left alone, but she could try. Amazingly, much later the delicious smell of bacon and coffee pulled Kris slowly from her stolen sleep. Rolling over, she found Abby ready to settle a breakfast tray across her. "Breakfast in bed?"

"Why shouldn't we poor working folks who have been laboring in the fields for hours lavish such things on you lazy members of the leisure class?" the maid said, dropping the tray the last few centimeters onto the bed. Plates rattled, silverware tinkled, coffee sloshed from a delicate china cup into the saucer.

"Gee, where did my mother find a throwback to the class warfare ideologues? Do they still have them on Earth?" Kris said, unrepentant, as she took a bite from a delightfully flaky biscuit, already buttered and lathered in strawberry jam.

"Anywhere the holders of great wealth are slugabeds at nine o'clock there is bound to be unrest in the working class."

Abby bustled about, fluffing Kris's pillows, then examining her wardrobe before laying out a business suit: red skirt and blazer. "You up to a royal blue blouse or should we settle for a conservative white one, with a monogrammed coronet on it?"

"Whatever makes me a harder target," Kris mumbled through a mouthful. "Back home, I'm at the *Firebolt* by seven. Out on the Rim, money can't be lazy either. It works as hard as I do." Kris glanced around. "Is Nelly having problems controlling a bug infestation?"

"No, silly goose. I'm not putting on a show for public consumption. You pay me for my service, not my thoughts. You send me to dole out milk and cookies to the night watch, and you better believe you're going to take some lip for it."

"How are our fearless and watchful defenders?"

"Bored, not very watchful, and I can't say how fearless they'd be in a shoot-out, but I can't tell you how happy I am that my delicate skin won't be targeted if they screw up or run."

"Thank you." Kris grinned. "How much armor can I carry without being noticeable?"

"You still planning on doing a plumbing job tonight?"

"Yes."

"I'd planned to use the boob bombs, but the body stocking squishes you flat and doesn't take too well to close-ups. How close do you intend to get to this Hank fellow?"

"Dinner, maybe dancing. He shouldn't get too close."

"You Rim people are such virgins. Back home my first date and I would have . . . well, never mind."

"Abby, you are the best stand-up liar I've ever met."

"Who says I'm lying?" Abby sniffed. "You going to take all day? Or maybe you want to call your fellow from bed. Back home, that's usually an invite to finish the date there."

"I'm finished," Kris said. "Let's do full armor with that suit. We can decide on tonight later."

Half an hour later, Kris was armored, dressed, and made up enough for Abby to permit her to make a phone call.

"Mr. Smythe-Peterwald is unavailable," a standard computer voice informed her.

"Please tell him that Princess Kristine Anne Longknife of Wardhaven would like to discuss a date with him."

"He will be so informed."

KEEP THAT RETARDED BUCKET OF CIRCUITS ON THE LINE A BIT LONGER, Nelly put in.

"Do you have any idea when he might answer my call? I have such a busy schedule," Kris lied.

"I am sorry, but I cannot offer any estimate. He is a busy businessman and often must respond to unscheduled priorities."

Kris hated talking to buffers. She really hated the ones that were following the new tact subroutines; they could waste your time by the yard. "Well, I really would like a call back before noon. If he is really delayed, maybe . . ." Kris rambled on. NELLY, HOW MUCH LONGER?

DONE!

Kris finished with the buffer, hung up, and turned around. "Okay, Nelly girl, what was that all about?"

"That block of wood was programmed to shortstop you. I corrected that minor fault. Now, when Hank next asks for his messages, yours will be at the top of the queue."

"More evidence Sandfire likes you where he has you?" Jack asked.

"If we needed any. Where's Tom?"

"He got away at six-fifteen," Jack said. "The guards were not too enthusiastic about that, but Abby just happened by with the coffee and donuts. What might have taken forever was resolved amazingly fast once the Sergeant commanding had food in his mouth. I've also arranged for chairs out there."

"Chairs!"

"Why not? Those kids will never be very good in a fight. At least this way they won't be cranky."

"When's Tom due back?"

"He'll stay out as long as he can, maybe until three if he can stretch it. He's dropping by the embassy to remind whatever officer is in charge of such matters that you and he are here and not intentionally missing ship movement or deserting."

"Oh Lord, I forgot about that stuff. I am supposed to check in once in a while, aren't I?"

"I can't picture the Navy booting you out for this," Penny said, standing at the door to her room, wearing one of Kris's nightgowns and robes. On her, they hung long.

"You don't know General McMorrison. Mac would love an excuse to be rid of me."

Penny raised her eyebrows, whether at the prospects of a Princess being given the heave-ho, or Kris's familiarity with the name of the Chief of Staff for all Wardhaven armed forces. Kris didn't bother to ask. Unless they got out of here, it wouldn't matter. And unless they figured out a way to blow up a nascent battle fleet, a lot of matters would change drastically.

But for the moment, Kris had absolutely nothing to do. She was, as comfortable as it looked, under house arrest. What she could do was already being done. She went down her list of things that might need doing and came up with a long list of answers that totaled "insufficient information."

Penny offered to play chess. "But not with Nelly. Just you." Halfway through the first game, it was clear Penny was far more experienced at this game than Kris ever wanted to be. Penny didn't mind when Abby took to kibitzing, offering suggestions and pointing out possibilities four and five moves in the future.

Kris minded. Standing, she waved a hand not at all as graciously as she wanted to. "Here, you take over."

"You've already lost the game," Abby pointed out.

"We can start a new one," Penny offered.

"You do that," Kris said, walking, not stomping, but walking gently to the screen. "Where is that call?"

"Earth girls don't wait to be called back," Abby pointed out, settling at the table and offering Penny two fists. Penny tapped one, got white, and they turned the board around.

"I thought the idea was for me to play her and help her stay calm," Penny said as she arranged her board.

"The woman is waiting for the man to call. Trust me," Abby said dryly. "There is no way to calm her. It's an X gene thing."

"I am not waiting for a man to call. I'm waiting for someone to call so I can go plant a bomb upstairs," Kris snapped.

"Looks like a moonstruck calf to me," Abby said, making her counter to Penny's opening move. "What do you think, Jack?"

"Be interesting to see if he calls. I suspect he's got Kris right where he and Sandfire and his papa want her. Locked up like a bird in a cage. Available to be plucked at their convenience."

Kris stuck out her tongue, but her heart wasn't in it. If Hank was his father's man, Jack was right. "I don't think Hank's in on all his father's schemes," Kris insisted. "He didn't know about the problem with the smart-metal boats he gave me."

"He got kind of quiet when you brought that up," Abby said as she quickly responded to Penny's move. Unlike Kris's game, Penny and Abby moved pieces around the board like it was greased.

"When you grow up in my neighborhood," Kris said, trotting over to bend down and get in Abby's face, "you learn real quick not to give anyone a sound bite they can use on the news or in a court of law against your father."

"Anyway," Jack said, stretching his legs out on the couch and picking up his reader, "it doesn't matter what plots he is or isn't in on. Whether you, young Princess, are moonstruck or not. If he doesn't call, nothing happens."

"He doesn't call, I have to figure out a new option for rearranging the plumbing upstairs," Kris pointed out.

Jack shrugged.

Nelly gave a kind of light buzz that startled Kris. "A call is coming in."

"Who?" Kris asked, struggling to swallow a grin. Abby brought her latest move to a roaring halt, a knight hovering in midair. Penny pulled her hand back from a move she was ready to make. Jack kept reading.

"Call has no identifier on it."

"Well, accept it," Kris said.

"Please hold a moment for Mr. Henry Smythe-Peterwald the Thirteenth," a computer voice announced. A coat of arms filled the screen Nelly had opened.

WAS THAT TRUMPETS?

I WOULD HAVE TO RERUN IT AND ANALYZE, Nelly said.

WHO'S THE ROYALTY HERE?

YOU ARE, Nelly said. Kris wondered how you snorted derision at a computer.

"Hi, Kris, sorry I missed your call." Hank actually did look sorry, a slight droop to the mouth, a bit of a slump to the shoulder. Breathlessly handsome, but tinged with regret.

"They keeping you busy?" Kris answered, trying to place the scene behind Hank, then realizing it was computer generated.

"Cal is up to his ears in things. I think he wants to impress me with his executive brilliance. Me, I'm wondering why he doesn't delegate the half of this. But then," he shrugged, "I've watched my dad in full fury a few times. Hope I don't get like that when I'm his age. What are you up to?"

"It's not what I'm up to. More like what I'd like to do for a while this evening. My social schedule kind of got lightened suddenly last night. You have any plans for tonight?"

"They're never any more my plans than they are yours. Are you hatching a conspiracy to slip our handlers and maybe steal a few hours just for ourselves?"

"Think we could get hung for treason?"

Hank glanced around like a bad video conspirator. "They have to catch us first," he whispered.

"Pick me up, say seven," Kris offered.

"Sounds great."

"What do I dress for, dinner, dancing, a movie?"

"Sitting alone with you for two hours while ghosts do all the speaking on a holostage is not what I want to do with you." He smiled. This one reached across his lips, swept up to his eyes, and didn't stop this side of his eyebrows. Nice smile.

"I'll wear something for dancing," Kris said.

"See you at seven."

"Call if you can't make it."

"The only way I won't make it is if somebody blows up the elevator and I get stuck on the ground."

"Hank, don't even think that! The way things have been going . . ." Kris let that thought wind down.

"Don't worry. I think Cal's had enough of the locals' bumbling. Nothing's going boom that he doesn't want. Bye for now, duty calls, and I'm gonna get duty wrestled and tied up in a big bow by seven."

Kris turned as the screen went blank. "He called," she said, letting her own grin out to romp and play.

"He's with Sandfire," Jack pointed out.

"As an observer," Kris countered.

"Maybe you can get him talking about a few of his observations," Abby said slowly.

"That's not what I want to do tonight."

Abby and Penny went back to their rapid-fire chess.

The day passed slowly. Abby paid a milk and cookies visit to the new guard shift and came back with an offer of a date from the Sergeant in charge. "Cupid seems to be going through arrows at an alarming pace," Jack drawled.

"You're just jealous 'cause I got a date and you don't," Abby said.

Jack shrugged her off with "Sergeant just isn't my type."

About three, Kris asked the obvious. "When is Tom due back?"

Penny paused, rook halfway to taking Abby's last bishop, gave a worried shrug, and went on with her game.

Jack took Kris aside. "I thought he'd be back by three. A quick stop at the embassy, then on to Penny's place."

"Could he have been held up at the embassy?"

Jack shook his head. "Your guess is as good as mine."

At four, Abby pushed back from the table. "Eight to eight. What do you say we leave it as a tie? There's always tomorrow."

"Just one more." Penny sighed.

"I really have to get Kris into a bath."

"Okay," had nothing but resignation.

"I'd offer to play you," Jack said, "but color me totally intimidated. I've never seen people play like you two."

"Saves me from thinking about anything but the game," Penny said, then snapped at the door. "Where is that man?"

"He'll call," Kris got out before she thought about it.

"I don't want him to call. I want him to walk his thin-skinned body through that door, preferably with no new black-and-blue marks on it."

Kris retreated to the bath; it wasn't nearly as relaxing. No sooner was Kris in the tub than Abby was showing her how to turn her falsies into bombs. "Stretch them out, or they'll totally block the pipes and never get to where they need to be."

Kris nodded. "How dangerous are those things to wear?"

"I only know of them going off prematurely once, and she shot her mouth off too much," Abby said, giving Kris a wicked grin.

"I'll take a vow of silence when I'm wearing them," Kris said, hefting a booby bomb with both hands. It was light; she slowly settled it into the water. It barely floated.

"You arm it by pushing down on the nipple; that arouses it," Abby said with a straight face. "Turn it three hundred sixty degrees, then depress it. Your breast is now dangerous."

Kris shook her head. "That's a disturbing picture."

"You are far too literal," Abby said, retrieving the bomb.

Kris relaxed, or at least soaked. Her mind spun. She was launching an attack on a sovereign planet. Did she have that right? Hell's bells, was there any chance she could trip up this planet's mad rush to war even after this crazy stunt? Where was Tommy? Where was some returned intel from the yard? How many girls going on a first date with a cute guy thought about these things? Kris just shook her head.

The real question was Hank. Was he out to kill, kidnap, or otherwise mess with her life? And most girls just worried about their hair and makeup at a time like this. "It would be nice to be just a girl sometime," Kris muttered, willing the jets to work their relaxing miracle on her muscles. But what could relax the tension between her ears?

After thirty minutes, Abby got her out, patted her dry, and started on her hair. About the time Kris was all sudsed up, Jack stuck his head in. "Tom called from the lobby. He says to stand by. If he needs help getting back in, he'll yelp." Abby went right on working Kris's hair.

Five minutes later, Nelly chimed from the edge of the dressing counter, "Tom's at the door. The new Sergeant doesn't want to let him in."

Kris stood up; Abby was already stepping back to give her room. Tightening her robe, Kris headed, water dripping and barefoot, for the suite entrance. Jack stood in the doorway, Penny beside him. A half-dozen guards blocked them from Tom. Armed only with his lopsided smile, the kid from Santa Maria faced the grays. Kris charged in, coming to a halt only when she stood beside Jack. "Is there a problem here, Agent, Sergeant?" she said, using The Face that Grampa Trouble might use to freeze a laser. Surprisingly, her hair didn't grow icicles.

"There seems to be," Jack said.

"No, ma'am," the Sergeant said, eyes flinching to the floor.

"If *our* security agent says so, there is," Kris said, invoking the imperial plural.

It had the desired effect. The Sergeant blanched and swallowed hard. The guards got a whole lot more interested in Kris than in Tom. He edged forward into their midst as Kris snapped, "*We* dispatched this young man to the surface of your planet because a member of *our* entourage required certain items from her home. Items required because she last came up here directly from the hospital, were she was being treated for a savage beating she received while supposedly under Turantic Security protection. Why are you delaying him?"

The Sergeant's Adam's apple was doing a full dervish dance. "Sorry, Your Highness, we were only trying to protect you."

"We appreciate your protection," Kris said, cutting him off even as she noted her transformation from "ma'am" to "Highness." "This matter has been well handled up to this moment. Let us leave it at that."

Tom moved through the guards with a regal dignity of his own, as befitted a Princess's courtier. The guards morphed from roadblock to honor guard without moving so much as a step. As Tom passed through, he rewarded them with a nod as royal as any Grampa Ray bestowed. Only when Jack had closed the door behind them did he deflate with a sigh that would have been the envy of all his Irish grandmothers. "Holy Mother of God, I thought they had me there," he said collapsing on the couch.

"We'd have retrieved you sooner or later," Kris assured him.

"You need me sooner. Can Nelly do her bug-catching thing?"

I AM WORKING ON IT. I AM WORKING ON IT, Nelly told Kris.

"Just a moment," Kris told the rest. The air sparkled and zapped around them.

HEY, SOME OF THESE ARE MINE! TOM BROUGHT BACK SOME RECON BUGS!

INTERROGATE THEM LATER. TOM NEEDS TO TELL US SOMETHING.

I AM VERY AWARE OF YOUR PRIORITIES, KRIS. JUST A MOMENT MORE, PLEASE.

Kris drummed her fingers on the end table as she knelt beside Tom. Penny had settled in beside Tom, an arm around his shoulders. Abby stood behind Kris. Jack moved around so he had a good view of Tom . . . and the door.

"All clear," Nelly said. "Tom, you brought back some of my recon nanos from the yard!"

"I was hoping to pick up a few. I borrowed Abby's second

computer, and it reported I got rid of all this morning's drop real fine. You can have yours back, Abby. I picked up new ones for Penny and myself at the embassy."

"Was that what took you so long?" Penny demanded, bouncing on the couch with impatience.

"Well, wouldn't you know but the Ambassador himself wanted to tell me to tell Kris not to do anything 'unseemly.' His word. 'We will work all of this out. We don't need her youthful exuberance leading her into some unseemly display.'"

"I'll try not to be unseemly," Kris said, adjusting her robe to make sure it was properly closed where she knelt.

"Penny's boss also took me aside for a little talk."

"Oh dear," Penny said.

"Kris, he also doesn't want you to do anything."

"Penny, you left me with the impression this boss of yours had guts. He sounds like a ninny who raids the Ambassador's long skirt collection."

"He usually isn't. Tom, did he give you a reason why Kris should lay low? Does he have some irons in the fire?"

"Doesn't he wish he had. He didn't say a lot, other than to make sure I was who I claimed to be and to get as much out of me about what Kris has been up to for the last week."

"What'd you tell him?" Kris growled.

"Only what he'd get from reading the papers," Tom said, primly brushing the legs of his slacks.

"So he didn't tell you why he wants us to be good little children and wave as the army marches off to war?" Kris said, letting the sarcasm run free.

"Yes, he did tell me," Tom said, real worry showing on his face. "I don't know how to tell you this, Kris. He wouldn't tell me how he knows it, but he says that Sandfire has something personal against you. I told him I knew a few good reasons. He seemed disturbed I knew so much about all that led up to the mess at the Paris system. Anyway, he says that Sandfire wants you personally in chains when this is over. Sandfire seems to think Hank Smythe-Peterwald's dad would love to have you served up naked to him. What happens next involves knives and doesn't end with you alive," Tom finished with a hard swallow.

That knocked Kris back. Literally. She settled into a cross-legged sit. She'd been afraid before, terrified even. It usually came before the shooting started. Once outgoing and incoming were flying, she was too busy staying alive to bother with fear. Suds rolled down her forehead; she wiped them away. Abby produced a towel and wrapped it expertly around Kris's head. Kris sat lotus and tried to calm the sudden roiling in her belly.

Sandfire wants me a prisoner, tortured, and dead, she said to herself, tasting it. Feeling it.

No surprise there; she knew she'd been dodging Sandfire's assassins for at least the last year. When Eddy was kidnapped and killed, was it Sandfire? *Was he going for the both of us? Did poor Eddy's demand for an ice cream cone save me?*

Sandfire, I hate you.

Kris stood up slowly, not leaning on anything, anyone.

"Sandfire wants a war started. I want it stopped. Sandfire wants me dead. I like being alive. Nothing's changed. Nelly, let us know when you have something to show us on the yard."

"Nelly," Jack said, "do you have any access to the lasers on this station?"

"What do you mean?" Kris growled.

"Nelly, do you have any way you could shut down the lasers they've got targeted for ships making for a jump out of here?

"Nelly, ignore that. Concentrate on the yard mapping."

"Kris, Jack, I can do both," Nelly said.

"Talk to me about the lasers," Jack demanded.

"Display what you have mapped of the yard," Kris said. AND DON'T YOU SAY A WORD TO JACK.

KRIS, I CAN DO BOTH, AND MAYBE IT WOULD BE A GOOD IDEA IF YOU AND I DID GET OUT OF HERE.

I DON'T WANT OUT OF HERE.

I DO! Great, now her computer wanted to live forever.

"Nelly, talk to me," Jack repeated.

DON'T. SHOW ME THE YARD.

"I have filled in the yard to some extent," Nelly began as the screen across the room turned from a lovely view of snow-capped mountains into a schematic of the station. "So far, our recon shows no other entry to the yard besides the elevators."

"Show me the lasers," Jack said softly.

A dozen batteries began flashing red.

"Where's the yard's power plant?" Kris demanded.

In the center of the yard a large block flashed yellow. "The fusion reactor is here," Nelly said. "The magnetohydrodynamic plasma track runs around the reactor."

"That is unsafe," Tom said, forming each word separately.

"As I said, this place was a rush job," Penny put in.

"Build it in a hurry, lose it in a second," Tom recited.

"Nelly, can you take out any of those lasers?" Jack asked.

"I have an eighty-five percent probability of penetrating the batteries on A and C levels," Nelly said. The eight lasers in the old section and the upper section flashed faster. "I have no access to the ones in the yard."

"They won't be there after we blow the yard," Kris said. "We can steal a ship and get out of here real easy then."

"And I don't think you or Tom will have any problem dodging the two or three yard lasers left active when we break out of here tonight," Jack said. "Tom, you good on defense?"

"Not as good as Kris is. Something about the hair on the back of her neck tells her just when to jink from a laser hit."

"We're not leaving tonight," Kris said firmly.

"My job is to keep you safe," Jack began slowly, as if talking to a very stubborn four-year-old. "This is not some Navy show. You heard Tom. The objective of this situation is you— your personal demise. My orders are to keep you alive, if necessary, in spite of yourself. You've known since this started there was more to it than Tom. You've known since the Ambassador passed along Sandfire's invite to the first ball that someone was showing an awful lot of interest in you. Now we know you are the target. I'm taking over, and you are leaving now."

"You did notice that someone is starting a war that will kill a hell of a lot more people than just little old me," Kris said. She started edging away from Jack . . . and backed into Abby. "Penny, you're with me."

The Lieutenant shook her head. "Kris, those had to be Sandfire's people who beat me up. Given a choice between another session with them and a fifty-fifty chance of being shot escaping, I think fifty-fifty are lovely odds. And did you hear Tom? They beat me up. Sandfire wants you dead."

"I heard. He's wanted me dead for a while now. I'm still breathing. He won't be much longer."

"Longknife to the end," Tom snorted. "You know, you can

be killed. Eddy died. Don't you have a few grandparents that weren't as lucky as General Trouble?"

"Eddy didn't have a chance. He was six. I'm not six," Kris said low, her voice sparking flint.

"I . . . want . . . you . . . out . . . of . . . here," Jack said.

"And I'll be out of here, once I blow the yards and docks."

"And kill Sandfire. It's personal now with you two."

"If I get a bead on Sandfire, he's dead." Kris nodded. "But priority one is blowing the yard and the damn fleet it's cobbling together. Jack, you know a hell of a lot of people are going to die if Sandfire gets what he wants. Klaggath's ready to throw himself at this mad drive to war. Klaggath and a couple of the Senators. They don't have a chance."

"What makes you think you do?" Jack shot at her.

Kris opened her mouth to shoot back a fast retort, then closed it. She couldn't claim she was the wild card in this game. Sandfire had dealt her in from the start . . . and she'd let herself be played. Kris's mind shot quickly through the last week. How much of it was her reacting to Sandfire? How much of it was her messing up his work? Little Nara Krief's kidnapping had not gone according to Sandfire's plan. What else?

"Jack, Sandfire has been running this place like it was his pet poodle. Yes, he ran me, too. He snagged Tom, and I walked right into his trap. But name me one person who could have pulled off the recon I did yesterday. One set of pictures, and everything Sandfire worked for went down the tubes."

"So he got his pet President to declare martial law, and he's right back running the show," Jack pointed out.

"Right." Kris paused. "Jack, you know I couldn't have gotten those pictures if a cabby hadn't been willing to stick his neck out. I wouldn't have gotten back here if a lot of women and men hadn't risked their lives for me."

"And now you're telling me you owe them," Jack snapped.

"I was going to." Kris sighed. "But maybe I ought to just leave it at this. There's a lot of people down there that deserve better. They want it. They've reached for it. I think we can give it to them. Why not try? What's so magic about us bugging out tonight? Why not tomorrow night, or the next one? Why can't we nibble a bit at Sandfire's god-awful plan?"

"Because you're bound to make Sandfire furious. And even

if he can't point a finger at you for this or that mess, he'll figure you for it and tighten the noose on you."

Kris nodded; Jack had an answer for everything she said. Without thinking, her hands came up to rest on her hips. "Then it comes down to this. We do this my way." There were glaciers on Wardhaven warmer than Kris felt at the moment. Ice cold. Determined. No alternative. No compromise.

"I can hog-tie you in five seconds," Jack whispered.

"Abby, don't even think of going for me," Kris said, taking a step away from her maid, even if it put her closer to Jack. "Anyone makes a grab for me, I start screaming. The guards will be in here before you can get a gag in me."

"That would really foul things up," Tom pointed out, maddeningly reasonable.

"No doubt about that," Kris agreed. "We do it my way, or I'll make sure we don't do it your way, Jack."

"You are a brat."

"Certified, Princess level," Kris agreed.

Jack locked eyes with Kris. She didn't blink. He finally shrugged. "Once we get home, I could ask for a reassignment."

So it had come to that, each of them playing their last card. Kris could scream and get them all locked away in the deepest dungeon Turantic had, able neither to escape nor wreck Sandfire's plans. And Jack could turn his back on Kris. Did he know how much she depended on him? How much she enjoyed him being around? Kris swallowed hard.

"That's something you'll have to decide when we're back."

"If we get back," Jack shot at her. "Abby, you better do something with her hair, or I'll get written up for causing serious damage to my primary." He scowled and turned away.

"Back to the sink, young woman. You may have the power to put my delicate flesh in a world of hurt, but I still am in charge of making you presentable."

Kris went where she was ordered . . . for a change. Tom's and Penny's eyes followed her. Was there desperation there, or just the usual expectation that she'd somehow get them all out of the mess she'd gotten them into?

21

Abby was putting the finishing touches on Kris's hair when the suite's doorbell rang. "I'll get it," Jack said, his voice the same cast-iron flat it had been since Kris balked his plan to get her off planet.

"Do I look all right?" Kris asked Abby in the mirror. The maid nodded, and Kris took a final look at herself. Abby had her hair up in swirls held in place by a diamond affair rented from the hotel jeweler. The aquamarine dress's thin waist ballooned in both directions. Petticoats assured the skirt would sway with every move she made. The bodice rose to just brush what it promised she had. With the bombs, Kris almost did. And once she got rid of them, no one would be the wiser.

Well, maybe Hank, depending on how close they danced.

Giving herself one last glance that proved her nose was no smaller—there were limits to even Abby' s magic—Kris advanced to see how things were developing.

The living room held no surprises. Three different security details were sniffing about, going through their dominance routines. Hank's was arrayed to the left of the door, the gray goons to the right, and Jack, with Tom in full Navy dinner dress at his elbow, held them all at bay while they each announced their intentions for the night. "We can handle everything," the head of Hank's detail said as if that settled it all. "Nobody told us about nobody going nowhere," the grays bleated, thereby losing all claim to control. "Kris goes nowhere without her detail," Jack said, which seemed to brighten up the grays' day until they realized Jack did not include them in that. Abby bustled out of Kris's room dressed in a severe dark gray suit and took station at Jack's other elbow.

"Are we ready?" she asked no one.

Hank gave Kris a knowing wink. "You look beautiful tonight," he said as if they were normal people, alone.

Kris did a little wiggle that set her entire ensemble to rustling and returned the favor. "You don't look half bad yourself." Which was definitely an understatement. His light tan tux was well set off by a red cummerbund. The deliciously ruffled shirt was dressed down for tonight with no tie and the last buttonhole empty.

Hank offered Kris an arm, proving chivalry was no longer dead, and led her through the still bickering security details as if they were not there. It took only a second of reflection for Kris to decide that might well be the way to handle tonight. Possibly every night. See how Jack liked that.

Hank's security had the slide car reserved. Hank missed the signal from the head of his detail that would have had Kris wait for the next car. Kris ignored the unseemly scrambling as she settled herself into the rear couch, Hank at her side.

"It's been quite a day," Hank said. "Have you been busy?"

"You may have noticed, Wardhaven isn't Turantic's favorite planet at the moment." Hank nodded attentively. "I've kind of been under house arrest today. After my schedule of late, it's rather relaxing." He shared in her laugh.

"Maybe I should try that approach. But Turantic has few ties with Greenfeld, so they don't quite know what to do with me."

"I thought your Mr. Sandfire was . . ." Kris left the words hanging.

"He's not my Mr. Sandfire. I'm not sure Cal is anybody's man." Hank sighed, and Kris could almost see him making a mental note to pass that observation along to his father. "He seems to have his irons in a lot of fires here, but a lot of people have been surprised to see me at his elbow these last few days. I think I'm part of some kind of coming out party. Not sure I really understand how I'm being used."

"But someone's always wanting to use us." Kris sighed.

"At least you get this Princess stuff." Hank flashed her an evil grin. "Makes it easy to save you. Me, I'm just another businessman's brat."

"Trade you," Kris shot back. "You can have it, crown and all."

"I'd want a few less diamonds," Hank said, glancing up at her present jewelry. "I don't think all that glitter would look good on a man."

"Hey, you or I make a fashion statement, everyone listens," Kris assured him. "But these are on loan for tonight. Didn't want to wear a crown out in public what with all the political currents washing around." *And I traded most of my crown for some pictures I thought might end this whole problem. Hope nobody misses that hat trick.*

The door opened, and the guards set up a perimeter before letting them out. Getting organized again took time; Abby and two of the grays missed the second car, and everyone waited until they arrived on a third. "I've seen better organized riots," Abby sniffed as she joined them.

"No doubt you organized them," Jack said, a second ahead of Kris.

Hank noticed the interplay and laughed. "I predict tonight will be very enjoyable."

"Have you done your usual exhaustive search of the available eateries to find the best . . . and probably most expensive?"

"But of course, since I'm paying."

"Hey, I called you up for the date. I pay," Kris growled, but she dropped it quickly. Not all the lines it would show on her face were laugh lines.

"But I'm an old-fashioned kind of guy. I would never let a lady pay for her supper."

"Yes, but my trust fund is bigger than your trust fund."

"You checked with your broker lately?" That brought a laugh to both. "I hate being out of communications," Hank finished.

"I really hate it. I'm in the second week of a one-week leave. My Captain's going to keelhaul me when I get back."

"I can't picture anyone wanting to sign your pink slip."

"Oh, I could name several Generals and at least one Admiral that would be delighted to be quit of me."

"That would have to be a career-ending move for them."

"It may sound that way to you, but there are several members of my father's opposition who would dearly love to see my family in that kind of media circus."

The restaurant was out of the way. The lighting was dim enough that Jack pulled out his low-vision glasses as he took a seat at a table with Tom and Abby between the door and the table Kris and Hank were led to by a hostess in a shimmering yellow sarong that may or may not have been translucent in good light. Hank seemed to find the view enticing.

"You plan to dance with the girl you brought or the help?" Kris asked, keeping a smile on her face.

"I never know with you Longknifes if I'll be leaving with you or be run off the planet. Figured I better keep an eye out for fallback options."

"Well let me get a good look at the waiter, and I may turn you loose."

"Who would take us?" Hank said, suddenly serious as he leaned forward so his words did not carry easily to the security details occupying tables three deep around them.

"We could buy this planet and everyone on it. You'd probably have change left over to upgrade that pet computer of yours. We could buy anyone, but could we get anyone here to have and to hold us?"

"Maybe we have to earn that," Kris said.

"How do we earn anything when we've inherited everything?"

"You sound like you've been giving this problem of ours," Kris said, knowing what she was saying could come out sounding so empty, "a lot of thought."

"You in counseling, too?"

"Navy frowns on its officers being emotionally unstable."

"Just like my old man. Let's say that I may have managed to find a friend or two that he doesn't know as much about as he thinks." Kris eyed the twitch of Hank's hand, the blink of his eyes. Sincerity wasn't there so much as hope.

"Your father coming on strong?"

"I think he's starting to feel old. All the rejuvenation we have these days, and men still seem to have their own menopause around fifty."

"Your grandfather's still alive."

"And Great-grandfather probably would be if he hadn't had that accident," Hank said. Kris had read Grampa Al's business intelligence report on that "accident." The final conclusion was fifty-fifty, a stockholder's revolt or Hank's father.

Interesting family.

But Hank didn't sound any more in love with his family than Kris was with hers. Was there any chance she could bring him into the mess she was in?

A waiter appeared at Hank's elbow. The young man was in a light blue sarong of his own. Shimmers and flesh played hide-and-seek with her eyes in the dim candlelight. Good pecs, good abs. Maybe even better than Jack's. Kris enjoyed the view while Hank ordered in a language that defied interpretation. NELLY?

IT MIGHT BE BALINESE, OR SOMETHING RELATED TO SOUTHEAST ASIA ON OLD EARTH, BUT IT ISN'T CLASSICAL. IT'S CHANGED IN SPACE.

What hadn't? Kris watched the fellow weave his way among the guards, then rose.

"You follow him, and I'll go hunting for the hostess," Hank said pointedly.

"I think that sign says the ladies' room is that way," Kris said, pointing. "While I've spent most of the afternoon in the bathroom, my maid doesn't believe in wasting time on old-fashioned uses of the place. I promise you, I'll be much better company if I'm several liters lighter."

"Say that five times and fast." Hank was his laughing self again. "But I swear, you stay gone too long, and I'll be in the back office with the hostess."

"I'll keep that in mind," Kris said as Abby attached herself to Kris's elbow.

"If I knew you were going to say bad things about me, I'd have demanded a higher wage."

"I thought the wages of your sins were already sky high." Now Jack was at Kris's other elbow, and a gray fog was stumbling from their seats to get in her way. "Fellows, you get between me and that door, and you get to clean up the mess," Kris threatened, and the gray opened before her like the Red Sea did for Moses.

NELLY, WE STILL HAVE DEFENSE NANOS WITH US?

WE HAVE NOT LOST A ONE FROM AMONG YOUR DIAMONDS.

RELEASE THEM AS SOON AS WE GET INSIDE THE DOOR. LET ME KNOW HOW MUCH COMPANY WE HAVE. READY?

READY, Nelly answered as Abby pushed the door open. Jack stopped in the doorway, which persuaded any doubting grays that Kris deserved *some* privacy.

SURVEILLANCE?

TWO CAMERAS SIGHTED DOWN THE SINKS TO SHOW YOU EN-TERING AND LEAVING THE STALLS. NOTHING OVER THE STALLS. FIVE FLYING NANOS.

TAKE THEM OVER, NELLY. TRY NOT TO KILL THEM.

WORKING ON THEM.

Abby checked the four stalls and found them empty. She stood back for a moment eyeing them dubiously, then muttered, "That looks like the cleanest." She pulled a bottle from her bag and sprayed down the place. Without a word, she stepped aside to allow Kris to enter.

The drill was to act pathologically terrified of germs. Hell-for-brimstone fighters could be quivering jelly where tiny bugs were concerned. It gave Kris an excuse to immediately flush the toilet, then flush it again. HOW WE DOING, NELLY?

ONE MORE.

DO YOU KNOW WHERE WE ARE? Kris thought as she settled down.

I HAVE LOCATED THIS RESTAURANT ON THE SCHEMATIC. THE FLOW BETWEEN HERE AND THE POTENTIALLY RICH METHANE TRAP SHOULD BE ABOUT TEN MINUTES. I CAN PROGRAM THE EX-PLOSIVES.

Drat, that might cut dinner short and certainly would mess with dancing. Then, of course, the security details might not react to a little trouble in the sewage treatment plant. *Right, my luck is bound to change before I'm an ancient spinster of thirty*. Kris laughed to herself.

DONE, Nelly reported.

Kris felt around, careful of the dress, and lifted out the left bomb, activated it, and let Nelly set its timer. She stretched it lengthwise until it was a good twenty centimeters, then slid it quietly into the water and flushed. A minute later, the second bomb was on its way. Kris took a moment to do what she'd come for—nothing like being scared spitless to fill a bladder—flushed again, and adjusted her dress. Abby waited outside to put the finishing touches on both the skirt and the top as well as help Kris wash her hands without getting water on the fabric. Done, Abby gave her a full once-over, then nodded. "I do damn good work."

"What, nothing about how easy it is to make someone like me beautiful?"

Abby fixed Kris with a puzzled eye. "You really need assurances from someone like me that you are beautiful?"

"Abby, I know I'm not." Kris sighed.

"Where were your mother and father, little girl, when you needed them?"

"Busy campaigning, or just busy," Kris said. "You going to open the door?" Abby did. Kris returned to her table, Hank rising as she sat down. "You're such a gentleman," she told him.

"What? I was just heading for the hostess. I figured you'd run off with the waiter."

Kris tapped a crystal goblet of water that hadn't been there when she left. "Someone's been working while I was gone."

"Water server. Cute little thing. Doesn't bother with that filmy sarong stuff. Eliminates all questions."

"You know, if I didn't know you better, I'd think you were some sort of rich spoiled brat who was afraid of commitment."

Hank said nothing for a long moment. "Boy, ain't that the truth." He sighed, then he glanced around, caught the eye of his chief security guard, and waved him close. "Nobody's going to kill me tonight. Her either. I need space. Back your people up to the walls. Wipe out bugs, then lie low."

"What about those gray fumble bums?"

"If you can't get them out of the way, I'll have somebody working your job tomorrow morning who can."

"No problem, Hank." The boss made quick, curt hand signals, and black-clad agents began quick-walking grays for the door. Where someone argued, money changed hands, and silence fell.

"Jack," Kris said over her shoulder.

"I don't like this," he said.

"I'm not asking you to. But I figure if you keep Hank's honcho company and Tom covers the other side, Abby can take a nap at the table next to the ladies' room."

"Kris, I'm dead serious. I can't be working my heart out trying to keep you alive and biting my nails every time you cheerfully ignore me. I don't want to be the one holding you while you die." He spoke as if he were watching her bleed out.

Almost Kris could see him, kneeling over her, feel his arms around her. Feel the blood draining from her. She shivered but would not change her mind. The rest of tonight was hers, hers and Hank's. "Go with Hank's man."

Jack did, his face a chiseled mask. Tom found a seat by the kitchen entrance at a table with another of Hank's men. That covered the three exits Kris had spotted as they entered.

"So, you do this often?" she asked cheerily.

Hank leaned back in his chair, seemed to sluff off a half ton of worry, and shook his head. "When Bertie was assigned to me, I told him I wanted to do this twice a year. He said he'd let me do it once a year. That was three years ago, and this is the first time I've actually done it."

"Hurray for you," Kris cheered.

"Yes, it is somehow maturing. Or selfish or risky. You think anyone will try to assassinate you tonight? You seem to get one of those as often as most people come down with colds."

"Now you're plum wrong on that," Kris said airily. "Why, that last brouhaha was really an attempt to kidnap that Senator's cute little daughter."

"Somebody had to be really stupid to try a snatch out from under you, of all people."

"Well, I don't think they were expecting to run into me." Kris shrugged. "Me, I was just trying to stay out of range of anyone who might be looking for me."

"And you walked into that. Dad's right. You Longknifes live wrong or something." That left Kris wondering what files the Peterwalds kept on the Longknifes and what they reported as the cause of death for a few of Kris' s ancestors. Somehow she doubted she'd ever read those files.

"And you Peterwalds lead such laid-back lives," Kris said. Hank scrubbed at his eyes, his beautiful face showing exhaustion. "Not this week. Cal wants me at his elbow every waking moment. Not as if he asks my opinion on anything. Just wants me there. I think he enjoys having me for an audience."

"Why would he want that?" Kris said. Maybe she would get some gossip for Abby.

"If I didn't know better, I'd say he wanted to impress me. Or intimidate me. 'Look at all the strings I can pull. Look at all the things I can make happen.' "

" 'You *really* want me running *your* show,' " Kris supplied.

"Maybe that's it. I'm not sure all he's doing is that impressive."

"Such as . . . ?"

Hank leaned back, eyed Kris up and down slowly, then shook his head. "Your dad has a few things he wouldn't share with his friendly opposition. You wouldn't talk about that, and I wouldn't push you. Don't push me." He almost sounded pleading.

"You're right; there's stuff I know about my father that I'd never want to see in the papers, but there's nothing he's ever done that I'd be ashamed to read, either."

"Nothing that you know of."

Now it was Kris's turn to shrug. "We are talking about what you and I know, aren't we?"

"Yes, but is everything done in your pop's name necessarily what he wants? With the message center hashed, I can't get a question off to my old man. Damn," Hank said, looking up into the void above and its star-covered night, eyes pleading as if the stars might answer the questions gnawing at him.

Might Hank be an ally? Could he help her bring this planet off its war boil? Dare she risk popping the question? She almost smiled at that. Girl meets boy, girl invites boy into world-shaking conspiracy. What follows from that?

The table trembled under her hands.

"What was that?" Hank asked the air around them.

How time flies when you're trying to have fun. Kris sighed. "Haven't felt anything like that since I got here. Think the spin stabilization is having problems? One of our embassy staff told me they slapped this station together pretty fast. Maybe they missed something?"

"Whatever it was, it wasn't good. Here come Bertie and

Jack. Why do I think your dance card just got filled up again?"

"Not if you say it hasn't," Kris said with what she hoped was a coy smile.

"I can only go so far against my security folks, then they invoke Dad."

"Bertie'd have a tough time phoning home tonight." Now her smile was pure imp.

"You are dangerous, Miss Longknife."

"Not nearly so bad since they made me Princess Kristine."

"And you expect me to believe that. So what is it, Bertie? The natives restless? That didn't sound like jungle drums."

"No, sir. There seems to have been a methane explosion in the waste treatment plant. The extent of the damage isn't clear, but I must suggest that you retire to your ship."

"You're not going to leave?" Kris said.

"Not likely," Hank told her, "but when there's any question of hull integrity, Dad wants me safe in the *Barbarossa*. You care to join us? It may be a while before they sound the all clear."

"I think Jack would have an epileptic fit if I did that," Kris said, eyeing her agent. He coughed gently into his fist.

"Right. Your man doesn't trust my men any more than . . . Tell me, Kris, have you ever seen an ancient play about two star-crossed lovers from families that hate each other?"

"*Romeo and Juliet,* isn't it?"

"I think so."

"They both end up dead, don't they?"

"Maybe we aren't that much like them," Hank said. Bertie cleared his throat. "Right. Kris, call me in the morning. Maybe we can do something tomorrow if they clean this thing up."

"They're going to have to do a lot of cleaning up," Tom said, joining them. "They had a water geyser up in the sinks. Really stinks in there."

Abby also appeared at Kris's elbow. "I hope you won't be requiring another visit to the ladies' room," she said. "The place is in some disarray."

The odor reached Kris. "I shall endeavor to hold it until we get back to the suite," Kris assured her.

Outside, her pack of gray surrounded her, apparently none the wiser about the problem. On the promenade, a glance up showed cracks in the mirror on the right-hand wall of the Top of

Turantic. Some couples were heading for the slide cars while others talked, as yet unaware of the extent of the problem.

"Sir, if we don't move fast, we could be stuck here for some time," Bertie said. Kris stayed on Hank's elbow as his men opened a path for them and her team. They only had to wait for one car and quickly filled it. The Sergeant commanding the grays was most distraught when there was no room for them.

"With luck, we won't see them for a while," Kris said as the door closed. "Abby, you want a night out? Tom, what about you?"

"I would prefer we were all in the suite, if that Sergeant does a bed check," Jack said behind his hand.

"Is it really that bad?" Hank said.

"Some newsies and grays seem to think Wardhaven should be treated as a cobelligerent with Hamilton," Kris said airily.

"Oh, right," Hank said, rather too easily reminded. That must have been among the things he'd watched Sandfire prance through today. How a business tycoon arranges the first moves of a profitable war. Basic and advanced course in one easy lesson. Of course, Sandfire would spare Hank the blood and the mud Kris knew as war. Definite oversight in Hank's education. Should she tell the guy he was being shortchanged? A glance at Bertie was enough to make Kris swallow the idea. That cold, bland face could hide a mountain of evil. She doubted she'd get three words out.

Hank might not know Sandfire wanted her dead. Bertie, now that was a different matter.

The slide car slowed to a stop. Kris and her people shuffled to the front. "You want to come in?" she offered Hank.

"We really must get you aboard ship, sir," Bertie said, an order if Kris ever heard one.

"I guess I better not," Hank said, not hiding the longing.

"We must try this again. Sometime when we can really talk."

"I hope so. Why would anyone blow up a sewage treatment plant?" Hank shook his head at the question.

"Was it blown up?" Tom put in. "Every waste plant has problems with methane buildup. You don't treat that smelly sludge with respect, things come back at you. I heard this was a rush job. Maybe some contractor cut the wrong corner," the space born finished, giving Hank something to think about other than what Sandfire would tell him.

"I'll see you tomorrow?" Hank asked as the door opened.

"Somehow I doubt I'll be all that busy." Kris smiled as she let Jack and Tom lead her out, Abby gently pushing from behind, the reluctant good night until the door closed.

22

"Let's get inside," Jack said. Kris followed him, twiddling her thumbs while three bug zappers helped Nelly clean up what they'd brought in. Kris's thoughts raced; they'd pulled off the first step of the plan. How quickly should she execute the next phase? She'd figured tomorrow, maybe later. Could she risk taking things slow? Would Sandfire give her that much time?

"All clear," Nelly said. "No new bug types in that mix."

"Something tells me its not going to take Sandfire very long to trace that back to us," Kris said immediately.

"We left him no trail back to here," Abby assured her.

"Sandfire doesn't need a reason to come after Kris," Jack said. "If we plan to do something, I vote for doing it now."

"Nelly, could you get a signal to the command bugs overseeing the recon in the yard?"

"We have that option. Kris, I must point out that—"

"That it will leave a trail to our door. Yes, Nelly, I know, but I don't intend to be here when they come knocking."

"What do you have in mind?" Jack said, a hint of a smile niggling at the formal frown he wore.

"Strike fast, strike hard, and get gone. Isn't that what they train us to do in the fast attack boats, Tom?"

"All the way!" he answered.

"Penny, how are you doing?"

The Lieutenant had joined them dressed in sweatpants and a shirt proclaiming, Go Navy. "I think I can keep up with the rest of you. I hear every task force needs a rear guard." Tom quickly was at her side, a concerned arm around her. She didn't flinch this time at his touch.

"We can handle the tail-in-Charlie slot," Tom said.

Kris left the two of them to a murmured argument. "Nelly, show me what we know about the yard upstairs." A schematic appeared, more filled in than last time. Kris ran her fingers over the outline. It was only five hundred feet up from her suite to the security wall that assured nothing in the hotel levels got into the yard. Actually, it was advertised the other way around. None of the chemicals or materials used in the yard could taint the pleasantness of the paying customers' air. Any way you cut it, it meant trouble for Kris tonight.

"We use a two-step daisy chain. First, one explosion to get everyone headed for the ground. Then, once anyone with good sense has got themselves gone, a second explosion for the kill. Nelly, calculate the time needed to evacuate the yard."

"Twenty-eight minutes and a few seconds," Nelly said. If a computer could sound reluctant, Nelly had the act down solid. "Kris, maybe Jack is right. Maybe we should move faster."

Kris glanced down to where Nelly hung on her hips and raised her eyebrows. Another one to report to Auntie Tru if they got out alive. "Jack, if we blow the yard without warning, we kill four to six thousand workers. That's what terrorists do. I didn't put on the uniform to do that kind of shit. I'm a sailor. When we fight, it's on the up-and-up. I say we pull off the first blow and start running. If we're being chased by the likes of those grays, we can stay a step ahead of them from now till doomsday. After thirty minutes, we do the big blow and run like hell. Any problems?" she said, facing her team.

"Putting it that way . . ." Jack shrugged. "I guess not."

"I do hate running with you Longknifes." Tom paused. "You come up with such good excuses to get everyone around you killed." But his smile was lopsided and about a klick wide.

"I think I know how you got that ship to dump its Captain

and follow you," Penny said. "Why don't I think my boss will believe my report . . . assuming I'm alive to write it." But she, too, was grinning like she'd taken leave of any claim to good sense. Now she truly was perfect for Naval Intelligence.

"You'll need to dress for the part," Abby said with a sniff and turned for Kris's room.

"We're ten minutes into the evacuation of Top of Turantic. Let's give them a full hour to get the kids down. There's some risk that Sandfire could react, but even he has to close down what he's doing now before he can launch anything new against us. Let's get dressed, as Abby said. We've got new parts to play."

There was a ring at the door. Jack glanced at his wrist. "Ten minutes. Not bad, considering the confusion."

"You handle them. I'm taking a bath to relax after the stress of being so close to a bomb," Kris said.

Closing the door behind her, Kris turned to Abby. "What does the well-dressed bomber wear?"

"I thought this little number might come in handy," Abby said, turning from Kris's wardrobe with a dark blue watermarked silk dress held across herself. The tight waist was marked off with silver filagree before petticoats swished out to a short skirt. That would leave a lot of leg to distract male eyes. But only if they pried them away from what little of the bodice there was. Deep scooped, it revealed enough cleavage to make Kris gulp. "Can I wear that?"

"Honey, this only makes it easy to get at your explosives."

"What is it with you and booby bombs?"

"Young woman, how can you expect Hollywood to make a spectacle of your life if you don't have lots of explosions?"

"And boobs."

"As someone nature failed to properly endow, I make it my mission in life to correct such shortcomings. Now strip, Miss Princess. Full body stocking is suggested with this getup."

Kris stripped but didn't stop arguing. It kept her mind off of what she was getting into. "How can I wear full armor with this and still get at those booby bombs of yours?"

"They have sticky backs to go on the outside of the suit."

"Why didn't you do that with the first batch tonight?"

"Because I had no idea how close you'd let that Hank Peterwald get."

"It was dinner, Abby. Dinner and dancing, maybe. Turned out not to even be dinner."

"Ah, the confidence of youth. You honestly believe you know exactly what you'll do from moment to moment, don't you?"

"Of course," Kris said, down to nothing and starting to pull on the body stocking. Like everything made of Super Spider Silk, it had no give; Abby talced Kris; the pain was almost bearable.

"Well, Baby Cakes, someday you're going to find that passion or hormones or just the raging fates can blow your plans away. When it does, remember Mamma Abby warned you. Oh, and don't forget to enjoy it."

"Aren't we here because of the raging fates?" Kris said.

"No, honey child, we are here because you still harbor the illusion you can snap your fingers and make anything happen."

"Am I that bad?" Kris said, feeling the pressure of what she'd gotten these people into closing in on her. Suddenly it was hard to breathe.

Abby glanced up from where she was working the suit up Kris's narrow hips, sighed, and let the hint of a smile cross her lower lip. "In case you haven't noticed, there's a whole lot of stuff going on around here. You're part of it. I, may the gods and goddesses have mercy on my misspent youth, am part of it. Even that poor Hank kid has his part. I believe you're trying to make it better for a whole lot of people who have a part in this, but no control over it. You, however, young woman, have the illusion that you can control it, and having that illusion, may very well gain control."

Kris shook her head and made a sour face at her maid. "Well, then, who do you think has control here? Sandfire?"

"Sandfire walks in the illusion of control, just as you do. Just as your Captain did on the *Typhoon*. But you grabbed the imagination of the rest of the crew so powerfully they were dragged right into your illusion. Look what happened. I can't wait to see whose illusion is the most powerful here."

Kris frowned as she worked her arms into the suit. Abby had just shown she knew a whale of a lot more about Kris's life than she should. Another thing to grill this woman on later. Right now, Abby had piqued Kris's curiosity. "If Sandfire and I only have the illusion of control, then who is running this lash-up? Tell me, oh suddenly wise and ancient monk of the mountain."

Abby actually laughed, a chuckle that shook her body from belly to hairline. "And what makes you so sure someone is in control? You put a single person in a room, and maybe they control themselves. Maybe, assuming they don't get in an argument with their father or mother and let someone not there control them. You put two, three, a dozen, a million people into a room, onto a planet, and Great Hera herself can't tell you who's running things. Does your dad run Wardhaven?"

"Heavens no. Wardhaven's a democracy. Father's only—"

"Got you there. Let's see how this dress falls." And Abby brought it, and Kris lifted her arms and let it settle around her. The waist was tight. The skirt swished, which Kris was finding delightful, and the bodice was a scandal. Or would have been if Kris filled it out. Abby did with two bombs that jiggled nicely for any male type suffering from testosterone poisoning.

"No bra?"

"Why spoil the view? Distracting a male eye could be half the battle tonight. Now, let's load you up." Kris's ten kilos of dumb metal went into a strap that rode high on her rump. The short, flounced skirt covered it nicely. Abby produced a laser.

"Where'd that come from?"

"That nice Jack brought it through security. You were planning on using the metal to drill, but why don't we avoid turning that hunk of not-so-smart metal into one thing, then another."

"Agreed," and Kris developed a pouch of a tummy.

"You're filling out nicely," Abby said. "You really should put on some weight. All bones and angles can't help but scare the guys away."

"And I always thought it was being able to buy and sell them from my petty change purse," Kris drawled.

"Can't really tell until you try it, can you?"

"Why don't we get out of this mess, then discuss my diet."

"Good idea," Abby said, settling Kris's Navy tiara on her piled-up hair, then running a wire down to Nelly at Kris's waist. "I've included the antennas in the tiara," the maid said.

"Too bad I don't have the fancy one tonight."

"I'll have backup crowns for you next time we go adventuring," Abby said, turning back to Kris with four small cylinders in hand. "Here are more nice booms. There're pockets for them just under the waist of your skirt. These are nice whizbangs, guaranteed to make anyone near them lose all interest in chasing you for a whole minute, maybe two."

Kris pocketed the four, noting their green strips. A close look at her skirt showed a dozen pockets. Abby presented four more. "These are sleepy bombs. Let us know when you use them, unless you want us to sleep along with the bad guys. Sorry, no masks, a slight oversight on my part."

"Has to be the first. I've got four empty pockets."

"These are deadly. Fragmentation bombs. Use them when you want a whole lot of people to quit bothering you." Kris handled them respectfully and made special note of where she put them and their red strips. Finally Abby handed Kris a small automatic and three clips. "Use them sparingly. That's all you have."

Kris checked the works. One clip of sleepy darts was already loaded. She clicked in a lethal load next to it. Switch the safety off, and it was sleepy darts. Move the switch another click, it was lethal. Kris left it at sleepy darts for a start.

It would not stay that way. Tonight she would kill someone— or be killed. Kris let the thought roll around in her head. Her stomach went sour; her heart took on a chill. She'd never been in a him-or-me situation before. Sandfire wanted her dead in the worst way. She liked breathing. Someday she might even want a family. *If I do things right tonight, the option stays open. Blow it, let Sandfire win, and I die.*

Kris holstered the small automatic on her right thigh, adjusted the fall of her skirt, and stood tall. "Let's go."

"Let me clean up a few things. I'll be right with you."

Kris opened the door of her suite. Outside, Tom was still in formal dress uniform. With a grin, he made two service automatics appear. Beside him, Penny was in like drill, white dress pants in place of the long skirt otherwise required. The cut of her tunic was loose enough to hide exactly where she produced a machine pistol from. Jack simply stood beside them, looking his usual friendly, deadly self.

"Are we ready?" Kris asked.

"Looks like it," "Ready as we'll ever be," was followed by Jack's simple "Yes."

"What do our guards look like out there?"

"I told the Sergeant we were in for the night. He dismissed half of them."

"We've evacuated the top of this thing. Nelly, order the nanos in the yard to link up and short out transformers."

"We can take out four and still have our command units and a few defenders left over for when the dust cloud arrives."

"Do it, Nelly, and call in your security nanos here. Don't leave any behind. They may come in handy."

Jack looked at his wrist unit. "Five minutes?"

"Probably sooner. Sandfire reacts fast," Kris said.

Abby joined them; twelve trunks rolled after her.

"Do we need those?" Jack growled.

"If we lose them, I won't weep, but why abandon what we don't have to?" Abby said with simple logic.

A minute crawled by. Kris settled into her chair. The others found seats of their own. The next minute took longer. Kris was committed. Somewhere in this station an alarm was blinking or clanging, screaming that a major message stream had been shot into the yard from Kris's suite. There was no benefit to second thoughts. Either she or Sandfire would get what they wanted tonight. No political compromise, no splitting the difference. That was why Kris chose the Navy over Father and his politics. Then, the clarity of alive or dead seemed better than settling for half a loaf. Half of what you wanted.

Maybe Father had a point.

If I get out of here, I'll have a sit-down talk with the man, Kris promised herself.

"Kris, there is major traffic on the security net."

Kris rose to her feet. "Jack, please invite in our guards."

Jack quickly stepped off the distance to the door, then paused. "It might be better if we really had a fire," he said.

"Right," Kris said. "Abby, get those crates into Jack's room." While the maid did, Kris took the four steps to her door and pulled a cylinder from her pocket. One red band. Big boom. *Take this, you screenwriter.* "Fire in the hole," she called, tossed it at her bathtub, and ducked back against the wall.

Three very noticeable seconds later, the bathroom exploded.

Jack waited a further second, then yanked open the door. Across the hall, two men were propped back in chairs, one snoring. Jack yelled "Fire!" and both came awake with a start. One fell out of his chair sideways; the other landed on his feet. The Sergeant appeared in the door, rubbing sleep from his eyes. He raced past Jack, followed by three others. Kris pointed them at the bathroom as alarms began pulsating in the room and the hall, drowning out even Kris's bellow of "Fire! In there!"

They charged into her bedroom, then came to a halt, gaping at the wreckage . . . and maybe realizing they had nothing to fight the fire. Kris waved Tom forward, automatic in hand. "Nonlethal," she whispered in his ear between bleats of the alarm.

Tom didn't change his ammunition selection. He shot; four grays crumpled. Kris examined the bath. The bomb had shattered the tub. Spray from the faucets was putting out most of what had caught fire. "Leave them," she ordered.

Penny and Tom took the lead for the door. Abby was already halfway down the hall, trunks rolling along behind her. As she punched for an elevator, one opened.

Trouble in spandex.

Eight of Sandfire's girls stood in red, form-fitting body suits. Utility belts showed wicked looking bulges. Most held machine pistols at the ready; one had only a long black staff. Another held a crossbow slung across her arm.

For a startled moment, the two groups stared at each other. As weapons came up, the adjacent elevator door opened for Abby. She led her boxes in as if she knew nothing of what was about to happen. However, the maid had not given Kris all her small and impressive packages. As Abby crossed the threshold of the elevator, she casually tossed a small cylinder into the next car.

It gave a loud pop, knocking the red beauties off their combat rhythm for a fraction of a second, and gave Kris's crew time to grab their weapons and dive for the floor.

Suddenly, the elevator was filled with swirling smoke lit by blinding flashes of light. If eyes weren't dazzled, ears were shattered by a high-pitched screech that warbled as it went up and down the scale.

Behind Kris, Penny's automatic pistol rattled from the doorway, hardly noticeable among the racket. Its slugs gouged plastic and plaster from the elevator wall where rounds missed

the car and its load. Jack produced a machine pistol and emptied the magazine. Kris felt a moment's compassion for the
reds until a slug ripped plaster from the wall beside her.

Kris wasn't the only one wearing body armor.

She spun on her belly and snaked herself down the hall toward an exit light just as a gray figure emerged from the elevator's smoke at a low crouch, weapon on full automatic. A stream
of rounds shot over Kris's head before the woman spun and fell
back into the smoke. Six hits on her body only knocked her
back. The one that exploded her face killed her.

Kris reached up to unlatch the stairwell door, then pushed it
open by rolling through it. Now with her pistol out, she worked
herself up to her knees, took aim, and sent single rounds at
anything in the smoke that looked like a face or bare flesh.

She didn't have many good shots, but she fired some of her
limited ammunition every few seconds to encourage heads to
stay down.

Weapons in both hands, Tom wiggled his way backwards
to the stairwell and joined Kris. "Those red outfits turn gray in
the smoke. Anybody notice an explosion in the yard?" he said
as he took station above Kris and sent a stream of slugs down
the hall.

"The red outfits are also bulletproof. Nelly, anything?"

"Three of the task units reported just before they self-
destructed," the computer reported. "There are alarms on all
levels of the station and verbal instructions to evacuate as
quickly as possible. I assume the same is going on in the yard."

"Good assumption. Tommy, me boy, the show is on."

"And did I ever doubt it for a second," he said, brogue
showing. "Now, how do we get the hell out of here?"

The smoke hung in the elevator. Normally, there should
have been a draft going into the stairwell. Not today. "Somebody's closed down the airflow."

"Only way to fight a fire," the spacer pointed out.

Penny was now on her belly, snaking her way toward Kris.
Jack kept up his fire even as he began a backward crawl. Someone in gray edged out of the elevator, but their face turned into
a messy pulp, and motion stopped.

Fire was slow and sporadic as Penny backed into the exit
door. Tom kept shooting, sending rounds into the smoke from

on high. Encouraged, most fire from the elevator was equally high.

Jack rolled himself into the stairwell just as something flew by Kris's head to explode at the far end of the hall. The back blast flashed toward Kris as she slammed the door shut.

"What was that?" Tom asked breathlessly.

"I don't think that crossbow is for friendly games of darts," Kris said as she opened the door a crack. Two gray figures came through the smoke at a crouch, machine pistols at the ready. "I'll take the one on the right."

"I got the left one," Tom said.

"On three. One, two, three," Kris said and squeezed off a burst directly at her target's face. She collapsed, to be covered by Tom's target. There was no more movement in the smoke.

Kris wasn't waiting for any, either. "Let's get upstairs."

"That takes us toward maintenance," Tom pointed out.

"Which is where they won't be expecting us," Kris said as she hiked up the first of a long flight of stairs, heels echoing on steel. Jack was right behind her, Penny and Tom farther back.

"Nelly, tell me what's happening."

"The station is being evacuated. Yard, too, from the level of power to the elevators. The security net is going wild."

"Any traffic near us?"

"No, Kris, but I did not get any signal traffic off the group in the elevator. Totally quiet."

"A different net would be my guess," Jack offered. "Look for something anywhere on the frequency band. Even something in the civilian net that isn't used here. These folks aren't going to be bothered by a minor thing like frequency allocation."

Kris brought her team to a halt on a landing. "We've got to split up. Tommy, you and Penny can't keep up with me and Jack."

"Yes we can," and "I'm with you," was their reply.

"I also want to complicate Sandfire's chase. We stay together, he's got one problem. We raise scatter hell, and he's not sure who's doing what where. Play with me," Kris said, pulling several of her cylinders from her dress. "We've got thirty minutes to run before I want to blow the yard. I've got to stay free that long."

"Make Sandfire's life miserable." Tom grinned. "I can do that."

Kris handed Penny half the bombs, explaining them as Penny pocketed each type. "Now, you walk or take a slide car down into the business section. Twenty minutes from now, meet us at Dock Eleven. That's where they park the private stuff. We hijack one and head for a jump gate before the station blows. Now, make tracks. I'm leaving a booby trap here for our friends."

Tom and Penny checked the hall, found it clear, and headed out. "What does that leave us?" Jack asked.

"There's a service belt at the next landing," Kris said, feeling inside her bodice and producing a booby trap.

"Real booby trap."

"Pity, now I'm off balance. Give me a lift." Jack made a foothold, and Kris stepped up just long enough to stick the explosives to the metal of the landing above them. *Wonder if Jack's a legs man?* "Nelly, leave a nano to blow this if it spots people in SureFire Security gray or red/gray ninja getups."

"Done."

"Let's make tracks." They headed up another flight, found a door that Nelly opened onto a floor between the floors, full of air ducts, cable runs, and all the other necessities of modern life that people ignored. Nelly projected a holograph map. This floor circled the station at the .75 gravity level. Open all the way, they could reach the yard wall from here, but Kris intended to work her way closer to the station hub. If she was going to blow out the yard, she'd do it from the center out.

"Cameras, Nelly?" Red points appeared on the map. "Lay out a walk that dodges as many of them as we can," Kris said, then glanced around at the gray walls, floor, and machinery. "I don't think my Princess camouflage quite fits here."

"Nelly, is there a locker room on the map?" Jack asked.

A block showed yellow. The locker room had security, but someone had stuck a picture in front of the lens of a naked guy mooning the camera. Jack only broke into three lockers before he had two sets of orange overalls and blue union baseball caps. A tool kit in the last locker provided the final element for their disguise. That, and Kris's skirt. Bunched around her middle, it gave her a world-class beer gut.

"You got to start exercising more, Bud," Jack said, elbowing her in her crinolines.

"It's not the beer," she shot back. "I was born this way."

"It's gonna be the death of you."

"You can say that again," Kris said, buying into it, double entendre and all.

Jack looked at a clipboard he'd found, handed Kris the tool kit to lug, and led off like he knew what he was doing. Kris followed, steering him as Nelly directed her. This lasted for most of five minutes, enough for Kris to start thinking they might make it. Then a hooter went off in the gray and dusty space between floors. After three blares, a computer voice announced all personnel were to leave the station. "A lockdown is being enforced. Anyone remaining will be subject to immediate arrest and detention. If you resist, you will be shot. All work is to cease. Go to the nearest descent station and exit the station." The hooter went back to hooting, then repeated the order.

"No surprise there. Sandfire is running scared."

"I would be about now if I was fighting you," Jack said.

"Maybe it's time to go with plan B. Get the nanos into the yard soonest and let them loiter up there while we run like hell."

"Best idea you've had all day. All month. Maybe all lifetime."

"I don't like leaving our nanos for them to attack," Kris said, starting to trot for the nearest exit like a good worker.

"Better than leaving ourselves out for them to attack."

"Let's try for the next exit. See if we get called on it."

"Why do I not want to say it's your call?" Jack scowled but trotted along as Kris took a right turn. Kris managed to skip three exits: a slide car, an elevator, and a stairwell.

She was working her way higher up the station, closer to the yard wall when the horn ahead of them quit hooting and a woman's voice squawked. "Work party on twenty-six B, what the hell do you think you're doing?"

"I forgot my lunch pail," Jack shouted. "I got this new thermos I don't want to lose."

"Forget your damn coffee, you idiot. This cheap ass pile of crap is falling apart, and there are goons all over looking for anyone they can shoot for a saboteur to cover the ass of the bloody idiot who built this mess. Don't be dumb; get the hell out. I'm leaving in two minutes."

"We're going, we're going," Kris shouted. "I told you your damn coffee wasn't worth my neck."

"You got it, honey. You tell him."

"Women," Jack snarled, but headed for the nearby exit.

"You're the fools what want to live with us," the horn blared back.

"Not live with you, just—"

Kris got Jack good in the ribs.

"Throw that one back where he came from, honey, we can get you a better work partner."

"The last one was all hands. I'll take him. He's just a lot of talk," Kris answered.

"Well, you hurry along. I'm out of here. There's a gray goon that wants my observation station, and he can have it. Maybe they're getting overtime. I sure ain't. Now hurry along."

Kris did, for about thirty seconds, then took a turn and headed up again.

"How long before a gray spots us?" Jack asked.

"Your guess is as good as mine. A gray can't know the plant layout like that nice woman did."

"Big mouth you mean."

"You're just mad 'cause she turned you down for a date."

"I assure you, young woman, when I offer a woman an evening, I do it most graciously, and I am never turned down."

"What'd that woman say? 'You're the fools what want to live with us.'"

"I don't want to live with her."

"Who does live with you?"

"No one. I'm never home anyway."

"So you live with me." That got no answer for several steps. Jack was just opening his mouth, Kris anticipating his reply.

"Freeze where you are," growled a voice behind them.

23

Kris froze in midstep. Jack, mouth open in mid banter, a statue beside her.

"Now turn around. Do it now. Do it slow. Nothing fast, or I'll shoot you both dead." The voice was high, tending to crack in the upper registers. Just what Kris needed, a nervous finger on a gun aimed at her. She turned slowly, one hand raising high. The other still holding the tool box. Jack did the same.

"We're doing what you want," Kris said in a soothing voice. "We don't want no problems here. We're leaving. We just wanted to get Jack here's new thermos. He paid one of those latte places to fill it," she rambled on, stepping forward and just casually coming between Jack and the gray-clad security guard.

"Everybody got told to get the hell out of here." The young man licked lips already raw and chapped. Very nervous type.

"Yeah, but when has the boss man ever meant what he says when he's panicking and ordering everyone around?" Kris said, seeking sympathy. "And we got really good coffee. You want a cup?" she said, stooping to put down her tool kit, giving him a good view down her only partially zipped overalls and the one falsie she still had.

The youngster stared, part distraction, part confusion, and no part alarm. He nodded. A split second later, he collapsed slowly as Jack put three sleepy darts into him.

Kris grabbed his automatic pistol before it hit the deck. She popped his ammo belt off and snatched his wrist unit, stuffing it down her bodice. "Nelly, crack that net. We got any bugs we can spare?"

"I have twelve. I am working on the net."

"Send one bug zigzagging off that way," Kris pointed. "Have it switch off every camera it can. Do the same with another bug in the opposite direction."

"Doing."

"Which direction are we going?" Jack asked.

"I think we're close enough to the wall. Time to take the exit like we were told," Kris said, dodging around the elevator.

"Right behind you."

"I had Corporal Stout report that he is pursuing two people and gave a bearing that follows my first decoy," Nelly reported.

"Good," Kris said as she opened the service hatch behind the bank of elevators. "In you go, Jack."

"I thought you were going to lead, and I got to follow."

"Change of plan. You missed Chivalry 101 and failed to open the door for me."

"Damn, and me out killing some of your dad's opposition the day it was taught. They said I'd never miss it if I worked for a Longknife."

"That'll teach you to trust what other people say about those damn Longknifes," Kris said, leaving a whizbang on a ledge next to the door. "Nelly, leave a nano. Blow the charge if something gray or ninja comes in here."

"That leaves us only nine," Nelly pointed out.

"Nine will have to do. What's happening on net?"

"SureFire Security is dividing its forces between problems on Level 26—that's us—and Levels 51 and 39. One of those must be Tom and Penny. There are also crowd control problems on five other levels. Kris, people are panicking."

Jack glanced down at her; she shrugged. She'd known when she started that evacuations were not orderly affairs; people got hurt. Whatever happened in the next twenty minutes had to be less deadly than what would happen when the station started whipping around as the yard blew out. Calculated risk.

Climbing went quickly. Gravity grew less the closer they got to the hub. Jack went hand over hand up the rungs, Kris right behind him. There was a shout from below them followed by a burst of rapid fire. A second later the whizbang went off. Noise, flashing light, and smoke turned the shaft into no place to be; Jack opened the next exit hatch and made good use of it.

"We're not quite at the hub," he told her. A glance showed a high ceiling, gray work spaces, heavy machinery, and from the smell, a wastewater treatment plant.

"Am I going to spend the rest of my life doing penance for that little bomb topside?" Kris snapped.

"I'm sure you'll earn worse karma," Jack said and ducked behind a whirling green generator.

Two grays were headed their way at their best attempt at a run in this gravity, arms and legs flying.

"Put your hands up," one bawled. Kris did. Jack snapped off two shots; the grays tumbled and slid along the deck.

"That cuts it," Kris said. "We fight the rest of the way."

"The security net has squawkers reporting those two down," Nelly added.

"That way," Kris pointed. "The wall can't be too far over."

Problem was, that direction had four grays coming around a corner at a run. Kris took them down in one burst that pounded shredded bodies against the wall. A glance at the gray pistol she'd picked up showed only one setting: deadly.

"This is for keeps," Jack said, switching his weapon from sleepy to lethal. That wasn't what Kris intended, but Sandfire was calling the tune now.

She half-trotted, half-skated for the corridor the grays had just left, careful with her steps in one-quarter gravity. A stairwell's door gaped open. Ahead of her loomed a long open space, dotted with the occasional humming machine, pipe run, stairwells, and control stations. The far side of this big space was the wall. She spotted a room built out from it and pointed it out to Jack. Kris tossed a sleepy bomb in the stairwell, closed the door, and made fast, tiny steps for the wall.

Kris heard footsteps before she saw them. Going to ground behind a large yellow pump, she searched to the left. The legs of the grays came in sight first. This close to the hub, the pronounced curve up of the floor made for a close horizon. Kris waited, then drilled them as their bodies came in view.

Jack caught up with her, paused for a second, then said, "Cover me," and launched himself for a pipe run.

Kris was up as soon as Jack got down, low trotted past him and across the floor to drop behind a compressor. Jack was up and moving while she was still bouncing.

On Kris's right, a gray turned the corner of a green-painted bank of pipes, seemed startled to find herself already in the fight, and turned to run as Kris dropped her. A fusillade of fire to Kris's left made a lot of noise and resulted in spent darts ricocheting off the ceiling but left no target for Kris. NELLY, GET A BUG OVER THERE.

ON ITS WAY.

It showed three grays squatting behind a very solid generator, occasionally sticking their machine pistols out enough to fire but never enough to aim. Kris chalked them down to a risk not worth pursuing. Maybe others would catch their attitude if they lived.

Far to Kris's right, an elevator door opened, followed by an explosion, smoke, and flashing lights. Kris snapped off a burst and waited. Jack dropped but held his fire. Nothing came out that Kris could see; she wiggled around to the other side of the compressor for cover.

KRIS, THERE ARE OBSERVER NANOS OUT NOW, Nelly announced.

KILL THEM.

I AM TRYING, BUT THEY ARE TOUGH FIGHTERS.

Kris risked a look. A red-clad body lay just outside the elevator doors. Sandfire's harem had caught up with them.

Kris backed off and half-ran, half-sailed for a spinning turbine. A grenade flew out of the car to smash itself against a piece of massive machinery. Smoke swirled to cover the entire elevator landing. Jack liberally hosed down the smoke, but now there was return fire, and it spread out. The reds were loose.

"Follow me, Jack," Kris shouted. The two of them dodged and weaved as they fired and ducked their way across the industrial floor. Rounds flew from both directions. A pump took punishment it wasn't designed for, sending a spray of oil or

other industrial-grade chemicals flying in lazy globules. Some
caught fire, adding smoke to the mess before the lack of nearby
oxygen suppressed the flame. The oil did send one swift-
moving red into a pratfall. Kris got a good shot at her face. Now
blood added its red to the wreckage.

Three grays came running down the decking over a wire
run to Kris's left. They emptied their magazines at Jack to no
apparent effect as Kris snapped off a fast volley in their direction. Suddenly, there were no more grays.

"Those damn fools," came from behind Kris. So the reds
didn't think much of the grays either. Kris loaded a new clip
and emptied it in cover fire as she lunged for the wire run.

Her orange coveralls ran red from the slaughter as she slid
under it, but the fire that chased her did not catch her. She
slammed a new magazine in. Shouldering two full ammo
satchels, she grabbed a machine pistol from one of the fallen,
reloaded it, stood, shouted, "I'm covering," and let loose with
both guns.

Jack did a fast trot for her. She waved her head, pointing him
for the stairwell the three dead grays had used, and he changed
directions. Snagging an extra machine pistol as he went by,
Jack sailed into the stairs as Kris emptied both magazines.

Now Jack covered her as she made the dash, crashing
into the stairwell as Jack slammed the door closed. A grenade
bounced off it with a clank followed by an explosion. Someone was at least using only low-order stuff; the door bowed in
but held.

Kris frowned. There should have been dents where darts
stuck in the outside. Lots of dents. "Somebody wants us alive?"
she muttered as she followed Jack up the stairs.

"That was the idea, remember? You naked, Sandfire and
Smythe-Peterwald with knives. Looks like his harem of red
ninja wanna-bes has got that word."

"I don't like this."

"I haven't liked it for some time. You got another one of
those whizbangs?" Kris passed it to him. He cracked the door
a bit and rolled it out. Three seconds later, noisy, flashy hell
broke loose. He counted to three. "We run now."

Staying low, he rolled right from the door. She rolled left,
then wiggled for cover behind a bank of pipes. This ring was

also industrial gray. Slugs cut the air over her head. She wiggled some more and spotted two attractive legs in red tights behind an elevated walkway. The legs led to a very intense face behind an assault rifle firing on full automatic. Kris was immediately in love with that rifle.

One shot, and a lovely face vanished.

Kris crawled forward, spotted another shooter, and knocked her down with a short burst, then finished her off with a single shot to the face. To Kris's right Jack handled similar problems. A few more wiggles, and Kris had the assault rifle. Not a Marine M-6, but it looked like a good knockoff. NELLY, CAN YOU UNLOCK THIS RIFLE'S FIRE CONTROL SYSTEM?

NO, KRIS, IT IS HIGHLY CODED WITH LOCKOUTS.

DAMN, DOESN'T SANDFIRE TRUST ANYONE?

Nelly did not grace that question with an answer.

Kris studied the manual controls. If it did mimic the M-6, this dial should jack up the power behind the darts, squirt more juice into the fire chamber. She maxed it to the right and looked around for someone to test it on. A red was working her way across the floor. Kris waited for her to make her next move. A shot to the chest sent her spinning; she did not get up.

Super Spider Silk might stop a pistol. A slug from an assault rifle on maximum power was something else.

She checked Jack's quarter, found two antagonists, and brought both down. The floor became suddenly quiet as even the echos of fire died off.

"Jack, I think we got them all."

"Wait one," came back tersely.

She did, keeping a roving eye on the gray on gray of the industrial plant. NELLY, YOU HAVE ANY SPIES IN JACK'S AREA?

YES.

YOU SEE ANYTHING?

NO.

Was Jack just spooked? Kris had a wall to drill and a plan to get moving. There had to be more trouble on its way. Time was wasting. But Jack knew what he was doing. If the hackles on the back of his neck said the bugs were missing something, Kris would trust his short hairs over Nelly's eyes.

A short burst came from behind Kris. She whirled to see a black-clad lump slowly tumble out of a long pipe, outfit changing to red as blood dripped slowly. A black staff, no a tube, crumbling under the fallen body.

"That's a blowgun, not a fighting staff like I thought," Jack said. "They do want you alive."

"Yep," Kris said, taking a look around. This floor had an office loft perched against the yard wall. Whether it was a su- pervisor's lookout or control station didn't matter; Kris wanted to be there. She pointed; Jack nodded and followed her as she trotted for it. He took short detours to pick up some ammo pouches and another long rifle.

Kris made it to the station and up the ladder with no more shots fired. Jack slammed the door behind him, then shoved a desk up to block it. Kris zipped down her coveralls and pulled out the laser.

"You didn't bother with underwear today, I see," Jack said, taking the other handle on the laser.

"I figured Super Spider Silk ought to protect me from catching anything. What are you doing, sneaking a peek? I thought you agents were beyond that," she said, turning the laser on and adjusting the beam down to its finest.

"Sometimes it helps to get a good look at the body we're protecting," Jack drawled. "Hold that laser steady," he added as Kris took one hand off it to give him a swat.

They steadied the beam. Around the hole, metal turned to liquid and splattered. In the center, it vaporized, giving color to an otherwise invisible beam.

"Kris, there is movement on the work floor," Nelly said.

"Can you hold this?" Kris asked.

"Pull that chair over here," Jack said. Kris gently gave up her hold on the laser. It dipped a bit, then Jack got it back to the hole they were working on.

She risked a glance out the window. A fusillade from several directions shattered the glass upper half of the office, showering her and Jack, but the metal bottom sent ricochets flying. Kris slid the chair in place. It wasn't quite high enough. She duck- walked to the desk, found some reports, and added them to get it the right height. Jack adjusted it, then reached for his rifle.

"There are three grays at fifty meters, say ten o'clock," Nelly told them. "A pair of reds are closer, one at one, the other at two o'clock."

"I'll take the reds," Jack said.

"You armored?"

"Isn't it a bit late to ask? But yes." Of course, neither of them had face protection. Kris and Jack fired out. The grays and reds fired back. Glass shattered into the small room, contributing nothing but making Kris move carefully as she changed her firing position from one volley to the next. The laser heated the room, even with the extra ventilation in the now windowless office. As the heat rose, the score stayed Christians 0, lions 0, but the lions had only to wait for dinner; time was on their side. Kris grew to dislike the present status as she bounced up to shoot, then ducked incoming. It was getting routine and boring.

"Time to do something to make life interesting," she muttered to herself.

"Ah gee, and I thought it already was," Jack said, ducking down as the space he vacated filled with darts.

"I'm bored. Can't you come up with anything more exciting to do?" Kris said, then snapped off a dozen rounds.

"Hate to tell you this, Princess, but this ain't the best evening I've ever had, either. Think that laser is through."

Kris glanced at it. No new fumes rose from the cut. She switched it off, careful not to move it. The metal looked plenty hot. "Nelly, can you send a scout in?"

"Did it as you were asking. It went through!"

Kris retrieved the ten pounds of only slightly dumb metal from her bustle and held it close to Nelly. "Gal, slight change of plans. Can you convert some of the metal into defensive nanos, no bigger than the dust motes we want? They'll need to fight their way in as well as contribute for the explosion."

"I am adjusting the construction as you wish. Seventy percent of the metal will be twenty-micron mobile units, optimum for coal or grain dust explosions. Twenty-nine percent will be defender units of forty microns. Still small enough to contribute to an explosion. One percent will be ignition units, also forty microns. Is that satisfactory?"

"Great, Nelly. Do it. I want to get out of here."

"Interesting problem, Princess," Jack said, snapping off a short volley, then settling back down. "We've got a solid wall to our back, albeit with one tiny hole in it, and five shooters, highly ineffective, but then I'm not really giving them much of a target to prove themselves on. I take it you have a plan?" Jack slid over, fired a few rounds, and was down before return fire could make holes in him.

"Is air moving much?" Kris asked as she watched the ten-kilogram cylinder of gray metal begin to melt away. She thought she could catch glints of light forming a path to the hole, but she wouldn't bet she was seeing anything but hope on the wing.

"Don't think so, why?"

"Wonder what two sleepy bombs would do out there?"

"I suspect I know what it would do in here."

"But I don't plan to be here," Kris said, settling the thinning bar of metal down in front of the hole. She picked up the laser, aimed it at the floor, and sliced a hole.

"We going to disappear into the wall?" Jack asked.

"Something like that." The chunk of floor bent back when she had three sides cut away. Beneath was a storage room, full of whatever the boss man felt needed to be kept under lock and key. It smelled musty and burnt now.

Kris dropped through and applied the laser to the next floor. It was metal also, old and apparently solid steel. It was also thin, probably predating the beanstalk, so it cost to get it here. She sliced through it quickly to find herself looking into some kind of isolated transformer room. She dropped into it, made her way quickly to the door, and took a peek out at the floor that had been the center of their firefight a few minutes before. A gray was helping a wounded comrade limp off, but no one seemed interested in policing up the wreckage.

The gray dead gave Kris some new options.

"Jack," she called up.

A quick volley answered her, then his scowling face showed at the hole. "You called?"

She found the last two sleepy cylinders and tossed them to Jack. In the low gravity, they made lazy circles; he caught them. "Toss them out there. Then get down here."

There was a longer volley, a loud pop, and Jack was falling through both floors to land easily beside her. "What now?"

"Nobody's bothering with the mess we made down here. What do you say we blow this transformer, cop a few gray uniforms off the dead, and go cruise chicks."

"Now that's a side of you I never expected to see," Jack said as Kris brought out her last booby trap. "You mean they were falsies all this time? You're breaking my heart."

"Nelly, leave a nano behind. Same drill, gray or red."

They made their way quickly across the work floor, Nelly directing them to first one gray, then another. Jack quickly found a uniform. "I think I goofed," Kris muttered. All the grays, males and females, wore pants. Kris would not give up her skirt.

"Don't worry, young woman, you are my prisoner."

"Damn, and we were having such a good time." Behind them, the transformer blew, plunging this area into darkness.

"Guess someone had a breather mask." Kris batted eyelashes at Jack. "Well, captor mine, what do you have in mind?"

"Grabbing the nearest slide car and heading down station."

"I am kind of looking forward to hot wiring a starship and going for a joy ride," Kris said, heading for a slide station.

"Nelly, how good are you at jiggling controls?" Jack asked.

"Usually quite good."

"I think the poor girl is having a crisis of confidence," Kris said.

"It is just that Mr. Sandfire is proving to be a very careful user of automatic systems," Nelly defended herself.

Kris found a slide station, punched for a car, and got one immediately. Jack hauled her in, strong grip on her forearm.

"What do you have?" a voice asked. Kris looked over to see a small screen and observation camera hastily slapped onto the control board.

"One of those idiot workers who kept jacking around rather than leaving like they were ordered."

"One?"

"Short fat woman. Nothing like we're looking for."

"They were shooting all over the place," Kris whined, pitching her voice high enough to shatter flint. "Good God, man, how's a woman supposed to find a ride out of here when there's these red dudes running around shooting up the place?"

"Oh shut up. Bring her down here. We got to talk to all of them now. See anything of the four we're hunting for? Things on the floor above you are confused."

"Hey, man, it's quiet on this floor. I'm just glad I wasn't

one of the first here. There's a whole lot of dead bodies. Oh, and a transformer just blew. It's dark!"

"Yeah, yeah, it's tough all over. Get down here." The light for stop five lit up, and the car began to move sideways.

"Docks are at stop eleven," Kris said, prying open the service panel on the control console. "Nelly, stop us between stop twelve and eleven." The computer reached a tendril of smart metal into the controls. The numbers flashing as stops went by suddenly stopped at "1—"

"What's wrong with your car?" came from the speaker grille. "I've lost your visual, and you're not moving."

"No power," Jack said. "Car's stopped, I don't know where."

"Looks like you're between ten and eleven. No, nine and ten. Just relax. We'll get you out."

"When?" Kris screeched. "This place is falling apart around us! I want out now!"

"I'll take care of this one," Jack shouted at the speaker.

"You can have her. I'm closing down your audio."

"Hmm, you're all mine," Jack whispered.

"That sounds wonderful. Got a knife to open this door?"

"All work and no play," Jack said, putting a stout blade to the door crack. He leaned. It opened on a thin metal walk.

"Nice place you got here. Invite folks up often?"

"Needs a bit of cleaning," Kris said, dropping her last red banded explosive into her ammunition satchel as she slipped out the door. She held it open for Jack to join her. "Nelly, leave a spare nano. Reactivate the car and take it to stop five. Then explode the charge."

Jack tossed his spare ammo bag onto the heap. Kris led him to an exit hatch, worked it open, and found herself in a small room filled with electrical cabling. A peek outside showed a corridor suited to the needs and fine tastes of the refined businessman or woman.

It was time to start looking like a Princess again.

24

The dress showed amazingly few wrinkles. As Abby said, the perfect little number for this evening.

"I'll stay in uniform a bit longer," Jack said and opened the door. The corridor was business charcoal and blue, very tastefully done. She led Jack, as if he was her escort, for stop twelve. There the hall emptied into a wide spiral concourse winding its way in a gentle slope toward Circle One, the outer skin of the station with its docks and ships. Being public, the concourse was carpeted in eye-appealing brown and beige. The ceiling was high, the walls impressive in what might be real marble.

The people they passed were businessmen and women, some being hustled along by security guards, others going their way without interference. This was where the movers worked and did their shaking. They kept their calm exterior even when the station trembled. OUR CAR HAS EXPLODED, Nelly reported.

Jack provided Kris all the probity she required. No one approached her; still, she kept within an easy dash of the right-hand wall with its occasional cross-corridors. Here and there a baggage cart sat parked and out of use for the last week, a few loaded with forlorn packages. Kris kept her pace down, her breath slow, covering the distance to Circle One. Get there, find a yacht or fast transport, and she was out of here.

A door opened in a cross-corridor; Tom stuck his head out, saw Kris, and waved. A moment later, Penny hurried out of the stairwell, a worried glance backward telling Kris all she needed to know. She waved Tom away, pointing him down the corridor and away from the concourse, while taking a step back and turning toward the wall herself.

Kris had broken contact. The last thing she wanted now was a shoot-out drawing ninjas and grays to this quiet and ignored section of the station. "Jack, get a baggage cart. Large, loaded, if you can."

The second nearest filled the bill. Jack pushed it; Kris pointed him down the corridor, then followed him. A lady putting her security to good use as a bellhop.

Two red-clad women bolted from the stairwell, dismissed the baggage cart with a glance, and spotted Tom and Penny as they disappeared around a corner. They took off running, but Jack tripped and sent the baggage cart careening into one, knocking her into the other. Kris had watched Sandfire's harem girls move with liquid grace, but these two were not expecting to tangle with a cart full of boxes. Both went down, one hard.

"My leg, you idiot gray-skull. Look where you're going."

"I'm sorry, ma'am," Jack said, all contrition and head down as he approached them, Kris in his shadow. "I tripped."

"Over your shoelaces, no doubt," the leader snapped, helping the other to her feet. "Can you run on that?"

The other took a step that turned into a hobble. The ankle of her tight body armor expanded to make a splint. "I'll try to keep up. You chase them."

"Listen, I'm sorry," Jack said, reaching out to offer support to the limping one.

Kris came around Jack, arm out for the other one, wrist limp to hide her automatic. "Listen, I know they rented me the worst excuse for security on the Rim, nothing like back on Earth. I feel like I owe you—"

The leader's eyes grew big. "You're—"

"Yes, I am," Kris said, putting three sleepy darts into her. At lowest power, her automatic was hardly louder than a series of pops. At this range, it shattered her skull. Jack gave the other one the same treatment. Quickly, they loaded the reds onto the cart and buried them under boxes. Tom ducked his head around the corner, grinned, and he and Penny hurried back.

"Anybody seen or heard from Abby?" Kris asked. Penny shook her head. In their travels, the other two had acquired new clothes as well. Penny now wore Security gray. Tom had acquired a light blue dinner jacket and red cummerbund that went well with his uniform pants. "Tom, you and Penny stay on this side of the concourse. Jack and I will edge toward the left. If anyone gets in trouble, we'll help as we can."

They got to where Concourse Twelve emptied onto Circle One with no further trouble.

"Abby says the private yacht basin is left," Nelly said.

"When?" Kris asked.

"I do not know, but she left a small message nano at the corner to tell me that."

Kris turned left.

The spin of the station was slow enough that huge freighters and liners had no problem catching their first mooring hitch and being pulled into the pier. Yachts and runabouts, smaller and more maneuverable, were expected to find their places along several landings that made up Pier Eleven. Kris wanted a large ship. That meant selecting one that paid extra for an outer birth. Finding the right one could take time she didn't have.

Abby exited a ladies' room, twelve steamer trunks docilely trailing behind her. "You're right on time," she told Kris. "There's a large yacht out on landing D. There's a slightly smaller one on landing C. Which do you want?"

"Which has the lighter security?" Jack asked.

"I don't know. It didn't seem wise to be noticed casing the place, what with all the trouble some people were causing."

"Ever the courageous one," Jack growled.

"We're all still alive," Abby pointed out cheerfully.

"Let's take the bigger one. I have a plan for getting through their security," Kris said.

"What might that be?" Tom said as he and Penny joined up.

"The same one we used the first night." Kris didn't try to swallow her evil grin. "You can't tell me wealthy yachts don't put calls out for strange, new, and interesting woman flesh?"

"I think I have created a monster," Abby moaned, but she

was rummaging in the side compartment of one of the trunks.

"Abby hasn't created a monster," Jack said. "She's only putting the finishing touches on Kris's own work of art."

"And speaking of finishing touches, you might want this," Abby said, tossing Kris a small hand purse.

Kris opened it. A compact with an old-fashioned mirror, six sticks of chewing gum and, Kris took a second to recognize the other items, four different kinds of condoms. "I think I can use some of this," she said with a slight cough.

Jack glanced over Kris's shoulder, then threw Abby a glare. "And you were acting surprised."

"Surprised, yes. Unprepared, never." And she produced a purse of her own. "Shall we go, Sister?" Abby tossed Jack the controller for the steamer trunks. "Don't misplace any of them, and please don't pick up luggage that is not your own. So many look alike," she beamed and led Kris into the landing tunnel.

Ten meters around, the landing spiral made a comfortable walkway with wide windows looking out over gaily painted runabouts and small overnighters. Just the thing for in-system travel. Kris jawed a growing wad of gum for a good hundred meters, got it under control, and flashed Abby a smile.

"I know I'm supposed to look like that loony vid Princess," Kris said, snapping her gum and putting a twang on each word, "but who'd go for you?" Kris knew she was letting the imp get her tongue, but she was seeing a new side of her maid and had to scratch that surface.

"There are men who go for prim, unbending women, and besides," Abby said, snapping her purse open and producing a fold-out whip, "I have other special skills."

"Men are crazy." Kris shook her head.

"Some men are crazy. So are some women. The trick is to match them up." The landing divided into two levels. Abby took the up ramp. Now the ships out the windows were larger, more impressive, and less flamboyantly painted. Clearly, the greater the value, the less the need for overstatement. At the end of the landing, two men in black suits and ties lounged at the entrance to a gangway elevator. Kris got her hips going, her dress swaying, and gave the sashay all she had.

"Don't overdo it," Abby whispered through her smile. "These guys are not the customer."

"Yeah, but ain't they hunks. I could go for them."

"You give nothing away for free, young woman. How can your dear mother make a living off you if you devalue what you sell?"

The words almost knocked Kris out of her walk. Had Abby just let something slip? *Yes, Mama,* Kris mouthed silently.

"Can we help you . . . ladies?" the guard with a shaved head said as the younger, cuter one, took a step back and rested his hand on what had to be his weapon.

"Our agency had a call from Pier eleven-d-one for a rush escort service," Abby said as Kris brought a hand up to her hair, put her hips in low and her gum on high. "They weren't quite sure what was required, so they sent us both."

"This is the right pier," the guard said, trying not to eye Kris. "What was requested?"

"Candy, get rid of that gum," Abby whispered from the side of her mouth, then smiled at the guards. "Someone with a certain media caché as a reward, though punishment might be required."

The guard paged through his hand unit. "I've got nothing."

"Yeah," the young one said, "but the kid's been having a lousy week. Maybe the boss is trying something new. You heard about tonight."

The two guards turned to exchange knowing grins. Abby sniffed—and she took down the hunk, leaving the closer guy to Kris. Three soft pops and enough sleepy drug was in their chests to keep them down for the night.

"What was that all about?" Kris said as she stepped over the guard.

"I have no idea, but we better be ready at the inside door." So they entered the elevator, pushed the one button, and slow and easy rode it down.

The elevator stopped at a landing facing what Kris thought of as the quarterdeck. Two men in dark suits, apparently the uniform of this ship's security, eyed them cautiously. "What brings you here, ah, ladies?" one with a bull neck asked. Beside him, seated at a console with blank monitors, was a smaller but equally muscled model of himself.

"My agency received a call for our services."

"We didn't make a call," the small one said, turning to his board and flipping through the one active screen.

"Yeah, Marko, but there's a lot of stuff you're not monitoring tonight," the other said, waving a hand at the blank screens. "Station lines were max flaky even before the boss hit the disconnect." A thick comm line lay on the gangway. Normally, it was one of the last things disconnected before getting under way. Tonight, someone had unplugged it, leaving the ship out of any land line loop and killing the camera feed covering the upper part of the gangway. Bit of luck for Kris and her team, she thought as she and Abby took advantage of bull neck's momentary concentration on winning his point with Marko to shoot the two of them full of sleepy darts.

Gun out, Kris stood guard while Abby lugged the two sleepers onto the landing, then rode the elevator up. She returned a moment later with Jack, Tom, and Penny.

"Jack, you and Abby secure the ship. The rest of you, with me. Let's see what the bridge looks like," Kris said, then halted. The only way to the command deck was an elevator. A good option for a ship under high acceleration, but being locked in a box was not an idea Kris liked tonight. "Penny, you stay down here. Tom, you're my pimp."

"Your what!"

"Stay close, keep your mouth closed, and gun ready."

"Where have I heard that order before?" he said, giving Kris a wry grin and Penny a quick kiss. Then he stepped into the elevator. Kris hit the top button, and the car started moving.

The doors opened on a dimly lit bridge that smelled of machine oil, rosin, sweat, and ozone. The rest of the ship might smell like an office, but here it was a working ship. Two chairs swiveled around to face the elevator. A man and woman in dark flight suits, pistols in shoulder holsters, eyed Kris.

Kris turned her entrance onto the bridge into an excited half hop and wiggle. "Wow, this really is maxi radi," she bubbled. "This is really what makes the thing go?" she asked, getting a peek around the side of the elevator. A third man worked at a console back there. Whatever it did, the board was up and held the man's attention.

"Excuse me, kid," the woman said, standing, "but haven't you taken a wrong turn somewhere?"

"I told her our client would be down, not up, but she pushed the button before I could stop her," Tom said. "Come on, Rosie, we've got a customer waiting."

"But this one's good-looking, and I bet he could tell me what all of those flashing lights mean," Kris gushed and took two steps closer to the controls.

"Honey child, you do look like fun," the still-seated man said, "but I am on duty, and this is not a sim. All this is working, and we can't have little girls playing with it."

"Little girls?" Kris pouted—and shot the fellow.

Tom brought down the woman. The fellow behind the elevator was just turning as Kris put three darts into him.

"I'm taller than you, little boy," Kris said as she turned the command chair and rolled the sleeping fellow out of it. "Tom, get Penny. We've got some controls to figure out."

Tom pulled the woman he'd shot into a fireman's carry and headed for the elevator. Kris studied the board, but, following the napping pilot's advice, touched nothing.

When the elevator returned, Abby was with Penny. "The ship's ours. There were only two more crew on board. A fellow claiming to be the cook told us most hands were dirtside on leave. They were recalled after you kids started blowing things up, but they aren't back yet."

"Let's close up the ship," Kris said.

"Give us a few minutes to get everyone off," Abby said, pulling sleepers into the elevator. "Oh, and what looks like the owner's cabin has been locked from the outside and the inside. Jack's working on the problem."

"Outside and inside," Kris muttered. "Nelly, can you do anything about that?"

"I am concentrating on access to the ship's main network," Kris's computer said slowly, as if ashamed to admit she wasn't already in. "This system is very well protected."

"Well, get in," Kris said. "The reactor is on a low trickle, but I'll have to add reaction mass for a good five minutes before we can get under way. When's the big boom scheduled?"

"Six point four two minutes."

Abby and Tom left with the last two sleepers. Penny settled down on the other side of the bridge, examining that working station. "Kris," she called half a minute later, "I think this is an intelligence gathering post. I seem to have access to a whole lot of police and military data flow."

"But they disconnected the land line from the main net. I saw the decoupled data line."

"It's coming in on a tight beam. If I didn't know better, I'd say someone has hacked the central security net."

"Curious and curiouser," Kris whispered, still eying the lights on the navigation board. "Nelly, it would be real nice to do a few things."

"I think I have broken the lock on your board, Kris. Try something."

Kris tapped for a slight increase in reactor power.

Access Denied.

"I will keep working on that, Kris."

"You do." Kris wanted to scream, pound on the workstation, run in circles. Instead, she walked slowly around the bridge. All stations faced the wall screens, a conventional merchant ship layout since no one put merchies into defensive battle spins. One station backed up the main nav position; that was where the woman had sat. The next few stations around the bridge circle were blank. One should have been sensors if this was a jump ship. Kris would wait until Nelly turned on all stations to make sure. The stations along the back were all data-gathering slots; some looked business, some scientific. Strange mix. Penny was deep into something, so Kris left her undisturbed.

The positions took on an engineering look as Kris made her way back to nav station . . . except the one next to navigation. It was totally blank, ready to be brought up and initialized. But as what?

Kris settled into the seat at nav. "Nelly, it would be real nice if we could light a fire on this rig."

"Try it again, please."

Kris edged up the reactor level from 5 percent to 10 percent. The reactor responded. Sitting forward in her chair, Kris further increased the flow of reaction mass to the reactor. The amount of plasma into the standby race tract increased, and the electricity generated by the Magnetohydrodynamics engines rose with it. Kris fed that into capacitors . . . and found this yacht had a very large capacity for storing spare electricity.

"Jack, you ready to seal the hatches?"

"Getting the last extras over the side and sealing the gangway as we speak."

"Break all connections except the mooring hold-downs. Then stand by. Nelly, how long until things get interesting on the station?"

"Three minutes or so," Nelly said.

"And why are you suddenly going general on me?" Kris asked as she checked out her maneuvering jets. The ship bucked a bit, but the mooring lines held it tight.

"I became aware that though the command nanos have their instructions, the possibility of opposition means that instructions may not be executed on the second I planned."

"Good, Nelly, you are catching on to how things work in the real world."

"Your 'real world' is messy."

"What parts of this control system don't we control?"

"I am still trying to bring up the jump point sensors," Nelly said. "They are under a different lockdown entirely."

"Probably the woman I shot," Tom said, crossing from the elevator to the secondary control station. He tapped several buttons, then tapped more, shaking his head slowly. "I see an atom laser gyro, but it won't initialize. Same for the gravimeter. Kris, we can't jump."

"Nelly, keep working."

"Kris"—Jack's words came through the ship's system—"I sure could use some help cracking into this last room."

"Anyone shooting at you from it?"

"Not at the moment."

"Then Nelly keeps hacking the jump station before she messes with anything else."

"Dock eleven-d-one, this is the Port Master's office. We read you powering up. We remind you this port is closed."

"Roger, Port Master," Kris drawled, "we understand this port is closed. We're just running some tests. We've been parked here a while and, if you'll excuse my comment, things are getting a bit interesting on your station. Just in case Pier Eleven were to, maybe, fall off, my owner wants to know I could maneuver to a new dock."

"I understand your owner is antsy. Just you understand I have orders to shoot anyone departing the station."

"Assuming they still have power," Kris whispered, resting her hand on the console mike. On it, but not totally over it.

"I heard that. We all have our problems tonight. Just you don't go adding any more to my growing list."

"Roger, Port Master, over and out." This time Kris did wait to say anything further until the mike showed a solid red light. "That ought to keep him off our back for a while."

"But did you have to give me a heart attack doing it?" Penny said, leaning back in her chair so she could see Kris. "I know getting out of here is like, top and highest priority, but you might want to see what I found."

"I can watch the board," Tom offered.

Kris trotted over to look at Penny's board.

"I have quite a comm set here," Penny began. "You want to know what the President is saying, listen here." She punched a button and the President's harsh twang came through solidly. "His accent gets worse when he's under pressure," Penny said, "and that's about as bad as I've ever heard it."

"What else do you have?"

"How about Sandfire?"

"Him!" came from both Kris and Tom.

"He doesn't say a lot, but when he does, he says it on this channel. Actually, it's about fifty-nine channels, but this rig knows his schedule for jumping as well as his code."

"You sure?"

"He's ordered his ninjas back to 'the castle.' He also ordered somebody named 'Bertie' and his team to the same location. I don't know where that is, but it doesn't sound like he's still hunting us."

"That's not good." Kris turned and walked slowly back to her station. While Sandfire was turning the station upside down, he was chasing the wrong fox. If he was pulling his teams back, that meant he'd given up and was trying something new. "Keep track of Sandfire. Let me know of any traffic from him. What's the President doing?"

"There seems to be an uprising going on dirtside. The Arab quarter was first to send people into the streets. Then the university district had a rally to hear some Senators, some of whom you've met. It got out of hand, and now other areas have streets jammed with people. When orders came to use force to break them up, a lot of the cops refused and joined the protestors. Our buddy Inspector Klaggath was on the net encouraging any doubters to 'jump in, the water's fine.' " Kris smiled at that, wondering if the Inspector had lake water in mind.

"Sandfire's insisting they can beat the revolt. Izzic's the nervous type who wants his problems solved yesterday. He's issuing a lot of orders. My guess is too many. Order, counterorder, disorder." Penny said, quoting the old military warning.

"Kris, we have a problem," Jack announced on ship net. "Somebody's come down the gangway and found our sleeping beauties. They're demanding we open up."

"I think that's our cue to leave," Kris said, slipping into her seat and belting herself in while her eyes checked her board. "I see a green board."

"I confirm a green board," Tom answered.

"I have the conn. Nelly, release all moorings," Kris said as she gave her forward reaction jet a light tap.

Nothing happened.

"I do not have control of the mooring points," Nelly answered. "I am working on them."

"Work fast, Nelly."

"Mooring eleven-d-one, this is the Port Master. We showing you trying to release your mooring points. All mooring points have been centrally locked. What do you think you're doing?"

"Sorry, Port Master," Kris said, tapping her mike on. "We were testing things, and a subroutine got activated. Computer error. Won't happen again."

"See that it doesn't. Wait one." The net went dead with a harsh click.

"Oh, oh," Tommy said. "I think someone just got through."

"Who am I talking to?" came in a new voice.

"Repeat your question," Kris said. "We're not on land line, and our radio traffic is breaking up. You know how it is." Kris tried to ramble on but was cut off.

"This is the Port Duty Officer. Who am I talking to?"

"Nelly Benteen," Kris said, taking the name of a friend from first grade.

"What's your ship?"

Kris tapped the mike. As it went red, she glanced around. "Anybody know the name of this bucket of bolts?"

"Terrorists on yacht at pier eleven-d-one. You are in violation of—"

"Nelly, kill that channel." It went quiet.

"Sandfire appears to have a couple of ships," Penny said. "He's ordering them to cast off and take station to keep us in port."

"Nelly, it would really be nice to get out of here."

"Try your jets."

Kris did.

"Try them harder."

Kris tapped the ship's speaker. "Jack, Abby, get ready for a hull breach. I'm backing out of here, and the pier isn't exactly cooperating."

Kris took a deep breath, gave Jack about as much time as she could to secure himself inboard from the hull, and ordered the bow thrusters to 25 percent. The ship trembled under her but went nowhere. Using her fingers, she edged the power line up slowly to 50 percent. The ship bucked in place. Somewhere metal tore. *Hope that's the dock.*

At 63 percent something let go. The ship creaked and groaned as the tie-downs trundled down the pier at three times the authorized speed. As the bridge passed the end of the pier and the station spin swung the landing away, Kris got a short glimpse of twisted metal and whipping cables. It didn't look like she was leaving much if any of her hull behind.

"Any castoff you can walk away from is a cause for celebration," Tom said. "Isn't that what the old Chief said?"

"I don't think he had this in mind," Kris muttered as she steadied ship, dampened her reverse headway, and looked for room to rotate ship.

"Are you sure?" Tom grinned.

"I'm sure I'd like to know if I'm being targeted," Kris said.

"None of the ranging lasers from the station are on us," Penny said. "I have their net, and it really sounds like a Tiger and Rabbit cartoon. Five will get you fifty they haven't had a live fire drill in years."

"You ready to bet your life?" Kris asked.

"Aren't we?"

"I hate to interrupt this validation that you both need to attend Gamblers Anonymous, but we have company," Tom said, pointing at the screen. Three long, thin hulls cruised slowly around the edge of the station.

Kris hit her reaction jets, spun ship, and put headway on fast.

"We've got a problem down here," Jack said from the ship's system.

"Sorry about that, Jack, but we've got worse problems up here. Sandfire has three ships on our tail."

"I really think you ought to see the problem I've got down here."

"I can't leave the pilot seat, Jack."

"I'll bring it up to you."

"How could you have a worse problem than mine?" Kris muttered as she fed the main engines all the plasma she could afford to lose at the moment. Her hands played on the directional jets, jinking a bit up, a bit down, anything to spoil a firing solution.

"Kris, I have a message from Sandfire," Penny announced.

"I'm listening," Kris said as the elevator opened behind her.

"Ah," Sandfire beamed confidently, "Princess Kristine, we can do this the quick way or the slow way. Either way, I have you. I have three heavily armed cruisers in range of your little runabout. Surrender, or I will blow you out of space."

"Cal, you can't fire on this ship while I'm on it," came from behind Kris.

She turned.

Hank Smythe-Peterwald flashed her one if his billion-dollar smiles. "Hi, Kris. I thought you passed on joining me on my yacht."

Kris swallowed hard. She'd planned to hijack a ship. She didn't plan to kidnap anyone. Definitely not Hank Peterwald.

Hank's smile wavered as a flash of light lit up his face. Kris whirled back to the screen. The station was blowing up.

The first explosion came from her ten kilos of dust mites. They exploded out one side of the yard. For a moment, the station rotated on, top fine, bottom fine, the yards and docks in the middle showing one huge bite out of it. Another, larger and slower explosion roiled around inside the yard, growing as it found more to feed on, casting light out the gaping hole that went from red to yellow to white. In quiet majesty, the walls of the yard bowed, then blew out almost lazily.

As if refreshed by that, the next round of fireworks was an expanding ball of explosives that shot through the growing cloud of wreckage with lightning speed, sending fragments of ships and station twisting and spinning into space. A big chunk clipped one of Sandfire's ships, sending it careening into the next.

"So that's what a signature Longknife job looks like." Hank breathed slowly.

25

"Grab anything handy," Kris shouted as she poured more plasma into her engines than she wanted to. Now was no time to blow out her reactor by using so much plasma that when the flood of cold reaction mass she was pouring in met what little plasma was left, the critical core temperature would plummet below the fusion level. *Maybe not, but I need to move now!*

The ship—correction: *Barbarossa*, Hank's yacht—took off with a lurch, sending Jack, Abby, and Hank to their knees. As Kris balanced reactor temperature against acceleration against a rapidly closing wall of gas and wreckage, the new arrivals crawled for seats: Hank on Kris's right, Jack right next to him, Abby next to Tom.

"What are you doing with my ship?" Hank asked, proprietorship showing as he strapped himself in.

"Trying to stay ahead of that mess," Kris answered, just remembering to change "my mess" to "that mess." Now was no time to bring Hank in on all she'd been up to of late. Boys tended to be slow and so excitable about such things.

"What happened?" Hank breathed as he took in the screens.

"Some sort of industrial accident I would guess," Kris evaded.

"And you're just running off in my ship."

Kris eyed the reactor and upped the feed from the fuel tanks. "It seemed like a good idea at the time, and it was available."

"Yes, there were only four or so guards protecting it. Father warned me you Longknifes have a very lackadaisical view of property rights when it suits you."

"Sorry if I disappoint you," Kris said, cutting the main engines and rotating ship so the power plant and engines weren't in the direct path of the fast-approaching shock wave. It did put the command deck face into it.

"Hold on, folks," Kris shouted. The wave front hit, slamming them against their restraints as it shoved the ship back, then sideways, trying to roll it. Gyros struggled against the forces arrayed against them. Kris added her own efforts to the battle, hitting the overrides and raising the power of the control jets, sending them more reaction mass, more electricity.

The ship held steady . . . or close enough.

Now came the big stuff. Chunks of station. Hunks of ships. Girders, walls . . . blessedly, Kris spotted no bodies. Now the control jets slid the ship up or right, left or down as Kris played a lethal game of dodge it.

"Alpha, gamma, seven, seven," Hank muttered in incantation beside Kris, "Omega, zed, epsilon, one, nine, eleven," he finished, and the board in front of him came to life. "Extra armor to the bow."

Eyes on the wreckage coming her way, Kris asked, "What are you doing?"

"I'm no Navy type like you, but I like to know enough about my ship to keep my hide in one piece when it matters. This is a smart metal ship, and I think I just thickened up the bow."

"Tom, I've got the conn. Slave your station to Hank's and see what you can do," Kris ordered. Tom's assigned station on the *Typhoon* was defense.

"I'm locked out," Tom shouted.

"I grant open access to all stations," Hank said.

"I'm in," Tom said.

"We're going to take a hit down our right side," Kris shouted.

"I'm on it," Tom said, hands dancing over his board. The

ship shuddered, then groaned as the glancing blow Kris had set-tled for tumbled down the right side of the hull.

"Damage?"

"I'm fixing it," Tom answered Kris.

"Good man," Hank whispered.

"Not a bad ship. Not bad at all," Tom said, giving high praise for a space born.

"Cost enough it ought to be," Hank said through gritted teeth as Kris slammed the ship sideways. A tumbling ship's stern, laser cannons twisting at the end of cables, struck a glancing blow.

"I'm on it," Tom said before Kris got a word out.

Kris took a moment to expand her collision avoidance screen. It looked clear, but she needed a bigger picture. "Any-one at a sensor suite station?" she asked and got no reply.

"My code should have released the entire command deck," Hank said, glancing around. "Isn't that a sensor suite your man is seated at?" he said, waving at Jack.

"I wouldn't know a sensor suite from a luxury suite," Jack grumbled.

"I'll slave the station next to me to that one," Penny said. "Yep, it's sensors. Kris, I'm sending you the overview screen."

A screen opened at Kris's left elbow. It rated more space than life support at the moment, so Kris squelched them to ex-pand the view. The area was a mess, about what she'd expected. She spared a quick glance at the station. The thick wall she'd sliced through to get her nanos in had channeled the explosion out, not up or down. The Hilton was probably well shaken, but it and the rest of the lower station still sat atop the beanstalk. The Top of Turantic was also there, now floating above a big chunk of empty space but holding on to a few tenuous connec-tions to the lower station.

The explosion had blown outward as Kris intended. She hoped that didn't exhaust her supply of luck for today. From the looks of things, she'd be needing a whole lot more.

A cruiser was making its way through the devastation, headed her way.

"Penny, anything new from Sandfire?"

"Nothing."

"Prepare to rotate ship. Let's get out of here." Kris spun the ship, picked a potential jump point, checked to see how much the reactor had heated up while she was using the lateral jets, liked the temperature she had, and put it to good use. "Here comes two g's" she told her crew.

"And here comes Sandfire," Penny announced.

"Put him on main screen."

Sandfire didn't look nearly as imperial strapped into an acceleration couch. It had been a rush job, two of the straps twisted, Kris saw. He'd be in for a miserable time at high g. His eyes were wide, his coloring florid. A vein on his forehead throbbed, but his words were no less demanding. "Surrender, take all acceleration off your ship and prepare to be boarded."

Kris shook her head. "Sorry, Sandfire, I've let you run me in circles long enough. I'm leaving your little trap."

Sandfire strained against his straps as he tried to get closer to the camera, loom larger on Kris's screen. That vein was pounding out a wild beat. "Refuse my orders, and I will blast you out of space."

Hank coughed twice. "Cal, this is my yacht, and I am on it. You will not fire at me or it."

Sandfire took Hank's mild words like a slap. He sat back in his seat for a moment, eyes going wild. Then he smiled, or let his lips turn into what Sandfire passed off as one. "You're a hostage."

"I am not a hostage."

"You're a hostage of that Longknife terrorist and Smythe-Peterwald policy is never to negotiate for hostages."

"I assure you, Cal, this may not be the evening I had intended to share with Miss Longknife, but I am in no way a hostage. Considering what just happened at the station, she may have saved my life."

"She's the one that blew it up," he screamed. "She's the one that nearly killed you and did kill thousands of workers. Ask her. You ask her. Those damn Longknifes have done it again. But this will be the last time that one does anything."

Kris tried not to react. She'd done everything she could to get people out of her target. Everything possible. What could she answer Hank?

But Hank was less interested in Kris than he was in his own man. "Cal, you need to calm down. I know the expansion on the station was your project. But I'm sure you insured it. You've been working hard on your Turantic projects. Don't let this one setback interfere with your overall business plan. Write it off, move on. There's more money to be made tomorrow."

"What would you know, you spoiled brat." Sandfire spat the words at the screen. Kris measured the arcs the spittle made, then glanced at her board. Yep, that cruiser was accelerating at two g's. She edged her acceleration up to two and a half.

Hank took two breaths, leaving the words out in the open between him and his associate as he formed his perfect face into friendly concern. "Calvin, you need to get a hold of yourself. You are saying things you'll regret in the morning. I'll do my best to forget them, but you have got to control yourself."

"You stupid kid," Sandfire shot back. "You don't know anything about what's going on here, do you? Longknife, you want to tell him what you just did? What I was about to do and you wrecked. You gunna tell him or shall I?"

Kris edged the acceleration up another quarter g. Whoever was skippering that cruiser was paying more attention to Kris's speed than Sandfire was. Now it was Kris's turn to take a deep breath, but at least Hank would learn about things in her words, not Sandfire's.

"I'm afraid your Mr. Sandfire is right. I have tossed a monkey wrench into his plans . . . again." She grinned at the screen and was rewarded with a snarl. "Sandfire here was converting every available Turantic merchant ship into a warship and outfitting them as a major battle fleet. Considering the nearly disarmed status of the surrounding planets, he would have cut quite a swath as Attila the Hun. Now his fleet is gone and what army he had President Iedinka raising has no place to go. Check and checkmate."

"But I've got you this time," Sandfire snapped from the screen. "Captain, fire on that terrorist ship."

"Firing," came from the screen as Kris put her ship into a right skid and spun it around its middle. The wild gyrations threw Kris against her straps, but she kept her hand on the acceleration bar, quickly dropping it to one g, then slamming it up to three as the attack board showed lasers missing high and ahead.

"He's firing on me," came from Hank. Shock and a gulp of fear told Kris this was a first for him.

"Not his first try for me, but it's a miss like the rest," Kris said, trying to sound encouraging.

"Beta, alfa, beta, Xray," Hank spat. "I don't know how to use the lasers on this tub, but I'm sure someone here does."

"Lasers!" Kris chortled in glee.

"Twelve-inch. Full military pulse. Did you notice the size of my capacitors?"

"I did, but some nervous nannies like them that way," Kris said, as a whole new set of screens appeared on Hank's station.

"Dad said Greenfeld would be needing a fleet someday, and we might as well have the first warship."

"Penny, you up to defense?"

"I'm trained. Not qualified."

"We'll qualify you today. Tom, you take the conn."

"I have the conn, executing defensive jinking as needed," he said.

"I have weapons," Kris muttered as she rearranged her board, calling up sections of sensors as well as the readouts on the two weapons she had. "Fire control computer is only taking feed from the radar and laser ranging gear."

"Dad said it was the best Singer AGR made." Hank sounded a bit defensive.

"Sorry, Hank, you get better ranges when you add in the gravimeter and atom laser." Kris brought those two readouts up on her board. With no time to program them into the range finder, she adjusted for them in her head.

"Missed us again," Tom said through clenched teeth.

"Ranging fire, one quarter pulse." Kris mashed her firing buttons. She missed as well, both shots high and to the right.

Kris, I CAN DO BETTER THAN THAT, Nelly said.

"Nelly taking over fire control," Kris announced to the crew.

"Merging all ranging data. Firing one-eighth pulse for ranging," Nelly announced. Kris raised an eyebrow. The board had only offered her one-quarter power shots. This would allow more and faster ranging fire. A glance at the screen showed even Nelly would need a lot of power for ranging shots. Her first salvo was closer, but still high.

"I am analyzing their defensive jitter pattern," Nelly said.

"Tom, what's our pattern?" Kris asked.

"I've got four random patterns, and I'm switching between them at random times."

"Were the patterns in the computer here?"

"Oops, yes."

"Nelly, generate new patterns for Tom."

"Feeding them to the system," Nelly said. "Firing double pattern, one-eighth power." Each laser shot out two bursts in a rapid staccato.

"Looks like one hit," but the cruiser danced away, leaving a trail of streaming metal.

"No ice," Kris snapped. "He's got no ice to shield him from our lasers."

"That bad?" Hank asked.

"We've at least got the smart metal to move around and thicken up our engaged quarter. He's got nothing but bare hull between him and our lasers. Nelly, do you have his pattern down?"

"It changed after that hit. Give me a moment to study them." Kris checked the capacitors. A bit over half a charge was left. Rapid fire might get enough beams out there to matter.

"Nelly, could we fire a fast four pulses, one-eighth power?"

"I do not think so, Kris. The lasers are heating up. I really do not think they were intended for this kind of use."

Kris glanced at Hank. "Dad figured two shots would be enough to take out anything."

"Your father is an optimist," Kris said, did a quick search inside the weapons menu, and found temperature. Yep. Those babies were warm. Not hot, but considering the shots she'd fired so far, a couple of more in quick succession just might melt them to slag.

Time for a new approach to this battle. Run.

"Tom, new course. Fast, low orbit to slingshot us around Turantic, get us headed in a new direction."

"And get our rockets anywhere but aimed right at Sandfire," the defense manager in Tom spoke. "Course plotted. Hold on to your underwear folks. Executing." The *Barbarossa* swung around under power and headed planetward. A broadside from Sandfire's cruiser filled the space they had been in.

"Good course change," Kris said.

"Right." Tom sighed.

"Sandfire is following us," Penny reported.

"Surprise, surprise," Jack said with a shake of his head.

"He can't be shooting at me," Hank said, still in shock.

"No, Hank, me boy." Tom's grin took a bitter turn at its edges. "He's firing at Kris here. He's been after her since he kidnapped me. Probably before that. He wants her dead, and you are just in the way like the rest of us mere mortals."

"Kris? Why would he be after you?"

"Hank, there's a lot of things your family or corporation does that maybe you aren't fully informed about."

"My dad would never let anything get as out of control as this."

"For what it's worth, I've of late discovered a few things about my family that don't exactly match the PR releases."

"I could have told you about some of the stunts you Longknifes have pulled."

"So maybe I can tell you a few things about the Smythe-Peterwalds that don't get mentioned in the annual report to stockholders."

"We're privately held, as is Nuu Enterprises."

"Just means we have to dig deeper, Hank. Dig deeper. Now, if you'll excuse me, I need to see about keeping us alive." Kris eyed the capacitors, temperature readouts, and ranging systems. "Penny, put Hank's buddy Cal on the main screen."

"Hailing them. Here he is."

"You ready to surrender?" Sandfire glowered.

"Nope. You've missed me every time. I've hit you once. Seems to me the honors are mine."

"You have no honor. You meddle where you have no business. You wreck what others are trying to build. Surrender or die."

"Break off or you die," Kris shot back. "We've got better ranging gear, better armor. You keep this up, and you and your entire crew," which was who Kris really was talking to, "will die. Remember, Sandfire, I've hit ships in space. I've got a combat-experienced crew on my bridge. Has anyone on that tub of yours ever fired a shot in anger?" *Keep talking. While we talk my capacitors fill, my lasers cool.* A glance at the target board also showed Tom opening up the range as well.

"My girls are all killers. I wouldn't hire them if they weren't. They'd rather slit your throat than put up with your smirk."

"But they're not facing me with a knife or pistol. They're in my space, under my lasers. This is Lieutenant JG Kris Longknife, United Sentients Navy. Cease your harassing fire, break off your pursuit, and you will live. Keep this up, and I will kill you."

"Fire! Damn you, fire!" Sandfire shouted. Someone off-screen yelled, "We're not recharged; just a second, now!" Someone finally remembered to cut off the transmission.

The cruiser fired, but Tom had the *Barbarossa* in a whole new set of slides, jinks, and twists. All missed.

Kris eyed her own board. "Nelly, fire six one-tenth or one-twelfth power pulses. Tight salvo pattern."

"Firing six pulses, one-twelfth power," Nelly said.

Two lasers stuttered and reached out with six beams of destruction. Two were near misses. One hit.

The cruiser slipped away from the hit, spinning and shedding metal. It shed other things, larger, that took off under power. "Long boat and several escape pods scattering from the cruiser. Apparently not everyone wants to die with Cal," Penny reported.

"They'd have to be crazy to," Hank snapped, head shaking. "I don't understand this."

"Pay attention and learn," Kris said. "Penny, raise me Sandfire."

"He's not responding."

"Try again. Tell him his rats are fleeing the ship."

"None of my loyal people would ever leave me." Sandfire was back, filling the screen. His face was red enough to match some of this evening's explosions. The vein on the right side of his forehead now was matched by one on his left. Kris would not want his blood pressure.

"You want to see what my sensors showed a minute ago? Long boat and survival pods dropping off your boat like petals off a dead daisy."

"My God, she's a poet, too," Tom said in feigned shock.

"And you think I'd believe a Longknife."

"You must admit I've been a bit busy staying alive to doctor media."

"Longknife, you've been causing us trouble since you were a kid and dodged our kidnappers. You should have died on that minefield months ago. Instead, you wrecked what we'd arranged with that ass of a Commodore at Paris. This time I have you in my sights, and I'll kill you myself. Fire, damn you, fire."

The ship slid and dodged under Kris. It didn't match the wild ride her own stomach was taking.

Who was the "us" Sandfire included in his plots? To kill a kid! Eddy? She was damn proud she'd saved her Marine platoon from landing in a minefield. She was even prouder to have messed up Commodore Sampson's taking AttackRon Six out of the Wardhaven battle line to spark a war between Earth and Wardhaven. For all those and what Sandfire had done to Tom and Penny and was trying to do to the people of Turantic, he deserved to die.

Now he put poor dead Eddy at the head of his list.

There had to be a way to kill Sandfire as many times as he deserved.

Kris swallowed hard on rage and commands that vented hate to no good end. There could be no room in her heart, in her head, in her gut for anything so human as anger, as vengeance. Emotions took up space, took up blood flow, took up brainpower.

Cold as space, Kris studied the man on the screen even as she widened her vision to take in her board, reactor temperature, mass available, laser temperature, and power reserve.

Someone was going to die very, very soon. That someone would be Sandfire.

"Missed again," she said, molding her lips into the cold, unfeeling grin that showed teeth but no cheer. "That the best you can do, Cal? Get close, but never touch me. You kidnap a kid and make me a hero. You plan a war, and I end up a Princess. Your hate for us Longknifes only makes us richer, more powerful, more admired. It must really eat your guts out," she said, watching flaming passion rise up and consume him.

He was screaming now, demanding the cruiser fire as he struggled against his restraints, hands out, fingers reaching like claws as he tried to climb through the screen, get his hands around Kris's neck.

Offscreen, Kris heard someone report the lasers were just coming up on a full charge. Again Tom put the *Barbarossa* into a wild dance as lasers reached out for them, missed them yet again.

Sandfire roared his grief.

Kris ignored him as she took in her weapons status. Sandfire had wasted two broadsides while she cooled her lasers, charged their capacitors. NELLY, FIRE SIX BURSTS AT ONE-TWELFTH POWER. IF ONE HITS, FOLLOW IT UP WITH TWO BURSTS, ONE-QUARTER POWER.

YES, MA'AM. On Kris's board, below the screen with Sandfire's twisted visage, six beams reached out. Two connected, staggering the cruiser. Before Kris could form the word *fire*, two more shots followed, pinning the cruiser, cutting it through. Sandfire's face vanished as the screen above Kris went blank.

For a moment, the attacking cruiser hung there against the black of space. Then the screen dimmed as the ship turned itself into a momentary star. The screen flashed back to normal, revealing an expanding cloud of gas that, even as they looked, vanished as if it had never been there.

Sandfire was gone. Only the evil of his passage remained.

"He's dead," Jack said slowly. "But so is Eddy."

"You can dispose of evil," Abby added, "but you never can reclaim what it has done."

Kris studied her threat board. There was nothing on it. "Tom, set a course for the main jump point. It's time we head back to Wardhaven."

"You want to know what's happening on Turantic?" Penny asked.

"That is Turantic's business. Not mine," Kris said. She knew something in her gut was growing hot. Like the ship, she was going to explode . . . but not yet. "If anyone needs me, I'll be in my cabin."

"Take mine," Hank offered. "Level five, right-hand."

"You'll need it," Kris said, unstrapping herself.

"Not like you need it," Hank said. "It's got a full relaxing tub."

"I can draw you a bath," Abby said, rising from her seat.

"No. I want to be alone."

"As you wish." Abby dropped back into her seat.

"I'll hold the ship at one g," Tom said. "If I have to change it, I'll let you know with plenty of warning."

Kris made it to the elevator, teeth locked against the emotions washing through her. She punched 5 rather than attempt to get a word past the constriction in her throat. The door opened on a pleasant, wood paneled hall, new enough to still smell of sawdust and varnish. A door on the right gaped open.

The room was large, taking up half of the ship's hull at this level. The bed was big enough for five. Kris fled to it, threw herself on it, and let the hell inside her rip loose.

Long hours later, Kris slipped into a chair in the dining area of the *Barbarossa*. She'd voided all the emotions she could for one morning. Now she needed something to fill the emptiness inside. "What's to eat?" she said, voice hoarse.

"I am rather amazing with a skillet and eggs," Abby said, poking her head out of the small galley.

"Scrambled eggs, bacon, and toast would be nice," Kris said.

"Toast coming up," she heard Tom announce from the galley. "Milk, orange juice, or apple juice?"

"Yes," Kris answered feeling dehydrated. She'd scrubbed her face; she would not go public with red, puffy eyes.

"Who's got the bridge watch?" she said, glancing around the empty dining room.

"Penny has it," Tom said, setting three glasses down on the table. "Hank's showing her what he knows about this boat. Jack's keeping an eye on him. I don't think he trusts the boy."

Kris drained the glass of apple juice. "He never has."

"Hey, Kris, you in the galley?" Penny said from the speaker.

"Seems so," Kris said.

"I have some message traffic for you. You know Abu Kartum, that cabby who helped us one night?"

"And a few other times," Kris added under her breath.

"He sent a message. Says you don't owe him anything. Him or his nephew. He considers everything paid in full. Oh, and Tina had a beautiful baby girl she's naming Kris. She and all the women of the rug factory send their best. Kris, is there something here I should know?"

"Not to report," Kris said. NELLY, CAN YOU ARRANGE $100,000 DONATION TO ONE OF THE CHARITIES ABU WORKS WITH?

CONSIDER IT DONE.

"Well, since you're so excited about that one, I'll pass along this one, too. Senator Krief says she never much believed those stories you hear about Longknifes. She says she's a believer now, and oh, yes, thanks from all her friends, even Dennis Showkowski can't find something to complain about."

"That's got to be a first." Kris smiled.

The elevator chimed softly. Hank and Jack joined Kris at the table. "Penny says she has the hang of my ship," Hank said, pride in ownership still showing. "It's heavily automated."

"We'll get you a crew on Wardhaven," Kris said. "Certainly a cook."

"I heard that," Abby said, raging pride in full pout. "How badly burned do you want your eggs?"

"Scrambled like the Hilton always did them."

"Such high standards for someone who has no respect for her hired help." Abby sniffed and went back to work.

"An interesting group you have here," Hank said, taking a chair across from Kris. Jack settled down at the end of the table with both Kris and Hank in easy reach. Then he pulled out his reader and seemed to vanish into the furniture.

"I don't think I could have asked for a better team for what they had to do."

"Just exactly what did you do?" Hank's eyes were wide; his head was angled for sincerity. Did he really not know what had just happened?

"What did you see happen?" Kris asked. Father said you can't show someone something they won't see. And it was amazing the size of things that vanished before some people's eyes.

Hank leaned forward, resting himself almost eagerly on his elbows. "I saw a space station blow up. I saw three, no, one cruiser attack me. I saw you blow that cruiser out of space. And I heard Cal say a lot of things that didn't make sense."

"Such as?"

"He hated you. He seemed to blame you for everything that had ever gone wrong with his life. I knew Cal as a hardheaded businessman. If it didn't add to the bottom line, he didn't give a fig for it. Yet he went chasing after you, insisting his crew kill you. He was way over some edge. Why?"

"Did I hear him right?" Kris said slowly. "Did he say that he and some other 'us' missed killing me when they killed my kid brother, Eddy?"

"I missed that," Hank said, leaning back into his chair.

"I didn't," Tom said, bringing toast from the kitchen and a pot of coffee. He offered Hank the coffee. Hank grabbed a mug from the center of the table and let Tom fill it. Jack came out of his reading long enough to wangle a mug, too. Tom poured for himself and settled down at the other end of the table.

"I've been with Kris much of a year. I know what Eddy meant to her. What she felt about his death. I may not have perked up my listening like Kris did when that son of a bitch mentioned the boy, but I paid attention good. He and someone else arranged to have Eddy killed. Who was that?"

Tom said the words so calmly, almost casually. Kris wanted to shout them. But at who?

"I don't know," Hank said, shaking his head. "I was what, ten, eleven when it happened? No way I could know."

"That's the first answer," Kris said, sipping the orange juice. "Lots of stuff I didn't know about the Longknifes I've been learning lately. Learning because I needed it to stay one step ahead of the assassins your friend Cal was sending my way."

"He was not my friend."

"He worked for your father. He arranged things for your father," Kris said, putting the juice down slowly, willing each muscle in her body to do just what she wanted, stomach not to revolt, arms not to throw things. Eyes not to tear. "He was your father's man. What had he done for your father before?"

"I don't know," Hank said, choking on his answer. "Dad always said good things about him, but nothing specific. This was my first time to work closely with him, Kris. I told you I didn't much care for him. Remember, I told you that before any of this happened."

"Yes, you did."

"What do you expect of me?" He left that question in the air for a moment, then glanced around the room. "I did what I could for you. I told him you weren't holding me hostage. Hey folks, I don't know how you got on my ship, but I don't think it would look all that good in a court of law."

"We're not in a court of law," Kris said. "We were at war."

"War!"

"That was what Sandfire was trying to get started. That's what we stopped. Just like we did at the Paris system."

"Kris, my old man is in business. He doesn't deal in war."

"Are you sure?" she asked softly. "Have you tipped over any rocks? Looked at the seamy underbelly of your family tree? Hank, those smart-metal boats you donated to me on Olympia almost killed me. Did you buy them?"

"Yes, I bought them. Well, I ordered them."

"Ordered them. We initiated an investigation into them. We tried to trace them to a specific company. No luck. No evidence they'd ever been bought. Who'd you buy them from?" Kris knew she was sounding like a prosecutor; she watched Hank close up like a castle under siege. This was no way to win friends and get a boy to ask her out. But she needed to know the truth more than she needed something to do Friday night.

"I ordered them. I told my personal assistant to get them."

"Personal assistant?" Kris said.

"Yeah, my computer, you know, this thing," he said, opening his shirt and tapping the computer around his shoulders. "I had it order the boats. It said it did it. I didn't think about it again until you gave me that cryptic report a few days ago."

"Who programs your computer?" Kris asked, already suspecting the answer.

"Ah, Ironclad Software. Every other year, they'd sell me a new computer, program it for me, straight turnkey operations. I don't have time to waste with a dumb machine or one that doesn't work. And I don't give mine silly names like Nelly."

"Fool you," Nelly whispered.

"Shush, Nelly. Hank, did you hear what you just said? Sandfire let you pay him for the privilege of having a computer that gave him a back door into everything you did. Did your father suggest Sandfire's company to you?"

"Yes, no, this whole mess is Sandfire's. Not my dad. Dad would have nothing to do with this." The young man's face twisted in pain no amount of genetic sculpturing could make beautiful as he fled to the elevator.

Wordlessly, Abby settled eggs in front of Kris, then rested a hand on her shoulder.

Kris eyed the food, but shook her head; her appetite was gone. Food would not fill the void inside her today.

It was a long trip to Wardhaven. The ship's smart-metal hull could not keep out the cold, silent emptiness of space.

26

Kris stood at the top of the stairs at Nuu House. Below her the black and white spiral swirled its way to a point in the middle of the foyer. Eddy had chased her down its twists, her on white, him always on black. What was it about black that drew the little boy of six?

A question she would never answer.

Strange how getting the answer to one question didn't give you the answer to others.

But today was a day if not for answers then for answering. She'd been called to General McMorrison's office to answer for what she had done.

Last time she'd been put on the hot seat, Grampa Trouble and Ray had been in the foyer, offering, if not support, then quiet acceptance that she'd done what had to be done in the best Longknife tradition.

Grampa Trouble was off doing General stuff. Grampa Ray had not returned her call of last night. Kings were busy people. And maybe it was better to get the Navy out of the way before she faced her family.

Auntie Tru had called only seconds behind Mac. Over

Nelly's objections, Tru was third on Kris's cleanup to-do list.

Jack stood at the foot of the stairs. "Your car's here."

She smoothed down her undress whites. Decorations were an option for this uniform; she chose to leave them behind. Whatever was the intention of this command performance, she'd rise or fall on herself, not glory that some said was borrowed. Heels clicking on the tile floor, she let Jack open the front door for her. He also opened the door of a modest sedan, no limo today, let her settle into the backseat, then joined Harvey in the front.

The old chauffeur knew this morning's destination. He speed-dialed Main Navy and set the car in motion. The silence went long, like a funeral might. Still, she was among friends, as close to friends as she might ever know.

Kris let her eyes rove the familiar streets of Wardhaven, watching the walls of new construction go up from deep pits. Those mimed the answer to some of her questions.

A wall of money separated her from Tom and Penny and Jack.

A deeper pit separated her from Hank. Kris'd had her fill of being one of those Longknifes long before she ran off to join the Navy. She'd had her fill of Father's politicking and Mother's socializing. She was ready to hunt for where the glitzy press releases ended and the truth began.

Hank was not there yet. Might never be there. Hank Smythe-Peterwald the Thirteenth was still the loving and trusting son of Henry Smythe-Peterwald the Twelfth. Maybe when Hank started eyeing the fine print on his birth certificate, started looking deeper into the family business than the official reports told him, maybe then there would be someone for Kris to talk to.

Now, he was just a balloon filled with his father's hot air.

The car came to a stop in front of Main Navy's old concrete facade. Pigeons flew as Jack opened the door for her. She passed through security quickly, then marched down the polished tile halls for the Chief of Staff's office. Today's appointment was for oh eight hundred. Not bad, considering she'd only disembarked from the *Barbarossa* at nine-thirty last night. Either Penny was filing reports very fast, or Mac had his own little birdies following her.

The Secretary passed her in without hesitation. Jack fell out to a chair, opened a magazine, and settled into his usual reading fake. Physically, Kris had nothing to worry about here. The only threat of death this morning was to her soul.

Cutting her corners sharp enough to warm the heart of any Gunny Sergeant, Kris presented herself at rigid attention. Her salute passed precisely up her gig line. Mac waved in the general direction of his forehead without looking up from the three flimsies he was reading at once.

He also didn't release her from attention.

Kris stood like a board as sweat trickled down her back.

"Quite a mess you left," General McMorrison said, still not looking up.

"Looked to be a bigger mess if I did nothing."

The general's "Hmm," told her nothing. "There's a revolution or rebellion or some such thing causing quite a dustup on Turantic."

"Yes, sir." Two days after Kris busted out of Turantic space, a rather large task force from Wardhaven made orbit above that troubled planet. The Navy brought vaccines against several kinds of Ebola and a new comm suite. The Navy had been welcomed with open hands by all factions, but stood aloof officially, while distributing the vaccine and getting the comm link back up between Turantic and the rest of human space. The last Kris heard, President Iedinka had suffered an accident, died of natural causes, or been assassinated. What all reports agreed upon was that he was no longer among the living. Now the people of Turantic were struggling to clean up the loose ends of his administration.

"You have anything to do with the President's death?" Mac said, for the first time looking up at her.

"Not to my knowledge, sir. I suspect I encountered several of the major players on Turantic, but I neither encouraged them to do anything nor promised anything in the name of Wardhaven."

"That's nice to know, Princess Kristine."

So it was going to be a "Princess" dressing down. There was no avenue for her to appeal that. She made none.

"You overstayed your leave. You also missed a ship's movement."

"I understood that the *Firebolt* was to be tied up for four weeks, sir, as Nuu Docks worked on the Uni-plex."

"Nope. *Firebolt*'s Engineer lit a fire under the yard. Also seems there's quite a bit of money to be made in the dumb metal stuff, and Nuu Enterprises moved ahead faster than they thought possible." Grampa Al must be looking at a lot of money to push matters that fast.

"They took the *Firebolt* out for its tests last week. Passed with flying colors."

"I didn't think the Engineer would go out without my personal computer riding shotgun on the tests, sir."

"Seems new computers for the test were financed out of another fund, Princess. You are not irreplaceable."

"No, sir. I didn't think I was, sir. However, sir, when I found myself quarantined on Turantic, I did check in with the local military authority at the embassy. There should be a report from them of my unusual circumstances."

The General leafed through his flimsies. "Nope, nothing here, Princess. Not a word. Oh, excuse me, here is a report from the embassy. Seems you played the Princess rather strongly. Tied up several of their people full time. Interfered with them making normal reports. Put several of them in life-threatening situations. On first read, it pretty much sounds like normal damn Longknife behavior."

"The embassy doesn't say anything about me checking in with them."

"Not a word, Princess."

There were a lot of things Kris could say. *I did, too. They're not being fair. Somebody's out to get me.* None sounded appropriate for a naval officer. She said nothing.

That got her another "Hmm."

"I understand Admiral Crossenshild made you a job offer. Offered you a job in intelligence gathering or analysis."

"Yes, sir, he did."

"You turned him down."

"Yes, sir, I did."

"At ease, Lieutenant. You want to explain why you did? Sit down, take a weight off your feet," he said, waving at a chair beside his desk.

Kris relaxed . . . about one tenth of a degree. She slipped

into the offered chair, tried to calm the storm raging in her stomach, her blood, her head. *This "counseling session" is not fair. It is not right.* But Lieutenants don't tell four-star Generals that, not even when they're the Prime Minister's brat and a Princess. Especially not when they have *that* family baggage.

"You know, Lieutenant, this latest, ah, experience of yours kind of points out something me and Crossie agree on. You've got the head for irregular situations. Damn, but you came up with an irregular solution to one hell of an irregular situation."

"Yes, sir. I did what I had to do. But that doesn't mean that I enjoyed it, or would be good at it on a regular basis."

"Why not?"

Kris took a deep breath. Could anyone understand what she was about to say? "Sir, the people in my family have made a tradition out of doing what has to be done in really crappy situations."

"That's one way of putting it," the General said, what might pass for a smile crinkling the edge of his mouth.

"None of them ever sought to be in that kind of mess." She laid that out, pure and simple. If Mac saw it, grasped what she meant, she didn't need more words. If he didn't get her meaning, more words wouldn't do her a lot of good.

He sat back in his chair, head slowly nodding. "You have a point there. I sometimes wonder if some of Crossie's folks don't get too much fun out of what they do."

"Sir, I don't want to become someone who enjoys that kind of stuff. I don't think it would be good for Wardhaven to have a damn Longknife who does."

"Now that is a scary picture. Say no more. I'll talk to Crossenshild. He won't bother you anymore." Mac tore up one of his flimsies. "But you are long overdue from your leave," he said, eyeing her like a vulture long overdue for dinner. "I can bring you up on charges, but I don't think your pappy would be very happy to have you splashed all over the newsies. You may have missed the latest from Wardhaven, but the Prime Minister's lost a few bielections, and the opposition is breathing hot down his neck. You could just resign for, shall we say, health reasons so you can concentrate on your regal obligations."

Kris did not need to think about his offer. "Sir, I will not resign, and I might caution you." Lieutenant JGs did not caution four-star Generals. That was the rule. Kris had not broken one of the damn rules this morning. It was time to reduce one to kindling. "If you bring me up on charges, it may be difficult to prove that I did not check in with the embassy as required by regs. I don't pass through anyplace without a whole lot of people noticing me."

Mac eyed another flimsy, sighed, and tore it up. "I told Crossie that wouldn't work. So, Princess, what do I do with you?"

"Sir, I am a serving Lieutenant, Junior Grade, and there have to be many places you can safely dump me," she said, risking a smile.

"I send you off to a wet, hot jungle, dump the worst excuse for sailors and Marines we've got, and you rehabilitate the damn command . . . including one of the best officers I've ever had to want a resignation from," he said, shaking his head.

"I make you a boot Ensign under a hard-driving Skipper . . . and you relieve him for charges and win a war I don't want to fight. I give you the worst excuse for ship duty, and then you run off, crash a diplomatic crisis, and hand me back a situation well on its way to comfortable normalization. Young woman, I can't think of anyplace I dare send you where I will get anything close to what I think I'm aiming for."

"There's got to be someplace," Kris squeaked before she remembered that Junior Officers don't plead with Generals.

Mac picked up another flimsy. "That was some interesting ship driving you did, shooting your way out against a six-inch cruiser."

"Sandfire did not have a trained crew," Kris pointed out. "And while mine was small, it was a small ship."

"But one with structural problems. Who would put lasers on a boat and not cool them? Even dinky twelve-inchers. And that fire control system. A piece of crap."

"Yes, sir."

"You put it through its teething problems rather quickly."

"Nothing like a cruiser bearing down on you to give you a strong incentive, sir, and concentrate your mind."

"I can imagine," he muttered as he eyed the last flimsy. "Twenty years ago, we tried to come up with a fast patrol boat, something just for planetary protection. To keep the politicians happy we wasted a small fortune on a fleet of a hundred boats. Ended up using them for customs work." He tossed a picture Kris's way. She glanced at it but did not recognize the ship.

"This Uni-plex stuff has some of our designers thinking they might try PFs again. Small, fast, high acceleration. Have to be young to stand the g's. Four eighteen-inch pulse lasers could put a dent in a battlewagon if handled right. Decent fire control, though you might have a different opinion. Interested in skippering your own boat?"

"Yes, sir," was out of Kris's mouth almost before she opened it.

"Why am I not surprised?" He leaned back in his chair. "Now you still won't be out from under the chain of command. Some poor Lieutenant Commander will be stuck with a bunch of prima donnas as bad as you, no doubt. Maybe if I put all you brash puppies in one place, you can keep yourselves busy chasing each other's tails."

That didn't require an answer. Kris just tightened her smile.

"I can't have a JG commanding a commissioned ship. The Skipper's slot is a full Lieutenant. So," he said, standing, "it looks like I'm going to have to promote you again."

"I can see how much it pains you, sir," she let slip.

From his top desk drawer, he pulled out a set of Lieutenant shoulder boards, two nicely thick strips, unlike the ones on Kris's shoulders where one strip was anemically thin. "I had my secretary get these for me this morning. There's nothing special about them. Just what she grabbed from the store downstairs."

"You knew you'd be giving them to me," Kris said, raising an eyebrow.

"Last time we had one of these little counseling sessions, you wouldn't quit. Remember why?"

Kris remembered only too well. When you finally find the words that contain your soul, you don't forget them. "I'm Navy, sir."

"And I'm beginning to think that you are."

Kris stood, accepted the boards, saluted, then left. Maybe

she was a bit dizzy. Maybe she didn't cut the corners quite as square as when she went in. And maybe she was just a bit starry-eyed.

In the waiting room, the secretary gave her the kind of sweet smile Kris dreamed of getting from her mother. Jack rose, took the Lieutenant's shoulder boards in, and raised an eyebrow.

"I'm getting my own ship," Kris crowed.

"Oh Lordy," Jack breathed. "The Navy is in for it now."

About the Author

Mike Shepherd grew up Navy. It taught him early about change and the chain of command. He's worked as a bartender and cabdriver, personnel adviser and labor negotiator. Now retired from building databases about the endangered critters of the Pacific Northwest, he's looking forward to some serious writing.

Mike lives in Vancouver, Washington, with his wife, Ellen, and her mother. He enjoys reading, writing, watching grandchildren for story ideas, and upgrading his computer—all are never ending.

Oh, and working on Kris's next book, *Kris Longknife: Intrepid.*

You may reach him at Mike_Shepherd@comcast.net or drop by www.mikemoscoe.com to check on how the next book is going.

THE ULTIMATE
IN SCIENCE FICTION

From tales of distant worlds to stories of tomorrow's technology, Ace and Roc have everything you need to stretch your imagination to its limits.

Alastair Reynolds
Allen Steele
Charles Stross
Robert Heinlein
Joe Haldeman
Jack McDevitt
John Varley
William C. Dietz
Harry Turtledove
S. M. Stirling
Simon R. Green
Chris Bunch
E. E. Knight
S. L. Viehl
Kristine Kathryn Rusch

penguin.com

RoC   ACE